D0182086

Seal of the Salamander

The wizard was fussing over the baby. Gil picked up the ancient binder of *Arrivals Macabre*. "Andre, do you think we'll find Bey?"

The wizard didn't turn, but answered, "You will have your moment with Bey. It's in both your destinies."

Gil's hands closed angrily on the binder. The rough edges of the seal rested under his fingertips. Unthinking, he dug at it. The outermost corner gave way with a minute pop.

The wizard spun, consternation on his face. "No!"

Gil was blown back with enormous force by a ball of swirling transplendence. The entity, freed from the seal, sizzled and lashed out, knocking him sideways. The thing floated toward the baby.

Suddenly the sword Blazetongue flared incandescent.

Also by Brian Daley
Published by Ballantine Books:

THE DOOMFARERS OF CORAMONDE

The
Starfollowers of
Coramonde

by Brian Daley

A Del Rey Book

BALLANTINE BOOKS • NEW YORK

For friends, John, and their respective ladies,
and
for Myra A. Daley, who knew

A Del Rey Book
Published by Ballantine Books

Copyright © 1979 by Brian Daley

All rights reserved under International and Pan-American
Copyright Conventions. Published in the United States by
Ballantine Books, a division of Random House, Inc., New York,
and simultaneously in Canada by Ballantine Books of Canada,
Ltd., Toronto, Canada.

Library of Congress Catalog Card Number: 78-61501

ISBN 0-345-27495-4

Manufactured in the United States of America

First Edition: February 1979

Cover art by Carl Lundgren

ACKNOWLEDGMENT

I am indebted to the following people for their assistance and information: James Luceno, Myra Di Blasio, Linda Lionetti, and Major John C. Speedy of the United States Military Academy, West Point.

And to my editor, Mr. Lester del Rey, for generous measures of his patience, prodding, guidance, candor, and encouragement; I owe thanks for whatever virtues this book may possess.

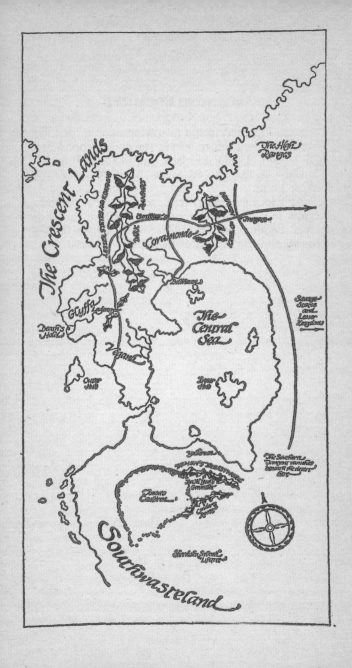

PART I

Protocols of the Sword

Prologue

IN a narrow ring of light in unmeasured darkness stood the Accused.

His head was bowed, hands clasped together within long sleeves—flesh seeking its own contact for reassurance, in vain. An arraignment in Shardishku-Salamá, these proceedings were unconcerned with justice. Their function was retribution. The Accused was aware of punishments available here; that was a form of punishment.

Yardiff Bey felt nothing change in the enormous Fane of the Masters. Yet between one moment and the next he knew the attention of the Five was upon him. No indication escaped to his face or posture, but in a shielded cinderbox in his soul, fears blew brighter.

He damped them down. Was he not first among sorcerers, subordinate only to the Masters? Brief, awful elation fanned up his spine at the thought. In flying back to Shardishku-Salamá in his demon-ship, *Cloud Ruler*: to plead before the vindictive Lords of the City, Yardiff Bey had taken his greatest dare. He was in more hideous danger than most men could envision in wildest speculation.

A waitingness hung around him, and cruel, dispassionate curiostity. He'd always exulted in the cold intellects of the Five, but now it was their displeasure directed at him. The single beam of light glinted from the strange ocular that was bound in place where his left eye had once been. He sent a stern command through every part of himself, physical and incorporeal: *Be still!*

He bowed deeply, unhurriedly. When his voice came, it was impeccable in its calm control.

"Masters, your servant has returned. Will he be heard?" He sensed mirthless amusement. Did They think he'd come on a fool's quest for mercy? There was a vast stirring somewhere in the colossal temple.

Yardiff Bey was slammed to his knees, by no force he could see. Without his will, his hands came up to rend the front of his robe, in mourning and contrition.

"List us your failures," came a disembodied command, "and number your faults."

He was cast headlong on the cold floor, held as a doll beneath a man's boot would be held, by the stacked, murderous weight of the will of the Masters of Shardishku-Salamá. He sobbed for breath that wouldn't come, and that weight retreated the merest bit. He knew a meager flicker of triumph; he hadn't been condemned out of hand, and so had the opportunity to say on. He brought his head up a degree, neck trembling with effort.

"Waste not the tool," he strained, "before it mends its errors. Let me make my reparations." He slumped again, drawing breath only with horrible exertion. He felt, by tingling of images not quite seen on his inner eye, that the Five were conferring.

The air was suddenly icy, carrying thick, infernal stenches. There was a new, an overwhelming Presence in the Fane. The sorcerer recognized its awesome savagery. His patron, Amon, a chief among demons, had come, after ignoring all previous pleas. Before Amon, even the Masters were silent, deferential in their intangible, unmistakable way.

When the demon spoke, words lashing like whips, the walls of the huge Fane shook in the lightlessness.

"More vainglorious plans, unworthy one? Are my agents in Salamá to be twice fools, and trust you a second time?" Amon asked. "List *me* your failures. You had the whole of Coramonde in your grasp. Your puppet-son was enthroned over the most important country in the Crescent Lands. You had the rightful Heir Springbuck trapped, along with the wizard Andre deCourteney and his enchantress sister Gabrielle. How was all that dashed asunder?"

Yardiff Bey groped for response. "I—I sent the dragon Chaffinch against them, oh Lord. He should have slaughtered them easily. But they had with them the alien Van Duyn . . ."

3

He faltered for a way to tell it. "You know there are other universes, mighty Amon, Realities sprouting from alternatives, like leaves from a tree. Van Duyn is from another, and from it he and the deCourteneys plucked soldiers, and a metal war-machine to slay Chaffinch."

"Your *first* failure," thundered the demon. "Masters of Shardishku-Salamá, witness it now!"

Yardiff Bey's senses jolted, as Amon conjured up those events again . . .

Through the eyes of Ibn-al-Yed, mask-slave to Yardiff Bey, they saw the castle where Springbuck, the deCourteneys and their little band were at bay. Ibn-al-Yed had only to keep them confined until the sorcerer sent the dragon Chaffinch.

But there was a disturbance in the air, a pushing-apart of the boundaries between worlds. A lumbering, drab-green vehicle came roaring into the meadow. From it a man emerged, confusion manifest on his face, some odd black implement cradled under his arm.

It was, in certainty, a trick of the deCourteneys. The Druid who'd accompanied Ibn-al-Yed called up an air elemental, to undo it. But as the were-wind ripped at him, the stranger brought up his implement. There were bright, stuttering explosions. Druid and horse toppled, dead, pierced with holes by the otherworldly weapon.

Ibn-al-Yed backed his horse away in shock and confusion. Yardiff Bey, his Masters and dread Amon looked back through time, at the indecision in the newcomer's features. He wiped his forehead once, quickly, on an olive-colored sleeve. Over his left breast pocket were cryptic letters no one there could decipher: US ARMY. Over the right was another strip of characters, whose meaning they would come to know: MACDONALD.

Through the eyes of the late Ibn-al-Yed, the sorcerer watched that early disruption of his careful design. The image receded, Amon summoned up another . . .

There was revelry in Hell.

The metal war vehicle had killed Chaffinch, but events had left Gabrielle deCourteney in the hands of Yardiff Bey. It was an occasion of tremendous importance, enormous success. In Amon's mansion on the infernal plane, the demon's votaries writhed, ecstatic, to insane music.

Without warning the cyclopean doors burst apart in a shower of wooden splinters and metal fragments. The armored personnel carrier revved down the center of the room, treads chewing stone, engine bellowing above the din.

The machine's weapons cut loose, flashing ruin in all directions. *Gunfire*, as Yardiff Bey was to hear it called later. The fugitive Prince Springbuck appeared, and Andre deCourteney. Gabrielle was rescued, as explosions and gunfire purged the chamber. Yardiff Bey had to flee, as Amon was humiliated by mad invasion.

The sorcerer quivered, experiencing it again. No one had affronted great Amon that way in an eternity. Now a last image . . .

Yardiff Bey sat in his own sanctum, high in the palace-fortress at Earthfast, laboring at a spell against the intruder, MacDonald, whose interference had persisted. Gil MacDonald of the bizarre innovations, unpredictable deceptions and unlooked-for influence, had thrown Bey's equations out of kilter.

With this invocation, sapping MacDonald's soul from his body, Yardiff Bey would remedy that. But he began to meet odd resistance; his enchantments were warped and subverted. There was howling from his supernatural servants.

An armed company appeared where the outlander's naked soul should have cringed. Springbuck, Andre deCourteney, Van Duyn and MacDonald himself, whole, were among them. In seconds the palace-fortress was filled with fighting and dying, crash of alien weapons, curses of combatants and belling of sword strokes. Yardiff Bey made his escape by a barest margin aboard his flying vessel *Cloud Ruler*. He'd lost, in minutes, his iron grip on Coramonde.

The taste of that catastrophe defiled his mouth once more. Then Amon let the retelling fade.

First among sorcerers, once the Hand of Shardishku-Salamá, Bey felt his breath heaving with terror and resentment.

"And all of that you will set right?" came the demon's challenge, on a sepulchral wind. The sorcerer raised himself to hands and knees with quaking hope. But his response held only firm conviction.

"I swear it! I have come back because I am needed. There approaches the time of greatest effort, but greatest risk also. Let me play my part in the Masters' mighty labor, Dark Father, as I was meant to!"

He couldn't hear the current of thoughts that passed among them. Amon's sawtooth voice came again. "I see what is in your thoughts, for they are open to me. Your Masters' might waxes plentiful now, but will be diverted more and more into the enchantment they forge as time goes on. They must work undisturbed, and though the chance of hindrance is slim, yet it must be eliminated. Begin your work, search out that last source of peril. But be warned: your Masters and I, and *my* terrible Overlord, are engaged in other struggles, other enterprises. You must be self-reliant, or be swallowed up in that final Night we shall found."

Then Amon was gone, between one heartbeat and another.

The ring of light began to move, to lead the sorcerer back out of the Fane. He lurched at first, drunk on the enormity of it, but his stride soon became surer, stronger, with his incredible good fortune. Raw power swelled him, of magic and personal force.

Yardiff Bey's feet were set, once more, on the thrill-path of conquest.

Chapter One

*What are MacDonald's antecedents, after all?
Dropout, drifter, product of popular-culture eclec-
ticism. His sole sustained adult endeavor revolved
around a war that estranged him from his society.
An absurd background for a young man caught up
in meta-events!*
     from EDWARD VAN DUYN's personal
     journal, *The Infinite Parallax*

TIRED, he chose not to sleep. Too often lately, he'd
awakened in saturating sweat, from tremulations of the
soul.

Gil MacDonald sat, without lamp or candle, before
the dying embers of the hearthfire in his room. In them,
he saw racing horsemen and swords making hornet-
darts of light in the night. On a night filled with just
those things, his lover had died.

He raised his right hand, the one that had held the
Lady Duskwind's as her wound had stolen her from him
by inches. He drew it across his eyes, to wipe away
memory; his thoughts could seldom go far from her.

He'd been snatched into Coramonde, with his crew
and their armored personnel carrier, by wizardry. After
they'd been returned to their own Reality, he alone had
chosen to come back. He hadn't counted on falling in
love. In love, he'd never thought he might lose Duskwind so cruelly. Bereft of her, he found his remaining
desires condensed, embittered.

He'd come back to the palace-fortress at Earthfast
only that evening. For weeks he'd combed the Dark
Rampart range, west of Earthfast, with an entire Legion
of Coramonde. It had been rumored that Yardiff Bey

kept his flying ship *Cloud Ruler* concealed there prior to his rise to power and subsequent overthrow.

Gil hadn't turned up a thing, not a whiff. Worn thin, short on the sleep he resisted these days and determined to find the sorcerer, he'd balked at the *Ku-Mor-Mai*'s urgent request that he go back to Earthfast. When he'd finally arrived, he'd found that Springbuck was closeted with some visiting big shot. He'd immediately gone off to be by himself.

A soft knock came at the door. Gil's hand dipped inside his loosened gambeson, fishing out the Browning automatic. He padded to the door, the clammy stone making his bare feet clench. The knock came again, discreet rapping a servant would use. Nevertheless, he stood to one side of the bolted door, cocking the pistol.

"Yeah?"

"Sir, the *Ku-Mor-Mai* craves your presence with all haste. He has tidings of import which you must needs hear."

" 'Craves my presence,' " Gil muttered. "Okay, tell him I'm coming, be right along."

He wondered why Springbuck would want conversation in the middle of the night. He sat on his wide, empty bed, sighing and pulling his boots on. A new thought made him pause. Maybe Springbuck had picked up on something about Bey?

His sword, byrnie and other gear he left on the floor, in a burst of enthusiasm born of enmity.

Springbuck, Protector-Suzerain of Coramonde—*Ku-Mor-Mai,* in the Old Tongue—had been up late with affairs of state, in his comfortable study. Its curtains were fastened across high windows, and a fire crackled in the hearth. Burnished lamps of brass and crystal lit it warmly, and thick furs and pelts were strewn on the floor.

He'd no sooner finished conferring with the envoy of the Mariners when his seneschal had announced Van Duyn and the Princess Katya. He'd had them admitted at once. Dirty, spent from days of hard riding, they'd told their story, their grave words interweaving.

Now Van Duyn, former Senior Fellow of the Grossen Institute for Advanced Studies, inter-universal traveler

8

and self-exile from his own Reality, ran a hand through disheveled gray hair, adjusting gold-rimmed glasses with the other. His heavy M-1, that otherworldly weapon, rested against the arm of his chair. For his help in the thronal war, Springbuck had granted the scholar stewardship over an impoverished collection of city-states, the Highlands Province, in the northwestern corner of Coramonde. The Princess Katya, who'd become enamored of the alien, had gone with him, to watch him apply his peculiar theories of government and organization. Van Duyn had made impressive progress in his few months there, but now the province was abandoned, its few survivors scattered.

"It can't be anyone's fault but mine," the outlander was saying. "The local commander, Roguespur, pleaded for more men, arms, patrols and fortifications. But I needed men for improvement projects, and iron and smiths for plows and equipment, and the border's been quiet for years. I knew the Druids were said to be there, but those were old tales." He shook his head. "I should have listened to them. I should have remembered—"

Katya put a pale hand on his. Her long, white-blonde hair swung around her with the gesture. Springbuck recalled the sobriquet given her in her own nation of Freegate—"the Snow Leopardess."

"Edward, how can you blame yourself?" she remonstrated. "No sword or spear laid waste to the Highlands Province, and none could have saved it. When magic comes, only magic can countervail it."

Springbuck pursued the point. "You're certain it was the Druids?"

The Snow Leopardess affirmed it. "Their spells haven't been seen in living memory, at least not on this side of the mountains. Yet, from whence else would come that magic of polar winds and an ice-elemental?"

Van Duyn concurred wearily. "When those clouds came down out of the mountains, we went from late summer to midwinter in minutes. No clothes or fire could protect us against that cold. When the ice-demon followed behind, nothing could withstand it. No one who got near it lived. I saw men shatter like icicles. All we could do was run for our lives." He remembered the

9

gallop, frozen grass shattering under their horses' hooves like filaments of glass, the air filled with a cold of such awful purity that each breath was torment and the reflex of breathing contested with the pain of the lungs and throat. The ice-elemental, liberated from some absolute-zero corner of Hell, continued to prowl the province for victims. And those who fell behind never caught up.

"Toward dawn, we passed out of the frozen zone," Katya went on. "We tried to return the next day, but it was beyond us, unendurable. 'Twill demand the deCourteneys' arts, I avow, to alter the situation back there."

Springbuck avoided their eyes noncommittally. "Other ears must hear this. Will you both withdraw to private chambers and take refreshment? Katya, your brother is in Earthfast. He'll want to see you at once, I know."

"Reacher is here? What brings him?"

"Several matters. He, too, has news. Many reports have come to me in recent weeks. Reacher will join you presently, as you dine."

When they left, Springbuck called for a council, then thrust aside the addenda for his latest Restoration Edicts and found himself staring at his sabre Bar, the sword called Never Blunted, which hung over the mantel.

Gil MacDonald, whom he summoned, entered in obvious haste. Unannounced and unaccompanied, as they both preferred it, the other alien slid into a chair. The *Ku-Mor-Mai* contemplated his friend.

The former sergeant's face was clean-shaven, his hair trimmed short. It gave prominence to the dark smear of powderburn on his cheek, the scar on his forehead. He'd gotten both in the throne room at Earthfast, when Springbuck had won his crown by rite of combat.

"Now what?" the American asked. He listened to these latest developments, sitting forward on his straight-backed chair, hoping to hear what he wanted so badly.

"That's gotta be it," he posited. "Bey's there, in the north, coming at us with his Druids." He hitched him-

10

self around eagerly. "How far did they come? We'll let Bey in far enough and *whap!*, the deCourteneys take a crack at him."

"You are less cautious than you once were," Springbuck observed.

"Huh? Look, I never said we shouldn't watch out. But this is Bey, man, *Bey!*"

"And you were certain he would be in the Dark Rampart range, remember? Before that, it was the far eastern provinces you wished to search, where he used to have many supporters—"

"And he wasn't there; I know! This deal though, this is the real item. Hell, the Druids used to work for Bey; isn't that what you told me? So why are we spinning our wheels? When do we move out?"

"Not yet, in truth. There are other factors."

Gil bristled. "Yardiff Bey arranged your folks' deaths, didn't he? Yeah, and Duskwind's, and that of how many others? And he snatched our pal Dunstan, and still has him, am I right? So what's gotten into you, saying 'take a break'?"

Springbuck stretched in his cumbersome robes to ease himself and measure his reply. Slightly shorter than average, with dark tones of skin and hair, he betrayed a fencer's sinuosity even when seated. As usual, he'd foregone the crown he seldom wore outside his Court. The corners of his eyes creased from time to time; he was nearsighted, part of the reason he liked to parley in his study.

The *Ku-Mor-Mai* owed the American a great deal, not the least of which was his life. There *was* substance to what Gil had said, too. Yardiff Bey was the creator of such suffering, pain and misery that his capture demanded high priority. And the sorcerer's being at large posed a threat to all the Crescent Lands, Coramonde in particular.

"Our situation is less secure now," he told the other. "My reign is being resisted in many quarters of the suzerainty. The military units upon which I may depend are spread in tenuous array. There are those who liked my predecessor far better than they do me. And there are partisans, irregulars from the late war, who have no

11

love of the commands of Earthfast. In some areas all authority has been swept away."

Gil understood, and berated himself for his own hard words, recognizing that his temper seemed more difficult to curb these days. In Coramonde, men sided with neighbors or relatives and obeyed their immediate superior, bound by oaths and honor to their liege, hetman, Legion-Marshal or whomever. Fealty to a remote, central monarch was less concrete. When local leaders came into contention, it was difficult for the *Ku-Mor-Mai* to settle things from the palace-fortress. Coramonde had known a number of wars arising from such squabbles, when the Legions had been sent in.

"There have been assassinations," Springbuck continued, "and defiance, unrest throughout the suzerainty. I will speak to you my secret fear: open revolt is not far beneath the surface. There have already been armed clashes, little short of rebellion. And here am I, with my reliable troops taxed to maintain order, deployed too thinly. Whether I can hold the center in this stress or not, and let things fly apart, is more in question every day."

Springbuck was in desperate need of dependable units and Gil had kept an entire Legion busy with his hunt, but the American could feel only guilty apprehension. His anxiety was that the young *Ku-Mor-Mai* would ask him to shelve the search for Bey.

Their talk was interrupted by people summoned to the council, taking seats at an oval table of gleaming spruce.

There was Ferrian, once Champion-at-arms of the Horseblooded, his long hair worn in the high horsetail his people favored; and Van Duyn and Katya, just returned, with Katya's brother, the King of Freegate, Lord of the Just and Sudden Reach.

Reacher was only a few inches over five feet, but broad-shouldered and long-legged for that. His hair was shades darker than Katya's, his eyes not such a lambent violet as hers. He wore fine mesh armor washed with gold for this state visit, but chafed in it. He'd been raised on the High Ranges among fleet-footed hunters, used to their sparse attire and their weapons, the cestus and claw-glove. He was undefeated in battle, armed or unarmed, preternaturally strong and fast. In exchanging greetings, he showed special enthusiasm for Ferrian, an old companion. Katya's arm was draped around her brother's neck affectionately.

Gil waved and said hello, but didn't go to them. He and Van Duyn had no particular liking for each other. Van Duyn considered the younger man irritating; Gil thought his countryman too dour.

Last to get there was Andre deCourteney, the wizard who'd done so much to counter Yardiff Bey. He merited esteem from all enemies of Shardishku-Salamá.

He was squat, balding, with a blue stubble on his heavy jowls. His arms and hands were matted with wiry black hair; stray curls escaped his collar to lie at his throat. He wore yeoman's breeches and tunic, resembling a teamster rather than a renowned wizard. The pudgy face was open and pleasant, though, and people had always trusted what they saw there.

"My sister Gabrielle could not be found," he explained, "and Lord Hightower seems also unavailable. All others are here, I think."

Springbuck had Van Duyn and the Snow Leopardess retell the devastation of the Highlands Province. Concern came into each mien. Questions were posed. Gil, out of turn, argued, "We're wasting time. Only Andre and Gabrielle can go head-to-head against Bey and those Druids."

Andre looked surprised. "I do not believe Bey is there, though I am sure I am intended to think so." Gil's expression grew chillier. "You are correct, I agree, in reasoning that Bey fostered the attack. But with the Hand of Salamá, you must never make those distressing leaps to conclusion. Ask, rather, 'Where is the deception here, where the trap?' " He smiled, barely. "I, too, learned that by harsh experience."

Gil had been overly irritated at the wizard. He reasserted self-control, wondering, *What's wrong with me?* His temper subdued, he said, "Okay then, let's hear it."

The wizard shook his head, jowls jiggling. "I have no theory, except that Yardiff Bey would like to see my sister and me go north with this." He pulled a chain from his tunic. Suspended from it was a gemstone of

13

changing colors in a silver setting, the mystic jewel Calundronius, one of the deCourteneys' prime instruments.
In close proximity, it negated all magic, dispersing all
spells.

"It would please the Hand of Salamá," Andre averred, "to see us take this into contest with the Druids,
but my thought is for alternatives. Where will Bey strike
in the meantime?"

It was, surprisingly, Reacher who answered. He
didn't often utter opinions, preferring to listen, reserving
comments in a shy way. Famous for cunning and prowess, he was uneasy in groups of people.

But he got to his feet now, working mailed shoulders
automatically. He wasn't used to the confinements of
civilized attire.

Reacher cleared his throat self-consciously. "We in
Freegate also feel encroachments of Salamá," he stated
softly. "Horsemen from the distant Southwastelands
harry and pillage, a virtual war. I am convinced they
are instigated by the Masters, in the City of Sorcery."

"Why does everyone equate Bey with Salamá?" Van
Duyn interposed. "Surely he fell from grace with the
Masters?"

"He was the supreme operative of the Five," Andre
answered. "Their best and shrewdest lieutenant. It is
barely conceivable, but he could have won their am-
nesty."

Reacher shifted restlessly from one foot to the other.
"I, too, think our woes stem from Salamá," he finished,
and sat down immediately.

The door opened again, and Gabrielle deCourteney
entered. As famous for her beauty as her sorcery, she
bore scant resemblance to her younger brother. Her
white skin was flawless, her hair amazingly red, thick
and heavy. She met their glances with eyes green as em-
eralds, her brows high-swept like gull's wings, her age
unguessable.

She wore a gown of brown Glyffan satin, of becoming folds and gatherings, belted with a cord of woven
copper. She settled herself next to the *Ku-Mor-Mai*. His
eyes stayed with her for a moment; he marveled, that
this woman was his paramour.

The others were waiting. Springbuck reassembled his

14

stream of thought. "There are other reports gathered here," he concluded, "which you may examine. Cora-monde's troubles, too, smack of outside influence. There is a final point."

He motioned to his aide, Captain Brodur, who rose and left. "An envoy from the Mariners came to me. I invited him to set it forth to you all."

Brodur re-entered with a tall, thickset man whose hair and beard hung in black, gleaming ringlets. His cloak was flowing, wine-red velvet, stylishly cut and vented. His beaded slippers were of finest Teebran leather, but a broad, businesslike cutlass hung at his sash.

Brodur announced, "I present Gale-Baiter, Captain of Mariners." The man made a minute bow. Face composed, he delivered his message, careful to keep emotion from it.

"Not long past, the Mariners declined to partake of your war on Yardiff Bey. Our Prince did not deem it wise, intruding in affairs of Landsmen.

"Now, war has sought us out. One of our two great Citadels is Citadel no more. It was laid waste to, its sea wall crushed, people massacred, homes destroyed. Fair vessels and sailormen lie at the bottom. Our maritime nation is cut by a fourth part, our safe berthings by half. We sifted the ashes, and know our enemies are the Southwastelanders, who serve Shardishku-Salamá.

"So we have put aside trade, fishnets and tally sheets, to take up the cutlass and the torch. What help we may render you against the Masters, you shall have. We mean to see all enemies swept from the sea, nothing less."

The *Ku-Mor-Mai* thanked Gale-Baiter. Brodur escorted him out. Conversations around the table were subdued, more lip movement than sound. Van Duyn, who'd expected reinforcements for the Highlands Province, saw that things would not go that way.

When Brodur came back, Lord Hightower was with him. Gil happened to be looking their way, noticing that the aide held himself stiffly, without expression.

Hightower lowered himself into the chair reserved for him. He was of heroic frame, deep-chested, thick-armed. His dense beard and long mustachios and hair

15

were white with age, hanging like snow on a mountain against his black hauberk. At his side was his great-sword, bigger than any other man would presume to carry, but they'd seen him ply it like a rapier. Past his eightieth year, he was the last pureblood of a gifted line. Like his ancestors, he'd been permitted to go into his age with undiminished vitality. He inclined his head to the *Ku-Mor-Mai*.

Springbuck welcomed him formally, then ticked off salient points of the meeting on his fingers. "The Druids and their wildmen are in our northernmost regions; Freegate is beset by raids and depredations; the Mariners have suffered the worst defeat in their history. Combat flares too, I am told, away in Veganá, at the southern tip of the Crescent Lands, but of that we ken little."

Katya said, "If you are leading to war against Salamá, it would be no easy undertaking. And will not our enemies consume our lands in our absence?"

"That is precisely why these attacks occur, I should say," Andre stated, "and why we must plan to send our vengeance south. Do you take it that Salamá simply wants new territory, or a few more subjects? I do not. They contrive to make it dangerous for us to prosecute war against them, for one motive. *They need time.* They have some design of their own, that brooks no interference. They give us our own preoccupations, so our alliance is pulled into fragments. Thus, they insure an uninterrupted span for themselves."

Katya inquired, "To what end?"

"I cannot divine its nature yet," the wizard shot back, "but something is taking shape in that dire city, of more peril than all these other incursions. The Masters decreed this screen, hiding larger danger in the south; in Shardishku-Salamá."

"The people of Coramonde—those who still support me—will want more proof than that," Springbuck said dubiously.

Andre responded carefully. "It is my hope and belief that they shall have confirmation, plain and unmistakable, in the correct moment. Other forces are in conflict here besides mere nations."

Reacher, head hung in thought, made up his mind.

16

"Andre deCourteney is the font of wisdom in opposing Bey and his Masters. Let us plan in concert our response to the strife he promises."

"Tomorrow," Springbuck concurred, "we begin." He grinned. "And there is one more pronouncement. In times as precarious as these, it has been the custom of the *Ku-Mor-Mai* to select a Warlord. For first officer in all matters military, I advance Hightower as Warlord over Coramonde, his authority issuing directly from my own."

The old man sputtered thanks. "Honeyed words are not my aptitude. My gratitude I will evince by service." He reddened at their applause.

The session ended. Gil avoided talking to the *Ku-Mor-Mai*, sore at himself for time wasted looking for Bey. That his temper had become so fragile worried him; he didn't want to discuss errors.

Ferrian of the Horseblooded stopped him in the corridor. The burly, one-time Champion-at-arms had made a remarkable recovery from the wound, suffered in the fight for the throne room, that had cost him his right arm. He was more inward-turning now. He beckoned Gil aside and pointed to where Captain Brodur took notes from Springbuck's instructions.

"Do you know him?"

"Uh, he's the guy who used to be one of—" Her name came with difficulty, even now. "One of Duskwind's agents, right? Tried to help her save Springbuck, back when Bey was going to have him killed?"

"Aye, and knows the palace-fortress and the city, and can tell you who reported to Bey, and carried out his commands. You are so intent on locating the sorcerer that I'd wondered if you shouldn't speak to him."

Gil checked the idea over, scratching the dark smear of powderburn on his cheek absentmindedly. "Good thinking. Not here though; Springbuck's already had enough of my Bey-hunt."

"Brodur drills at the fields every morning, at about the sixth hour. That would, perhaps, be the place."

"Got it." He yawned, jaw cracking. Things were moving again; maybe he could sleep. "I'm headed back for the rack. See you tomorrow."

He'd taken less than four steps when a hulking form

17

blocked his way, hissing loudly. The thing, nearly seven feet tall, was reptilian, covered with a thick, green-scaled hide. Knifelike fangs curved from its jaws, and its heavy tail was encased in caudal armor of spikes and sharp-edged flanges. At its back was slung a greatsword even larger than Hightower's.

Gil goggled, then composed himself. "Oh, hey, Kisst-Haa. Hi."

The reptile-man's fearsome head dipped once in reply; he had no speech but his own sibilant tongue. Gil had forgotten that Kisst-Haa was in Earthfast, having come along on the raid on the throne room. That must be one of the reasons Reacher had come, the American concluded—to take his faithful bodyguard home with him.

Reacher's keen ears had picked out Kisst-Haa's hiss. The King appeared, Van Duyn and the Snow Leopardess with him. It occurred to Gil, eyeing the reptile-man more closely, that the thing that made him more human than animal was his eyes. They were manlike, expressive, with whites, yellow irises and tiny dots of pupil. But it was weird to see the diminutive Lord of the Just and Sudden Reach trade glad hugs with the monster, who rumbled happily.

Gil shook hands perfunctorily with Van Duyn, clasped forearms with Katya, then with her brother. Reacher became grave. "Duskwind was given every honor," he assured Gil, "and her ashes lie with her family's. Her kinsmen wished you to know that—"

The American broke away, shaking his head. "No, Reacher. It's fine, I'm sure, whatever, but no more, please." He brushed past Kisst-Haa. "I have to go. Got an early date on the drill field."

The next morning, he put on soft, close-fitting blouse and pants and his Browning. He also strapped on the sword left behind by his friend Dunstan the Berserker, who'd been abducted by Yardiff Bey. *Just like the Froggy goin' courtin'*, he thought, settling the weapons. Reacher had inadvertently evoked a ghost, and Gil had only salvaged a few hours' sleep.

Knights and other fighting men sweated and strained in rigorous rehearsal. They'd left their finery at home, using older armor and accouterments for practice.

They swung swords at pells, tilted at quintains, hurled javelins, launched arrows, hefted axes. They feinted slyly with knives and toppled each other with dented shields. Dust rose, feet shuffled; man-nets were cast, like sinews of clouds, to bag or miss their quarry. There were wounds and other injuries, mostly among overzealous younger men.

Gil spotted Ferrian to one side, a distant look in his eyes. Gil had seen the rugged Horseblooded fight like a devil during the raid on the throne room. Now he stood apart, longing to be among the warriors again.

Ferrian noticed him, eyeing the Browning in its shoulder holster, and the sword of Dunstan. "Why bear a blade, when you have that, ah, gun?"

Gil resettled the holster. "See, there aren't many rounds left for it, or the Mauser either. High-speed nine-millimeter ammo doesn't grow on trees; I'd better be ready when the last shot goes."

Ferrian, not much older than the American but a veteran of uncounted duels, agreed wryly, "Wisdom indeed."

"Where's Brodur?"

"I was just watching him. See there, yes, where men are come together to fence with light blades in the new fashion? Brodur is there, in gray hose."

"Got him now. Who's he talking to there, Gale-whatshisname?"

"Gale-Baiter, the Mariner envoy, yes. The seaman has been dueling, with lesser opponents for the most part, and wagering heavily. Brodur's decided to try his luck. He is quite the betting man himself, you know; he insists no respectable gentleman can live on his pay alone."

Gale-Baiter was bigger, burlier than a fencer should be, whipping a heavy cavalry rapier through the air, expounding swordcraft. Brodur, long hair braided and fastened out of his way, paid close heed. He was compact, had a short-cropped beard and was smooth in movement.

19

The two observers couldn't hear what was being said—some difference of opinion over a fine point. With swords at hand, the theoretical discussion didn't last long. Gil could picture it, some lofty remark like, "Sir, if you are so very accomplished, you would perhaps vouchsafe a demonstration?"

Bets were going down right and left as the two squared off. Four judges were selected, and a president of the match, from the onlookers. The contestants placed themselves on the *piste,* held up dulled swords in their right hands to salute, and began.

They felt one another out, their dialogue of blades sporadic. Brodur showed an inclination to retreat, so Gale-Baiter tried a sudden flèche. Brodur, with less skill than Gil would have expected from a money fencer, managed a firm, blocking parry-in-retreat. But he failed to advance into an attack. He didn't seem to be toying with the Mariner or taking it easy, but in the next few moments the envoy pressed him sharply. The bigger man carried Brodur's blade from a high line to a low in bind, barely failing to hit in opposition to the blade.

The interplay became more rapid. Gale-Baiter indulged in flourishes, stamping his foot, striking Brodur's weapon with repeated beats and calling for him to come, fence boldly, show heart. Brodur stayed calm, counterattacked, and the jury followed the action along the *piste.* The younger man was quick, but not as confident as he should have been. Gale-Baiter began using vigorous stop- and time-thrusts. Brodur made a false attack and his lunge drew the Mariner out in parry-riposte. Brodur parried, hit on the counter-riposte so quickly that Gil missed it. Both judges watching Gale-Baiter spotted it, though. The president analyzed the phrase and gave the match to Brodur.

Ferrian and Gil went over. Gale-Baiter was disputing the decision. "Come, sir," he blustered to the president, "did you not see the man cover his target-parts with his shoulder? What swordsmanship is in that?"

The president, a dignified master-of-arms, held himself rigidly. "There was no covering, my Lord. We but officiated the duel as we saw it fought, well and fairly."

The Mariner flushed. He whirled on Brodur, who

was toweling his face. "You, sir; admit it! You touched me lucky, and not within the rules. Let us see who's best two times out of three!"

Brodur regarded the Mariner with a grin. "Beg pardon, my Lord Envoy, but shall we go from there to three of five? I should be delighted to teach you how it is done, but alas, I lack the time." He extended his palm. "My winnings, please."

Interesting shade of heliotrope, thought Gil, watching Gale-Baiter's face.

"Pestilence take your money, Brodur! You fight only for gold, then? Would it interest you if the bet were tenfold? Or did you beat me by guile and luck alone? Or are you afraid?"

Brodur balled his hands, compressing the towel. "If I beat you once, my Lord, I can do it twice. A man who can ignore your jigging and squawking could beat you every time and, if I may say so, with either hand."

"So? Done! Jury to their places, please. Tenfold's the bet, and if you can defeat me with either hand, let me see you do it with your left."

Brodur looked around embarrassedly, a sense of error in his face. He stepped hesitantly to his end of the *piste,* taking his sword in his left hand.

"I thought Brodur was a sharpie," Gil said to Ferrian.

The big Horseblooded laughed. "Nay, now, you are always and ever the one for private jests, eh? This time you must wait."

Gale-Baiter and Brodur crossed points again. This time there was little hesitation. The Mariner advanced confidently, saying, "Now *I* shall instruct *you!*"

Brodur stopped the attack with a perfect stop-thrust, easily avoiding the double-hit. Gale-Baiter tried for a bind. Brodur passed his point underneath the envoy's with surgical precision and met him with arm extended, point still in line. Gale-Baiter elected to retreat out of fencing distance, to ascertain just what was happening to him. Brodur attacked-in-advance into scoring range, pressed, and hit punctually on the redoublement, one fluid moment.

Neither man bothered to glance at the judges. Brodur lowered his weapon. Gale-Baiter held his up for a moment, staring at the younger man. Then, with a snort, he took his blade through an exacting salute. He motioned to two men at the sideline, his attendants. One was a red-bearded bear of a man, the other an apple-cheeked little guy with sandy curls. The smaller one dashed to hand Brodur a jingling purse. Gale-Baiter, spinning his heel, left without a word. Gil stopped the aide.

"I heard you used to work for the Lady Duskwind."

Captain Brodur eyed him for a moment. "That is essentially correct. How is it of interest to you?"

"Do you still have contacts in the city? I want to know about Yardiff Bey, where he is and how I can get to him."

"A hazardous line of inquiry."

"Didn't ask you that." He realized he was being brusque again.

Brodur smiled knowingly. "Vengeance has spurs with sharpest rowels, has it not? Very well, meet me at the Arborway at the tenth hour this evening." Taking his cloak, he left.

Watching him go, Gil said, "All right, Ferrian, cut me loose. What was the big joke?"

The Horseblooded laughed, full and loud. "Brodur, you see, is left-handed. He fought Gale-Baiter with his right to build his confidence and bump him to higher stakes for the left-handed match, a sure wager."

The American guffawed. Shaking his head at the departing Brodur, he declared, "Now *that,* Ferrian, is what you call a *hustler.*"

Chapter Two

Thou shalt not swear falsely, but fulfill thy oaths.
St. Matthew
Chapter 5, verse 33

GIL used up the brass-bright afternoon and coral evening prowling Kee-Amaine, the city spread at the feet of the palace-fortress. He liked hanging out, voluntarily lost, in Kee-Amaine's fabulous, twilight labyrinth of a bazaar. He browsed guardedly past the glitter of copper utensils and stained-glass lanterns, bolts of rich silks and bales of prize furs, the sparkle of jeweled hilts and the glint of blue steel blades. There was the omnipresent clink of vigilantly counted coins and pay-tokens. The place smelled of cheap incense, avaricious sweat, rare perfumes, old dung, hundreds of pungent foods, and unhappy livestock of every species.

He kept the heel of his left hand conspicuously on the pommel of his sword. It was a more certain insurance against trouble than his pistol; few people here would have heard of firearms, much less been able to recognize one, but all knew cold steel well. It was a simple, utilitarian blade, belonging to his friend Dunstan the Berserker. The American was determined that its owner would have it again.

The confused uproar in the bazaar was constant. Each vendor had a song or call, and bartering was animated, almost theatrical. Voices and chatter here interested him. People in the Crescent Lands spoke more rapidly, more vividly than he was used to. Theirs was a verbal culture, and this, very much, a world of the ear and the spoken word.

He sampled a skewer of grease-popping cubed meat. He found it—like many foods here—so highly spiced

23

that it brought tears. Lacking preservatives, people fought gamey flavor with a tongue-searing array of seasonings.

He eventually threaded his way through the bazaar to the Arborway, main path through the rambling commons known as the Tarryinground. Trees of many kinds arched above, a corridor of the diverse hues and textures of leaves and bark.

At the entrance he met Brodur, just after the tenth hour had resounded. "You received my message?" the captain asked.

"Yes. I've got the money; I grubbed it off Springbuck."

"Good. The man we want is to meet us in a taproom, the White Tern. I thought a walk there might be salutary. Too, I shall have to know more in order to be of assistance to you. Any dealing concerned with Yardiff Bey must be presumed to have its pitfalls."

Brodur, who wore a hooded cloak, held up a broad-brimmed hat. "I took the liberty of selecting this for you, apropos of our excursion. The man we go to see was in the throne room the night you and Springbuck and the others invaded it. May I point out that the brim can be tilted quite low across the face?"

Gil's respect for Brodur increased. They set off, their way among the strollers lit by flaming cressets.

Gil began, "When Yardiff Bey bugged out in that airship of his, he had Dunstan prisoner. I think Bey'll hang onto him as a hedge or hostage, or for interrogation." Their boots crunched over the gravel path as he thought out his next words. "Thing is, I've got this *feeling* Dunstan's alive, y'know? So I have to find Bey to spring Dunstan."

Brodur glanced sidelong at him. "Pardon my saying this, but you are said to harbor another reason as well. It is rumored you require vengeance."

Gil stopped and faced Brodur. "You knew her too, right?"

"Gil MacDonald, I conspired with the Lady Duskwind. I served her, held her in highest regard and in some measure, I tell you, she was dear to me."

"I'm not sure what you're getting at, here."

"That I, too, want requittal for gentle Duskwind's

24

death. I shall advance your purpose and abet you in whatever manner you may need. Whatever manner. I trust I make myself clear?"

"Shake." They clasped hands, then resumed their way.

At the end of the Arborway a fountain played in the glare of torches. There were wide playing fields, where children charged back and forth in giggling games of chase-ball, hampered by darkness. Others played a new favorite, "the Game of Springbuck," re-enacting the *Ku-Mor-Mai*'s flight and eventual return. Gil could see their bright clothes intermittently, like Chinese kites on a night breeze.

Farther along, adults congregated to chat, see and be seen, or just linger. Food and drink were sold, but no other paying enterprise was permitted except entertainment. Beyond, in a meadow, musicians at the foot of a statue of Springbuck's father Surehand mingled notes, accompanied occasionally by voices lifted in song. Off to one side a puppet show was in progress.

They passed through groves of trees onto a greensward. Public speakers were free to address matters of conviction or caprice here, an acclaimed innovation of Springbuck's, but several pikemen were stationed nearby to squelch the brawls that often ignited from impassioned debate.

Skirting a quiet lake with a tiny, exquisite chapel of the Bright Mistress on its rim, they came to another access path, and left the commons for what Gil knew was a raunchy section of the city, Lowlintel Road.

Lighting was sparser, buildings more tightly packed. There were enclaves crowded together, of people from the many subdominions of polyglot Coramonde. Here, no bedding was aired on balconies by day, nor washing hung out at night, for fear of theft. Both loosened swords in their scabbards. Gil made sure his cloak didn't impede access to the Browning.

There were loiterers, usually outside a hell-raising tavern or dimly lit house with a red wreath on its door and women beckoning from the windows.

They came to the White Tern. Its interior was a scene of faded charms; beautiful starmolding around the door had been allowed to crack and chip away and the rushes serving as a floor hadn't been changed recently. Ceiling, rafters and tiny roundel windows were all coated with greasy smoke. Odors reported too many people, too close, over much too long a time. There was a sweetish thickness in the air. Gil knew it for the scent of the drug Earnai, the Dreamdrowse.

Boisterous arguments vied with harsh laughter. An arm-wrestling match between a Teebran archer and an Alebowrenian bravo spurred rabid rooting and wagering. Gil trailed Brodur into the snug at the back, and they took a booth.

Candles guttered low; customers were solo and silent. A harassed-looking girl brushed a lock of limp hair from her eyes and took their order, a toss of brandy for Brodur, jack of beer for the American. The aide made an elaborate ceremony of inhaling the brandy, eyes closed. Gil just drank.

The captain got back to their errand. "The man is called Wintereye. He is an Oathbreaker, stripped of sword and status, but I knew him in the days of his prosperity. Now he roots out his living as best he may. While Bey was in power he often—"

A man had come to their booth. He was unkempt; a stale stink drifting from him. His eyes darted nervously, reconning the room. At the captain's invitation he seated himself next to Brodur, refusing a drink. He kept his head lowered, disheveled hair hiding his face.

"I am glad to see you, Wintereye," said the aide. "It is some space of time since last we met. You are slimmer now but tired, I venture."

Wintereye lifted his gaze. His cheek was branded with a stylized Faith Cup, broken at the stem, stigma of the Oathbreaker. The man scowled.

"These days, Captain Brodur, living's lean and skittish. In fact, you may know someone who can use this?"

From some inner fold of his ragged shirt his left hand brought a pellet the size of a pea, of a waxy, kneaded material. Gil noticed Wintereye wore odd tubes of painted leather on his fingertips.

"Finest Earnai from the south, and at a reasonable price. No? What makes two gallants deny the Dreamdrowse? Life is sweet but ah, visions sweeter still! Open the Doors that lie Between; here is the Key that unlocks

26

fastnesses of the mind. With it, you'll see inward, and Beyond, and find your Answers."

Brodur refused a second time. "As you will," Wintereye surrendered. "The Dreamdrowse always comes to him for whom it is destined." He left the Dreamdrowse conspicuously on the table.

"Permit me to present my associate," Brodur went on. The American tilted his hat brim lower. "My associate's name has no importance, but he is interested in where he might reasonably seek a former employer of yours."

Wintereye thought a moment. "There are few things, very few, worse than the life I lead, yet one is the enmity of Yardiff Bey."

"Ah, money could take you even beyond the reach of the Hand of Salamá."

Wintereye shuddered. "*Nothing* can take a man that far!"

Brodur showed his teeth, his suave mask dropping. "You once drank a Faith Cup with Springbuck's father. Then you betrayed the son, would have murdered him, given the chance."

He caught Wintereye's right forearm and held it up. The hand had been lopped off, its wrist bound in leather. "I convinced the *Ku-Mor-Mai* you were not worth executing, traitor. Others were impaled and hung outside the Iron Hook Gate for less." The angry captain released the arm. "The hour is too late for you to begin protecting your trusts, Wintereye."

It drove home to Gil just how serious oathbreaking was. In a world with few written contracts a man was, quite literally, only as good as his word. A violation of that word placed on him a mark no decent person would wear. Wintereye, with missing hand and branded cheek, would never know honest companions, and was ejected from the profession of arms forever. His face twitched with anger.

Gil looked away, and noticed a bulky man, face cowled and hidden like Brodur's, enter the snug. The man seated himself, scanning the room.

Wintereye, glowering at Brodur, asked, "You have money?" Gil brought out the wallet of coins Springbuck had given him without inquiring how the American would use it. Brodur had his hand on his sword, insuring that Wintereye wouldn't bolt. But when the informer had tucked his fee inside his tattered shirt, he set his forearms on the table and leaned forward.

"Now, as to my master Yardiff Bey—" He stopped suddenly, lurching at Brodur, catching the aide's swordhand. His accomplice must have stolen up very softly; a leering face and a burlap-wrapped arm and torso appeared around the edge of the high-backed bench. The man swung a heavy cudgel at Gil.

The American's reflexes were good. If he hadn't been so intent on Wintereye, he might have dodged. But he only managed to avoid having his head bashed open. The heavy, knotted cudgel connected glancingly with his outside shoulder, his right. He screamed in anguish and his arm went numb. The man tried to close on him, but Gil dragged himself farther into the booth. Whipping his drinking jack at his attacker, he got his legs up to fend him off, clawing futilely with his left hand for the Browning that hung beneath his left armpit.

Brodur broke Wintereye's desperate grip and would have thrown him aside and swept his sword free, but the back room of the White Tern sprouted more enemies. Most of the patrons, wanting no part of it, stampeded for the doors, but four others rushed into the fight with daggers and clubs. Three swarmed up behind Wintereye at Brodur, who had just time to snatch his own dagger. Wintereye seized the dagger hand, beating the captain with his wrist, but inadvertently shielded him from the rest.

There was more movement, this time from the front wall. The hooded man whom Gil had noticed entering barreled into the fray, cutlass held high. Gil squirmed to avoid another blow, keeping his assailant at bay with kicking feet. The cudgel battered his thigh. Next thing, his opponent dropped to the floor, holding his side in a spreading pool of blood. His mouth appeared to work and strain, but no sound came.

One of the attackers reached around Wintereye, and slashed. His aim was off; the blade plowed along the flesh of Brodur's upper chest, stopped by the collarbone with a nauseating grate. Gil got the Browning with his left hand. Extending it across the table, he fired point-

28

blank at the informer. In the confinement of the booth, the report was more concussion than sound, slamming deafness. Brain tissue and bone chips exploded in a mist of blood. Wintereye crashed hard against the back of the bench and fell across the table, a hideous exit hole in his skull. His other cheek, covering the candle, snuffed it.

The assassins fell back, yowling. The smell of gunpowder replaced all others in the snug. Gil wriggled into a sitting position and swung the muzzle to bear on the man who had stabbed Brodur. His left hand and pistol shook badly. The first shot had rung a world of silence down around him. With effort, he locked his elbow steady and shot the man, as Brodur tried to clasp his gushing wound together with his hands. The second shot battered Gil's ears and began an acute ache. The man flew backward in a heap, a burbling puncture in his chest.

Gil managed to thrust his useless right hand into his shirtfront, crouching to hold it there, then slid from the booth. A thought occurred to him, and he groped around the darkened space, searching.

Brodur, in shock, was being helped to his feet by their benefactor, whose hood had fallen back. A dark beard of oiled ringlets glistened. It was Gale-Baiter, envoy of the Mariners. He supported the captain as Gil stumbled after. None of the other attackers remained. The door swung lazily on rawhide hinges.

The front room of the White Tern was empty. Gil thought dazedly that he'd never gotten more mileage out of two rounds. Gale-Baiter's coach was waiting outside. The driver and footman had gotten down to help. Gil recognized them from the drill field, the towering redbeard and the little guy, the envoy's attendants. They hoisted Brodur into the coach; all boarded and clattered away quickly.

Gale-Baiter banged the roof of the carriage with the basket hilt of his cutlass. "Skewerskean, rot you, don't jostle this biscuit box around! This is a wounded man in here!" The ride steadied. Gil had scarcely been able to hear the command, his ears pounded so.

"Wound's not too serious," Gale-Baiter decided,

which, Gil supposed, only meant Brodur wouldn't die right away.

"You want to tell me about your being here just now?" the American hollered over the rumble of the coach and his own deafness. The automatic was still in his hand.

"I was trailing this fella here. I thought I had a right to call him out, after the way he did me this morning, but the *Ku-Mor-Mai* frowns on dueling inside the city anymore. I reckoned it that we could re-examine the outcome of the match, him and me. Still, I could not very well watch the pair of you laid by the heels and carved up, could I now?"

Gil reflected that Gale-Baiter could very well have done just that; lots of people would have. The envoy brought a liquor flask from beneath his seat cushion. He gave Brodur a sip, then he and Gil each took a swig. It was thick, cordial-tasting stuff Gil wouldn't ordinarily have liked, but welcomed now.

Gilbert A., old son, he told himself, *Brodur was right. Bey sure hasn't lost his touch.*

Brodur was holding his wound, teeth gritted, clinging to consciousness. Gale-Baiter slipped his scarf off, helping stop the seeping blood. It was decided the aide must go to Earthfast, where Springbuck's physicians could treat him.

"Sorry am I," husked Brodur, "that Yardiff Bey's control still extends so far. We wasted your silver and you are no farther toward the Hand of Salamá."

"Don't bet on that." Gil tucked the pistol away, carefully retaining the pellet of Earnai he'd snatched from the booth with two fingers, just before leaving the snug. He held the Dreamdrowse up to the fitful light of torches and cressets as the coach tore along.

"No, don't be too sure of that at all."

Chapter Three

So much the rather thou celestial light
Shine inward, and the mind through all her powers
Irradiate, there plant eyes, all mist from thence
Purge and disperse, that I may see and tell
Of things invisible to mortal sight.

> John Milton
> *Paradise Lost,* Book III

GABRIELLE deCourteney had been installed in lush rooms, luxury appropriate to the sovereign's mistress and a pre-eminent sorceress.

The knock surprised her. Springbuck had said he'd be occupied with counsels, and would see her at breakfast. Her handmaiden opened the door and Gil MacDonald stepped in, right arm in a sling, a limp in his stride. Gabrielle inspected him coldly; there'd never been much liking between them.

"Can I talk to you alone? Please."

Dismissing the handmaiden, she curtly invited him to sit. "Have you had an accident? You have seen the chirurgeons?"

He skirted her questions. "I'll be okay. The arm's numb, and my hook shot's ruined, but I'm bound up tight, and it'll do."

Gabrielle wore a gown of softest white kid, embroidered in the flowery, intricate Teebran style. Masses of red curls tumbled around her shoulders, and the deep, green eyes held him. He'd always felt jumpy around her. Her aloofness knocked him off stride; she was too good at manipulating people.

He told her what had happened, words tumbling over each other, up to where he'd left Brodur sitting propped

31

up in bed, wound sutured closed, puffing on an old, deep-bowled pipe, out of danger. Gil finished by holding up the waxy bead of Earnai. Soliciting his permission with a lift of an eyebrow, she took the Dream-drowse, and held it up to a candle.

"Why me? Why not Springbuck or Andre?"

"Springbuck's preoccupied and—no offense—your brother's too cautious. He might not go for what I've got in mind."

"And I?"

He hesitated. "I figure you'll try anything that sounds interesting. That's the way you strike me." She didn't reply. He knew he'd have to say it all without prompting; that much she would demand.

"I was sitting in the White Tern, thinking about what Wintereye was saying. I'm running around Coramonde like a monkey in a hardware store. You have to understand, I was brought up to go from 'one' to 'two' to 'and so on.' You've got necromancy and tiromancy and all those other 'mancies, but I always steered clear of 'em. But this Earnai, it was like *it* found *me*. I thought maybe I could tap in on whatever, uh, insights I can unlock." He made a vague gesture, hand dropping to the chair arm. "I want in on those Doors Between and Beyond. I need the mystical connection. I want to perceive things a different way."

She scrutinized him coolly. It was, she thought, a decision that could as easily have come from desperation as from reason. "Do you think you would find Dunstan? Or Yardiff Bey?"

He shrugged. "I've seen you do things a million times weirder. At one time or another, I've believed in nuclear fusion and Virgin Birth, but I never saw either one. I admit possibilities. Look, we've never been great pals, but I thought it might intrigue you."

She rose and glided from the room. He waited. In a moment she returned with a tarot deck. She held the Earnai up to the candle again and smiled. "And I thought this would be an idle evening. Come."

She led him to an inner chamber, furbished to suit her, not a sanctum, but a personal place of solitude. The carpet was deep; the door seemed to shut airtight. She'd arranged lamps, shades and mirrors to decorate with illuminated and shadowed spaces. Gil found himself studying unidentifiable knickknacks, paintings, and objects that might be musical instruments or, equally likely, rococo mobile sculptures. Or something utterly else. Nobody really knew how old she was. What might a finely alert mind, living for centuries, light upon as curious?

"There are many forms of Earnai." She brought out a tiny brazier carved from a block of onyx, its basin no larger than a teacup. She lit a flame beneath it. "It comes from the heart of a plant found throughout the southern reaches, did you know that? Some Southwastelanders call it 'mahónn,' which means 'rescue.' Among others it is 'k'nual, the visitor.' It is, in different places and climes, 'Vision Flower,' 'God-call,' and 'the Passageway.' But it takes a measure of art to use it safely. A single mote of the pure substance would slay you, me, and anyone else in the room. It must be diluted, it must be handled carefully, like a cunning beast. It is used in countless ways, you see. Effects depend on concentration and combination."

She dropped the pellet into the brazier. Thin ribbons of smoke curled up into the air. "It can be a euphoric, or make you giddy. It can banish pain or render the strongest man unconscious. It has been used in aphrodisiacs, and inquisitor's compounds."

At her invitation, they arranged themselves on thick pillows on opposite sides of a low table of old, pleasant-feeling mahogany. "That pellet, that is a thing of the south, but the Horseblooded sometimes use it. Did Wintereye wear thimbles or coverings on his fingertips? Ah, then he worked it from the pure himself. The Dreamdrowse is mingled with one of the noropianics. Its color and inner striations are good, its odor untainted, perfect for what you have in mind. Have you ever experienced the Other Sides?"

Not certain what she meant, he kept it to the issue at hand. "Guess not. Do we stick our heads over it, catch it in a bag, or what?"

"What do you taste?"

He rolled his tongue experimentally. "Musk. A little tartlike, I think."

"Dreamdrowse. It entered your pores, and your
33

blood has carried it to your tongue already." She put the tarot deck down precisely between them. Her fingers stroked and patted the deck slowly, renewing old ties.

Perhaps the Dreamdrowse was working, or the events of the night had exhausted his restraint. On impulse, he clapped his hand down on the deck before she could take it up. She withheld her objections, recognizing inspiration. Gabrielle had no qualms about subordinating ceremony to revelation.

In a motion he never questioned, he fanned the cards out, faces down, an arc from one side of the table to the other. She said nothing, but her green eyes flashed at him again.

He let his hand rove the deck. He felt warmth rising against his palm, and picked up the card from which it radiated. She took it gently.

"The Ace of Swords. Hmm." She laid it before him. On it, a hand emerging from a cloud held a greatsword encircled by a crown. In the background, tongues of flame blazed in the sky like a firmament. Every feature screamed possible interpretations at him. He sensed an outpouring from himself toward the tarot. A small part of him saw its resemblance to the regimental crest of his old outfit, the 32d.

Gabrielle whispered piercingly, "Your card—it is yours now—says 'All power to the extremes!' Dare to seize your moment, the prize, the victory. Card of conquest, of excess in love and hatred, love of haunting intensity, but also hatred of terrible immutability.

"Reversed, it takes on other connotations, proliferation and increase, variety and, perhaps, tragedy. But you pulled this tarot yourself and I cannot tell which message is intended. You are not meant to know yet, Gil MacDonald. There are things especially pertinent to the Ace of Swords; the glow on a lover's face, and blood on a steel blade."

The tarot rose through his senses. Gabrielle's voice was a narrative faculty for it. He opened himself to it. It enveloped him.

Then there were quick images, like a slide show. An enormous fortification spread before him on a level plain facing a gray, wind-chased sea. It stretched in grim angles and martial tessellations. It was, he intuited, a repository of fear.

From far away, words drifted to him.

Forget the fear.

There is no fear.

And the fear was gone. The American almost identified the voice, but the scene shifted. Another view, of a dark, vaulted ceiling in a dank, subterranean room. It was lit by banked fires. There was the creak and clash of equipment of torture. In a white-hot universe of agony, the voice returned.

Reject the pain.

There is no pain.

The anguish retreated. Gil knew it as Dunstan's voice, and tried to call, but had no voice of his own in the eerie pseudo-world of the Ace. He sensed cruel bindings against wronged flesh. The words persisted.

Banish restraint.

There is no restraint.

But there was a note of doubt to it. The restraint didn't disappear.

A last vision came, of a fluttering banner. Its device was a flaming wheel, half black, half white, on a black-and-white field, so that each half of the wheel was against the opposite color. Then the world faded before his eyes.

He was at Gabrielle's table, had never left it. She watched him with an attitude very much like pity. From stellar distances he heard her say, "You are no thaumaturge, yet rarely, rarely have I seen the Cards do that for anyone. The Sudden Enlightenment, it was. We are very much alike, you and I."

His eyes were still drifting. His brain overloaded with speculation, mystical synapses, cognitive spasm-shocks. Ideas strobing in his head left tantalizing residues of after-image.

But one fact was manifest. He knew whose banner he'd seen through Dunstan's eyes, without himself ever having seen or heard of it before. Gabrielle watched the lips form a single word under vacant, murderous eyes.

Bey.

Springbuck was alone in his cavernous throne room, without crown or pageantry, steps clacking hollowly.

It was the first time he'd ever been in the chamber without anyone else. He could feel echoes of the past pressing in; it was for that reason he'd come. He saw the darker spot on the floor where, months before, the younger Hightower, the old hero's son, had been beheaded by the ogre Archog. Peering hard to accommodate weak vision, he could see places where Gil's and Van Duyn's shots had blasted chips of stone from the walls.

He climbed the dais where he and Strongblade had fought. In the ornate wood of the throne was a deep penetration where the *Ku-Mor-Mai* had left his knife when he'd chosen to face the usurper with only his sword Bar.

There was a bare spot where Strongblade's portrait had been. Throughout Earthfast and the city, statues, paintings, busts and plaques of him had, in fear or anger, been unceremoniously removed. Traditionalists had wanted to strike the name from history; Springbuck had forbidden that. Strongblade's name, deeds and fate would be an infamous lesson for posterity.

Gil entered, the only person besides Gabrielle and Hightower whom the door warders would let interrupt the *Ku-Mor-Mai*'s musings. He saw that the young monarch was lost in introspection. "Hey, I could catch you later."

"No, come in. I hungered for early-morning silence before the day's obligations. They are bringing Midwis before me today, a thorny problem, one of the Legion-Marshals who went against me. He's been decorated half a hundred times, and his battle standard's heavy with ribbons of valor. His family's influential as well, and at the very last he renounced the conspiracy. I can neither deny him some measure of clemency, nor let him go unpunished. A twisty dilemma."

"You'll think of something."

"May it be so. Tonight will be little less busy. A famous poet will be here. Court will be crowded and last late." He sat on the top step of the dais. "Gil, do you remember Freegate, in my exile? Reacher brought in that prestigious harper, but you and Duskwind were tipsy. You insisted the poor man come with the two of you to the kitchens, and teach the scullions to dance? What music was that?"

"A slide. A Kerry slide."

"Oh yes, slide." Springbuck chuckled. "The courtiers were quite astonished."

"Yeah, but Katya liked it. And it was the only time I ever saw Reacher dance." Gil, too, chortled.

"And in the end, didn't that harper add it to his repertoire? Aha, and offer you both places with his company?" He burst into mirth again.

Gil sobered, nodding to himself, speaking so the other could hardly hear. "We had ourselves some times, then."

He went up the dais and plopped down on the throne, one leg dangling nonchalantly over its arm. Springbuck was no longer shocked at such irreverence.

"Gil, I should like to hear your version of what happened last night with Brodur. He's mending nicely, by the way."

Recounting the incident at the White Tern and the séance, the other became strained and brittle. There was anger, curbed violence, just beneath the surface of him. As he spoke, he felt with his forefinger the scar on his forehead.

When he'd heard it all, Springbuck said, "A foolish idea. You could have died, you idiot!"

"Sue me. I just tried for a lead on Bey. How was I supposed to know we'd be set up?"

"I did not mean going to the White Tern, though that was no stroke of genius either. I meant using the Dreamdrowse. It could easily have been poisoned; Bey's traps are subtlety itself."

"Gabe would have spotted it if it had been a hotshot. Besides, I figure it was worth it."

"Ah, marvelous epitaph! 'He figured it was worth it.' Splendid!"

"Hey, take it easy. Don't be such a hardcase." There was a tray of food and a pitcher set out on a small table. Gil poured them each a stone mug of lager. "Here, put some money in your meter. What I did doesn't matter. Bey does." He drew breath for the big question. "How many men can you spare me?"

37

Springbuck took a long bowie knife from beneath his robes and toyed with it. It had been a gift from Gil, a genuine Hibben, and had left that mark in the wood of the throne.

"Have you considered this in detail?" he finally asked.

"What's to consider? I got through to Dunstan. Gabe felt it too. She thinks he's at a place called Death's Hold, an old hangout of Bey's." He pointed vaguely southwest. "It's thataway, on the coast of the Outer Sea. I'm going. Do I get men, or not?"

Springbuck put the tips of his fingers together and pressed them to his lips. He avoided the American's glance, racked between commitment to his friend and duty to the suzerainty.

He spoke into the little steeple of fingers, resenting what he must say. "Had I left that Legion under you, when first you returned from the Dark Rampart, you would have taken it back into the mountains, would you not? Hearing Van Duyn's news, you'd have had us all depart for the Highlands Province, is that not true also? But this morning you are of the persuasion that Death's Hold is the place. Gil, my very hold on Coramonde is in jeopardy. Subject-states threaten to fall, not one by one but in rows. Where you would have been wrong the first time, and the second, how can you ask me to squander a Legion I need so badly? Every man under arms is crucial." He faltered, then met the American's glare. "Had you not returned with that Legion when you did, I'd have dispatched orders to its Marshal."

Gil whitened, the scar and powderburn standing out vividly. "All right, Coramonde's in trouble; so are you. Where do you think it's coming from? Bey, where else? Nail him and you settle all your hassles right there and then. Are you too dumb to see we have to get him for your sake too?"

"Which Yardiff Bey?" the *Ku-Mor-Mai* shouted back. "The one in the Dark Rampart? In the Highlands Province? Death's Hold? I dare not be prodigal with what loyal units are left me. If you were in command you'd say the same."

The American lost hold of his bitterness. "You're going to do nothing while Bey and his people chip away

38

at you? When are you going to learn to take the first swing? Are you scared to go after him for a change?"

Both knew they were on their way to irrevocable words. Springbuck was first to avert it.

"Yes, I am afraid. I fear for Coramonde, and myself as well. Everything I ever learned about the sorcerer makes me wary. He can do more damage with a lie than most men could with a regiment at their back. He draws out that ductile gullibility in all of us. You've deceived him, because you used tricks of war altogether new here, but he never makes the same error twice. Never. I am afraid this fresh spoor is one more trick. There are uncounted lives hinging on this; I cannot divert Coramonde's remaining manpower, not on such tenuous grounds."

Gil, too, pulled back, ashamed. The *Ku-Mor-Mai* was right; in his place Gil would have been just as cautious; the man in charge had to be. He scratched his cheek, and thought.

"Springbuck, I'm sorry. You had it straight, I had it garbled. I never meant you're, y'know, a coward." He sat down alongside the other. They knocked mugs.

"It's funny about Dunstan, he was so full of contradictions. He'd be so placid, introverted really, until he flew into one of those berserkergangs. I took it into my head that somehow he was like a key to the Crescent Lands; if I could understand him, it would clarify everything for me here. And when he began hanging out with us, when he'd learned how to laugh, I felt this Chinese Obligation."

Gil drew himself back to the present. "Springbuck, it was so clear, Dunstan in Death's Hold. You'd have believed it too."

The son of Surehand shook his head. "I believe you as much as myself. I trust not my own senses either, where the Hand of Salamá is involved. What's needed is proof."

Gil jumped up, pacing the thick carpet. "Proof? All right, now we're clicking. You want hard evidence, I'll get it."

He broke off. "Do you still think you'll have to go south, against Shardishku-Salamá?"

39

"I am uncertain. The question is whether or not I will be able to. Coramonde's upheavals continue."

"But if we take Bey out of the picture, it'll take pressure off you."

"Past all question."

"So when I find Bey, be set to move fast. The next problem's how to get to Death's Hold. What's the normal route?"

The *Ku-Mor-Mai* rubbed his jaw. "Most trading fell off during the thronal war, but the Western Tangent is open. I would be dubious of traveling with merchant convoys, though; insecure. An alternative suggests itself. You might go south with Andre deCourteney."

"Andre? Why's Andre going south?"

"To bring the sword Blazetongue back to its rightful owner, as I told you he would. He insists Blazetongue has important consequences in the struggle against Salamá. He and a small party are leaving within days."

"How many?"

"A minimal number. He, too, knows no men can be spared, but requires few. There are a number of borders between here and Veganá, where he's going. Foreign governments would respect Coramonde's letter of transit, but they're hardly likely to permit a large armed force to enter their territories. Andre wants no regular soldiers; he could not take enough to guarantee safety, only enough to insure conspicuousness."

Gil had missed that angle. He saw now that any large group would make travel harder. "Smart. But would Andre go out of his way and check out Death's Hold?"

"Not before he delivers Blazetongue. He is adamant. But he is as eager to break and hinder Bey as you are. If you accompany him, he will probably be more than ready to investigate Death's Hold afterward."

Gil sorted it out. If he couldn't use a large escort, the next best thing was Andre deCourteney. No one in the Crescent Lands had a more formidable constellation of skills and experience.

"Okay, quit shoveling. It's a deal. Where's Andre? I'll give him the pitch."

Andre deCourteney had appropriated Yardiff Bey's abandoned sanctum sanctorum, at the summit of Earth-

40

fast, to examine its contents and learn what he could from them. He still hadn't replaced the door that had been bent back on its hinges by the reptile-man Kisst-Haa.

Gil knocked on the frame, and went in to find the wizard at a puzzling piece of apparatus. The American sat on a bench to watch. The room was filled with jars, bottles, scrolls, astrolabes and star charts. Blazetongue, the huge onetime Sword of the *Ku-Mor-Mai,* rested against the bench.

"I have plumbed a riddle here, I think," Andre said, "but it has generated another. Behold."

He lit a flame under each of two retorts. The liquids in them boiled, one forming a yellow gas, the other a red. Opening two petcocks, he let them blend. A faint orange mist rose from a nozzle at the top of the equipment.

"Now, see." He held a piece of parchment into the orange flow. It was old, with a ragged edge as if it had been ripped from a book.

Andre fanned the sheet in the orange vapor, which began to peel a covering from the parchment in flakes. Soon there was a little snowdrift of them on the worktable, and a page-within-a-page was revealed. Andre held it up proudly. Gil politely applauded.

"Andre, I thought science projects are Van Duyn's line."

"This is of interest to me because it was important to Yardiff Bey." He held up the binding from which the page had come. It was richly embossed, encircled by a wide metallic strip. A thick, raised seal was impressed on the strip, filled with runes and sigils, in wax the color of burgundy. Bey had apparently removed the pages somehow without disturbing it.

"This is the cover from Rydolomo's *Arrivals Macabre,*" Andre explained. "It survived the Great Blow. There are not more than two or three copies in existence; Rydolomo was an arch-mage and premier thinker. Bey is, by appearances, under the impression Rydolomo left some in one of his books. The sorcerer circumvented its guardian seal somehow."

The page he held was blank, but Gil understood.

Somewhere, a book of Rydolomo's had something Bey coveted, hidden within.

A servant appeared at the door frame. Andre went, and accepted a blanket-wrapped bundle. It was a baby, a chubby girl.

"Recognize her? She's the one we brought back from the Infernal Plane, the one the demon Amon had been holding."

Gil inspected her from a distance, not used to children. Andre began tickling and chucking her under the chin, making senseless, happy sounds. "Isn't she the charmer? Oh, come on, Gil; say something to her."

"Goo," offered the American solemnly. "Why's she here?"

"Reacher brought her from Freegate. I believe she's tied in with all this, the endeavors of Bey and the Masters. I wanted her here while I go through Yardiff Bey's things, to see if there are correlations." He put her in a makeshift bassinet, a dry-sink. "But now, what brings you up here?"

Gil jabbed a thumb at Blazetongue. It was a long, imperial-looking weapon, its blade chased with inscriptions and enchantment. "I've been elected. I'm going to Death's Hold, but first I'm going with you to Veganá."

"Your company will be welcome; we share common goals beside Veganá. As to Blazetongue, there are some things I could tell, and one thing for certain I cannot. I do not have the spell that makes the blade burn, as Bey and Strongblade did."

"Well, Springbuck told me the rest. Too bad; that would be a handy trick to have." His eye fell on *Arrivals Macabre*.

"Delivering Blazetongue is a job that has wanted doing for a long time," the wizard assured him. He went back to playing with the child, chuckling at her giggles.

"Your sister and I both think Bey is in Death's Hold. Are you interested in seeing?"

"After delivering Blazetongue? Hmm, yes, if evidence points to it. First, I must think it through. Speaking of the Hand of Salamá, Bey's sword Dirge is there on the chest."

Gil spied it, a shorter sword than Blazetongue, with a vicious, runcinate blade. The sorcerer had dropped it in his fight with Dunstan. Terrible properties were attributed to it. It occurred to Gil that it might be linked to Bey's magic; weapons and owners had strange affinities here.

Andre was still fussing over the baby. Gil picked up the binder of *Arrivals Macabre*, feeling its ancient weight.

"Andre, do you think we'll find Bey?"

The wizard didn't turn. He bounced the child, answering, "You will have your moment with Bey. The hatred is mutual, and in both your destinies."

Hearing it cut Gil to the bone. His hand closed angrily on the binder. The rough edges of the seal rested under his fingertips.

"What kind of crack's that, Andre?" His nails had detected a slight give in the seal's edge. Unthinkingly, framing his next words, he dug at it. The outermost corner gave way with a minute pop, but Andre somehow heard.

The wizard spun, consternation on his face, shouting "No!"

Gil was blown back off the bench with enormous force by something that had suddenly come into the room. He twisted to avoid landing on his injured side, but was still jarred by shooting pain. He sat up awkwardly to a hair-raising scene, with those feelings so characteristic of his Coramonde experience, utter astonishment mixed with stark terror.

Between Andre and Gil a ball of swirling transplendence hung, a miniature sun. Andre had taken in the situation—which Gil hadn't sorted out yet—and acted. Putting the baby back in the dry-sink he began mystic passes, uttering words from a dead language. As he did, he backed away, deliberately shoving the dry-sink toward the door with his legs and plump buttocks, wishing he hadn't left the occult jewel Calundronius with his sister.

Gil found time to think, *He's such a homey little guy, balding and fat. You forget he's the man of action.*

Andre's spell had been hasty or incomplete. The entity sizzled, and lashed out at him, knocking him sideways. The baby began wailing, attracting the thing's attention. It floated in that direction.

43

Gil grabbed for his pistol, then stopped. It wasn't likely to do much good. Andre was still groggy. As a tendril of energy edged into the dry-sink, the child's complaint shifted register from dismay to rage

Blazetongue, still lying against the bench, flared incandescent. Flame licked up and down its glowing blade.

The being instantly pulled back, compressing into an alarmed ball. Gil snatched up Blazetongue, leaping sparks singeing his hands. The bench had begun to burn where the sword had rested against it.

Gil circled, the short-hairs of his neck on end with electricity, trying to get between the child and the thing that hovered near it. Instead, the thing floated over the dry-sink and retreated to the far wall, dangerously at bay, gathering itself to strike out. He followed, waving the weapon dubiously. Putting himself to block the baby from immediate harm, he tried to decide what to do.

A hand on his shoulder; Andre. The hand was steady as stone, its grip imperatively strong. Gil gave him room. Andre moved nearer the being, pointed his index finger at it. It swelled to attack. He roared a string of syllables that meant nothing to the American, and the intruder was rent like smoke in the wind. It pulled itself together again, radiating its perturbation. Gil waved Blazetongue, cheering. "Eat him up, deCourteney!"

Wrath, usually a stranger to Andre's face, had transformed it. His lips quivered, his eyes slitted, but the finger was unswerving. He loosed the string of syllables again. This time the being was dissipated beyond its ability to recover, dismissed.

It was the old, unscary Andre who took the baby to his shoulder, to soothe her. Gil watched fire die along Blazetongue.

"What—what was that thing?" he got out finally. The wizard ignored him. "Y'know, Andre, you could have just said you didn't want to give out the burning spell. You didn't have to lie."

The thaumaturge came to him, bouncing up and down a fraction, which the baby enjoyed. "What in the world are you talking about?"

"The goddam *sword's* what I'm talking about, man! You did one helluva job just now, but you were still

44

jazzing me about not knowing the spell of the sword."

Andre stopped bouncing. Gil tensed.

"Let me inform you of two facts," the wizard said. "The first is that what you saw was a guardian entity. It appeared when you meddled with Rydolomo's seal; it was to avoid just such an accident that I forebore to wear Calundronius today. Next time you go poking about such perils, I should be grateful if you would arrange to deal with whatever problems arise by yourself."

Gil eyed the disturbed seal of Rydolomo guiltily. Andre plodded on. "And the second item is that, as I said, I do not know the conjuration for the fire of Blazetongue. Do I make myself quite lucid?"

"So, who lit it up? 'Cause *I* sure as hell didn't."

Andre smiled smugly and patted the baby's back. She burped softly. Gil stared in disbelief from wizard to child and back.

"You're kidding. Aren't you? Kidding?"

The other sighed. "I am not certain how, yet it was indisputably she. Now, I presume you have no objections to my cleaning up here. You have, I take it, other things to which you should be attending?"

"I'm going. I've gone."

In the stairwell, he blew thoughtfully on his blistering hands. *One other item's for damn sure; the next thing I unseal's going to have a drink inside it.*

Chapter Four

*Thou'rt slave to fate, chance, kings and desperate
men.*

John Donne
"Death, Be Not Proud"

ON his way to Springbuck's study the next day Gil met
Van Duyn.

"MacDonald, I, ah—"

"You craved my presence?"

The scholar agreed wryly. "There're things you and I
should clear up; it may be awhile before we see one
another again."

They found a window seat. Gil sat gingerly, protecting his shoulder. His occult contact with Dunstan, and
the belief that he was on the right track, had calmed
him. He'd been able to sleep, a dreamless rest that had
refreshed him. The lacerating feeling of futility was
gone.

Van Duyn rubbed his hands. He wasn't sure he cred-
ited his countryman's alleged *samadhi*-experience, his
Enlightenment. "Katya is going back to Freegate. With
her country on a wartime footing she has little option.
I've decided to go with her. The Highlands Province
will be untenable so long as Shardishku-Salamá engages
in Fabian policies. I will do what I can for Katya and
Reacher. I am taking the contiguity device. I was separated from it once, to my sorrow. I won't risk leaving it
here. But before we part, it's only fair to offer you one
last opportunity to leave the Crescent Lands."

Van Duyn's machine was the only certain way back
to their home Reality. The deCourteneys' spells might
suffice, but would be hazardous. Gil considered for a
moment.

"I can't, just now. I'll have to take a raincheck."

"The choice is yours."

"Thanks for asking though. I remember, before I returned to Coramonde, I threw together the stuff I was bringing here with me. My brother Ralph wandered in when I had it all laid out, the traveling gear, guns and all. Right away he flashed on it that I was heading 'way out into the tall timber someplace. I almost told him how far short that fell, but he'd never have bought it. He knew me though; I had nothing to keep me back there. Oh, I'll go back one day, but there's no rush."

"I see. By the way, you shouldn't have gone off so quickly the other day. Not all Reacher's news was so unfortunate. He brought General Stuart back from Freegate with him."

"Jeb? Outstanding!" Jeb Stuart was the name Gil had given the war-horse assigned him from the stables of Freegate. Jeb had borne up well under travails of the thronal war.

"The King thought you'd want him. Now, I suggest we join the others."

They assembled in Springbuck's airy, high-windowed study, where long slants of sunlight irradiated the stained-glass scenes and breathed life into the tapestries and selected pieces of sculpture.

Hightower and the deCourteneys were present, with the *Ku-Mor-Mai,* Katya and Reacher. Gil settled into a chair, making his shoulder comfortable, and Van Duyn sat and fiddled with his glasses. The last participant arrived, Angorman, Saint-Commander of the Order of the Axe.

Gil had been introduced to him earlier. The Order was one of two rival sects of warrior-priests sworn in worship and errantry to the female deity called the Bright Lady. The Brotherhood of the Bright Lady, the other sect, was an older organization whose Divine Vicar Balagon was at odds with Angorman on a running basis. Outright violence between the two groups was absolutely prohibited, and so occurred only rarely. But there was an ongoing, pious antagonism.

Angorman greeted them all and eased himself with a grunt into the last vacant seat. He was dressed in his usual brown forager's cloak, an old man bald as an egg

47

except for thick, flaring white eyebrows. He retained his wide-brimmed slouch hat with the brassard of the Order on its high crown, an axehead superimposed on a cresent moon, worked in heavy silver. The Saint-Commander rested his famous greataxe against his chair. Gil recalled its name, Red Pilgrim. Six feet of wooden haft, braced with iron langets, held a double-flanged bit, gracefully curved to lend cutting power and leverage.

Springbuck had shucked the hated robes of state. Barefoot among the furs and pelts, he wore loose, soft trousers and sash, and a wraparound jacket. The hilt of the Hibben bowie nosed from his waistband.

Gabrielle sat at the *Ku-Mor-Mai*'s right, in deep conversation with Andre. Seeing her, Gil unconsciously put a finger to the chain around his neck. After the tarot séance, she'd taken the Ace of Swords from the deck, put it on a fine chain and given it to him, saying it was truly his. He'd accepted it reluctantly, committing himself to something he didn't understand. It was not made of paper or parchment, but a flexible material he couldn't identify.

Andre was sitting tailor-fashion on Springbuck's tall writing table. Gil saw that the protector-suzerain had been working again on *The Antechamber Ballads*, a collection of poetry, essays and autobiographical writings.

Angorman spoke. "Blazetongue is our subject first, is it not? It belongs in Veganá, we know. It is therefore an object of the Bright Lady, for they follow the Blessed Way down there. It is hence of interest to my Order to see the sword—and the child—safely back where they belong."

Gil sat up. "Child? You mean you want the kid to go? How can I—"

"We!" Angorman interjected. "*We* will accomplish this. The baby did conjure the fire of Blazetongue. By that we know she must be of the royal house of Veganá; only they command the sword's enchantment by inherent right."

So, Angorman was in the party. Gil turned to Springbuck. "What d'you say? How'd *you* like to pack a kid around with you?"

48

"Have you forgotten? I have already traveled with her."

"Oh. Yeah, but that was 'way before, when there was no choice. This is now, and this is me."

"I shall be responsible for the infant," Angorman declared, "and so you need not fear for her." His gnarled, sinewy hands played along the length of Red Pilgrim like some musician exercising before concert. "She shall be safe."

Gil slumped. If he backed out now he'd lose his best crack at finding Bey and Dunstan. It was a simple go/no-go.

He lost the floor to Andre. "Gil, is it not clear, after all she has been through, held captive along with Gabrielle in Amon's halls, that she will never be safe anywhere but with her own people? There are impetuses at work here that are not to be questioned. Attempts to harm or recapture her may be foiled simply by dint of quick, quiet departure. Does that alter your attitude?"

"Dunno." He thought of Dunstan. He couldn't afford to debate, or delay. "I suppose so."

Angorman said, "Andre and I envision a small party, several members and no more. Going quickly, inconspicuously, we go safest."

"That would be okay." Without enough men to insure safety, there was no point overburdening themselves.

"Then," Gabrielle cut in with her lovely, mocking smile, "you have accepted your first two-bard commission."

"My what? My too-what?"

Angorman cracked a vestigial smile of his own. "A 'two-bard commission' is something of an insider's jest in my Order. It denotes an errand of service so arduous that one poet alone could never recount it all. But of course, the Lady deCourteney was speaking humorously."

Gil let it pass. "Who would be in charge? There's only one Walking Boss."

"Andre," Springbuck answered, before Angorman could speak. The Saint-Commander considered the *Ku-Mor-Mai* from beneath bushy brows, then the American, then concurred.

The wizard coughed. "Well of course, I should be happy for both Gil's advice and the counsel of Lord Angorman."

Gil looked glum, but knew he would have made even more concessions.

Andre was tolling the fingers of his left hand. "We shall need maps and extra clothing, since we won't be far enough south soon enough to avoid cold weather. Food, weapons, medicines and general provisions. My Lord Angorman, how does this sound: Gil, yourself, me, the child and one or two others, with two pack-horses besides our own mounts?"

"Quite sufficient. Gil?"

"Okay. What about the rest of you?"

The Snow Leopardess responded, "Coramonde and Freegate may still have to go to war against Salamá, in two lines of advance. We of the Free City would thrust south along the eastern coast of the Central Sea, while Coramonde takes to the ocean, perhaps in league with the Mariners."

"When?"

"We are not certain," Springbuck admitted. "Soon, we think. Every day the writ of Earthfast erodes a little more. Preparations have already begun." He tugged a bell cord.

A servant entered, bearing a Faith Cup. The *Ku-Mor-Mai* took the deep, ornamented chalice with two hands, drank, and passed it to Gabrielle. She sipped and passed it to her brother, her green eyes never leaving Springbuck's.

Gil watched the Faith Cup make its ritualistic way around their circle. Andre was earnest and sober in drinking, but Katya took a flamboyant hoist. Reacher contemplated for a moment, then drank. Van Duyn took his draught indifferently, and handed it to Gil.

For a moment, the former sergeant had the daunting image of Wintereye before him. He'd come too far, though; swallowing the traditionally thick, bitter wine, he made himself a part of this Faith Cup. He gave it to Angorman, and his hand went again to the Ace of Swords lying against his chest. He suddenly felt optimistic.

Angorman, eyes closed, moved his lips in prayer before taking his part. Hightower, the last, raised the bulky chalice in one hand. "Confusion and death to Salamá!" He drained it as Angorman and Katya echoed him. Upturning the Faith Cup, he licked the last droplets from its rim and gave it to the servant.

Gil soon left, to find some time alone. He was intercepted in the corridor by Gale-Baiter. With the Mariner captain were his two crew members whose names Gil caught this time. The hulking redbeard was Wavewatcher the Harpooner, the smaller one Skewerskean the Chanteyman, whatever that meant.

Gale-Baiter began, "I have heard it privily that you wish to go to Death's Hold."

"What if I do?"

"Then you may come there with me, if you wish it. Our course should take us that way."

"Are you sure you'll be going there?"

"Not positive, but in prosecuting war on the seas against Salamá, we will in all likelihood come to it at last. Some vassals of the Masters are still said to linger there."

"And better a full sail above you," Wavewatcher rumbled, "than a stinking horse beneath." Skewerskean snickered. But Gil saw that any number of things could happen to screw up the sea voyage. He had no desire to be involved in an ocean battle, or get sidetracked on blockade duty or some such. Besides, he'd drunk the Faith Cup. He shook his head.

"Sorry, no. Thanks anyway for thinking of me."

Gale-Baiter waved his hand. "Not at all. We leave this evening for Boldhaven and our ship. If our courses ever cross again, you've always the offer of passage aboard the *Long-Dock Gal*."

Gil said good-bye to him, and to Wavewatcher and Skewerskean. "Fair winds to you," the harpooner boomed. "Until our courses cross again," added the chanteyman.

Springbuck had traveling arrangements quietly completed by morning. His seneschal made life miserable for many people in Earthfast that night. No one, aside from partakers in the Faith Cup, knew what it all meant. Springbuck's orders included a good deal of misdirection. He'd taken to wearing Bar once more.

The rising sun found them in a deserted corner of the bailey, puttering with the last-minute incidentals preceding any trip. Reacher, Katya and Van Duyn had come out to see them off. The three would depart a day later.

Gil had decided to abandon his suit of woven mesh armor. It had an insignia on its breast, copied from the 32d's crest, that Duskwind had put there; he preferred not to see it again. Instead, he wore a light, short-sleeved byrnie under his shirt. The sword of Dunstan the Berserker knocked at his left hip, the Mauser pistol at his right in a canvas holster. The Browning was in its shoulder holster. He'd prudently worn a steel cap, but had tucked the hat given him by Captain Brodur into his saddlebag. At the back of his belt was the trench knife he'd carried from home, with brass knuckles on its grip. He patted the neck of the waiting Jeb Stuart, a sturdy chestnut he trusted as much as he could anything with hooves. He had Dirge cased and slung at the side of his saddle, partly hidden by the chapelets, hoping Yardiff Bey's sword would be of use in tracing the sorcerer. Andre had agreed it might be so.

Angorman, wrapped against the cold, moved stiffly. Blazetongue, concealed in wrappings, was fastened to Andre's other gear. The wizard had his own ancient sword, sheathed, in hand, and another belted on over his coarse clothing. He also carried a powerful Horse-blooded composite bow and quiver of arrows.

He opened the pommel-knob of his old sword. Removing Calundronius from around his neck, he dropped it into the compartment there. Gil knew that the mystic jewel's influence was confined in that manner. The wizard was leaving it in Gabrielle's care, deeming that she might have greater need of it if war erupted.

Another companion appeared, whom Gil greeted with mixed reactions. It was Ferrian. The Horseblooded had a scimitar secured to his cantle, by his left hand, his cloak covering the pinned-up right sleeve. Gil wasn't so sure he was a good choice. The American couldn't very well object, however, and assumed Andre had reasons for picking him.

Gil was about to ask where the baby was when a last

traveler rode up. The newcomer was a woman in conservative road clothes, riding sidesaddle on a speckled
mare whose trappings were decorated with swatches of
bright red bunting. She was erect in a way suggesting
discipline, bearing harness supporting some burden on
her back. She had a kindly, rounded face, so fair that
her eyebrows and lashes were nearly invisible. Her
hair, free of its hood, was touched with much gray.

Gil, curious, walked to one side to see what cargo she
carried. He cursed when he saw the infant there, in a
sort of papoose rig.

He spun on Andre. "What the hell's she doing here
with that?"

She answered for herself. "My name is Woodsinger,
young man; I am to carry the child. Did you expect me
to bear her on my hip for our entire journey?"

"*Our* journey? No way; that's out, hear? Out!"

"Ahem," Springbuck intervened. "Gil, there is the
matter of the baby's care and feeding."

"Then," the American roared, pointing at Andre,
"let him do it. It's all his idea anyway."

"Not mine entirely," protested the wizard.

"And," added Woodsinger, "can he lactate?"

Gil spat on the cobbles and glared at the *Ku-Mor-
Mai*. At last he said, "We're wasting time."

"I am sure things will work out well," Springbuck
soothed. "She brought the child from Freegate."

"First it was the kid, now a nursie. This is giving me
a lot of grief, pal."

With injured dignity, Woodsinger proclaimed, "I
have been on farings to wear down better men than you,
with the heirs of Kings at my paps! Furthermore, I—"

Gil stopped her with a forefinger. "Save it! Just pull
your own weight."

He left her gaping, outraged, and said farewell to
Springbuck, who obviously envied him a bit, tired of
being chanceried at Court.

Suddenly there came a furor of growling, barking and
baying. A pack of dogs burst from the distant kennels
and swarmed toward them, bristling in hatred, bellies
low to the ground. The dogs were big, wolfish-looking
hounds, giving a confused impression of glinting eyes,

red tongues behind white, killing teeth and salivary foam.

The pack, eleven in all, threw themselves at Woodsinger's mount. The leader sprang for the nurse while the others caught the terrified horse's legs and flanks, sinking fangs in deep. Woodsinger kept the presence of mind to yank on her rein, though, and spoiled the lead dog's first attack, slashing at it with her riding crop as her horse fought madly to break free. She twisted her body to shield the child from the dog's jaws, fighting the horse at the same time.

Then Reacher was in among the pack. He avoided the snapping hounds and tore their leader away from Woodsinger, closing his fierce grip on its neck. Katya was behind him, sword flashing in the morning light, downing a dog with her first stroke, driving the others back for an instant. Reacher flung the body of the leader at two of its fellows, but another landed on his shoulders from behind. He went down, rolling over and over while it bit at the chain-mail collar of his armor.

Springbuck had drawn Bar and leapt in after the royal siblings. Woodsinger's horse was being dragged to the ground despite her efforts to keep it upright. Growls and shrill whinnies added to the total chaos.

Gil was afraid to risk a shot with Springbuck and the others intermingled with the pack. For the same reason Van Duyn held fire, and Angorman and Andre hesitated to strike. Gil took Jeb Stuart into the savagery. The war-horse, practiced combatant with hooves and teeth, instantly took a dog out of the fight, trampling it to bleeding shapelessness. Gil slipped his right hand from its sling.

Springbuck took another hound out of midair with Bar. The sword's enchantment of unfailing keenness was as effective as ever; the canine head and body fell away in different directions. Reacher had grappled the dog that had knocked him down into a bear hug. He applied his remarkable strength; the dog howled as its spine splintered.

Katya had lost her sword and now had a long combat knife in each hand. She dropped to one knee to evade a leaping hound. Her right-hand knife darted up to gut it as it passed overhead.

Two dogs had Woodsinger's horse by its nose and neck, another its tail, pulling it down. Ferrian's left hand blurred. A whirling metal loop struck down the tail-end dog in a welter of blood.

Gil, gripping his saddle tightly, leaned far over with the Browning in his hand. One dog had stopped pulling the nurse's horse, gathering itself to spring. The American stiffened his elbow and wrist, fired at a range of five feet. The dog somersaulted and fell dead.

Andre and Angorman had gotten to Woodsinger's side, pulling her from her floundering horse, keeping her safe between broadsword and greataxe. Reacher had plucked up another dog and raised it above his head. Now he flung it down against the cobbles with all his strength. It lay in death spasms, many of its bones shattered.

The two remaining hounds were still at the horse, pulling its tack, chewing at the red bunting with maniacal hatred. Springbuck smote the first down, while Reacher wrestled the second to the ground and held it immobile, arms locked around its throat, legs around its body. Guards had come to investigate; at Springbuck's command they took ropes and tied the dog, binding its muzzle.

"What the hell was all that about?" Gil demanded, shaken. Gabrielle, examining the baby, was satisfied she hadn't been harmed.

"I cannot say," the *Ku-Mor-Mai* answered, wiping Bar on a dog's coat. "These animals were all trained, and none had ever set upon a human being."

"They may not simply have attacked Woodsinger," Andre countered. "They were at her horse too. When we pulled her from her mount, the pack did not pursue her."

Katya, returning her cleaned knives to their sheaths strapped to her thighs, asked, "How now, then; did they go mad?"

"It is more to be suspected that they were driven to it." The wizard tore a strip of the red bunting from Woodsinger's saddle. He held it close to the bound dog; it growled, straining to tear into him.

"This, then, prompted the attack."

Gabrielle examined it. "There are procedures," she

55

agreed, "spells of no difficulty to Bey or his more adept followers. Yes, the dogs would assail anyone bearing this cloth. From whence did it come?"

The nurse was mystified. "I became impatient at awaiting my mount, so I went and found it myself, saddled and decked out so. I do not know who draped it, and thought it some good-fortune wish or send-off decoration."

Van Duyn had taken the bunting, sniffing it. "Your impatience saved you. The horse would probably have been brought around to the main steps, and the hounds released. You would have been killed before we could have gotten to you. Whoever planned this had no choice, after you'd taken your horse, but to set the dogs on you here."

The *Ku-Mor-Mai* dispatched a detail to search the kennels and stables for the one responsible, but doubted the person would still be close by. Gil now held the strip of bunting. He wadded it up and tucked it down into his saddlebag, one more piece of the sorcerer's trail.

Ferrian was holding the war-quoit he'd thrown, a Horseblooded weapon much like a Sikh chakram. Springbuck inquired whether Woodsinger would resume the trip or prefer to be relieved of her duty.

"We can switch her stuff to another horse and be on our way in a quarter of an hour," Gil broke in. Woodsinger stared at him. "Uh, right?"

Her round face showed a small, lopsided smile. "Quite so. Are we to be deterred by a dogfight?"

Gabrielle chuckled, one hand on Ferrian's shoulder, the other on Woodsinger's. "So, the Ace of Swords goes forth in suit."

"Gung ho," commented Gil MacDonald sourly.

Chapter Five

When in disgrace with fortune and men's eyes,
I all alone beweep my outcast state . . .
                                   William Shakespeare

THE *Ku-Mor-Mai* considered life, considered death.

Over his throne hung the snarling crimson tiger banner of Coramonde. Before him knelt Midwis, a Legion-Marshal.

"What mitigation can you offer," Springbuck demanded, "that you should not be hung from the Iron Hook Gate, and your family evicted from their lands?"

Midwis licked his lips and cast about for an answer. "Sire, I broke my ties with your enemies at the last, lifted the siege on your allies at Freegate, yea, and at the Hightower too."

"Yes, after you'd heard I had taken Earthfast."

"I concede it. Please, ask of me no merit; I have none, except some martial aptitude. Do as you will with me."

Which was precisely the problem. Midwis was a much-admired-officer, his battle standard weighted with campaign streamers won in service of Coramonde. His family was wealthy, ancient and influential. And, as the Marshal had said, he was a talented commander with a hardened Legion. Every resource was vital now, but Springbuck could no more let Midwis go unpunished than impose death upon him. He had a middle road in mind.

"Legion-Marshal, you and your men fought unjustly against me. Yet you may win back your honor by reverting to the sworn duty that is yours."

Midwis looked up hopefully. Springbuck went on,

"The Highlands Province suffers from depredations of the wildmen and the Druids. They are undermanned in the Highlands; it is in my mind to dispatch a Legion there. It will be a long, cold, perilous task. If the Druids use their polar magic again, despite the enchanters I've sent against them at Andre deCourteney's suggestion, it may come a disaster. But there must be armed units to check the wildmen."

Midwis was on his feet. "Give me your let to go there! Naive and wrongful in statecraft though I have been, no man can say Midwis is unschooled in conflict."

The solution had advantages. Springbuck hadn't enough loyal men to reinforce the Highlands Province and, left near Earthfast, Midwis' host was potentially dangerous. If he would renew his allegiance in truth, he would be a great help, and his powerful family and friends would be well disposed toward the *Ku-Mor-Mai*.

"You are dispatched with these provisos. Your host goes with its colors cased, and all blazonry covered. Until you reach the Highlands Province you march with arms reversed, without trump, drum or cymbal. Silent will be your route. When you unfurl your standard in combat it will show the bar sinister. If you do well by Coramonde, that will be revoked when you are come again to Earthfast. Do you agree?"

"Without qualm, *Ku-Mor-Mai*." Midwis bowed, then squared his shoulders, and retreated from the throne room.

It had been a long morning, beginning with the departure of Andre and his companions. Springbuck decided to take his midday meal. Courtiers rose, and servitors. He waved them away; having foregone his formal robes of state and taken to wearing Bar at his side again, he wasn't inclined to be pestered and indulged like a wealthy aunt.

Passing alone through an empty gallery, he heard low voices to one side, in a window-seat booth. Its curtains had been drawn, but had fallen back a bit. He squinted, crinkling his face, and made out a glimpse of brilliant red hair and milky skin. He went over, thinking to speak to Gabrielle. Then something blocked his partial view of her pale, perfect face. It was a mass of white hair and a black, chain-mailed shoulder.

The shoulder moved away. Gabrielle's eye, fluttering open from what could only have been a kiss, fell on him. She said something softly; the curtain was thrown back. There stood Hightower, hand on his broadsword hilt.

The Warlord stopped in surprise. His hand instantly dropped from the weapon. Springbuck, too, was immobilized; only Gabrielle's calm was unfailing.

"Yes, Springbuck?" Her eyes didn't avoid his.

He condemned himself for not having seen it sooner. On several occasions now, she and Hightower had been absent at the same time. She'd always made it quite clear that she was her own woman.

"You did not bid good-bye to Andre," he reminded her lamely.

"We made our farewells last evening. I mislike partings."

He turned to go. "My Lord," called the old warrior, halting Springbuck, "for what it may mean, Gabrielle and I had been—close, in times far back. We never did this to wound your feelings, and indeed, denied one another so long as we could. But there are ties that may not be gainsaid."

Springbuck resolved to be as ungrudging as Van Duyn had been when the scholar had lost Gabrielle to him. "Neither of you owe me explanations, my Lord. We are all free souls." Gabrielle's expression, hearing that, was satisfied. It made him feel no better.

"There are matters of policy that need advice from both of you," he continued, drawing a shaky breath. "Until later, then, good day."

He went his solitary way. She faced the Warlord. "I said as much; he is an older man in a young one's skin. He understands."

Hightower disagreed. "He accepts. I doubt he understands. Be that as it may, all courses turn toward Salamá, as in days long gone. Will they hold as much tragedy as they did then?" His arm went around her. "It begins anew."

Within the ironclad circle, she leaned against his chest. "For us, it never ceased."

59

On an occasion of rare self-indulgence, in the Hour of the Drug, Yardiff Bey, satisfied with his revivified plans, drifted in reverie back across the centuries.

He saw a small boy squatting in the dust of a teeming marketplace, scene of variegated color, bewildering sounds. A wandering illusionist was playing with tongues of flame and momentary flowers plucked from the air. The watching boy's father was the Bey, regional governor, Prince in his own right, but the boy had crept away from his manor house and teachers to watch this small magic.

The boy was fine-featured, destined to be aristocratically handsome. His cheekbones were high, lips full and dark. His eyes, watching minor enchantments with consuming interest—though he knew these were barely magics at all—were black, liquid with fascination.

It had been his misfortune or accidental lot to be born under ominous stars. The portents had spoken of disorder, ruin, cataclysm. His name would dominate the mightiest struggles. His mother had grieved for that, but the boy found it intriguing. His father discounted any words that didn't lend themselves to his own will. It was to occur to the boy, Yardiff, later in life, to speculate whether he'd made those prophesies come true by accepting them.

The boy, being groomed for his father's lofty station, had already decided he would never assume it. There were no magicians in his background, so it was hard to say from whence his preoccupation had come. His forebears and father were lordly, arrogant men, subtle warriors, merciless in battle. But in this generation, in this boy, under dire signs, the union of cold intellect and imperial pride had taken a new bent.

The nomadic magician was leaping and capering, half the fool, half the prestidigitator. He skipped around the circle of watching people, offering flowers that faded instantly away. He extended his fingers with tiny spits of flame that didn't burn. Most onlookers were afraid to touch them; those brave souls who did found that the flames evaporated at once.

Until he came to the boy.

A hand extended, and the clown-magician waited, scoffing. Yardiff's wide eyes shifted from the man to his pyrotechnic fingers, and back to the man. He put his hand forth calmly; uncertainty and apprehension had long since been driven out of him.

Tongues of fire were somehow transferred; it wasn't clear to the crowd just how. Now he held them, but the fires didn't disappear as they had for others. Instead they burned high, higher than for the magician himself. They flickered brightly in colors, then Yardiff waved his hand, dismissing them with a gesture of impatience. The crowd murmured. Some few dropped coins in the dust. Others covertly thrust forefinger and little finger at the wanderer, to fend off any evil he might harbor.

The magician scrambled in unseemly haste again, to gather meager pickings. People went their various ways, except the boy. When they were alone, the wanderer came to him. There was, in his features, the joy of a miner who's found a rich gemstone. He took the small hand that had so recently accepted his fire, pressed it for a moment, left something there. Then he twirled to go, once more the capering fool.

Yardiff didn't move, watching him until he was out of sight. Only then did he open dark, delicate fingers to see what was there. It was a plaque of malachite; picked out on it in silvery material was a flaming wheel, a mandala. The thing he'd so vaguely longed for had now found him. He tucked the token into his safest inner pocket and set out for his father's manor house. There were deceptions to work, lip service to pay, eventual disengagement to be made from the career being forced upon him. His destiny had made itself known; he embraced it fervently.

Centuries before the Great Blow, Yardiff's thin brown legs carried him home tiredly through sun-baked streets.

Sorcery was his contagion.

His delights were the coruscating spells that bent men and the world to his will. He rejoiced in them as viands, as he thought, for some inner hunger.

It was inevitable from the start that he should enter the service of the darker influences, the more terrible forces.

As journeyman, he'd roamed the world, contesting,

learning, along the hidden orbits of enchanters. He faced spells, demons, strange beasts, and hostile men and women. He grew from each incident.

He heard of a mountain bandit who'd devised a clever means of binding men to him. Disguised, he went to spy it out for himself. The outlaw would slip a prospective follower food drugged with Earnai, then have him borne into a secret garden. There the initiate would awaken, in seeming paradise, to eat and drink his fill and take his way with compliant women. Drugged again, he'd be returned to the "mortal plane" and made the simple offer of eternal joy in exchange for unquestioning loyalty. The technique seldom failed to produce a fanatically willing vassal.

Revealing his puissance to the bandit, Yardiff Bey showed him true sorcery: The bandit—Ibn-al-Yed, who later became Bey's mask-slave—threw himself at the magician's feet. His burgeoning realm of criminals and murderers became a keystone in Yardiff Bey's own concealed empire.

Bey had gone from task to task, always climbing in the dangerous favors of his Liege, the demon Amon, until the mighty attempt of the Great Blow. Then, the Masters had uprooted the Lifetree and made their fearsome effort to open the way between mortal plane and infernal, to summon up hordes from Hell. But it had been despoiled, though the world had been transformed forever in the disaster, and the Unity ended.

In the wake of that failure, with the darker forces harried closely by their opponents, Yardiff Bey had risen in perilous, opportunistic service; he'd kept the Crescent Lands from driving out every vestige of the Masters' influence. Eventually, the Five had solidified their power, and foremost among their agents stood Yardiff Bey. They'd revealed to him a fragment of his destiny, that his hope for ultimate success lay in three children he would beget, the first a girl, the second a boychild, and the third both, yet neither.

He'd subverted the many Southwasteland tribes, forging them into True Believers for his Masters. He'd brought down the vengeance of the Bright Lady on Glyffa by encouraging its king in the suppression of women. He'd distorted matters to Springbuck's great-

62

grandfather, so that Blazetongue was wrongly taken from Veganá in a battle that should never have been fought. In disguise, he'd prompted Hightower into that defiance that had left him blinded, hateful and disillusioned for decades. Bey had raised the great fortress at Death's Hold, on the westernmost shore of the Crescent Lands, and filled it with vicious armsmen, only to see it fall once it had served its purpose.

A great challenge had come, when the Deep-Rock Folk, the clans of tiny subterraneans, had cried out for protection. His name had long gone abroad; he'd answered their plea, for few heroes had survived.

The Deep-Rock Folk had been set upon by a creature from the lower Depths. Bey fought it in a lone combat through the strata of the earth, he and his adversary stalking and attacking one another in a series of duels that had lasted weeks.

Yardiff Bey's hand came up to the silver-and-malachite ocular he wore where his own left eye had been. The price of victory had been that eye. As replacement, he'd taken the single eye of his monstrous antagonist, confining its terrible energies and making it his own with the eyepiece he'd fashioned.

Then he'd stated his price. The Deep-Rock Folk had labored for twelve years to build a vessel, an adamantine shell in which he could imprison a fire-elemental and harness it. In the end he'd had *Cloud Ruler*, his flying ship.

He'd insinuated his way into the confidence of generations of the *Ku-Mor-Mai*. At last, he put his own bastard son, Strongblade, on the throne.

Then things had begun to go wrong. First the madman Van Duyn had appeared. Next, Springbuck had escaped house arrest at Earthfast. The Five had lifted their attention from darkling meditations to a premonition of *divergence*. But Bey had convinced them he still controlled events, and thought he did.

Gil MacDonald had come, summoned by the de-Courteneys and Van Duyn, to shake the whole network of ordinations. Bey's plans had been destroyed before his eyes in Court at Earthfast, by magic and force of arms. Compelled to flee, he had seen his world unravel.

Yardiff Bey thought about that, in the Hour of the

Drug. He recalled those last moments, striking down Dunstan and abducting him, escaping in *Cloud Ruler,* seeking sanctuary among his remaining supporters. At last he'd sought refuge in Death's Hold, gathering a few loyal adherents. But exile had held no fulfillment; he literally would rather have been dead. He'd come at last to Salamá, to the Five, and been granted another chance, a reprieve. Who else but Yardiff Bey was suited to ferret out the secret of the ancient mage Rydolomo?

His plans were meshing again. It had been unfortunate that the deCourteneys hadn't been lured north together, but at least they were separated; their whole was greater than the sum of its parts.

Better, the Heir of Veganá and the sword Blazetongue were on the move, occupying the attention of Andre deCourteney, permitting Bey to hunt out the secret he needed so badly. Once he'd secured it, no opposition would matter.

Let child and sword come south. In time they, too, would fall into his fist. He thought with special, shuddering savor of how good it would be to have the wizard, the baby, the sword and MacDonald in hand.

An eternally lucid part of him told him the Hour of the Dreamdrowse was drawing to a close. His last indulgence was a pulse of satisfaction. The endless effort would soon yield a final product.

He rose to go. There was an incredible amount to do yet, in order to become as a god among the new Masters of Reality.

PART II

❧

Jeopardies of a
Two-Bard Commission

Chapter Six

I struck the board, and cried "No more;
I will abroad!"

George Herbert
"The Collar"

AT first, the going was pleasant.

Springbuck's letter of transit, bearing false names and authentic seals, let the party go without interference, barely noticed. The silver brassard of Angorman's Order opened many doors, to busy inns, lonely huts and spartan outposts. Gil got used to seeing caps doffed to the Saint-Commander and the badge of his Order, but remained suspicious of everyone. Angorman was sometimes asked for a special benediction, which he never failed to impart. Andre, too, usually seemed to know a good stopping place not too far away. Gil never knew whether the evening would give him a straw mattress in a priory cell, a hard, narrow bench before a tavern hearth, or a comfortable bed in a local Lord's keep. Wherever they stopped, one of the four men would sleep near Woodsinger, or stretch out with his back to her door. Despite Angorman's prestige and Andre's providence, they were sometimes compelled to bivouac under the sky, with Woodsinger and her charge inside the one small tent they'd brought.

Andre, Ferrian and Angorman relieved Woodsinger of her burden from time to time, quieting the baby if she woke by night but wasn't hungry.

Gil didn't. He shared any other chore or problem, but flatly refused to become involved with the infant herself. No one pressed him to do differently. To make up for it, he always bore the carry-rack when Woodsinger rode with the baby held inside her cloak; it was his tacit apology. The child took the trip well. Woodsinger was extremely capable, looking after her well-being, keeping her healthy, clean and fed without commotion.

They rode with Angorman at their head, leading one packhorse's rein, Red Pilgrim usually propped butt-in-rest like a lance. Gil followed, with Woodsinger and the baby behind. Ferrian was next, leading the other pack-horse, guiding his own mount with his knees, Horse-blooded style. Andre brought up the rear, bow in hand, watchful at their backs.

Coramonde's diversity amazed the American. He met dashing, egotistical bravoes from Alebowrene, in the Fifty Lakes Territory, and reserved, puritanical men of Matloo, patrolling their flat, grassy province in huge, armored war-drays. Passing through the Fens of Hinn, marshes abundant with fish and game, he kept sharp watch, but saw few of the elusive, cantankerous people who inhabited them. Then, for eight solid days, they passed under the tangled, gloomy forest canopy of Tee-bra, famous for its eagle-eyed archers.

The Tangent frequently held some traffic: a trapper with furs, a farmer with produce, wary shepherds with their flocks or a boisterous column of Free Mercenaries off to their next job. Now and then a wealthy man or Lord would go by in a polished coach drawn by a matched team of six or eight horses. They encountered bands of tinkers, bangled and sly, who offered goods of dubious origin and mules and horses with cleverly doc-tored markings. Every so often the party was forced to make way for a military dispatch rider, his straining mount throwing off flecks of foam. They overtook pon-derous convoys of merchants' wains, leaving them be-hind quickly. These were guarded, but Gil still thought they were a fat, inviting target. Springbuck had been right; joining one would have been a mistake.

There were roadside shrines, most of them the Bright Lady's, and no two images of Her were quite alike. One statue embodied Her as highborn, hair arranged pains-takingly, with a haughty tilt to her chin and a patroniz-ing smile; the next represented Her as a big-boned peas-ant woman, bobbed hair gathered in a kerchief, skirts tucked up for field labor, barefoot and laughing heartily. But all Her many personae were quite clearly one, the ever-changing, omnipresent Lady.

The party stayed, by and large, to the Western Tangent. Its straight, unobstructed course made the going far easier than any local road could have. Gil had been worried that the Tangent's hard, tractive surface would harm the horses' hooves, but the others reassured him there was nothing to fear, and were right. Apparently, that was one of the qualities of the Tangent, a highway predating the Great Blow, the Unity's most visible single artifact, certainly its most useful one.

Everywhere were signs of doubt or discontent. The corrosion of Springbuck's authority was more advanced on the fringes of Coramonde. Twice, nearing the Dark Rampart, the travelers left the Tangent to skirt areas where, they'd been warned, warfare had erupted. They saw thick, dark smoke smudge the sky, from battle and siege. Once, a distant fire lit the night, a burning village.

People were storing food frantically; this promised to be a severe winter. The American became used to eating as his companions did, with the left hand. The right stayed free, theirs near hilts and helve, and his close to the grip of the Mauser, his holster flap left open.

They were even more cautious traversing the Dark Rampart range. There, the Tangent cut between sheer mountain walls or spanned stomach-wrenching chasms on delicate-looking arches. Refugees, fugitives and deserters had fled up here during the war to hide and live as they must. The party came across graves from which the bodies had been stolen by the starving. When they camped at night, they picked as defensible a spot as they could, even if they had to stop early or go on in dusk. Three times, it took the flash of swords and greataxe to discourage small bands of shabby, sunken-cheeked men who blocked their way. They saw no other women or children, and Gil assumed none had survived up here. Armored, mounted, the party wasn't pursued or molested.

All hospitality had ended, and any amenity they hadn't brought with them. They all began to reek, their clothes and gambesons stained and itchy.

Their stocks grew low. Soon, thcy had only a dwindling supply of dried fruit and rock-hard travelers' loaves that reminded Gil of Logan Bread. They cut consumption drastically, except Woodsinger, who must nurse the baby. All game had disappeared, prey and predator alike. Angorman and Andre were adept at gathering edible roots and plants, but even these were scarce. They came on a hermit's cabin, high in the chilly peaks. Andre managed to barter, at scandalous price, a supply of the only meat the old recluse had, dog. It was salty, chewy and greasy, but far from the worst thing Gil or the others had ever eaten. By the time the last of it was gone, Gil found that he missed it, thinking of their shrunken stock of fruit and stony loaves.

They came down out of the mountains the next day, just as the first snows threatened the heights. At the merestone that marked the boundary of Coramonde, they came to the first foreign border.

They were met with suspicion. The lesser states and kingdoms had turned back virtually everyone, but the letters of transit and Angorman's badge got the party past.

Gil saw Andre's wisdom in not taking more men. Four, with a woman and child, were enough to guard and provide. There was an inner resonance to two pairs of armed men, the implied capacity to defend at all points. Still, they were few enough so that border guards were inclined to permit them by. A military escort, in this climate, could have proceeded only by force.

They sold one packhorse, no longer needing it. The wide, straight Western Tangent took them quickly south, sometimes passing through an entire lesser kingdom in a day. They were able to buy food, particularly the proteins Woodsinger needed. The nurse allowed as how the child was old enough to begin taking small samples of regular foods, and began feeding her mushed bits of egg, cheese and fruit.

Morale improved; conversation became more lively. One afternoon Ferrian brought down a pheasant with his war-quoit, the first fresh game they'd had in weeks. It only afforded each a small portion, but put them in an exceptional mood.

"How come," Gil asked Andre that night, tossing a bone into the fire, "you do that? When you were talking about your sister just now, you said 'sorcery.' But you always call your stuff 'wizardry,' and they always say Bey's a sorcerer."

Andre leaned back against his saddle. "All those terms denote diverse methods of dealing with the same thing. They are different paths of approach. Never would I make a living sacrifice."

"You mean human beings?"

"I mean any life." The wizard stretched his legs out. Woodsinger, halfway through a feeding, burped the baby. "I am no newcomer to strife, Gil. I have laid more than one man low in open battle. But I will not use up life as an ingredient in conjuration."

"But Gabe's a sorceress. She has?"

"Of that you must ask her. I will only say there are times when the life of an enemy, a malefactor, can be used to save the life of a friend, by mystic procedure. It has been known for such an exchange to be made, and for the person who did it to be acclaimed. Few object to the loss of an evil life if it saves a good one. Yet that operation is sorcery, and there is no disguising it. Beyond this, you will have to query Gabrielle."

Angorman spoke, firelight shadowing his face under his big slouch hat. "You will hear it said that Andre deCourteney is too meek for transcendent magics, not hardhearted enough to cope with them. It is not so; he never swayed from any trial or test, nor failed any. If you want the long and short of it, Gil MacDonald, there are boundaries over which a wizard will not step, things he will not do, to make enchantments work, however puissant he is. But if man or woman overstep, it is sorcery, however slight the trespass."

The talk was getting to Andre. "There is little more to the topic than that." Throwing another piece of wood on their fire, he huddled down in his cloak.

The baby was full. Woodsinger inserted her finger gently at the side of the child's mouth to break suction. She laved her nipple with a cloth, closed her voluminous robes and retired to her cramped tent.

The first watch was Gil's. He stared into the fire, the Mauser under his hand. It was all well and good that Andre was principled, but what if that meant Bey had him outclassed? It would be best, the American decided, if the wizard finally faced his age-old enemy with his sister by his side. No one could afford to grant any advantage to the Hand of Salamá.

They were in a country of fields and vineyards. Though the nights had been cold the days were warm here. Jeb Stuart's breath would shoot jets of steam from his nostrils when he was being saddled, but later he'd be in danger of overheating, and Gil would feel sweat trickling under his byrnie.

One afternoon a wind came up, an angry storm on its heels. Andre had some weather cantations but didn't want to use them, to avoid attracting any notice. The land was fairly flat, with few trees and no apparent shelter. Angorman left the road, carefully examining the face of a low rock wall, the only prominent feature in the area. He announced that they could sit out the storm in the lee of the cliff. It looked just like more ground to Gil, but Andre and Ferrian accepted the Saint-Commander's word. They moved rubble and crowded a close little camp against the rock wall.

The storm broke. Just as Angorman had promised, they huddled, riders and animals, in a dry margin six feet wide, while rain soaked the ground just beyond.

The rain stopped and started all night, refusing to go or break. But it had slackened by the time they were breaking camp. Andre said they'd reach the border of Glyffa in two days.

The companions rode stretching, working their muscles to drive out the chill. Woodsinger held the baby inside her robes, as she sometimes did to warm her. Gil took the rack from her and slipped it on his back. They made no effort to hurry, watching droplets make their way down leaves and grasses. The pitched Tangent, already drained, was drying slowly.

Gil was swaying along, fitting himself unconsciously to Jeb Stuart's gait. He had nothing in particular in mind, even the distance to Death's Hold and Bey.

An unexpected blow to his back sent him against his saddle bow as his head was buffeted on either side. There was less pain than astonishment; he thought for a moment that Andre or Ferrian had ridden by to slap him, but he'd heard no hoofbeats. He pushed himself upright as Jeb gave a disturbed whicker. A screech sounded overhead and a shadow crossed quickly, alarmingly, in semaphore on the edge of his vision.

Gil spotted his attacker looping in the air for another pass. He had difficulty telling what it was—some large hawk or eagle, or something else. His immediate impulse was to let it go; it had done him no damage. But a note of unmixed hatred in its call warned him.

He yanked the Mauser out, led his target and squeezed off a round. The other horses jumped at the shot; Jeb took it stolidly.

It was a miss; the flier had selected that instant to wheel in midair for another run. Gil cursed. *Sumbitch can turn like he has one wingtip nailed down.*

It veered at him. His aim wavered overhastily. There was a hiss of fletching in heavy air, and an eerie piping. The bird spun toward the ground, the tension of its flight changing to helpless fluttering, feathers gyrating free.

It hit the Tangent with a limp roll, eyes still lit with the intensity of the unalloyed hunter. It was no species they'd ever seen. Andre's arrow stood from its breast, a Horseblooded shaft that had made its piping moan by a trick of carving the Wild Riders used. Gil holstered the handgun, musing that reflexes and coordination were more important than instrumentality.

He shrugged off the carrying rack to check it. Diamond-hard talons had scored long, deep tears in the tough hide and torn splinters from the wooden frame. An extra blanket, rolled and stored inside, had been slashed in strips.

"The bird's target was the rack." Andre surmised. They looked to Woodsinger, who drew her cloak more closely around herself and her charge.

Hearing a wave of trilling sound, they craned their heads upward. Then they were surrounded by small birds who rushed past and hovered around them, a multicolored tempest of feathers, a gale of small wings. Tiny beaks ripped at them in passing; wings stung their faces.

Gil yelped and slapped at them, his hand coming away bloody. Woodsinger swatted with her crop, pulling her head down among the folds of her collar. They all fought to master their horses, realizing they were under

72

no natural attack. Gil fired two rounds into the air, not counting on hitting anything, to scatter the tiny furies. They exploded away in every direction, but circled and swarmed like bees, and drew closer again.

Ferrian let the packhorse's rein fall. He pulled Woodsinger's hood down close to her face and swirled her cloak around her tightly. Taking her mount's reins in his teeth, the Horseblooded drew his scimitar, guiding his horse with his knees.

Andre had put away his bow. He, too, pulled his sword. With no time for spellcasting, they had to get out of the open.

Gil, the Browning Hi-Power in his right hand now, also took his reins in his teeth, as Dunstan the Berserker had taught him. He peered around for any sort of cover, a cave, trees, anything. There was none. It was the perfect spot for ambush.

The flock swept around in unison and came back in their direction. More birds were joining them every moment. "The cliff face," Ferrian called. " 'Tis better protection than none!"

They galloped back, knowing they couldn't outrun their pursuers. The birds ignored the riderless packhorse and were on them in seconds, many species commingled. Streaking by, they blotted all sounds with their calls and wounded men and horses. Gil fired twice from each handgun. The birds peeled off from the blasts, then gathered again, more rapidly this time.

In the shelter of the cliff face, they fastened up their cloaks for what little protection it meant. The horses whinnied, tossing their heads and showing the whites of their rolling eyes. Ferrian pinned Woodsinger's mount up against the rock with his own and waited, light racing up and down his scimitar. "Is there a conjuration that would help?" he shouted.

Andre's brow creased. "It is difficult to say. These are no supernatural foes, only living creatures following some imposed will. I have no ready spell for it. It must be a thorough enchantment." Given time, he could disperse it, but he had no time.

Gil watched the flock come in again. "Andre, it's with you now. This cliff won't protect us from anything but rain."

"Rain!" echoed Ferrian. "Andre, bring a downpour!"

The squat mage looked up dubiously. The clouds were still overburdened with moisture, but he wasn't sure mere rain would stop the attackers.

He dismounted, as Angorman took his horse's bridle. His mystic passes began; the sky rumbled.

The birds hit them again, landing and clinging to whatever skin or clothing they could grasp. Even Woodsinger was hurt, as beaks found her legs and feet. Another salvo drove some off, but the rest hovered and pecked and clung. The companions slapped at themselves and each other. Faces and hands were wounded, and the plunging horses were near insanity.

Ducking and thrashing, Andre completed his spell with a syllable of Command. Rain came in sheets, battering the fliers but not deterring them, though it struck with driving force.

Covered with them, Andre opened his palm. A brilliant flash of light broke forth, scattering them. It was a spell of sight more than substance; they sensed it, and resumed.

Andre was reduced to despair. Harnessing his arts, he might fell individual birds in large numbers, but they would eliminate him long before he could finish them.

Woodsinger screamed and began slapping at a starling that had fixed its claws near an opening in her cloak, stabbing its beak at the child's struggling arm. Wincing in pain, the baby began to bawl. The nurse brushed the starling away and covered her charge again, but the wails continued.

Gil heard. He slid from Jeb and lurched to Andre's horse, hoping the wrapped Blazetongue would show signs of its fire. He couldn't get to it; the bucking, terrified animal wouldn't allow it, though Angorman held its bridle. The American heard Ferrian shout for him to beware. Batting at the unavoidable birds, he got out of the way. The Horseblooded leaned over, slicing with his scimitar. Thongs parted as one; Blazetongue dropped to the ground.

Another round, fired into the air, won Gil more space and time. He snatched the sword and sprinted to

Andre. The wizard was stumbling toward the cliff, covered with feathered attackers. One of his wounds, over his temple, had blinded his left eye with his own blood. Gil helped him beat himself free.

"Andre, the baby's scared. Can you get the sword working?"

The wizard shielded his face and tore the coverings from the weapon, while birds whirled, pecking. "I know not; its fire is not nigh, so far as I can detect."

He unsheathed the greatsword and tried to hold it up in both hands, the phrases of a conjuration tumbling from his lips. He was soon buried under the fliers, his spell stopped cold. He jabbed the blade's point into the ground and stumbled back.

Gil dropped to his knees. Together they punched and pounded at maddened jackdaws, sparrows, linnets and jays. There was a crackle from Blazetongue. Blue effulgence whooshed up its blade like smoke up a flue, leaping off its pommel, disappearing.

The splashing rain threw up a curtain of steam. As if poured from a kettle it came, boiling hot. The flock's wrath became mortal pain. Humans and horses cowered against the cliff. Birds dropped, slaughtered in thousands. Those that found clear space by the cliff rebounded from the rock, blundering back to their deaths.

Gil pressed his face to the cool stone, fearing his lungs would be cooked. White steam filled the world, but the birds' cacophony dropped away. Only the hissing of superheated rain remained.

Andre gasped his foremost spell of Dismissal. Within seconds the torrent subsided. The horses began to quiet. The travelers uncovered their red, glistening faces.

Hot curls of vapor rose from soaked ground. Remains of plants and fallen birds floated in a muddy, foul-smelling soup. Dazed, the party hunkered in the lee of the cliff, staring at the scalded landscape.

"Andre, you far surpassed my expectations," Angorman confessed.

The wizard, watching the ground drain, waved the remark away. "I called the rain down, but our survival may be laid to Blazetongue. I did not release its force."

"The kid, then?" Gil asked.

"You saw the weapon's energies fly up out of it. Blazetongue itself is responsible; I did not activate it, and neither did the child."

He picked himself up, dabbing at his wounds, and rummaged through his saddlebags. "I have ointments somewhere, albeit none of us seems too badly burned or injured."

"But what about the rain?" Angorman persisted.

Andre stopped. "My Lord, I informed you in Earthfast; there are more than mere nations in opposition. Blazetongue is the Bright Lady's instrument. Those birds, bloodlusting on the wing, reeked of Amon, and the Five. The sword put forth its energies to advance its ends. Two primal forces clashed on this heath; the Perfect Mistress carried the day."

The Saint-Commander made a sign of thanksgiving. Andre observed, "This party is of enormous consequence, we have seen. I profess to understand little, just now." He scanned the steamy distance. "Our packhorse is gone, or dead perhaps; her burden was nothing we cannot replace, if needs be."

Gil blew his breath out wearily. "You mean you want to go on? What if we're walking into another ambush?"

"Going on is safer than going back. Ahead, in Glyffa, where the Divine Mistress' sway is greatest. Behind, it is less."

Gil, hand to his eyes, shook his head slowly. "How much longer will we have the option?"

Angorman's chin came up, harshly. "When one accepts a commission of service, one is *past* the point of no return. Or have you forgotten the Faith Cup?"

Instead of answering, the American got up to make sure Jeb was all right. A cool breeze was carrying away wreaths of steam and stench. The water had receded and the ground had cooled considerably.

Gil concluded that his only hope was that pressure would be off the party once they'd delivered the child. They rapidly prepared to leave this area, blighted by the confrontation of the gods.

76

Chapter Seven

I gave the day to Angorman, and showed to him my
  heel,
and prayed he would forego the chase
(and vowed me nevermore to face
his bright, moon-bitted Pilgrim, poet-cleaving Red
  ordeal) . . .

> from "The Lay of the Axe and the Rose,"
> by the hedge-robber and self-styled
> poet, Kidsheerer

TOWARD evening of the next day, they came to a towering cedar next to the Tangent. On its face an area was roughly planed off. Graven there was an intertwined rose and double-bitted axehead. The carving was old, but the tree's growth hadn't obliterated it.

Angorman ran a hand over the aged scars. Gil assumed the tree had been planed by Red Pilgrim. They left the Tangent for a well-used side road, on the warrior-priest's assurances of good accommodations.

The vineyards here boasted an exotic strain of oversized grapes nearly as big as figs. The workers had no guards or weapons, and weren't too surprised at the sight of wayfarers. The road ran past an old manor house, more or less a stronghold. Angorman entered its gate. They followed him into a pleasant courtyard that hadn't seen military activity in years. The house had plainly been grand in its day.

Their arrival had been signaled ahead somehow. An elderly woman waited on the front steps to greet them. She was slender and stately, with white hair caught in a bun. Her unadorned robes were as cheerless as a nun's habit. There was a ring of large keys at her belt, a pair of scissors and a little capped jar, the kind scholars used as a portable inkwell. She held a writing quill. Her features were lined with humor; a glint in her eye said she'd laugh readily. She seemed frail, but healthy and active. Dismounting, Angorman laid his axe down—the first time Gil had ever seen him do that—and bent knee to her stiffly.

"Welcome," the woman proclaimed to him alone. "My heart is happy you are here, and remembers much that makes it glad." She turned to the others. "Thank you, all, for the joy of your arrival. All that is here is yours to use."

Angorman made introductions, telling the others that their hostess' name was the Lady Dulcet. A footman showed up to take their horses. Dulcet apologized for their wait, saying her chief servitor was nowhere to be found. The travelers carried their own sparse luggage. Gil took Dirge along, and his saddlebags. Andre tucked the bundle of Blazetongue under his arm.

Dulcet led them to a high-ceilinged dining chamber floored with walnut, gleaming in age. In a hearth that must be twenty feet long, whole logs burned. In the middle of the hall was a dining table where thirty people could sit to eat with room left over. Candelabra lit the place, and close by the fire plush, pewlike benches sat on carpets of subtle weave.

"You have done well by your fief, Dulcet," Angorman told her.

"It is my nephew's now. Property in these parts is kept by those who can defend it. I steward it for him."

The Saint-Commander frowned. "It should be yours, and your heirs'."

"But I've none, and never shall have, shall I? That was fated long ago, the day you saved me from Kidsheerer. If I cannot have the mate I chose, I will have none."

The old man looked away, his features a doleful monument. Gil knew the Order, like the Brotherhood of the Bright Lady, swore celibacy. That tenet must have come under stress here, with Dulcet wanting Angorman and no one else. Having seen what life was like for an Oathbreaker like Wintereye, Gil wasn't surprised by the tragedy he saw.

The Lady Dulcet called for food, then insisted on

seeing the baby. She and Woodsinger agreed the child was a perfect treasure. Her questions were few; it was enough to know that they were bound for Veganá.

"My nephew Newshield should be back soon," Dulcet was saying. "He went out hunting this afternoon, all at once. He's something of a scholar lately. A terror in his younger days, but he has come along nicely, I think. He has even had men of learning here, to consult with him."

They took seats together at one end of the long table. White wine was brought in fluted goblets of lavender glass, a vintage from the giant grapes of the local vineyards. Then they were served hot bowls of stuff like thick bouillabaisse, which they scooped up with crisp shells of breadcrust.

It was dark when they settled at the hearthside benches, telling of late developments on the far side of the Dark Ramparts. Woodsinger began to yawn, the baby asleep on her lap. When Dulcet had her shown to a room, Ferrian and Andre went with her, saying they were tired, meaning they'd be on guard.

Gil had removed guns, sword and byrnie, stacking them with his gear and Angorman's along with Red Pilgrim in a corner. He relaxed, ecstatic at being able to scratch his chest and back at last.

Angorman had always confined his conversation to matters of travel and stories of his Order, tales of errantry with moral overtones. Now he made an effort to be breezy, witty, to entertain Dulcet. Their talk kept turning down old, private paths. To keep Gil involved, she inquired, "Has Lord Angorman told you how he came to be here in the warmlands? Few are the times he has told that story. Come, Saint-Commander; give us that rare treat."

Only because it was Dulcet who asked, Angorman settled himself deeper in his seat, to conjure the story. "Where I come from, it is dark for months of the year. In spiked boots we crossed the ice fields, hunting the white bear, the seal and breaching whale-fish. Of ten children, perhaps four lived to the graying of their hair. There, the wildmen of your northern isles were what *we* called warmlanders.

"In due time, at seventeen, I inherited the axe of my

father. He had died battling the white bear, and the weapon's helve was snapped in two. I fared out to seek a new one, but became lost in a blizzard. Then the weather broke, and I happened upon a ship stuck in the ice, her crew in embossed armor and silken remnants, frozen in the yards and rime-fastened to her deck. How far she had come I cannot imagine, but she had been there a long, long time.

"On her bow sprit was a figurehead. Its shape was the Bright Lady. The bowsprit had struck the ice, and the figurehead was cracked along its length. One great splinter stood out, straight and sharp in its rime jacket. I had found my axe-haft. I broke it off with much effort; the wood was tough as metal. I had my bearings, so I went to find my people, to share my incredible find.

"But the blizzard settled in again. We could not stir out of our ice-lodges for a day and a night. I passed the time mounting Red Pilgrim's new helve. It was another day before we could start for the ship. We had no trouble finding her; a column of smoke marked where she had struck the ice. My tribesmen halted, wondering how many enemies must be there; in the far north fire means men, and men are most often adversaries. I left the others behind, bellowing a war challenge. In my mind was the ethereal face on the bowsprit, that must come to no harm. But I was too late.

"There were raiders, wildmen from the Isles who go abroad to steal and slay. They follow the Druids, hating the Bright Lady and all Her works. They had lit fire all round the ship, fed with oil. Craftsmanship that had survived for—perhaps centuries—was blackened, withered in coils of flame." Angorman's thoughts were far away, holding some of the anguish he'd felt that day.

"I do not know how many there were. They had a large, outrigged sea-canoe drawn up, outfitted for winter voyaging. I went among the lot with my axe. I was young then, coming into my strength, faster with the greataxe than anyone. Many died.

"The rest, fearing a trap, or maybe my madness, launched their canoe and dug their paddles with vim. I saw the ship was past saving, a framework of fire. That proud, holy figurehead was consumed, the ice sizzling under the hull. The ship burned for an hour more, then slid down into the sea, the ice around her melted through. Her chains and metal fittings, molten hot, hissed like dragons at combat as they hit the water.

"But my heart revived. Here was a reason to live, and not just eke out existence. I would find that Lady, whoever she was, and put myself at Her disposal. I set out with my axe and little else, having come upon my Destiny."

His face creased in a moment's introspection. "I came at last to join the Brotherhood of the Bright Lady, which Balagon led, and leads still. They all agreed I was worthy, but they numbered one hundred, and are allowed no more members under their bylaws. This inadequate patience of mine soon wore out, so off I went to found the Order of the Axe. You will hear them curse me as a heretic or call on me for miracles, Gil MacDonald, but I am nothing more than a man who, like most, needed a dream. Finding it, I have held fast to it, grateful that She chose me."

Dulcet had lain a hand on his arm. He covered it with his. The candles burned low.

Gil came back from the story, uncomfortable. He shifted uneasily, studying weapons, shields, trophies and paintings hung on the walls. On a huge disk over the hearth was the device of Dulcet's family, a single rose.

Dulcet said, "Perhaps you would care to see my nephew's study? He is a collector of rare books and scrolls. You will find it at the top of those stairs there. Shall I have a servant show you?"

"No. Thanks, I'll find it." They wanted to be alone. He decided he'd find a place to rack out after he'd looked in on the study.

It was an odd place, more given to discarded clothing and empty cups than to books. He wandered through it lackadaisically, by candlelight. A few of the scrolls there were very old indeed.

There was a clatter of hooves and baying of hounds in the courtyard. Figuring it would be Newshield, Dulcet's nephew, he laid down the codex he'd been skimming. His glance crossed the table where he put the codex, went beyond, then back to the loose page lying there. He held it up to the light.

It was the title page from *Arrivals Macabre*.

He made a fast search, yanking curtains aside, opening chests and cabinets. He pulled up the lid on an ornate oaken box and saw what he'd sought, a glass apparatus of twin retorts like the one in Yardiff Bey's sanctum at Earthfast. There were voices, loudly, from downstairs. He wished he hadn't taken off his pistols.

He went back down hesitantly. His first impulse was to get to his guns, and warn Angorman. Moreover, he had to pass through the dining hall to get to Andre and the others. Drawing a deep breath, he re-entered the hall.

Newshield—it must be he—was a young man with pouchy eyes too old for him. He wore mud-caked boots and a fine, ermine-bordered cloak of embroidered silk over a gilt cuirass. Behind him, men hung around the main doors, hands close to swords. Two of them held straining, leashed hounds with either hand. The dogs' slaver stained the carpet; their muddy paws left tracks. Precipitous tension hung in the air.

"These premises are not my aunt's, Lord Angorman, but mine." Newshield's tone was unreasoning. "I do not like my hospitality extended without my let."

The Saint-Commander's effort to control his temper was visible. "I knew your aunt in days gone by. Surely her kindness can be no great transgression."

Gil came to their notice. "Where has this fellow been?" Newshield snapped. "My study? Oh, that is beyond the beyonds!"

"Then," answered Angorman, "we will get us gone. Our apologies." Gil, hoping Newshield would buy it, headed for his guns. But Dulcet's nephew raised his hand, and swords were drawn.

"No, Lord Angorman. Having come, you must stay." The heavies at the door ranged themselves frankly around the room, waiting. Gil's stomach clenched, but he hesitated to make a long move for the pistols; Dulcet and Newshield were both in his way. There were just too many men, too near, with bared blades. Newshield shed his cloak and loosened his own weapon.

"The rest of this party will doubtless be in guest quarters," he said, picking six of his men with a sweep of his arm. "You come with me." He selected four

82

more. "And you others make your way round, through the garden. Post yourselves beneath their window, against escape."

Dulcet was stunned. "You . . . you knew they would be here?"

"He's got pages from *Arrivals Macabre* upstairs," Gil told Angorman. Newshield appraised the American.

"Yes, I harbored a very important patron when he was in need. He did not find what he sought in the loose pages he brought, and so left them behind." He smirked. "We would have taken you when you first came, but my aunt's chief servitor got wind of it somehow. He fled, and would have betrayed me. It took us all afternoon to track him down in the marshes. He perished with the Bright Lady's name on his lips, stupid zealot."

He turned back to his men. "You know what is expected. Bear up; within the hour, the Flaming Wheel will be on the wing to the Hand of Salamá. In one hundred heartbeats we will go in at them. Harrowfoot, you will stay here with the remaining men and guard these three."

They took torches and moved out, six to the staircase that led to the guest quarters, behind Newshield, and four more for the garden. That left eight in the dining hall. They waited with unsheathed swords, leaving no doubt what would happen if someone shouted a warning. Gil felt sick to his stomach, angry at himself, very much afraid.

Perhaps the other servants would help? No, not against so many men-at-arms. He felt a split second's pity for the hapless chief servitor, driven to desperate courage by faith in the Bright Lady, run to ground by horsemen and baying dogs.

Something clicked. Short on time, he didn't even stop to look for flaws. "Harrowfoot, you look like a reasonable guy to me." The man, hard-bitten ugly whose midsection had gone to paunch, glared suspiciously.

"I mean, who doesn't want to turn an honest profit?" Gil hastened. Angorman eyed him noncommittally, but Harrowfoot's interest had been piqued.

"What profit is that, witling?"

"Hey, listen, I'm not with these people. Why can't you

83

just let me walk? It'd be worthwhile for you; there're a hundred gold bits in my saddlebag. You take 'em and I'll take off, how's that? Newshield won't care; he's got what he wants."

Harrowfoot plucked the saddlebags out of the pile of gear in the corner, set them on the table and rummaged through them. Gil tried to estimate how much time he had. *Hurry!* "The right bag, the one that's tied off. They're at the bottom." He bit his lip, trying to tell Angorman with eye contact, *It's coming, get set.* The Saint-Commander only displayed contempt.

Harrowfoot, tearing things out of the bag, grinned to himself. If there were money, he'd take it, but the outlander would never leave the room alive. He pulled items out and tossed them aside: a spare shirt, socks, a whetstone, a wadded swatch of red cloth.

Gil saw that, and gathered himself. The dogs growled, showed fangs and fought to break free with insane ferocity. One handler was dragged headlong, losing his hold. His two dogs flung themselves directly at Harrowfoot and the strip of red bunting Gil had saved from the attack on Woodsinger at Earthfast.

Harrowfoot went down with a scream. Everyone in the room was shouting. The armsman nearest Gil was distracted. The American took a long step inside his guard to knee him. He jumped the next man, whose sword pointed at Dulcet's heart. The man was just turning, having heard the thud of the kneeing and the first guard's moan. Gil clamped an arm around his throat and, kicking the back of his knee, hauled him back off balance. He bellowed to Andre and Ferrian, wherever they were, to watch out. To Angorman he screamed, "Go for it!"

The Saint-Commander wrestled the sword from the second man, thrust Dulcet over to the wall, and wove through confused foemen toward his axe.

The second handler's animals had turned on him and savaged him. They, too, now threw themselves at Harrowfoot. Two guards were trying to beat them off him with the flats of their blades. Men and hounds stabbed, bit, growled, cursed and fought.

Gil put his second man away with a hammer blow to the base of the skull, but the first was stumbling to his feet. The American damned himself for not having nailed him right. Another guard came around the table. Caught between them, Gil dove under the long, wide dining board, strawberrying his hands and forearms.

Angorman had eluded one opponent. The melee of dogs and men diverted most attention from him. Another foe closed with him. They flailed at each other, using their broadswords two-handed. Angorman, used to his axe, was forced on the defensive. He managed to draw his adversary around until their positions were reversed. Cautiously withdrawing out of dueling distance, he threw his weapon at the man, pivoted, and seized his greataxe.

The swordsman stepped back. One of his comrades, chasing Gil, broke off and came around the table to his aid. Red Pilgrim was in the old man's hands. He nodded to himself.

"Now, we shall see," he told them.

Gil, scuttling along between the table's ornate legs as blades whistled past him blindly, heard a new sound, an ululating war cry. He realized it was Angorman, and spotted the swirl of the old man's robes and the shuffle of feet as the fight resumed. There was the metal-to-metal clash of the duel. A man hit the floor, blood running from his side.

Gil took a quick survey of stamping feet and running boots, rolled past polished wooden griffin's limbs, and came up where he thought he'd be least noticed.

The hall was filled with turmoil. Harrowfoot was wheezing out his life, and the dogs were dead or dying. Several of the opposition were down; as he watched, Angorman dropped another.

Gil saw no stiffness in the Saint-Commander now. There was only lethal precision, a facility with the six-foot axe that was nearly gymnastic. It whipped through the air, taking red stains coming and going. It changed direction in midair, hitting from any arc and every quarter, as if Angorman had transcended gravity and velocity, ignoring or employing them at his pleasure. Sheer dexterity was at work.

He advanced up the hall, his flickering shadow thrown huge on the walls by light from the hearth. Red Pilgrim spun through loops and angles of its own fatal geometries. Another armsman jumped forward, broadsword raised. The crescent axehead eluded him, flew through his rib cage. Blood spurted and he toppled sideways. Gil, ignored, back to a wall, caught his bearings.

Angorman stopped his advance, having reached Dulcet's side. She was white-faced, hands gripped together, but her gaze never left the Saint-Commander. He swept her behind him. Newshield and his men swarmed back into the room, recalled by the fracas.

"Surrender," ordered Newshield, "or I will surely kill you."

Angorman, holding his eye, took the legendary greataxe around in a flourish that left an arc of light in the air.

The men with Newshield set their torches aside and advanced. The old man flicked Red Pilgrim through a dazzling figure eight and came on again like a nimble, deadly machine. One adroit change-vector and a man was down, his leg sliced open. The rest became more cautious, spreading to encircle him. He laughed, a wild gleam in his eye, and tossed his weapon into the air one-handed. It spun quickly, its center of gravity just below its head, and returned to his hands. He feinted in one direction, shifted his grip, and struck in another so fast that Gil lost track of it. Angorman met sword cuts with the axe's head or langets, or eluded them completely. He'd insert a flourish for love of it, but the bewildering ellipses were always murderous.

Two men had pulled bucklers from the wall, coming at him from the sides. He drove one back with an eager attack, then planted his feet firmly and swung on the other. The buckler split; the arm beneath was nearly halved, its ulna and radius both parted. The Saint-Commander had the axe back instantly as if, Gil thought, it were made of bamboo and aluminum foil.

Another man had skirted the table, having spotted the American. Gil chucked a footstool at him. Seeing his way was clear, he dashed to the corner and burrowed for his holster. He fished the Browning out and cocked it, but when he turned around again, the situation had changed. His pursuer had stopped and gone back, Angorman having driven the other men off; but

Newshield had slipped around the Saint-Commander and now held his swordpoint up under Dulcet's chin.

Red Pilgrim froze. Angorman's shoulders slumped as defeat came into his carriage. Gil took up a stance, right shoulder to his target, feet planted solidly. He set his left hand on his hip and brought the Browning up, straight and steady, with his right. He inhaled, exhaled half a breath and held it. Sighting, he squeezed the trigger slowly. A fierce delight swept through him. He wanted to get the Mauser too, and empty both pistols, then take Dunstan's sword and swing it until he was exhausted. His blood coursed like electricity. He fought the feeling down, needing composure.

He eased tension off his forefinger, lowering the barrel. The room was too dim, and Dulcet and Newshield, in the shadows, too close together. Gil wasn't expert enough to be sure he'd make the shot. Angorman was about to lay his weapon down again.

Gil pointed the pistol's muzzle to the ceiling and let go twice. Everyone was startled, but Angorman recovered almost at once. Changing his grasp, he whisked the greataxe around, deep into Newshield's shoulder. The swordpoint, already away from Dulcet's throat, fell. The younger man tottered, eyes bulging. A second stroke opened his gullet. He collapsed. Dulcet sank her head into her hands, weeping.

The others, terrified at the gunshots, jammed the door. Gil let them go, more as a denial of his bloodlust than an act of mercy. Andre and Ferrian appeared, the Horseblooded bearing his scimitar, the wizard with bow strung and arrow nocked. Gil picked up a discarded torch and relit it from the hearth. Angorman awkwardly tried to comfort Dulcet.

She shook him off, sobbing. "It is as it has always been. Death abides in you!" He winced and withdrew his hand.

Frightened servants returned and worked to remove signs of the carnage. In time, the story was pieced together. Newshield had sheltered Yardiff Bey after the sorcerer had fled Earthfast. He had been one of the "Scholars" guested in the manor house. The Hand of Salamá had foreseen that the baby and Blazetongue would come this way.

"Who would be better for Bey to recruit," Angorman asked Dulcet, "than a member of your household?"

"That would be in character," Andre seconded. "Angorman would be bound to stop here on the way south, but Newshield would have come after us had we not come to him."

"There's something else," Gil maintained. "Newshield was talking to his crew about how word would be winging to Bey. Within the hour, he said. What'd he mean?"

Wrapped in grief, Dulcet managed, "He keeps—*kept,* birds, pigeons of the message-bearing kind. Perhaps that is it."

More questions led Gil and Andre to a tower room where cages held a half-dozen carrier pigeons. They searched by torchlight, and discovered a wooden chest. The wizard smashed the lock off it with one blow of his pommel.

Inside they found leg bands, hollow metal capsules and strips of foil with characters written on them.

"Prearranged messages," Gil said. "Does one of those strips have a flaming wheel?"

There were three strips with the mandala of Yardiff Bey.

"Which strip do we send, Andre?"

"All, for one or even two may be lost along the way."

"How do we know they'll fly to the right place?"

Andre deftly drew one bird from the cage. "They are all cooped together; it is unlikely any would home to a different spot." He secured a band, with its capsule, to the bird's leg and slipped in a strip with the mandala on it. Throwing a heavy shutter open to the night, he let the pigeon fly. "A great pity we cannot trace its route." The bird circled the tower twice then flew southward. "But at least Bey should be deceived for a time."

"We could wait for him," Gil whispered, fingering the Ace of Swords on its chain. "When he shows to collect us, we could take him out." The simmering rage he'd felt down in the hall washed through him again.

Andre tut-tutted. "He might arrive with enough men to take *us* out, despite your weapons and my enchantments. Again, he may send someone else to do this errand, or it may have been agreed Newshield was to bring his captives south himself. We shall have to warn Dulcet to engage new guardsmen."

He'd readied another bird. It joined the first. "Be content that, in all this, we salvaged a respite from Yardiff Bey's traps. We shall soon be in Glyffa, where his influence will be far less."

Gil yielded the point. Andre banded a third pigeon. Looking southward, the American gripped the tarot around his neck. Andre was glad for the American that sheer hatred did not bestow wings.

Chapter Eight

What has there been, to this Man's life of yours,
  but war upon Woman?

                                        Anonymous
                                        Kasara's Plea

THEY left Dulcet's under a gunmetal sky. Sleep, food, baths and clean clothing hadn't dispelled the gloom that had settled over them. Dulcet had been restrained with Angorman, pitying him; the incident had underscored an earlier rift in their lives. She said her good-byes with determined reserve, and went to see to the burial of her nephew, and the summoning of the justiciary.

Going south, the party ran into increased traffic, commercial and military. They threaded their way past carriages and around boat-bodied wagons, and saw a column of light cavalry that had halted while its rittmaster bartered with a food vendor for rations. The brassard of the Order and transit letters got them by unimpeded. A wide river valley brought them to the borders of Glyffa where, as Gil had heard it, women ruled.

The frontier guardpost contained only two sentinels. They were helmeted women in ringmail hauberks cov-

ered by blue tabbards. They carried cross-hilted hand-
and-a-half swords, and one held a glave, the other a
bow. Both bore themselves in martial fashion with a
succinct, no-nonsense air. There was a wooden gate
blocking the road, but the women made no move to lift
it. Gil had expected Andre to parley, but the pudgy wizard hung back.

"This border is closed to all," announced the glave
carrier.

"And might one inquire why?" asked Angorman.

"War. It has overrun Veganá, and come into Glyffa.
The men of that nation were driven into our territories
by invaders from the Southwastelands."

"And what will Glyffa do?"

"My own opinion, you mean? Make common cause
with them, most likely. As may be, this border is
sealed."

"It'd be a cakewalk to sneak in or out by staying off
the road," Gil pointed out.

"Those who attempt it will find it risky business. We
have our safeguards. But enough; you cannot pass, and
must perforce turn back."

"Our avowed way lies ahead, to Veganá," Angorman
replied.

The bow was drawn, the polearm raised. "Your chosen path has led you on hazardous ground, stranger,"
said the archer softly.

Gil broke in, "Hold it, whoa. Isn't there somebody
we can talk to? It's really important."

It was enough like concession to placate them. The
arrowhead lowered a degree. "Our High Constable, administrator of the region, is due here later today. You
may make your plea to her if you will. But heed: On
that side of the barrier must you remain."

The travelers tree-hitched their horses, then made
themselves comfortable on the grass at the side of the
road. The guardswomen re-entered their station house,
peeking out often to check up on them.

As the party passed waterskins around, Gil noticed
autumn hadn't touched here yet. Angorman sat cross-
legged, drawing a hone across his axe blade with the
patience of years. The wizard sat like a Buddha, staring

out over Glyffa. Ferrian went aside a few paces to lie down and study clouds, head pillowed on his arm. Woodsinger took the child and suckled her.

"How's it happen to be women in charge here?" Gil asked Andre. The honing stopped a second, while Angorman gazed at the wizard. Gil hadn't caught what had passed between them.

Andre was a storyteller, always enjoying it, but now he had a distracted, unwilling look. Gil had heard that Andre's mother was from Glyffa, but he'd never asked either of the deCourteneys about it. Glyffa was just one more obstacle between Gil MacDonald and Yardiff Bey.

Andre got started. "This was a place not much worse or better than most, over a century ago. Its king paramount was young and headstrong, named Sunfavor. Handsome, vain, doughty fighter, he thought himself irresistible to women. His fancy lit on a courtier. Promised to another, she refused him. Her name was Kasara.

"He grew wroth. To his own end, he instituted legal sanctions against the rights of her sex. To him rallied men who concurred with him, or stood to gain by his new laws. Soon, a woman couldn't own property, choose her own mate or cite any birthright. To travel required consent of father, husband or brother. She was forbidden reading, writing and numbers. Aye, and speaking out in public, too; that pleased many men.

"Women who resisted and men who objected were squelched. Kasara escaped with her fiancé, who was a resourceful fellow, I suppose. She might have changed things with a word and a brief surrender, but did not. Well, she was in love, you see, and her lover could not bear the thought any more than she.

"From her exile she reviled Sunfavor; that provoked even greater excesses. Suppression became slavery outright. Two aborted insurrections led to mass arrest and wholesale slaughter. Women were chattels, as cattle would be. Old evils appeared, the piercing Virtue Ring, the locked chastity belt, whispered moronisms about women's cycles and life-change. Punishment was meted for the simple misfortune of infertility.

91

"Worship of the Bright Lady was, of course, outlawed. Even the Brotherhood could not alter that. Sunfavor left his mark forever, making his name and country an obscenity on the lips of any sane person.

"Late in life Kasara reappeared at the direction of dreams sent by the Goddess. She declared that neither sex could rule the other, any more than the right hand could chain the left. Kasara went unhindered, protected by unseen powers. A day came when she entered Sunfavor's courtroom.

"She bade him end his crimes. He blanched with fright, and struck her down with his scepter. A funeral pyre was built. The King lit it himself. Her husband lay in chains, proscribed from interfering, though it might have been within his ability.

"Flame blossomed. The final wrong was done.

"When it was finished, the Bright Lady made herself manifest to all of Glyffa. They shrank from her in sudden anguish. All her glory was made into blinding fury.

"Sunfavor's mind snapped. He threw himself on the pyre and was consumed. The Bright Lady mandated that for one hundred years, men of Glyffa were to meditate on what they had done. They would bear no arms, hunt no game, eat no meat, own no property and do no harm to anyone. They were never to ride, nor take a wife. They could engender children, but never know them.

"So that is the Mandate of Glyffa, and why its men are monkish and withdrawn. But when the Mandate ends, and men have searched their consciences, they will reveal what form they think life here should take. That is called the Reconciliation. Until then, women conduct the country's affairs."

Something occurred to Gil. "Wait, you're from Glyffa, aren't you? How's it you're not under that Mandate?"

The wizard's face closed up. "My sister and I have our own destinies to follow, given long ago."

Gil rolled over on his back, sucking at a blade of grass. How much of that was legend, how much verbatim truth? In the Crescent Lands, bald-faced lies and unlaundered gospel were equally likely.

Ferrian correctly saw the dust cloud to be cavalry. A troop came at the trot, drawing up to the checkpoint. Its leader alighted.

She was taller than her two sentinels. Like them, she wore a long hauberk, but her helmet was a brightly polished bascinet with white, spread wings fixed to its sides. Throwing back her billowing sky-blue cape, she uncovered a wide belt of tooled leather with bronze filigree. From it hung a hand-and-a-half sword and gleaming dagger sheath. Removing her helmet, she asked her guardswomen questions while they pointed to the party from Coramonde. Her skin was a light olive, her face open and high-cheeked. A dark birthmark spilled down from the hairline over her right ear to her collarbone.

She gave her women permission to dismount and rest, then came to the travelers. Her blue-black hair was pinned in mounds to pad her bascinet, Gil saw, and as she scrutinized them her face creased, flashing white teeth. Her brown eyes had a heavy-lidded look, but her posture was unsparingly correct.

"What is your business in Glyffa?" she asked.

Once more it was Angorman to the barrier. "Our endeavor enjoys the auspices of the Crescent Moon."

She inspected the brassard on his slouch hat. Her mouth pursed in thought, lips fuller than when she'd narrowed her eyes at them. She tugged off mailed gauntlets and leaned her elbows on the gate. Her hands were graceful, and slim. "What bona fides do you offer?"

"May I ask to whom I speak?"

"I am High Constable of Region Blue, this Region. Yourself?"

A deep bow from the Saint-Commander. "Angorman, of the Order of the Axe."

Her eyes widened. "I thought you might be. We have only had tales of you here. Is that Red Pilgrim then? The original one?"

He smiled benignly. "There is only one. But I am unused to your warm clime. If we might continue our conversation inside—?"

She straightened and gave a thumbs-up behind her. The gate swung away. They all trailed her into the checkpoint building. Andre had Blazetongue, wrapped, on his shoulder.

There was a spare sort of mess hall there, built for more troops than used it now. She seated herself at a bench, inviting them to do the same, keeping her dark birthmark to the wall.

"We have spread ourselves thinly along the border. I suppose that much is evident. Most of my troop strength had been reassigned southward. I am going there myself, directly."

Gil spoke for the first time. "Your—your guardswomen said there's been some kind of invasion."

She checked him over frankly. "The men of Veganá have been thrown back over our border by Southwastelanders. We have made common cause with Veganá, not a moment early. Now, what errand takes you through Glyffa? I must have the tale."

"We are on our way," Angorman said, "to bring this child back where she belongs."

"And why is she so important?"

"Because she's connected to this," Gil answered, taking Blazetongue from Andre. He unwrapped it and held it out. Andre had assured them they could trust the women of Glyffa; they might as well find out.

She didn't try to take Blazetongue, but ran her fingertips down the rune-written blade, perhaps seeing if it would burn at her touch. She whispered the sword's name.

Gil nodded. "They used to call it Flarecore in Coramonde. This goes home too."

She looked from weapon to child. "We had heard the last survivor of the Royal House of Veganá had been spirited away months ago. A baby girl, she was. This is the same?"

"Without question," Angorman stated.

"Then, there will be jubilation in that beaten army." Her brow furrowed in thought. "But this transcends my authority. You cannot be turned back, and I certainly shan't allow you to go unaccompanied with Southwastelanders abroad. Ah, Red Pilgrim and Blazetongue side by side, when they are most needed. What a goddess-sending! I live to see interesting times."

"The way to Veganá is closed?"

"Veganá is occupied soil. Still, the tide of battle will ebb after it carves its sea-marks. We Sisters of the Line have withdrawn and withdrawn, beckoning the South-wastelanders onto ground we chose. The battle will begin soon; I go there with my contingent."

"Do the Southwastelanders not overextend themselves?" Angorman asked.

"We think so, for they have moved up every man for this coming fight."

"What about Death's Hold?" Gil interrupted.

She shrugged. "What of it?"

"We heard it was reoccupied, that Yardiff Bey was there."

"No. Or rather, not now. Death's Hold had been cleared of enemies in years long gone by. Months ago, activity began there again, but we were too busy to go in and dig the troublemakers out. Then, less than a week ago, the Mariners landed in strength. Our news is that they cleaned it up, dispersing the evil there."

So, the Mariners had made good their promise to pursue their enemies wherever they had to. Gil wondered if that meant Dunstan had been taken somewhere else; it didn't sound as if Yardiff Bey had been located. The High Constable knew nothing of his whereabouts nor had anyone sighted his demon-ship, *Cloud Ruler*.

Gil pondered. Did it mean Bey had never been in Death's Hold? He'd hidden out with Newshield after his flight from Barthfast, failing to find the secret he'd hoped to uncover in his copy of *Arrivals Macabre*. Where had he gone from there, back to Salamá? But what about the insights of the Dreamdrowse? Muddled, the American tried to rearrange the new data to make some sense.

The High Constable was saying, "You must continue your commission under my protection. Whatever is left of the government of Veganá will be with my Liege, the Trustee. Thus our two paths are one." She stood, tucking her gauntlets through her belt. "We leave in short order."

Everyone concurred, glad for escort. Gil thought about going off on his own to Death's Hold, but she'd sounded definite, telling him it was now empty. Besides, there was the Faith Cup.

Andre was watching him, knowing what he was thinking. "If Bey is hidden, should you not look for him where his minions are most numerous? If a Southwaste-lander army is assembled, his attention must bear on it somehow. Your direction still lies with ours."

Woodsinger and Ferrian were puttering around the child's rack, talking about rigging a dustcover for her, since she'd be in the cavalry column. The High Constable gauged the light as her troops scurried to their horses.

"We have another three hours' light before we must stop," she judged. To the two sentinels she commanded, "This border's clear to the west; do your duty here as best you can. Do not throw your lives away foolishly if numbers are against you; you are a watching detail only."

They lifted their hilts in salute. She turned, slipping an arm through Angorman's elbow on one side and Woodsinger's on the other. "By the Lady, but the men of Veganá will be delirious with these tidings!"

The travelers got their horses, joining her at the head of her column.

"Excuse me," Gil remembered to ask as they moved out, "what do we call you?"

"I am Swan," she threw back over her blue-caped shoulder.

The ride was punctuated with clinking accouter-ments, tintinnabulation of bits, beating hooves on the Tangent and the slap of scabbards. It was interspersed with walks to rest the horses, and occasional stops for water. Swan had a single-minded approach to her job.

They camped as the sun was setting. Swan stood to one side, hands clasped behind her back, to insure that her troops were fed and squared away to her satisfaction. The Sisters of the Line, regular soldiery of Glyffa, were as proficient as any Gil had seen in the Crescent Lands, but made less banter than most.

That night, Angorman conducted a ritual of worship to the Bright Lady. Woodsinger joined Swan and most Sisters of the Line. Against his habit, Gil lingered near, watching along with Ferrian and Andre. The service

96

was subdued, much given to silent prayer and meditation, but there were sweet songs too.

It ended with each worshiper going off to spend time alone. Gil went to check Jeb Stuart and found Swan standing by the picket line, blue cape pulled around her. Memories jumped up in his face of the Lady Duskwind, whom he'd met under similar circumstances. Where he'd been about to talk to Swan, he turned away, propelled by recollections and brooding.

Their breakfast was hard biscuit and strips of dry, plastic-tasting jerky. Gil used a stiff little pig-bristled brush he carried to clean his teeth, but the brackish taste remained in his mouth. He decided not to shave; he usually let his beard go for a few days before using the sliver of a straight razor he had. But he never let his beard hide the powderburn on his cheek, and kept his hair trimmed back from the scar on his forehead. Seeing them in his reflection was a regular reminder he wished to maintain.

He knuckled his eyes, and saddled Jeb, yawning. Rubbing the scar, he tried to estimate how much closer he was to Yardiff Bey today than yesterday.

"Which way's Death's Hold?" he asked Andre.

The wizard pointed westward. "There, along the shore of the Outer Sea. We'll be going away from it soon."

Gil gnawed his lip. Andre added, "If Bey's at Death's Hold, he will be there for a time to come. But if he is behind enemy lines, he may not be there for long. You have set the most likely course."

"Why should he be with the army? Why wouldn't he sneak through in one of his disguises or use magic? Or even fly in, in *Cloud Ruler?*"

Andre averted his glance, muttering. "His arts are less efficacious here. Rely upon it; he will not use his demon-ship, nor wish to employ spells."

Swan came to them. "We link up with my Liege in four days, but there is a stretch of ground to cover."

Gil watched the sunrise. Time and distance from home, hanging over him from the service of the preceding night, descended without warning. His parents' faces were hard to summon up, his brother's impossible. Had

97

the transition to this Reality deadened him down inside, where his feelings lived? Or did it have to do with his single-mindedness, hunting Bey? He fingered the chain that held the Ace, shook the mood off and mounted.

The day's ride took them down through a forest of venerable old lindens that hadn't heard an axe in generations, then across a dry, arid plain of red earth and brown scrub. Toward evening they came into a string of shallow valleys where narrow streams moved quickly. They saw lumbering supply trains bound southward, weighted with supplies for the war effort. It was odd to see a sweating teamster cuss out her horses, and have a broken strap on Jeb's headstall repaired by a handy-woman quartermaster sergeant.

He drew no conclusions about the men of Glyffa, because he met none. They were there to be seen, usually in groups, cowled and cloaked, walking silently along the side of the road, but they eschewed contact with anyone but themselves.

They moved hard again, all through the next day. Terrain became drier and weather hotter. On the third day they passed once more into lands that were well watered. They pitched camp in a stand of pine where beds of dead brown needles muffled hoofbeats, their mounts kicking up clots of them packed with black humus.

The American had seen to Jeb. Passing a large boulder up-cropping in the middle of the bivouac, he noticed a man sitting on it. Gil was sure the guy hadn't been there when they'd stopped, but couldn't understand how he'd gotten through the sentry cordons.

A young man, the stranger sat on the rock, slightly above the American's head, resting buttocks on heels with hands on knees, like a judoka waiting for a match. He wore a simple green robe and toque of weighty, twisted gold cable around his neck. He was lean, with the olive skin and straight, coal-black hair of Glyffa, trimmed at his shoulders. His feet were bare, used to constant walking. He was somehow familiar, but not in a way Gil could pin down. He exuded inner calm.

Gil found the Browning had gotten into his hand. He put it away with chagrin. Though others had noticed the man now, there wasn't any outcry. Presently, Swan arrived. The visitor slipped down to speak to her. Gil figured out what that vague familiarity had been.

"Jade," she said, "brother, how good in my heart to see you."

"Sister, it is good."

"What brings you here, Jade?" Swan's brother was the first Glyffan male Gil had seen up close, aside from Andre, who was obviously the all-around exception. He stuck around.

"I saw your troop as I meditated in the hills, and came down, thinking it might be you. What has come to pass? Your aura is of battle."

"You know that is not for you to ask, brother. The hour for men to enter everyday affairs is not yet."

"Yet we may think, Swan. What will we find?"

She answered, "When the Mandate is done and you men have made your decision, what shall we women discover?"

His eyes were veiled. "The last of the old have died, or will soon. The Mandate will be complete, and you will know our minds."

His glance caught the American. Gil had been puzzling over his last remark, thinking it might have something to do with Andre; now he held himself carefully, watching Jade.

"You move in rarefied circles now, Swan," her brother told her. "Here I see a restless Seeker, who outdoes us all." He backed away, only half talking to Gil. "You have come a far way, and have even farther to go." His right hand went through a rapid, intricate Sign. Then he went to Swan, who presented her cheek for his chaste kiss. He strode from camp.

"Odd dude," Gil remarked to fill the silence.

She made a sound, neither agreement nor objection. She had half-turned from him, used to keeping her birthmark from the sight of others. He moved casually to stand to her left; she relaxed perceptibly.

"Not like yourself at the very least, eh?" she replied. "We are permitted little contact with male siblings in Glyffa, but Jade searched me out from curiosity about our mother. She died birthing him, when I was young, but I remember her well. He and I have spoken, oh, five times or more now. A very close relationship, in

99

Glyffa." She clasped her hands behind her back, head tilted down, debating whether she wished to finish. She did.

"I brought the column by this route, some small measure from its way, because, for some reason, I wished to see him. I knew he would probably be up among the hillsides; his favorite places are there."

"What was that hand-signal thing he did to me before he went?"

"It was a blessing of sorts, but—" She hesitated. "It means he wishes the pity of the Bright Lady for you."

He looked to where Jade had disappeared into the gloaming. "I'd like to know what they're coming up with, Jade and the others."

"I, too. Whatever their decision, it is Mandated that we abide by it. We hold the country in trust, until that time comes. That is *our* learning Trial." Her face shone, but Gil retained his conviction that all final solutions were suspect.

"Are they all as remote as Jade?"

"Many. Their paths lie deep within themselves. Others are not, doing what they can to aid and sustain their fellows. Some are formed in mendicant or praying orders, but many operate vast retreats where they care for anyone who is sick or injured. They set aside chambers where a woman may come and conceive a child, but she must depart when it is accomplished, and never see the man again."

Gil chewed that one over. "The population's down since a hundred years ago, right?"

She confirmed it. "But not dangerously so." Mischief crept into her face. "That will change with the Reconciliation."

Sadness retook her. Gil wanted to ask why, with a battle looming, she'd detoured to have a word with her brother. To see him a last time? He dismissed the question; her own affair. As he often did with profundities, he changed the subject.

"We get to your boss' camp tomorrow?"

"Aye. There may already be fighting. The Southwastelanders are in great array."

"Who're they anyway, these Southwastelanders?"

"How can you not know? They are enlisted of

Shardishku-Salamá, a broad term for many tribes from lands south of the Central Sea. They ward the Masters against invasion, and used to make the occasional raid into Veganá. But now they aggress in hordes, mustering a mighty corps for this enterprise."

"Wait a minute; Salamá's mounting major campaigns in the Crescent Lands?"

"You are not the least perceptive of listeners."

"I'm a dipstick." He'd never thought the Masters could mass that much manpower, or why would Bey have spent decades weaseling control of Coramonde? Apparently they'd just wanted to save their best shot for the main event. Gil knew he was spitballing. His attention went back to Swan. "You, however, aren't. You're about a pure talent."

She inclined her head in mocking gratitude. He colored in embarrassment. She laughed. "And what uncommon fellow are you? Old Sir Angorman, with his far-northern accent, still speaks with less novelty than you. You are altogether odder than your companions."

He couldn't think of a pat way to explain alternate Realities. He swiped a line from Van Duyn. "I, uh, I hail from different probabilities than you."

She shrugged, "As you like."

"Hey, no offense. It's tough to run down for you. I'm outside my own place and time. Yeah, I guess that's it."

"Seeking what?" He didn't get it. "Jade said it; what are you seeking, seeker?"

He thought hidden thoughts feeling the Ace against his chest. She stretched and yawned. "You are a mystery, open and yet closed. Do not speak from social grace, but I should be interested in hearing what you have to say, when you are truthing."

She made prompt departure. He went to find his campfire. Angorman and Andre were gone; they'd been spending time off on their own in earnest conversation since they'd hit Glyffa. Woodsinger and the baby had been allocated a bigger tent, ringed by guards, close to where Swan bunked. That left Ferrian reclining by the fire. Gil eased himself down.

"We have gone from skirmish to battle," Ferrian said, not turning from contemplation of the flames. "Shall we then go from battle to war?"

"Looks like."

The disquiet in Ferrian was finding its way out. "When I was Champion-at-arms of the Wild Riders, always I counseled against war. I thought, *If I am strongest, no man dare deride my rede; the Horseblooded will stay at peace.*" He put his hand to his empty sleeve. "No man has that strength. I grow to hate the sword and spear, Gil MacDonald."

Gil said nothing. Ferrian rolled over to sleep, but his despondency was infectious. The American pulled the chain up, held the Ace. He tilted the tarot and watched firelight lick across the sword, the firmament. It was as if a universe were burning.

Chapter Nine

I am nearer home today
  Than I have ever been before . . .

Phoebe Cary
"Nearer Home"

"THE outlanders, your Grace." The travelers entered the tent on cue.

When they'd arrived at the camp of the Trustee of Glyffa, spread over a high saddle of land above a broad river, Swan had been admitted immediately to the pavilion that was her Liege's headquarters. Gil, beating dust off himself, saw many wounded around him and concluded that the Sisters of the Line had been mauled. There were about seven thousand of them, not counting however many were farther downslope in the camp of the ousted army of occupied Veganá.

The Trustee turned out to be a slender old woman with an oval face, green eyes, and gray hair shot through with white. She wore no armor, though the women clustered around her did. She was seated, dressed in flowing vestments of springtime colors, gathered at her waist by a broad yellow sash set with lapis lazuli. She held a tall shepherdess' crook which, Swan had said, was her staff of office. It was inscribed with cursive spell-phrases and curlicued sigils.

She swept them with her gaze. It paused on Angorman and his cockaded hat, but when the Trustee rose, it was to Woodsinger she went, asking to see the baby. Her voice was reedy, but measured. After she'd looked at the child and heard her laugh, she addressed the others.

"Please pardon me. So much strife have I seen these last weeks that I had to take myself a moment to focus on life." She looked around again. "But, did Swan not say you were five besides the infant?"

Andre wasn't with them. He'd hung back, at the entrance. The Trustee's glance found him, and her face lost animation. Swan was as mystified as anyone.

The wizard came slowly into the room and stood before the Trustee. "Greetings, Andre," she said at last. There was emotional weight to it. "You could not be more desperately needed. You have my gratitude."

His voice strained. "Phases end, lives converge. This reunion was due . . . Mother."

She reached out, and he put his hand in hers. Gil saw now how closely the green of her eyes matched Gabrielle's. He'd heard the deCourteneys' mother was a famous enchantress, but it had never occurred to him she'd be Trustee. Chairs were brought, and Andre seated to her right. His plump, stubbled face was at peace for the first time in days.

The Trustee turned to her son's companions. "Pardon us; we have not had one another's company for—how long, Andre?" Her eyes fell away from his. "Since your Kasara was taken from you." She sighed. "Foolish anger of the moment, and my fault, I acknowledge it."

Gil was fitting in the pieces. So Andre had been Kasara's lover, later her husband. When she'd been executed, when the Bright Lady had imposed her Mandate on Glyffa, Andre must have defied it, exempted himself. The falling-out with his mother had lasted nearly a century.

103

"And your sister, Andre? I have word from her only very infrequently. Is she well?"

"Quite. And happy, I believe."

"Then I am content. I worried when she went with you from Glyffa, but knew you two would need one another."

Angorman cleared his throat; they were all feeling uncomfortable. "The campaign has gone ill, madam?"

"Not well, say rather. Would you not all take somewhat to drink?" They accepted tots of brandy. Swan performed introductions as chairs were brought.

"Your bringing Blazetongue and the heiress is good hearing," the Trustee declared. "The Veganán commander is due for council. I know he will find this more to his liking."

Gil was worried about Salamá's manpower. "How bad are you outnumbered?"

"Badly enough, though we have pruned down the odds a bit since the beginning. Many landings were made on Veganá's southern coasts. They lost several ports, and the Masters poured in more men. They swept Veganá and hold most of it, if uneasily."

"Which Southwastelanders are these?" Angorman inquired.

"They are of the Occhlon, once a peaceful race. The Five recruited them through Yardiff Bey; now they are truest fanatics, avid to lay down their lives for the Masters, foremost in the favor of Salamá.

"They took Veganá in four pitched battles. We have fought them twice within our borders, drawing them on. They are eager for us though; I suspect they would relish an opportunity to trounce us rowdy bitches who have emptied so many of their saddles, pour souls." She shifted her shepherdess' crook. "This war must be resolved; the Reconciliation is not far off, eh, Swan?"

The High Constable of Region Blue agreed. Hands clasped behind her back, she went to the pavilion's entrance, her thoughts on her many ideas to improve life in Glyffa for all. "Your legacy will be human weal," she said to the Trustee at length, "and fulfillment. Your name will live forever."

Swan stepped back from the entrance, seeing someone coming. A man marched into the tent, the Com-

104

mander of Veganá, Lord Blacktarget. He was barrel-chested, with eyes ringed with proclamations of fatigue. He doffed his helmet, holding it in his left arm. His head was shaved smooth, gleaming in the light. His hand went up to touch back his long mustachios, which were waxed stiff. He wore an unusual blazonry, a red circle with a heart done in jet, like a fencing mark. His broadsword hilt was set with a carnelian-eyed basilisk, and his cloak was stained and muddy from the campaign.

The Trustee rose. "Please welcome new friends, my Lord Blacktarget. They bear best tidings to us all." The travelers were quickly named.

"What tidings are they?" Blacktarget asked curtly. Andre took the wrappings from Blazetongue. He handed it to the astonished general.

"But—the Sword of Kings. This is past belief! I know it from old songs, but I never thought I—" His gaze caressed the blade, then suspicion showed on his face. "From whence comes it?"

"Sword and owner found their way to one another," Andre said, "in a time of convergences."

"Yes, but how?" Andre's words suddenly penetrated. "Owner, did you say? The Princess has been found?"

Woodsinger came forward. In the middle of the drama the baby had fallen asleep. Blacktarget's shock was visible. "Stolen the night her parents were killed," he recalled, "but I have held the Princess Cynosure myself, and I know her. Note the shape of her ear. It is indisputably Cynosure. How many prayers entreated for our sovereign and our symbol of fortune at war?"

He took a seat, unsettled, even while he exulted. "These are the things I need, at the moment I need them. Now will Veganá triumph." He jumped up again, his arms wide over Cynosure, so the shadow of Blazetongue fell across her. "Blacktarget the fool! The fates have thrown back the night, just when I despaired most!" He swung around, laughing, impetuous enough in that moment to catch up the Trustee and give her a hug; they'd had their share of disagreements during the campaign. She stopped him with a little *ahem!*, and he sobered.

"Stories are to be told, I think," she said.

105

There was jubilation in the camp of Veganá. Lord Blacktarget had gone before them holding the baby and Blazetongue, basking in their hurrahs. But the South-wastelanders were moving up, and the next day would bring battle.

While the Veganáns were cheering Blacktarget, the Trustee was telling Swan and the company. "They shall need all their fervor tomorrow. The enemy has more horse than we, some of it heavily armored warriors like knights of Coramonde. I pray we will see Sword and Princess in their appointed place. Andre is right; there are vast forces moving those two toward Veganá, for reasons that we do not fully understand."

Angorman averred, "The Order of the Axe will work to that, and you may rely upon my help tomorrow." Andre and Ferrian seconded him.

Gil was smoothing up a diplomatic way to steer clear of the impending battle. "What if it's a decoy? Bey's used sorcery trying to get at the baby and sword. Why not again?"

Andre, Swan and the Trustee became grave. The High Constable beckoned him, saying, "Come, I shall show you the disposition of the camp, and where you may shelter."

She led him to the northern face of the hill. He waited, knowing he'd committed a gaffe, but not seeing how. She began, "You know of Gabrielle, Andre's sister? Good, and you are familiar with the details of her parentage?"

"Springbuck told me something about it, the *Ku-Mor-Mai,* that is. Her father was Yardiff Bey, right?"

"Before the Mandate, long before she was Trustee, the deCourteneys' mother was an enchantress, an aristo-crat of Glyffa. She took for husband the man whose name Gabrielle and Andre bear, the first deCourteney, who came from Outside, a different place and time, as you did. He had some talent in magic. To make the tale quick, he grew jealous; he was the lesser magician and she the enchantress paramount.

"Dissatisfied, he closed an infernal contract. He was deluded, and his forfeiture was to be his soul. But an alternative was granted, that he could escape if he yielded his wife and her favors for a night. Her love

106

must have been strong; she agreed. Gabrielle was begat. As you say, it was discovered later that the succubus who fathered Gabrielle was Yardiff Bey in a borrowed shape, furthering his plans.

"Gabrielle has been in communication with her mother. The Trustee is aware now that it was the Hand of Salamá who ill-used her."

Gil interrupted, "I got all that. I'm sorry I brought it up to her, but the question remains. How do we know Bey's not moving around Glyffa already?"

"Do you not see? During that poisoned union the Trustee listened and observed the inner workings of his sorcery. She heard his oaths, the Powers he invoked. She learned the concealed lines of promise and commitment. In a contest of spell and counterspell, she would have a weighty advantage by that, for she has penetrated her enemy's most guarded activities. Bey would not much care to face her here, I am certain, or even come nigh in *Cloud Ruler*. This is Glyffa, where all hearts and minds serve the Bright Lady, and his might is less here."

Gil digested that. "What about someplace else? Could she beat him outside Glyffa?"

"That is moot. They would be close-matched, but the Trustee is old, old beyond anyone's reckoning, and weary. In Glyffa no foe could stand against her, but outside—well, I pray it is not tested."

"Swan, d'you think Bey is with the Southwastelanders?"

"It might be so. There is such a stench of the Masters hanging over them that the Hand could be among them and not be detected even by the Trustee. It may be that he directs them, to retake the sword and the child and break asunder the focal point of the Bright Lady's influence, at once."

The former sergeant saw he'd have to hang on with the Glyffans. Cynosure and Blazetongue were important to Bey, and now the Southwastelanders had suddenly driven deep into the Crescent Lands. What could that mean, except that Yardiff Bey was out to recover them? Could that mean Dunstan the Berserker was being held somewhere close by?

Staring, thinking, Gil spied a motley collection of

shabby tents to the north. A constant trickle of people was coming up from the plain below the camp, adding to the makeshift village. He asked who they were.

"Displaced persons, flying before the Occhlon," Swan explained.

"Have they been checked out?"

"Lord Blacktarget has men posted on the plain, and in the mountains. He says no Southwastelander could masquerade and fool Crescent Landers; their accents are too barbarous and their stink too conspicuous."

"Do you feel like betting on it?"

"We cannot leave them on the plain; when the sun rises it will be a battleground. See, there is even a troupe of wandering entertainers among them."

There was a ludicrous clown, a red-clad acrobat, and a fire-eater. A fat brown bear danced, and a tall, skeletally lean juggler kept a fountain of knives and apples going.

"Worry not, they will be watched tonight. By tomorrow they will have decamped. None of them want to be near the encounter that will come with the sun."

Yeah, he told himself, resigned that he had to stick around, *neither do I.*

Since the army was short on horses, Gil was requested to serve as a courier. He was no expert rider, but it suited him better than direct involvement. Angorman and Woodsinger yielded their horses to others, she to remain under guard with little Cynosure in the Veganán camp, he to command a company of infantry from Veganá whose captain had been killed. Ferrian, for reasons of his own, declined to follow any banner, but would serve with the orderlies whose job was to drag the wounded from battle and get them to medical stations at the rear. It was risky work; orderlies were themselves often cut down in the heat of the struggle.

Andre was another question, the only living Glyffan male who'd seen combat. He was a seasoned leader, aside from talents of magic. Reconsidering the Mandate, the Trustee admitted Andre had always been exempt from its bans. He was placed over a squadron of heavy cavalry, to ride before a Glyffan flag for the first time in nearly a century.

Dawn came chilly and hazy. Gil reported to the Trustee's pavilion after a restless night. It was swarming with officers and functionaries, and High Constables with capes colored for their Regions in red, yellow, brown and gray.

The Trustee sat across a little table from Swan, both of them ignoring the hubbub, playing chess as if they were alone, and this an idle day. The chesspieces were large and topped by little lighted candles. The game was going rapidly, moves coming with unusual haste, with little or no lag between. Swan's hair was pinned up, to fit her bascinet; her armor glinted from diligent polishing.

An aide stepped in Gil's way, demanding his business. The Trustee looked up, saying he could be admitted. She asked if Woodsinger and Cynosure were guarded; he said they were, in the tent of Blacktarget himself. "What are the candles for?"

Sunrise wasn't far off. The two women began snuffing out the flames. Swan explained. "It is a variation developed by the Trustee. When a candle goes out, its piece is eliminated from the game. Wicks are of assorted duration, and we pick which pieces get which lifespans at random, except that the king goes untimed."

"Sounds like a fast game."

"Verily," she replied, moving her chair back, "and a martial one. It has the merciless pressure of time, an uncaring randomness and rude unpredictability."

The Trustee was on her feet now. "I enjoyed that, my dear; it is helpful to put one's concerns aside. You are becoming good at this wildcard game. How much do you owe me?"

"More than I can pay. But this time I shall win."

The Trustee patted her arm. "I shall checkmate you in three moves when we return, you have my promise. If not, consider us even."

"Done."

The old woman took up the crook of her office. People in the tent became totally attentive. "Each of you has her particular instructions," she said, "and if you but keep them in mind, all will be well." She lifted the crook. Everybody but Gil bowed to receive her benediction. As she recited the blessing her eye caught the American's. He dipped his head to her once, politely. Gravely, she winked in return.

Then everyone was moving. Swan went past, bidding him good fortune hastily. Someone shoved an armload of hardware into his hands. He found himself holding a lance of polished ebony and a shield of brightly painted leather, rimmed and studded with iron, bearing the Trustee's device of a green unicorn. There was also a pair of greaves, rusty ones whose dark stains suggested their previous owner hadn't been very lucky.

He was about to protest; he'd be no match for an experienced opponent. Then he saw that he could throw the stuff away if he wanted, and—who knew?—he might need it. Outside, he buckled the greaves on clumsily, took the lance and tested its balance. His muscles tensed unconsciously, ready for impact. He felt a twinge of the ferocity that had filled him in Dulcet's hall.

The conjoined armies were drawn up, waiting. There was movement far out across the plain, the Occhlon leaving their camp and taking up positions.

Lord Blacktarget and the men of Veganá were to take the right flank, stretching down to the river's side. The general could be seen haranguing his men, waving Blazetongue, though he intended to leave the sword behind.

The left flank, to be anchored at the foot of the slopes, was under Swan. She had two thousand troops, mostly light cavalry and archers, backed by four companies of pikewomen.

Gil watched the Occhlon assembly writhing its way into order. He couldn't see much, except that there seemed to be an awful lot of them. The Trustee called for her horse; she would command the center herself. The women closest to her repeated the call. They were all veteran commanders, wily fighters.

He mounted Jeb Stuart and trailed the Trustee and her knot of advisors and aides to her position at the center. They passed through ranks of waiting soldiers of both sexes, who resembled those he'd known in his own world, in a way. Young, worried, they were examining their feelings, thinking ten thousand thoughts of how the day would go. He caught snatches of conversation.

110

"What should I do if—"; "Suppose my enemy comes at me so—"; "The grip of the lance is the thing, remember it and you will be—."

He passed squatting pike-bearers and straight-backed lancers, and ranks of nervous sword-and-buckler infantry anticipating the order to shield-lock. The Trustee was greeted with some cheers, but more silence. This army had lost before and might again today, portents or no portents. These were all people who would die if it did.

The Trustee took her place on slightly higher ground, her green unicorn banner nearby. She took one last look right, left and behind, then raised her crook. Trumpets blared around him, and Gil's belly twisted. The entire army began a slow walking pace across the plain. Early-morning stillness left battle pennons limp on staffs and spears. He wiggled the lance to seat it in its rest. His hands were damp; his heart banged in his chest. He hated the idea of a large-scale clash, where he could get himself wasted from any direction.

The enemy stepped off with crashing cymbals and thundering drums. Gil noticed that the point of his lance was bobbing around and realized he'd crouched in the saddle and clamped it to his side in anticipation. If he actually had to use it, a rigid grip would spoil his aim. He sat erect again. His fingers flexed at the en-armes of his shield.

The enemy stopped when their right flank, facing Swan and her Sisters of the Line along the slope, came to high ground of its own. Then the Occhlon center advanced to stand and form a salient point. The men at the river bank, fronting Lord Blacktarget, stayed put. The river ran swiftly, deeply at this point, offering no fording place for miles, and that was one of the reasons for which the Trustee had chosen this spot.

Both sides halted. They exchanged challenges of a sort, soaring horn blasts of the Crescent Lands and cymbals and drums of the Southwastelanders. Then there was silence, and for the next ten minutes nothing happened at all.

Gil knew this was common in the Crescent Lands; these were people who trusted in defense, fortification, armor, shields. They preferred to let their opponents

111

make the first move. He fidgeted as sweat ran down from the padded brim of his cap.

The Trustee conferred with her privy councilors. Finally, she ordered: "Archers forward." There was no need for riders to carry the word this early, when trumpets could be heard and movements clearly seen. All along the lines of the North, bowmen and bowwomen stepped out, limbering strings, drawing shafts. The battle's first phase had started.

Chapter Ten

Dream of battled fields no more,
Days of danger, nights of waking . . .
                    Sir Walter Scott
                    The Lady of the Lake

THE archers stopped about ten paces out, taking maul-hammers from their backs. Sharpened stakes were pounded into the ground at a forward cant as defense against cavalry. Lengthy pavise shields, protection from enemy missiles, were held by assistants while the archers shook out their quivers, arranging their arrows at their feet.

The Sisters of the Line were armed with slightly lighter bows; few had the height and length of arm to pull the heavyweights some men preferred. The range was extreme. The archers began lofting long flight arrows in high arcs, saving their livery shafts for closer combat. Gil could hear bowstrings snapping on leather bracers up and down the line, and the whizz of pile-headed arrows. They flew beyond the wall of enemy shields, but he couldn't tell how much effect they had. The shooting went on for a minute, then bowmen emerged from the Occhlon ranks, set themselves up in much the same way and returned fire. The Southwastelanders' bows were giant recurve weapons, over six feet long, but simple "self" bows, not composite; they lacked the range of the Crescent Landers'. Moreover, the Occhlon used a pinch-draw in their release, less effective than the northern two- and three-fingered draws. Only a few of their shots found their way among the Crescent Landers. Gil raised his shield whenever he saw a salvo coming, but no shaft dropped near him.

As the Trustee had hoped, the uneven archery duel tweaked the Southwastelanders to move. A sally of fleet horsemen swept up the river bank, their places in the ranks taken immediately by reserves. Some of the southerners wore mottled armor with bizarre patterns of decoration. Swan had told Gil that there were warriors among the enemy who fashioned their panoply from skins of the huge snakes and lizards of their desert.

Lord Blacktarget and his men swept their swords out. Their war-horses, hearing the sound, danced and reared in anticipation. The men of Veganá rode out to meet the foe before the Occhlon could get in among the stakes and take a toll of archers. The two sides hit with scores of individual collisions. A dust cloud went up in the hazy light while cries and chants mixed with the horns and cymbals. Gil expected to see the Trustee rush reinforcements in, but it didn't happen. The ruler of Glyffa regarded this as an early probe and held back from committing herself. The Occhlon pressed hard, but Gil heard a thousand throats hollering *Veganá!* above the melee. The attempt to roll up the Trustee's right flank faltered, reduced to maddened charge and countercharge over short distances, with swords, maces and axes in sharp opposition at close quarters.

Off to the left an attack was launched against Swan's command, but because the land dipped and rose that way, Gil couldn't see clearly. He began to appreciate the importance of gonfalons and banners. Everyone in the armies—himself included—depended on the battle flags to tell if their side was moving forward, making a stand or being driven back. The Trustee told him to go tell a particular cavalry unit to stand ready. He spurred away, trying to keep some speed and still not gallop over massed soldiers in his way. He found the correct outfit and relayed the order. The Sisters of the Line

113

were already in their files, nervously adjusting helmets, lances and shields.

Finding his way back, he went along the seam of the two armies on the right flank, where men of Veganá marked time next to Glyffan women. Gil was amazed again at their youth. They called to him for news but he couldn't stop. He knew, though, that in their place he'd have ripped a bypasser out of the saddle and clubbed the latest reports out of him.

The leader of the reserve element came up and awaited orders to move. The Trustee instructed her to go in either direction when the next probe came, but to wait toward the left flank. Then she ordered Gil to see how things were going on the Veganán flank.

He barrel-rode off again, cutting deeply behind his own lines. The front might shift down there, and he was a messenger, not a grunt. The arrow showers had stopped nearer the river, the sides being too intermingled.

The fighting had overflowed into the river. The clay bank and bed were too treacherous to maneuver on with a horse; men were clashing on foot, the river running around their legs, muddy-red. Then he spotted Lord Blacktarget.

The general had dismounted and waded out chest-deep, holding the extreme end of his flank himself. A rope around his waist ran back and slightly upstream, belayed by two husky squires. He was jubilant, sure that the battle would go his way. He'd called for his piper, who stood on the river bank blowing a lusty war-song. Lord Blacktarget would occasionally bellow a snatch of the lyrics, waiting for the next adversary.

His two-handed broadsword whirled and chopped, throwing back every opponent. Further downstream, Gil could see corpses of men and horses being whisked away in the current. The Occhlon had lost an ambitious gambit, trying to outflank through the river itself. As he watched, Blacktarget lost his footing and was yanked up again by the two squires.

The river bank was in the firm control of Veganá again, so the general had himself hauled in. Dripping and wounded, he accepted his wineskin from an aide

114

and drank deeply, while his injuries were being bound. His pink skull gleamed with sweat and muddy water.

In response to the Trustee's inquiry, he leaned on his broadsword and studied the front. "This may have been the feint, or may be a feint-in-deception. We will hold here against any attack, but I will retain my reserves. Tell her Veganá needs no succor." Forgetting Gil completely, he called for his horse. The piper struck up another song.

The Trustee heard the reply while monitoring her worrisome left flank. "Needs no succor, eh?" she repeated, as her aides muttered among themselves. "That was not his claim a fortnight ago. He hates subordinating himself to me, but if he holds his end of things I am content." She peered more closely to the left. "The Southwastelanders do not like it there, by the water with Blacktarget; he is secure. Send the first reserve element to Swan." It wasn't Gil's turn yet, so another rider galloped off.

The sky had become overcast. Gil looked down to the center where Andre should be and saw the heavy cavalry was no longer there, replaced by a new unit. He asked one of the aides about it.

"There was a quick, impudent sally while you were gone," she said. She disapproved of his inquisitiveness, but knew he was somehow favored by the Trustee. "Andre deCourteney was hurt, taken back in one of the wagons, his contingent replaced." Gil fought the impulse to rein around and go see how the wizard was, unsure that he could even find him.

More commanders were coming up now, as units were rotated in gradual attrition. The Trustee still hesitated to group her main strength. Gil viewed the fitful migrations of the banners, forward in conquest or backward in disarray. This wasn't his kind of military action, chafing on an open field while slow, sometimes hours-long maneuvers took shape. He'd served in an army of tactical radios, air observers, choppers, artillery and personnel carriers. Operations had been mobile, fast-breaking. Sitting on a horse marking time had worn his patience out quickly.

He noticed the Trustee was unoccupied. "Any word on Andre?" he asked. Aides glowered.

"None," she said, having forgotten her son in the absorptions of the day. "If you would do me a service, go rear and inquire." Her mind reverted at once to the battle.

He threaded his way back through waiting soldiers, cavalry who stood in their stirrups and infantry who held one another on their shoulders, craning for a view. Further to the rear, those waiting were more relaxed, passing time. At the very edge of the plain the chirurgeons had set up their crude field operations in an open tent with wooden slabs on which they performed desperate surgery. A constant flow of wounded was the engagement's yield.

Gil spotted Ferrian. Answering to his name, the Horseblooded didn't stop his work. He carried men and women groaning and screaming their pain to where they must wait until they could be attended to. Gil finally halted him by grabbing his shoulder over an empty sleeve. There was a vacant look in the brawny Horseblooded's eyes. He motioned to the wounded, "So many, so very many."

Gil shook him. "Forget that. Where's deCourteney?"

The left hand pointed; Gil released him.

The wizard was sitting beside a water barrel, rewrapping his wounded side more to his liking. Seeing Gil, he achieved a wan grin. "I shall live, it seems," he conceded. Gil heard sounds of the wounded being treated with measures nearly as sanguinary as the battle itself. He avoided looking into the tent.

"Where's your horse?"

"Appropriated as soon as ever I fell. Ferrian was first to my side, and carried me to safety."

"Ferrian better be cool. He's losing his grip."

Andre stood up angrily. "Do you know what he has dealt with today? Then go, behind the tent."

Training his eyes to the ground, he did as Andre bid him, unwillingly. In the area behind the tent were rows of the dead, butchered and savaged in a hundred ways, darkening the earth with blood. To the side was a pile of what he thought at first to be wood, or discarded armor. Closer, he saw they were human limbs, blackening as they lay, arms and legs and hands and feet too ruined to salvage. White bone poked from bloated flesh;

116

clouds of big, shiny black flies covered the piles. The steamy reek drove him back.

He caught shaky balance with one hand on a tent post and fought his compulsion to retch until his stomach inverted. Andre pulled him away. He was breathing harder, heart racing. "I'm clearing out of here; let's go." When Gil had remounted, the wizard climbed up on Jeb's croup. Gil caught a last look at Ferrian, assisting a stumbling lancer who was pressing her intestines back in and crying like a lost child. The American kicked hard. With a peevish snort, Jeb Stuart bolted away.

"Why don't you and your mother use magic?" he called, as they cantered along. The wind of their passage took away much of the reply.

"Too close . . . preparation . . . on their side too."

It began to drizzle. Gil reined in to find he'd drifted too far left. There was intense fighting along the foot of the slopes. He could see Swan's banner, with her white-winged namesake. He decided things were going to go the way they were going to go, no matter where Gilbert A. MacDonald was, and wanted to see if the High Constable was all right. Andre made no objection.

Others were going that way. The two rode past a detachment of infantry with Angorman at its head, and swapped news.

The assault on Lord Blacktarget had indeed been a feint, the light sally at Swan a screen for the advance of a larger force. The whole left flank could be rolled back if it wasn't stopped. Angorman was bringing up his sword-and-shield men to protect the archers. Gil hurried on.

The Sisters of the Line must have repelled the attack and gained ground; there were trampled Occhlon corpses at the rear of their position. It was Gil's first sight of them close up. They weren't unusual, just men who were dead. They were a taller race than the Veganáns, with slightly darker skin and hair. These wore armor of *cuir bolli*, faced and shaped with metal. Their weapons looked light, slender swords both curved and straight, and shorter lances. But, Gil remembered, there were supposed to be more heavily armed and armored Southwastelanders somewhere.

He worked forward, Andre clinging to him, past groups of archers and strings of pikewomen crouching behind mantlets. Dust swirled thickly; they heard the ringing of swords and yells of combatants. A captain rode by, not noticing they weren't part of her unit. "Up! Up to the line and 'ware. Their knights come against us now. We broke their last onset, but another will come soon."

The wounded were being dragged away from a point in the line where it had thinned. Swan was there, dismounted for a rest. She'd taken off her helmet, and an aide dashed a bucket of water on her face, cooling her in her stifling armor.

She waved wearily. "How goes the day?" Gil told her as much as he knew. She listened, again turning her head to hold her birthmark away. "Those clanking ironclads will be down on us again," she admitted. "I had never dealt with plate armor before. It seems rather clumsy. We shall stop them."

Gil, who'd seen knights of Coramonde in full career, wasn't so sure. He couldn't see many of them, though; maybe two hundred had drawn up on a rise a quarter-mile away and formed a wedge, probably to be followed by the more numerous heavy cavalry.

"And what of your pikewomen?" Andre asked.

She motioned rearward with a thumb. "There. I thought they stood no chance against those behemoths in plate."

"How long are their pikes?"

"Ten, or perhaps eleven feet."

"Mmm, not good, but perhaps sufficient. I advise you to bring them up in support, High Constable. Let the enemy through your center, stop the knights with pikewomen and try carving them up from their flanks."

She ordered the infantry up, then looked to Gil. "What do you think, Seeker?"

He shrugged. "Ask me tonight." He was still in turmoil, angry at what he'd seen and heard through the morning.

"I will. They say fighting on the river bank has gotten sharper, but the men of Veganá are happy for that. I believe the day will be decided here."

Angorman arrived and dispersed his swordsmen

among the pikewomen, placing himself at the head of their formation. Someone shouted; the enemy knights were moving out at a trot. Swan mounted at once, and Gil let Andre down.

That vicious something that had been hovering at the outer circle of his thoughts began to take form. Seeing the charge, Gil felt his pulse hammer. It was as if the Occhlon advance was the final affront, obscene provocation. Ignoring Andre's call, he fell in at the end of Swan's riders, wanting to see what would happen.

They moved forward at a walk, then a canter. A horn winded. Dressed and aligned, they broke into the charge, Swan in the van. The High Constable of Region Blue hunkered down behind spear and shield and met her antagonist, who led the Occhlon. She downed him at first impact, her point skillfully catching his helmet on its crest, bursting its retaining laces and carrying him backward off his horse. He landed with a clang.

The two sides rammed into each other while Swan stopped to recover her own balance. Gil raced by, all restraint gone, hunting an opponent, calling out, "Nice lick!" She shouted something, but he didn't catch it.

He spotted an enemy on a roan charger. They bore in on each other by unspoken consent. The man crouched behind his triangular shield. Jeb's mane was stiff as a flag in Gil's face. He knew he should have been scared, but wasn't. The new thing on the rim of his awareness was overriding fear with volcanic anger.

As trained, they came in on each other's left side, shield to shield, lances held loosely until the last instant. The American kept his point more or less aligned, knowing he'd have to target in the last moment before meeting. The drizzle had made the lance slippery. Jeb, more experienced than his rider, gathered himself for collision just before it happened. The two men clamped knees to their horses' sides, clutched their weapons and threw all their weight forward. The Occhlon let go a battle cry that the American, in his emotional transport, never heard.

Their spears transversed into shields. Gil's skidded; the Occhlon's didn't. The jolt was like being clotheslined, blind-sided and body-blocked at the same time. The man felt Gil going and gave his point a clever twist,

119

to kill him right then. Jeb did a kind of change-step,
and Gil almost found his balance. Then he toppled sideways and backward as the Southwastelander came
around to finish him.

The fall released that thing that had waited in the
American. He ignored the pain of the fall and came up
in a fit of virulence so vivid he felt he could murder
with his will alone. He'd dropped his shield and lance,
and took no notice of Jeb, who stood waiting for him.
He drew the Browning, raised it in sidelong stance and
shot the Occhlon. It gave him an awful elation he'd
never known before.

There were outcries all around him. Horses
screamed, panic-stricken from the shot and smell. The
heavy knights had cut a swath through the Sisters of
the Line, and he was surrounded by foemen. It suited
him well. He emptied the Browning a shot at a time,
with a feral care that he kill as many as he could. He
barely noticed the autoloader's buck, greeting its explosions, a form of malign homecoming.

Swan came up, having lost her spear, to engage an
Occhlon with sword and shield. She slashed, striking
sparks from the other's blade, their horses whistling angrily and battering one another. Her shield was dented
and her sword notched, and it seemed the knight would
win. Gil hardly noticed it was the High Constable in
jeopardy when he smoked her opponent. He was in a
separate world of misted ebullition.

Angorman dashed up with swordsmen and pikewomen at his heels, the trap ruined by Gil's madness.
The Saint-Commander made do as best he could, bringing the fight out to them. A knight charged; Angorman
dodged to one side, chopping with Red Pilgrim. The
Occhlon's leg was severed, and the chausse that covered
it. The leg toppled to one side of his horse, the knight to
the other. Angorman was already busy with his next antagonist.

Swan's banner went forward. Assorted elements under her scrambled to fill the gap and close up after the
cavalry. The Occhlon had been stopped by the countercharge and the terror effect of the Browning. Now they
drew back. Gil ran after them, forgetting Jeb. He'd reloaded, and began howling, firing as he went.

Glyffan cavalry pounded past him. Swan might not know exactly what had happened, but she'd seen the opening and knew how to use that. Enemy archers and infantry had followed in the wake of the knights. Now they were milling around. The Sisters of the Line came down on them like harpies, driving them back into each other in a rain of sword strokes.

Some Southwasteland halberdiers made a stand. The High Constable dismounted with a troop of her riders and, with swords and parrying daggers, slipped in among the flashing polearms. Several of them fell, but once the Glyffans were past the halberd heads, the Occhlons were defenseless. Many dropped their weapons and fled. The remnant was quickly overrun.

Gil ran to join, dropping his empty pistol. He'd nearly forgotten what the conflict was about, but wanted passionately to be part of it. But as he ran he felt an ebbing. It became more difficult to think. He slowed to a walk, then stopped. The rain dripped from his face.

His sense of equilibrium waffled. He caught his balance with a sidestep. It seemed extremely hot and bright, as if the sun were out, filling the sky. His legs gave, and he found himself sitting on the ground. Then he keeled over. In his state, it was a relief.

Chapter Eleven

A book may be as great a thing as a battle.
                                Benjamin Disraeli
                                Memoir of Isaac D'Israeli

HIS head was propped against a rock, its graininess scraping the skin beneath his hair. He opened his eyes, expecting a dizzy spin to start, but none did. His steel cap had been removed, the Browning placed by his side.

The field was cluttered with bodies of allies and enemies, and wounded of both sides. The victors were doing what they could for all.

Swan, the Trustee and Angorman were near. The High Constable went down on one knee to study him with untelling brown eyes.

"The Saint-Commander explained your weapons to us," she said. "They helped break the charge. But why did you not tell us you are Berserker?"

Who, me? he thought, as Andre appeared. "All it was, was I lost my head. I'm not berserk, I know, 'cause I have this friend Dunstan who—"

He stopped and gaped. Andre had found a disk of polished metal, a trapping of some kind. He held it to reflect Gil's face, or what looked like it, drastically altered. There was saliva drying on his chin and at the corners of his mouth. His skin was waxy, his eyes huge and glassy. From fresh cuts he saw he'd chewed and bitten his lips. The scar on his forehead and the dark smear of powderburn stood out starkly on pale flesh. He'd never seen himself like this, but had seen someone in this condition exactly.

Dunstan after the Berserkergang; I look just like him. Then a flood of horror pried at his sanity. *God, please, no!* He knew it was true though; it had been waiting to flare up in him.

Andre said, "Some of Dunstan's Rage must have passed to you when you essayed to pull him from Bey's mystic circle in Earthfast. I do not know more." The American moaned. "But you can live with it, as Dunstan did, and control it. You must; it will come more strongly hereafter."

Gil's face was buried in his hands. A new thought occurred; did this mean Dunstan was still alive? Was it some shared bond with his friend? Some calm returned. "Was there any sign of Bey, Andre?"

"None whatsoever."

The Trustee was telling Swan to examine the enemy camp; the Occhlon had been routed when their flank was rolled back along the heights. "We shall pursue them as soon as we may," the old woman was saying. "It is not beyond chance that they may stand to fight again. Lord Blacktarget promises we shall gather more strength in Veganá with word of Blazetongue and Cynosure, and victory." She looked at Gil, then away.

Andre helped him to his feet, handed him his pistol and got him onto Jeb Stuart. The wizard didn't seem disabled by his wound at all. Keeping their pace slow, they all rode to the Southwastelanders' abandoned pavilions. Inside the biggest tent, Gil let himself down among some cushions. Energy was creeping back into him as the others started sorting through the enemy commander's property. He supposed he might as well help search; there might be a hint on Bey's whereabouts. They were poking around sacks, cases and portable shelves when Andre called. He held a small wooden chest. In it were jars and boxes, stained with painty stuff that he said was makeup, and weighted balls that a juggler might use. They all thought about the traveling troupe, in the refugee camp. Among them and perhaps among other displaced persons as well, there had been Occhlon. And maybe, Gil thought, Yardiff Bey.

"We should not delay the pursuit of the Occhlon," the Trustee said, "but neither can we let southern spies go unhunted."

"What can they be after?" Andre asked himself aloud. "Blazetongue and the child?"

"No," the Trustee responded, "I have word that all is well in the camp."

"What would the Southwastelanders be so hot to get their hands on?" Gil puzzled.

"There is *Arrivals Macabre*," Andre replied. "Bey is eager to get it."

"What is this?" the Trustee snapped. They told her of Bey's obsession with Rydolomo's book. "There is a copy at Ladentree," she said.

"What's Ladentree?" Gil wanted to know.

"It is our great library."

"My God, that's it!" He glared at Andre. "Why didn't you tell us about the library?"

The wizard ran a hand over his balding head. "When last I was in Glyffa, Ladentree was a monastery, but had no great store of books."

Swan told him, "It was made a center of study and thought when the Mandate was imposed. Precious

123

books and documents were brought there from every corner of Glyffa."

"That's where he'll go," Gil stated flatly. *Goddam Bey's got more disguises than a Chinese fox.*

The Trustee became brisk. "We act immediately. Swan, take your best women and give chase. Be alert; they may have changed guises yet again. I shall secure this area and follow."

"I'm going too," Gil told her. He didn't have to worry about joining combat; numbers would be on the side of the Sisters of the Line. Worrying about what to do if Bey were there, he looked expectantly at Andre.

"I shall accompany you, of course," the wizard said.

"Good enough. Uh, what about Woodsinger and the kid?"

"I shall stay with her for now," Angorman volunteered. "Then I will come along with the Trustee."

Swan set out a subaltern to gather the Sisters she wanted. A horse was found for Andre. Ferrian appeared, having gotten his mount back, to see how they'd fared. The Horseblooded was taciturn, avoiding their eyes; Andre explained what they'd discovered, finishing, "We leave for Ladentree now. Would you come?" Ferrian frowned in thought.

"C'mon, man," the American shouted. "There's nothing you can do here. Let it go."

"Your aid would be appreciated," Swan said. Gil looked at her in some surprise.

"Then you shall have it," Ferrian replied.

The High Constable had chosen fifty of her personal guardswomen, an elite. They found, as expected, that the entertainers had decamped as soon as battle had begun and left behind tents, baggage and the trained bear. Gil stopped long enough to pick up Dirge.

It was just over seven miles to Ladentree. The southern army must have been maneuvering to get as close to the library as it could. Had the Glyffans waited much longer before engaging them, the Southwastelanders might well have taken it.

The countryside was quiet and empty, with everyone either recruited or in hiding. Gil began to hope that they could trap Bey or even get Dunstan back alive. In any case, the book mustn't fall into enemy hands.

124

He was pleased in a tiredly dispassionate way that Cynosure and Blazetongue were safe, but glad to be free of them. As with Dunstan, the lethargy that had replaced Berserkergang passed away, leaving reflective calm.

They sighted Ladentree silhouetted against the setting sun, a rambling, airy place on a hill above a diminutive lake. It sprawled grandly in galleries, courtyards, repositories, study chambers, vaults, shelf rooms, auditoriums and copy studios. Its walls were blue-black stone, its roofs of thick orange tile.

They came to the front of the place, a tall arch of amandola marble. There were fresh hoofprints, deep and wide-spaced from speed, leading into the building itself. They left their own horses outside and Swan posted ten cavalrywomen to hold the gate. Gil left Dirge and Dunstan's sword behind, not to be slowed up.

The main corridor was broad as a city street, roofed in elaborate groining and fan-tracery, lit by wide windows.

There were fresh marks on the time-worn floors, pale dints of iron horseshoes on the darker surface. A word from Swan, and her Sisters of the Line drew swords. They raced along the corridors past paneled doors, their boot scuffs barely disturbing the vast quiet. They came on a body curled on the floor, a man with a broken length of wood beside him. He was dying, a deep wound in his side. Swan cried out, recognizing her brother Jade.

Some of the glaze left his eyes when he saw his sister. "Swan, you are needed; you are here." He strayed into unconsciousness for a second, but forced himself back out of it. "They came hours ago, riding their horses through our halls. We couldn't stop them. But we would not help them look for what they wanted, and they could not find it. At last they became angry, beyond temper. Silverquill—" He paused for a fit of coughing on his own blood. "The Senior Sage tried to run. They chased him."

Gil wanted to tell him to save his strength but there was no point; the wound had as good as killed him already. "Oh Swan, I broke the Mandate. I fought them with that length of wood to make them stop. The temperance of years ruined in a moment of—" He was racked with coughs again. The blood ran freely from his mouth now.

She hugged his head to her. "You did what you must," she said softly. "Warrior-spirit, you did what you could, no sin." He looked up in hope, his last exertion. He slumped, breathing leaving him. She looked up at the sound of boot heels.

It was Gil MacDonald, pistol in his fist. She thought at first that the Berserkergang was on him, but he was composed. Voices had attracted his attention, drifting from an inner courtyard. Ferrian, Andre and the guardswomen went after the American. Swan remained at her brother's side. Stern war captain, shrewd administrator, she was lenient with herself for once, taking a moment out for mourning.

Gil came to a pair of beautiful doors of reticulated carving. Through them he could see Sages of Ladentree, cowering from three members of the troupe. One of the intruders, the bear trainer, stood aside, holding some tiny white thing in his hand. Gil saw it was some minuscule songbird.

The Occhlon dropped the bird and clapped his hands together loudly. There was an exaltation of white wings up from the trees. Some birds flew to safety but many, close to the man, dropped with helpless paroxysms of wings to lie on the turf. Apparently they were so fragile that loud noises would stop their hearts. The Occhlon found that entertaining. He unslung a horn, to see how many he could frighten in adjoining courts and rafters.

The doors were latched from the outside. Gil took a step back and kicked. The painful rebound of his foot felt good, making him assert control; he intended never to capitulate to the Berserkergang again. There was a splintering of old wood. The doors slammed open.

The bear handler saw him, dropped the horn and put hand to hilt. The Mauser's muzzle came up.

"Give it up," Gil offered, "or I'll kill you. It wouldn't bother me. Decide!"

The Southwastelander's blade came free. Before Gil could get a shot off, Ferrian dodged around him, scimitar in his left hand, for a revenge of his own. Gil lowered the pistol.

The two fought up and back, hard boots scoring soft turf meant for bare feet or slippers. The other Southwastelanders, juggler and clown, waited, outnumbered. Ferrian was plainly the better fencer, with a flexible wrist and inspired sense of timing. The other, with a husky build much like the Horseblooded's, using his accustomed hand, found himself losing. Their blades wound, rang and rang again, investigating the scenarios of death. Ferrian's scimitar was first to execute one. The curved blade leapt at the Southwastelander's heart. The man died in cruel surprise.

The surviving members of the troupe drew together; cavalrywomen moved to disarm them. Then one of the Glyffans dropped, a long war arrow's fletch at her back, a pale-head sticking out of her mailed breast. Gil searched upward, saw an archer on a rooftop and cursed himself—*Screw-up!*—for not being more cautious. He brought the Mauser up, fired, missed. A second arrow found Ferrian's thigh; Gil squeezed off three more shots. The bowman's body hurled from its perch.

The American demanded of the quailed Sages where the other Southwastelanders were. "Abroad in the library," one answered. "There were many of them."

Swan arrived to investigate the shots. She split her troops into search teams. Gil went with seven Glyffans, to help. He never knew how many rooms he ran through, doors he yanked open, praying Bey's inhumanly calm, one-eyed stare would meet him on the other side. There were racks of clay tablets whose age he couldn't even guess, ages-old works of art. There were enormous books bound in gold, set with precious gems to show their rarity and worth. There were piles of scrolls and illuminated folios, maps and charts. He saw plant specimens and items of natural history, but ignored them all. He went on, dreamlike, ripping aside endless curtains, turning countless door handles, running, ever running through the maze of corridors.

Twilight turned as they searched. They had divided the offshoots among them. Gil fell behind, making his inspections thoroughly. The Sisters had outdistanced him and gone to the next stretch of corridors when he heard a whisper.

Pistol ready, he traced it back to an unlighted alcove.

127

Then he recognized a skinny frame and lean, melancholy face.

"Dunstan!" He lowered the handgun and would've let out a yell, but the Horseblooded, at the far end of a hidden hallway, hushed him with a finger sign. He was armed with a short stabbing sword, and wanted quiet. "Is Bey here?" Gil mouthed silently. With a nod and a signal to follow, Dunstan slipped down a flight of stairs. Gil complied.

Trailing the Horseblooded's fleet figure, he was only a few yards behind when Dunstan slipped through a door. Gil came more slowly, then jumped into the doorway. His glance skimmed past shelf on shelf of giant books, an ancient suit of armor on a display pedestal in a corner, an iron lance in its gauntlet, and a hearth. Then he saw Dunstan.

His friend stood, sword at the breast of Yardiff Bey. With the sorcerer at gunpoint, Gil knew fear and elation; the Hand of Salamá had forced his hatred far beyond what Gil had thought were its extreme limits. Here was his brilliant, elusive nemesis, everything that made him awaken in sweat and clouded his thought.

"Move away, Dunstan." He lifted his pistols, both muzzles leveled at Bey. His friend didn't move from his line of fire.

"Stay your hand a moment," said the Horseblooded.

"I said stand clear." His thumbs were moving the hammers back to half-cock. Whatever reasons Dunstan had, he didn't want to hear them.

"Nay, I will say my piece," the other insisted.

"No!" The muzzles shook now. Yardiff Bey glared at the American, unmoved. Gil took another step, meaning to angle around for an unobstructed line of fire. "Look out; I'm gonna—"

A terrific weight hit his shoulders, driving him to the floor. Something crashed off his steel cap; star clusters went off in his eyes. His arms were wrenched back, the pistols torn from his hands. By the time he could focus there were sharp points at each side of his neck, just behind the jaw. He croaked his friend's name.

The Horseblooded stepped away from the sorcerer. Yardiff Bey blithely waved a hand. Dunstan shimmered and became a stranger, a dark-skinned Occhlon. Gil hung his head abjectly. "Oh no; oh no, no." There were more Southwastelanders, who began to laugh.

"You would not have been deceived by so hasty a glamour," Bey told him, "had you not wanted to see Dunstan so very much. I did but work with what was already in your mind."

They shoved him against the hearth and held blades at his waist and throat. In this moment of complete disaster, he accepted it listlessly. There was a large worktable in the room, cluttered with books, low-burned candles and a long parchment list. Gil stared without seeing it, while Bey gathered implements, preparing for hasty departure. On the table was a huge leather binder, another intact jacket of *Arrivals Macabre*. It was empty, though its raised seal was undisturbed, and its stacked pages, bundled securely, lay near it.

"Be intelligent for once, insect," the sorcerer was saying. "You were observed, led astray and captured; it is accomplished fact. If needs be, you are our safe passage past the Glyffans. You may yet see Dunstan in the flesh. Simply obey."

Gil's scalp burned. *Insect?* He fought vertigo, a little less punchy. "You blew it when you came to Ladentree. They'll never let you walk."

The Hand of Salamá permitted himself an indulgent smile, the least retaliation. More than that would have been undue credit to the outlander, whose deception by carrier pigeon had caused the sorcerer to cancel standby plans to take Cynosure and Blazetongue. Bey had, at last, the prize secreted by Rydolomo. "Take the pages and put them in my pouch," he ordered, "and leave the sealed cover. It is of no use to me. We depart through the rear gates."

Gil shuddered. He would have opened himself to the Berserkergang in that moment, but it wasn't in him and he didn't know how to exert it. He made an effort to push the fuzz back in his brain, staring down at the empty covers of Rydolomo's book, his fright making every detail of binder and seal leap up at him with abnormal clarity. Then it struck him exactly what he was seeing. He pressed slightly against the weapons pricking him. He would need room, a piddling bit of leeway.

"You'll never make it," he told the sorcerer, "Andre deCourteney's here."

Yardiff Bey looked at him as if he were crazy. "What care I for an imbecile like deCourteney?"

"He and the Glyffans will stop you, but it's not too late to make a deal. Otherwise they'll bring you down before you can get out of Glyffa." He was making it up as he went, playing to his guards. If they were distracted, he had one chance. "Maybe Andre can't stop you," he leaned forward at the waist and dagger points backed off fractions of an inch, "but the Trustee can, can't she?"

The Southwastelanders looked to their leader. Gil's heart flip-flopped. They didn't have to buy it; they just had to see he was in a dialogue with the Hand of Salamá.

"*She* is not nigh," Bey replied, "or I should know it. I will be long away long before she is."

"Oh yeah? There's something you should know." Locking in on the sorcerer's ocular and the dark, liquid eye beside it, he leaned forward even more. The blades retreated one more degree. It was high-voltage triumph when his hand touched the table's edge. "The Trustee knows you're Gabrielle's father. She'll have your ass." His other hand got to the table. "You and these poor slobs are through." He eased down, forearms resting on the table, torso over it. "And Salamá's going down for good." The two points pressing his ribs didn't matter; he'd gone as far as he needed to. The sorcerer, bored with him, turned to fasten his bags, gathering thaumaturgical tools.

"So save yourself, Bey." Gil pushed himself backward, bringing his hands back toward himself, brushing the cover of *Arrivals Macabre* with his wrist. "And tell these scumbags to let loose."

He dared not look at the table now, and could only hope he'd gauged it right, and that Bey wouldn't see. He perspired, waiting, lost control of his impulse, and his eyes strayed to the empty binder. He'd moved it just enough to bring Rydolomo's seal up to a candle stub's flame. The men holding him hadn't noticed. He held his breath.

That alerted Yardiff Bey. He turned, wondering what

130

had made the American go silent. He followed Gil's eyes, saw it all. His voice was a whiplash. "The seal, fools!" A thread of melted wax ran from it, even as he lunged at the binder. The Occhlon stirred, mystified, indecisive.

There was an explosion over the table. The Occhlons flinched back. Gil, braced for it, threw them off, spun, and dodged around the corner of the hearth, crouching in its momentary protection.

The guardian entity confined by the seal of Rydolomo hovered in the air. Its tendrils flailed at one astounded Southwastelander, then another. They bounced through the air like tennis balls, one crunching up against the mantelpiece, the other dumping the table over, landing five feet beyond. The two handguns jumped from his clutch. Yardiff Bey ducked in to scoop up the bundled pages of *Arrivals Macabre*.

Another Occhlon, the acrobat in red who'd perched over the lintel and taken Gil, sprang in and hewed at the guardian with his yataghan. A pulse of light crackled down the blade. The Southwastelander dropped, arm charred, and there was the smell of smoking flesh.

Gil, peeking around the corner of the hearth, saw Yardiff Bey slide himself across the polished floor. The window at the opposite end of the shelf room was too far away. The sorcerer's hand was near the latch of his ocular, as if he debated unleashing whatever was contained there. Then he turned and swung the door open.

The entity whirled angrily, tracking the movement. It went drifting after him. Yardiff Bey tumbled through the door and hauled it shut behind him; without time to ready a spell, he chose to escape with his treasure. Perhaps the guardian would finish the American, perhaps not; the overriding priority was to bear away the secret he'd won.

One of his men tried to do the same, but collided with the closing door. The entity flowed over and around him. He shrilled in agony and collapsed backward, blackened. The door's wood burned where the thing had touched it.

The guardian throbbed darkly for a moment, then flared brighter. The last Southwastelander flattened against the wall, whites showing all around his eyes.

131

The sunball drifted nearer. He sidled along the shelf, slowly. It played with him for a moment, then rushed to block his way. He reversed field, and it circled to stop him again. The Occhlon's mind snapped; he ran at it with his blade high, screaming, "Bey-yyy!" This time the guardian flashed, blindingly. The desert man became a human firebrand, dropping to the floor, his sword twisted and molten.

Gil knelt, quivering with the need to fight or run. The guardian rotated slowly, waiting. He saw a straight run for the door would be suicide, but he'd noticed that the being recovered for a second or two after each discharge. It wafted toward him gently. He rose to his feet.

He scrambled around the pedestal on which the armor suit stood. The guardian detected him, came at him. He tugged hard, and hopped to the side as the armor tottered forward. The entity stopped short, but the iron lance clamped in the suit's gauntlet plunged into it. Streamers of energy spun out, dancing down the lance and armor, which began to soften and run, glowing, in abrupt thermoplasticity. Waves of heat filled the room and globs of scoria, blasted free, started more fires. For a heartbeat, the thing was dimmer.

He charged past the guardian, doubled over. An instant later its effulgence returned. The guardian circled and dove at him from behind just as he leapt one Southwastelander's charred corpse and threw the burning door open. Realizing he couldn't get through in time, he pushed himself to one side. The sunball boiled past, into the corridor, searing him.

It raged against the stone opposite the door. He slammed the door shut and, absurdly, shot the bolt. Backing away, watching the portal, he paid no attention to the fires and stench of burned flesh. As he'd feared, the door began to crackle more earnestly; smoke and flame seeped in around it, indicating the guardian's effort to re-enter and continue its vigilance. He scooped up his pistols and headed for the window.

There was a drop into darkness; he had no idea how far up he was. But the decision was easy; the cuckolded guardian was nearly through the door. He hung by his fingers from the sill and let go. He fell less than ten feet.

He rose and stumbled through blackness. Red light

flickering from the window didn't help much, but at least the guardian evinced no interest in coming after him. Wading blindly through shrubs and flower beds, he found a wall and groped along until he came to a door. Inside, he trotted slowly, pistols out, and picked up his bearings. He raced to the juncture of corridors where the search teams had divided.

There he found Andre, Swan and some of the Sages along with Sisters of the Line. He gasped his story; they had to chase Bey at once. But Andre rapped, "The guardian must be stopped first, and the fires. They will destroy lives, and Ladentree." He pounded away, Swan and some of the Glyffans at his back, over Gil's violent protests.

Ferrian was reclining against a wall, leg bandaged. "One of the teams was set upon by more Occhlon," he informed the American, "and a skirmish was fought. The Southwastelanders killed and injured many."

"If we don't nab Bey right now there'll be lots worse than that. He's got what he came for." His eye fell on the Sages. He grabbed one, a slender old man with a carefully trimmed beard and high, smooth forehead.

"Take me through this damn maze, to the rear gates." The Sage drew himself up.

"Remove your hand," he ordered, his expression saying he meant it, even though fighting was prohibited to him. Gil complied. The Sage turned to his fellows. "Go, help the Sisters of the Line in any way you may." He immediately set off down the main corridor. In time, through twisting hallways and wide passages, he guided Gil to a final door. The American edged past, drew both guns and eased it open. Horseshoes battered the earth.

He got to the open gates and fired at shadows from frustration, but heard the hoofbeats dying away into the night. *Maggie's drawers*, he chided himself; *I missed.* There was no other horse there. The Mauser was empty. He dashed back the way he'd come.

It wasn't hard to find Swan and Andre; smoke and commotion drew him to them. The wizard had used a Dismissal on the guardian, but the fires had taken hold, endangering the library. Swan directed the Sisters in fighting the blaze, the Sages working side by side with

133

them, using sand, water and their own robes. Gil got the High Constable's attention, relating what had happened.

"We cannot hie after him now," she said, wiping her smudged cheek with a blistered hand. Her blue cape was scorched.

He grated, "We can't do anything else. We can only collar him if we start now."

She blew up. "I have casualties to think about! My brother's dead, and if Ladentree is consumed Glyffa loses half its heritage. So go, chase him yourself if you must; I have no time to waste beating the bushes in the night. Now leave me be!" She pushed past him.

He went to the wizard. "It's you and me. We have to take Bey ourselves."

Andre shook his head regretfully. "He has more Southwastelanders with him, and we know not where he is gone. He trapped you once tonight; would you make it twice?"

Gil was disbelieving. "What's wrong with you?"

Andre's tone was hard. "I have been against Bey for longer years than you can imagine. This is not the closest I have come to him, only to lose him." Andre, too, went back to fighting the fire.

Gil, ready to take up the chase by himself, was stopped by common sense. He hadn't the vaguest idea which way the sorcerer had gone, and he'd never even tracked anybody by day, much less pitch darkness. He'd made one dumb move that night, he admitted; a second one wouldn't cancel that. Tearing off his steel cap, he hurled it at the floor; it rebounded with a belling sound.

Swan was commanding Sisters of the Line to tote more ancient codices and folios out of danger. Gil fell in with them. "You're right," he conceded gruffly. Now it was her turn to stare in surprise.

They fought the fire under control by phases. Gil tried to imagine what special advantage the Hand of Salamá had carried into the night.

Chapter Twelve

Although it fall and die that night—
It was the plant and flower of light . . .
                    Ben Jonson
                    "It Is Not Growing Like a Tree"

WHEN they were sure no last spark remained, Gil
trudged off tiredly through the smoke with the others.
No one could calculate how much irreplaceable knowledge had been incinerated.

Andre went off to see how Ferrian was. Gil found
space at a bench where two Sisters of the Line and a
few Sages sat numbly. Someone had left food on the
table, dark bread and jars of cold well water, sliced
fresh fuit from the library's orchards and slabs of
cheese. He helped himself mechanically, and asked
where Swan was.

A cavalrywoman told him, "She has gone to the
chapel, to do prayer for her brother. We are billeted for
the night; our casualties are being attended by Sages of
Healing and the Trustee's son, deCourteney. The High
Constable commanded that your baggage be set there,
by the door. Your horse has been seen to."

Dirge was among the things they'd brought. He faced
the Sages. One of them was the man who'd led him to
the rear gates.

"Hey, any of you know anything about swords?"

They stopped talking and looked among themselves.
The Sage Gil knew stood. "I am Silverquill, chief savant
here. I have some familiarity with metal working and
the various master smiths."

Gil got Dirge, unscabbarded it and threw it onto the
polished wood. It landed on the table with a gong that
hung in the air. There was a sinister glitter to the black,

runcinate blade, as if its sawing teeth waited to bite flesh. Sages and cavalrywomen alike examined it. None tried to touch.

Silverquill leaned over it, yellowed nail tracing one glyph, a flaming mandala. "This mark and the stamp of the weapon wrights of Death's Hold, I know, are inscribed in implements of dark renown. This is Dirge, is it not?" Gil confirmed it. "Then take great care; this hanger will do nothing but harm, wounds that only its dreaded owner may heal. Dirge seldom cuts but that it kills, by its edge and its runes of death. Yardiff Bey is said in the texts to hold it in highest merit."

Gil sat staring at the blade, speculating how he might use that. The others became uncomfortable. One by one they drifted away to stand guard duty, rest, or just leave Dirge and the morose outlander. Presently, he was alone in the small sphere of light from the candelabrum.

He touched the mandala glyph cautiously, feeling its cool fire. Then he slammed Dirge back into its scabbard, roused himself and began digging through his saddlebags.

Finding the oily rag and cleaning kit he carried, he took down the Browning and cleaned it, his mind elsewhere. When the Hi-Power was reloaded and returned to the shoulder rig, he stripped the Mauser, working proficiently. There were three rounds left for it, two for the Browning. They were both nine-millimeter weapons, but their ammo wasn't interchangeable. He was nearly done with the Mauser when he realized he wasn't alone. Replacing the magazine base plate, he saw Swan standing at the edge of the light.

She'd shed her armor, washed and combed out the straight, glossy black hair until its ends floated around her waist. She'd found a robe somewhere, simple black muslin, caught around her hips with an antique belt of beaten silver plaques. He was startled to see how young she looked, standing with the right half of her face in shadow. He finished quickly and holstered the pistol. "I'm sorry about Jade," he faltered, "truly sorry."

She took a seat across from him. Her long brown fingers interlocked. "He was so close," she told him softly. "Jade lived for the Reconciliation; to make it work. The Trustee knew his name, thought him an important

136

thought-shaper among the men. Do you know how many times we spoke? I have reckoned it. Today, finding him dying there in the corridor, was seven. Precisely seven times."

Her cheek gave a tug. "Why should death find Jade on the eve of Reconciliation?"

He wondered if he should leave, but it came to him that if she'd wanted solitude, Ladentree was full of it. He was accosted by his own griefs and regrets, evoked by hers. To deny them, he got up and took her hand and the candelabrum. She came to her feet. Taking the light from him, she led the way to the room she'd chosen in the secluded upper reaches of Ladentree, over the Sixth Hall of Antiquities.

When they stood together, he tilted her chin to see her full face in the glow. She resisted, catching his hands with a tight grip. He moved closer, brushed her hair away and kissed the hot curve of her throat. She had some second thought, or misplaced spasm of propriety in mourning. He stopped her when she might have pushed him away, drawing her arms around his neck. She locked her mouth to his.

There was little sense of transition. They left clothes behind and matched themselves along each other on the short, narrow bed. Its mean confines were an environment severed from any other. Both had worried about their own awkwardness. But uncertainties fell away; hesitations hadn't followed them. They made trusting, unhurried exploration, through levels of excitement. In their vergency he heard a victorious sound low in her throat.

They were left with a fragile tenderness. He went to brush the hair back from her birth-badge; she ducked away. He laid her fingertips to the powderburn tattoo on his cheek. She shook back black tresses, defiantly. He pretended to examine it closely, then nipped her nose. She throbbed with laughter.

After a while, she said, "It is some time that you have not been with a woman." She felt his nod against her cheek. "Nor I with a man. Once, I thought to put aside my duties and bear a child. But it was not to be; as it came out, I have contributed more to Glyffa this way."

She stretched up for a kiss. "But you, outlander, exemption, I am glad you came here." He was sorry he hadn't said it first, but seconding her now would sound lame. Instead, he reciprocated the kiss, and caressed the angry red wash of flesh on her neck.

"When I was young," she confided, "the other girls made sport of it. So, when we practiced at swords, I would tie back my hair and make a face at them, so." She showed him, the coal-gleaming mane gripped back in her left hand, imaginary rapier in her right. She grimaced savagely, eyes bulging. He laughed, then she did. "But it was effective, yes. I was ever the attacker, the winner. They ceased japing." She became reflective. "Then the Trustee saw me, and said, 'Little one with your warrior-mark, we have enough of lasses handy with a sword. Let us see if there is in you a leader.' "

Conversation slackened soon; desire took hold again.

At length, they held one another, warm and lazy. Gil's last thought was that he would least have thought that this particular day would bring him peace, however ephemeral.

He was awakened by a hand on his mouth. It would normally have sent his hand burrowing for the pistol under his pillow, but the love-pax had survived the discontinuity of sleep. Swan pulled him up to come with her. Goosefleshing, they went to the window. Dawn just touched the horizon. He knew unhappily that he'd have to leave soon.

Some of the little white birds he'd seen terrorized the day before were in the courtyard below, trilling a haunting song.

"What are they?"

"Those are the Birds of Accord. Once, ages ago, they nested and bred in the branches of the Lifetree itself. When it was destroyed, they fled here to Ladentree, sensing its tranquility. They live out their long lives, but when they die it will be the end of their kind. The Birds of Accord mated only among the branches of the Lifetree."

The floor under his bare feet sent him looking for his clothes. She wrapped herself in a blanket and sat on the bed, hugging her knees, watching him. As he sat lacing his shirt, she spoke suddenly.

138

"Did you leave her, or she you? Or did she die, or did you argue? Or are you going back to her?"

He stopped. "Her name was Duskwind. She died; I did too, a little. Bey's fault. I'm going to kill him for it, and free a friend of mine he's holding."

"You mentioned your friend second." There was coolness in her voice. "Is revenge more important?"

"I—" He went back to the lacings. "I don't know. I can't separate them." She saw the Ace of Swords as he slipped it around his neck.

There was a blast of trumpets. She sprang to her feet. Her persona was now High Constable; she was into her armor, white-wing-helmeted, before he finished dressing.

Downstairs, they found Andre greeting the Trustee, Angorman and two squadrons of cavalry. The Trustee demanded, "All is secured?"

Swan answered, "There is more to matters than that, but yes."

"Then," said the old woman, "let us go rest from all this whooping about. It is always a treat to visit Ladentree."

They went to an inner garden of the library. Silver-quill appeared, and welcomed the Trustee with a deep bow. She returned it equally. "Please be comfortable," the Sage invited, "but I ask you to put weapons aside. There have been enough tools of war brandished here in Ladentree."

Swan and Andre laid aside their swords and Gil put down his guns. Angorman looked stubborn; he was thinking of his last separation from Red Pilgrim, at Dulcet's. "Come, Saint-Commander," beckoned the Trustee, "lay your axe against the rose trellis. It will not be alone." She leaned her rune-carved Crook of Office next to it. They all found places on benches of agate centuries old.

Swan told what had happened in crisp, accurate style.

"This misfortune is less than it could have been," the ruler of Glyffa decided. "Bey's information was faulty; he lost much time in his hunting. Since he came himself, trusting no subordinate, a major advantage must have been at stake. I would give a pretty to ken what he won last night."

139

Swan asked, "How stand things with the Southwaste-landers?"

"The Occhlon withdrew, but regrouped, positioned at a certain disadvantage, inviting us to close with them." The old woman shook her head in wry humor. "I can recognize a pig in the parlor when I see one there, or a worm on a hook. They wanted to engage us, thus I sought elsewhere for their real motive. Setting my Lord Blacktarget to keep surveillance, I came here to find it, but not in time to strive against Yardiff Bey."

She drew on memories for a moment, then decided they were something the others there should hear. "I remember the Hand of Salamá in his youth, ere his foul affiliations were known, an avaricious boy, hungry for power. I was foremost among the Adepts then, having earned my Crook. Where Salamá stands now, the center of the Unity was then. The Lifetree bloomed nearby, its upper branches in the clouds, its roots delving to the earth's core, holding all spheres in its grand equilibrium. Gift of the Bright Lady, it was the demonstration of the Unity's office. Sojourners from every earthly quarter saw it; it is in most religions still. We held high hopes for the human race in those days."

"And the sorcerer?" prodded Angorman.

"Bey, yes; a willful one, even then. But of course, it was the demon Amon who seduced the Five. While the rest of us sat in the shade of the Lifetree, complacent or preoccupied with higher knowledge, Amon stole among the Lords Paramount of the Unity. Even Dorodor, central figure of the Unity, more demigod than man, failed to detect it.

"First of the demon's levers was Skaranx, whose high honor was to warder the Lifetree, but who destroyed it. Then there was Temopon, trusted Seer, who delivered false counsel. So too fell Vorwoda, taken with Amon's promises, betraying her husband Dorodor; she had been his mainstay. She lusted for Kaytaynor, Dorodor's closest friend, who slew him for envy of his wife and took her. Lastly was Dorodeen, the Flawed Hero who, failing to win the loftiest seat in the Unity, would take no second place, and set about to bring it low.

"Together, the Five compacted to annihilate the Lifetree and slay the Unity's most puissant overlords. They

140

would throw open the Infernal Plane, unleashing the hordes of the lower regions. In those first two aspirations they succeeded; the flower of the Unity perished, and the Lifetree with them. But in the final days of the Masters' plan, their Great Blow, remnants of us gathered to rob them of total victory. A portent appeared in the sky, the Trailingsword, to call together all persons of good intent. We won our resistance, but the world was tottered and changed forever.

"There are omens showing themselves," the Trustee finished, "which are products of those bygone days. I cannot share my every datum with you; proof will be forthcoming."

"We worry not," Angorman said in confidence; "chip by chip is the oak hewn."

As the Trustee was about to respond, Birds of Accord flocked down through the garden in a soft-winged cloud. Gil was nervous, remembering the aerial attack on the Tangent, but these Birds only lilted their song. Many hopped through the trellis, flitting from it to Red Pilgrim, then the Trustee's Crook and back again. One perched on the old woman's extended finger, singing as if telling her something, but she didn't have its language.

"Here is a good omen, surely," Angorman remarked.

"Aye," she answered, "they bode good luck."

"How lucky can they be?" Gil injected. "They're dying out."

The Trustee told him, "You may yet learn. It is sometimes the inoffensive, the forgotten creatures who set the gears of fate turning."

Gil felt squirmy. "What about Yardiff Bey?"

"He did not come back south, or I would have known it. Among his own kind I could not single him out, but if he were abroad near me in these lands of the Bright Lady, I could not have failed to. Thus, he meant me to stay occupied with battle."

"We have a two-edged problem," Andre declared. "Yardiff Bey must be found, but it is as important that Blazetongue and Cynosure be taken to Veganá."

"You cannot ignore the sorcerer," Swan objected.

"We will not," the Trustee proclaimed. "Here, his magic is small. Force of arms will net him. You will

141

supply that, High Constable. Where we mean to take Cynosure and Blazetongue there will be magic in plenty; Andre, the Saint Commander and I will all be needed. You take to Bey's spoor with half this force I brought; run him to ground if you can. He may be in Glyffa still, but I cannot permit that to divert me. What's more, I do not have full confidence in my Lord Blacktarget. He already has his harpers composing odes to his own bravery yesterday. I fear his vainglory may lead him to folly."

Gil was thinking it over. Andre and Angorman were still determined to escort the baby and the sword to their final destination. But if Swan was going after the Hand of Salamá with a full squadron, Gil no longer needed his companions. He'd be content with those odds; if Bey were caught here in Glyffa, Gil MacDonald meant to be there.

"All these things were best done as soon as may be," Andre was saying.

Gil told him, "I'm going after Bey."

"You have seen our charges into friendly hands, where they belong," Angorman announced, "and you go now to chase their enemy. You are no longer bound to us by the Faith Cup, therefore."

"Thanks." *As if that'd stop me!* He went off to collect his gear. On his way back, he remembered Ferrian. Asking around, he found his way to where the Horse-blooded lay in bed, leg bandaged. In his lap was a book. Gil told the former Champion-at-arms what had happened, then asked how he was.

"I shall survive, and walk again. There may be a limp, the Sages tell me, but a Horseblooded's feet are only for stirrups anyway, is it not so?"

Gil left the subject. "When you leave Ladentree, you'll have to figure out what to do by yourself. If I can, I'll come back this way, so leave word."

"I shall." Ferrian swept his hand at the shelves of books. "There are worse places to convalesce. How many days and nights would you have to listen, how far would you have to ride, to gather the wisdom that is met here?"

Gil admitted he didn't know.

"Exactly! Strange for a Wild Rider to say, but I have

come to love the elderly mustiness here. Thus, mending will be quick." His face was luminous, but then lost its rapture. "Gil, Andre has told me of your Berserker-gang."

Gil's features clouded; the Horseblooded hurried on. "That was less a betrayal than it seems. It was, in part, for fear that Dunstan's fits of the Rage had passed to you that Andre wanted me in the traveling party. I am Dunstan's kinsman, you see; the wizard thought I might be of some help. But all I can lay forth is that Dunstan had the seizures of his father, though he could often channel and control them."

"Does it mean Dunstan's alive?"

"There is good chance of it, aye."

"Then, I'll find him. Be seeing you when you're up and around." They traded grips. Gil left Ferrian bent over his book.

The Trustee, Andre and Angorman were back on their horses. They made quick good-byes, then the de-Courteneys' mother turned to Gil. "You are not unimportant in this. Kindly consider your every action accordingly." She called to Swan. "High Constable, what was that you did say in my tent, two nights gone? My legacy will be human weal?"

"And your name will live forever," Swan finished in subdued voice. She withheld her concern, that her Liege was overtaxed. The Trustee took the thought with her, lifting her Crook. Half the Sisters of the line wheeled into ranks and followed her away smartly, banners popping on the breeze.

With Swan's contingent readying for speedy departure, Gil stepped inside to fetch his baggage. His steel cap had been dented. He'd dug out the wide-brimmed, weather-beaten hat Brodur had given him in Earthfast; he'd wear it for shade and protection until he could find another helm that would fit him.

Silverquill came to say good-bye. The American tried to apologize for his rudeness; the savant set it aside. "I hope your way is clear, your hardship small. I have no proper leave-taking gift for you; accept, if you will, this token, to say there is no resentment betwixt us two." He handed the other a writing plume, silver-tipped for his name's sake. Gil thanked him. Silverquill went off about

143

his duties, and the younger man took the plume and pinned up the left side of his hat brim with it.

Swan appeared, pulling on gauntlets. She wore a baleful look; he asked what was wrong.

She eyed him ruefully. "The Trustee took me aside for a moment. She said my *lips* are puffy."

Then she broke up. They roared together, out of the sight of the Sisters of the Line. Making himself straight-faced for the ride, he began to think what life could hold if he lived to see the Hand of Salamá die.

Chapter Thirteen

Bright star! would I were as steadfast as thou art!
John Keats
"Bright Star"

WYVERN Boulevard was alive again, decked for celebration. Deliverance had come to Veganá.

For months the city of Midmount, capital of the country, had been somber in its captivity. Today a parade of triumph marched down the boulevard, through myriad flower petals drifting down from its balconies. People crowded twenty deep at either side, screamed, laughed, wept, hugged one another, waved pennants and hailed the captains or lords they recognized, scanning the ranks hopefully for the face of a loved one. Panegyric songs filled the air, many of them to Lord Blacktarget, propagated by his own advance guard. Occhlon banners could be seen, trampled and burned, in the gutters.

Weeks of sharp clashes had dislodged the Southwaste-landers from resolute positions just south of the Glyffan border. The returning army of Veganá and the Sisters of the Line, fueled by shattering wins to the north, had sent the desert men reeling in one onset after another.

Their numbers had swollen with militiawomen from liberated regions of Glyffa, and Veganán men freed from the southern yoke. These had been the most aggressive fighters, out for redress.

The Southwastelanders had been thrown out of central Veganá. Crows had circled, blotting the sky, awaiting a rare feast. Shrewd gray wolves skulking in the hills had licked their white chops, knowing their time would come. The Occhlon had lost nearly fifteen thousand men since the cream of their army had marched north to screen Yardiff Bey's stealthy mission to Ladentree.

Lord Blacktarget led the parade to a halt before the temple of the Bright Lady, lifting his hand to the cheers. He raised Blazetongue aloft, and Woodsinger held Cynosure. Veganáns were not far from a happy brand of hysteria.

After the general came the Trustee, who'd actually directed the campaign, with Andre deCourteney and Angorman, both risen as commanders in their own right. The crowd pressed in against their honor guard as they dismounted.

The temple reared above them, largest in the Crescent Lands; late-afternoon sun splashed from its gilded domes. Atop the front steps stood its archdeacon. When they came up, he kowtowed. "All praise for this day. I will take charge of the babe; she goes to the keeping of the temple virgins."

Woodsinger didn't move. "It is not yet the time for that," the Trustee said.

Lord Blacktarget became incensed. "Come, madam, your prerogatives do not run to this."

Patiently, she explained, "There is more to her homecoming than that. Prophesies must be observed, a Rite performed."

Their uneasy alliance was close to fracture. He'd never liked taking a secondary post to hers, and no longer needed to. But the archdeacon said, "If the Trustee refers to the child's Vigil, that would be commensurate with custom. Cynosure is, after all, the last of the Blood Royal."

Blacktarget yielded one last time. At the foot of the steps, a Glyffan captain let herself breathe; the call to arms hadn't been far from her lips. Her Liege had been specific; nothing was to keep the child from her Vigil. Woodsinger gave the child over to the archdeacon.

Andre, Angorman and the Trustee accompanied the old churchman inside. Lord Blacktarget insisted on coming too. Climbing from stairway to stairway, on stone worn away by ages of footfalls, they made a winding ascent to the little chapel where only royalty of Veganá held ceremony. Its walls and roof were all of glass roundels, like distorted gray lenses, that created an eerie half-world as the sun set.

The new monarch must, by tradition, stand a nightwatch. For the first time in generations it could be done, as it was supposed to be, with the ancestral sword. Usually, the Vigil was kept in solitude; tonight was the most singular exception in Veganá's history.

The chapel's altar was a waist-high cube of jasper. Inset at its center was the emblem of Cynosure's house, a wyvern picked out in gold on a black field. A short rod supported the crescent moon of the Bright Lady over it. The archdeacon set the baby down between the sparkling claws of the inlaid wyvern, then went away, having discharged his duty.

The others knelt or took seats on low divans. Andre removed the rod and in its aperture he stood Blazetongue. The child made no sound, attuned to the moment. "That is a liberty to take," commented Blacktarget, "with a sword not your own."

"Yet he has, by rights, some ties with it," the Trustee observed, "for it was forged by his grandsire, my father, for a King far back in Cynosure's line." The general was incredulous. "Yes, Lord Blacktarget, our magic is there, and far mightier enchantment besides, though Andre never knew any of that until I told him. Blazetongue is a vessel of the Bright Lady's energies, and complies with her still. Did you think it came into my hands at random? There is transcendent purpose to it all."

"What do you hope for, from it?" Lord Blacktarget snapped.

"The keeping of a promise given long ago. The Celestial Mistress brings many threads together tonight."

They were closeted with their own thoughts. Andre

fretted about Gil MacDonald, and wondered, too, how things boded for Springbuck, for Reacher, Katya and Van Duyn. He said a prayer for Gabrielle.

The stars appeared, warped and rearranged by the roundels. The crescent moon rose, magnified in the roundels, hanging over Cynosure and Blazetongue. The Trustee watched it carefully. Angorman chanted softly to himself, Lord Blacktarget halted his devotions. Andre simply waited.

Blazetongue came to life in this appointed moment; it had no ruinous flames to spew, but rather a blue aurora that made them shield their eyes, and a high-pitched humming, music of the spheres. All of them knew their deity had come.

Angorman was about to raise his voice in praise. The Trustee shushed him and stepped to the altar.

Her arms lifted imploringly. "We are assailed, hard-put even as we were long ago. One great portent must we have, to lift hopes, and set hands against the Masters. We look to your promised Omen."

The humming grew louder, Blazetongue's aura more brilliant. The baby didn't seem to mind at all. Monarch of Veganá, she'd been born for this, an hour implicit in Blazetongue's forging. Among the crowds keeping their own nightwatch in the streets below, a shout went up. They'd marked the glass-walled chapel's radiance.

The Sending subsided. Andre took his hand from his eyes. Cynosure was quiet, and Blazetongue dark. Angorman cried, "See!"

In the sky hung an awesome Sign, a comet stretched down through the firmament like a sword, the fiery head for its pommel, its tail aimed directly down where Shardishku-Salamá wove its spells. It outshone the moon, planets and stars, making night more like day.

They rushed out onto the balcony. Angorman and Blacktarget offered up thanks to the sky; Andre and his mother hung back. "What visitation is that?" voices called from the streets. Others answered, "The Trailingsword! It is as in days of long ago!"

"You see?" inquired the Trustee. "The old stories survive. Everywhere, there will be those who know the tale. Seven times seven days after the first Trailingsword appeared, our decisive battle was fought, where its tail pointed us."

"Did Bey know this would happen?" Andre asked.

"Suspected it, I should think. Still, he ignored it in his plotting to get the thing he sought at Ladentree; that disquiets me. Now the sword has rendered the second of the two great services for which it was created, and they are complete, though Blazetongue may render a final aid in its unmaking."

"I will remember," he promised. She was sharing what knowledge she could with him because all lives would soon be in danger again.

"Your prowess has increased, Andre," she remarked, "but that is a mixed gift. It says more arduous burdens shall be laid upon you."

"I welcome that. I owe Salamá no less than does Gil MacDonald. This Omen suits me well."

Across the Crescent Lands, men and women peered at the sky. The Trailingsword gleamed, and timeless tales came to mind, of the Great Blow and the last defense that was made there where it bid its supporters to rally. At every latitude it appeared the same, urging them toward Salamá. Seven times seven days was the measure of its time. There would be those who would ignore it, and those who would oppose it. But for many, it was a morsel of hope in desperately hungry days.

PART III

�

Children of the
Wind-Roads

Chapter Fourteen

But pleasures are like poppies spread—
You seize the flower, its bloom is shed . . .

Robert Burns
"Tam o' Shanter"

YARDIFF Bey was making for Death's Hold. His trail, read by astute Glyffan trackers, made no secret of that.

Swan shook her head in perplexity. "The Mariners gutted his fortress with their sea-and-land assault. There is only smoking rubble there; how can Bey hope to profit?"

A woodcutter, dwelling near the roadside, said she'd heard riders gallop by in the night. Gil tried to guess how much lead that gave the sorcerer, as Swan stepped up the pace. Stopping the occasional traveler, they met no one who'd seen Bey.

They'd covered twenty-five miles on rutted roads, much tougher going than the Western Tangent, when darkness forced them to halt, the trail no fresher than when they'd taken it up. Swan considered going on by torchlight, but feared that the way would be lost or their pursuit misdirected somehow by the Hand of Salamá. He might use such minor magic, though it chanced detection if the Trustee were near, and tricks like that were far more likely at night. Too, the horses must rest.

When he'd unsaddled Jeb, Gil made his way to Swan's spot in the bivouac. She'd dispensed with her tent, making do with a tarp set up as a crude lean-to. He found her in a huddle with subordinates, naming relief commanders for the night's guard. Maps were spread before her in a lamp's glow. All faces turned to Gil, then Swan.

"Yes?" she asked in neutral tones. She was all High Constable now, intent on her work. He saw he'd intruded, remembering how he'd hated people looking over his own shoulder. He excused himself and went off to sleep, curling at the base of a tree some distance from the Sisters of the Line.

The first relief had yielded to replacements when he woke to find her by his side. She slid into the warm cocoon of his cloak, adding her blue cape to their covers. They made wordless, exigent love unconnected, he knew now, with what they might do or whom they might be by daylight. He was, as she had called him, her exemption; in a way not wholly different, she was his.

Lounging afterward in the tangled clothing, the mingled aromas, the sudden heat that left them with less regard for that warmth mere cloaks and capes provide, he apprehended that areas of mutual consent had been defined. They slept in each other's arms, and just after the last relief came on, she rose and went off, picking her way surely among recumbent cavalrywomen. The squadron departed in first light.

On the second day of the chase, they had word from two men, cowled Sages on their way to Ladentree, that confirmed their route. The Sages said ten mounted men had passed them the preceding day, bearing westward in haste. The savants had been surprised, but assumed them to be outland allies. The gap between hunters and hunted hadn't closed at all.

"Squadron's too slow," Gil opined. "If we drop the heavy cavalry we could catch him."

"With less than a company of light horse," Swan pointed out. "We are going into unpoliced territory, where he may have arranged for reinforcements; my instructions direct me not to be drawn out headlong. There will likely be traps; so says the Trustee."

Though they were south of her own Region, her blue cape and flashing, winged bascinet gave Swan clout. Despite that, there were no fresh mounts to be had, the country having been stripped of every worthwhile horse for the Trustee's army. The fact cut both ways; the sorcerer wouldn't be able to obtain remounts either.

The chase stretched into grueling days and exhausted

151

nights. They strained their eyes in dazzling sun and saturating, dispiriting rain, hoping the next hill would
bring sight of the Hand of Salamá. It never did. Gil
didn't see how the horses of the sorcerer's party could
endure it. Jeb Stuart and the Glyffans' were close to the
limits of their means to comply. Swan thought magic
might be involved. Wolfing rations, sleeping and other
amenities became major luxuries, infrequently enjoyed.
But the merciless pursuit didn't keep Swan from coming
to him when responsibilities permitted. Both were
amazed at how little fatigue mattered when, together,
they were enfolded by the night. If Swan's subordinates
knew of the affair, none gave any sign.

But after a time they began to narrow the southerners' lead. The spoor grew fresher, Bey's brief campsites
more recently abandoned. The day came when the
hunters followed the Wheywater River around a bend
to see Final Graces, once a trading port, deserted when
Death's Hold, downriver, had revived its menacing activity. No Glyffans had yet re-entered it. The tracks
veered that way, rather than on along the river bank
road toward Bey's onetime stronghold.

Swan had expected to find no one there, but over the
little cluster of rooftops inside its wooden stockade, they
saw two masts, sails furled. The gates were closed; the
trumpeter blew a fanfare while the squadron deployed
itself along the wall. There was no reply; the High Constable had the call repeated.

A face appeared at the wall. Gil had the Browning
out, hoping it would be Bey or one of his men. He was
disappointed; he gradually recognized Gale-Baiter, the
Mariner captain who'd intervened to rescue Brodur and
himself in Earthfast.

"What would you?" demanded the captain.

"Open those gates," the trumpeter directed. "The
High Constable of Region Blue will enter."

Gale-Baiter hefted a cutlass. Other Mariners appeared on the wall, with bows and javelins. Among
them were Wavewatcher, the giant red-haired harpooner and Skewerskean, his smaller partner. "Be you
gone," the captain told the Sisters of the Line, "for we
know you to be no true Glyffans."

Some cavalrywomen had bows out, nocking arrows;

others shook lances, hollering angry denials. Gil dismounted, a sure sign that a cavalryman wanted no trouble and offered none. He swept off his battered hat with its bobbing quill.

"Gale-Baiter, it's me, Gil MacDonald, remember? I swear, these are really Glyffans. We're dogging Yardiff Bey. You'll let us in, right?"

The Mariner was taken off guard. He swapped uncertain looks with Wavewatcher and Skewerskean. " 'Tis assuredly he," the harpooner admitted. Gale-Baiter ordered the gates opened. Swan was pondering the American.

"You have friends in unlooked-for quarters," she remarked. He bowed.

"We had been told you would be enemies," Gale-Baiter explained when they'd joined him inside. There were twenty or so seafarers. They were swaggerers, dashing figures. They wore embroidered shirts and brocaded tunics, bibs of coins at their necks, chains of them at their wrists. Thick armlets and bracelets glittered, and on their buckles gemstones sparkled. But their cutlasses, bows and javelins were unadorned and well-used. Wavewatcher and Skewerskean stood warily to either side of their captain. The harpooner wore a sealskin shirt and a big scrimshawed whale's tooth on a thong against his hairy chest, and his barbed throwing-iron was in his hand. His smaller friend's sleeves were sewn with tiny bells that jingled as Skewerskean moved.

"It was said impostors were abroad," the captain said.

"By whom?" Swan rapped.

"Our Prince's special ambassador, who set sail this morning, after arriving in great hurly-burly."

Gil blasphemed, clenching his fist in the air. Soon, it was established what had happened. The Mariners' fleet had shattered Southwastelander sea power in a two-day engagement in the Central Sea, then pursued remnants to this area. The seafarers had laid waste to Death's Hold, to deny the southerners future sanctuary and erase their foothold in Glyffa. Afterward, the bulk of the Mariners had sailed northward after their surviving foes, leaving several ships on patrol in local waters. Gale-Baiter, remembering what Gil had said in Earthfast, had mentioned to his Prince that travelers from Coramonde might be coming to the ruined fortress. The Prince of the Mariners had assigned him to the patrol, ordering him to check upriver at Final Graces periodically, where wayfarers would logically stop first, to gather any recent news. Gale-Baiter had done so once, a week before. Three days ago he'd returned, but his ship had been damaged by a submerged rock, barely making Final Graces.

He and his men had hove down their ship, the *Long-Dock Gal*, for repairs. The following day, another craft had appeared flying Mariner colors, bearing the ensign of an ambassador extraordinary. Her master's papers showed she was on a mission for the Prince of the Mariners, awaiting a diplomatic entourage from the Glyffans and Veganáns. The newcomer's crew couldn't even aid Gale-Baiter's in repairing the *Gal*; their orders were to stand ready for instant departure.

Only hours before Swan's squadron arrived, the expected party had appeared, worn from strenuous riding, and ducked aboard their ship. Hooded and cloaked, they hadn't been seen by Gale-Baiter's men. Their horses, used up, had died at their tethers within minutes. Before their summary departure, the entourage had dispatched word that they might have been trailed by Southwastelanders masquerading as Glyffans.

It had to have been Bey and his men, using a contingency plan. But in leaving Gale-Baiter to cover his withdrawal, Bey had been unaware that Gil had met the captain, and could dissuade him from a bloodletting.

Gale-Baiter testified, "I had seen the papers they bore. Their ring-seal proved their mission was of highest priority. I was angry they would not assist our repairs, but could make no objection. Unhappy am I that I cannot go on their wake right this moment."

" 'Tis well-sent that you were repairing damage," Swan observed, "or they might have worked some ill to stave off pursuit."

"Rot him! I shall set sail on that liar's course. The body of the fleet is overdue to return, and there are other ships patrolling. We will take him; the Prince boasts vessels swifter still than mine."

Gil pounced on that. "You'll be ready that soon?"

"Aye, and if those were Occhlon scum, they can set only one course. North of here Mariners still scour the oceans. There is but unending water to the west. South will they voyage; the first hospitable landfall they can make is Veganá."

"Uh-uh," Gil told him, "Veganá's no good anymore. The Occhlon got whipped by the Crescent Landers."

"Then, to be safe, they can make no nearer port than the Isle of Keys. We shall catch them in open seas."

"But where would Yardiff Bey have gotten Mariners' safe-passage letters and seals?" Swan mused.

"There is only one place I wot of," Gale-Baiter said darkly. "The Inner Hub, whose destruction started this war."

Gil concurred. He himself had fooled enemies during the thronal war with phonied dispatches. That the scam had been turned around proved how fast Bey learned.

" 'Tis to be sea chase," the captain was telling Wave-watcher. The hulking redbeard nodded happily, scratching the tangle of rust-red curls on his chest. "See the repairs finished," Gale-Baiter continued, "with all speed." The harpooner went off, Skewerskean by his side.

Gil took the captain's elbow. "Hey, hey; I've gotta go along."

Gale-Baiter sized him up. Gil avoided meeting Swan's gaze, proceeding: "You're headed south and the seas belong to the Mariners, right? You'll overhaul Bey, most likely; if you don't, you'll still get me south a lot faster than I could get there on land. The Crescent Landers have a whole load of real estate yet to take back from the southerners. I can't wait that long; you promised me passage whenever I wanted."

The Mariner scratched his head. "Very well. I gauge the Isle of Keys will be our next objective, saved for last."

They all went to the dock. The *Long-Dock Gal* had been moved to the quayside for final work. Seamen were laboring with caulking irons, mallets and grease wells. Braces and bits, carpenter's hatchets, rave hooks and augers lay nearby. She was a small brig, carvel-built of finely sawn, smoothly trimmed planks, more a thing of the sea than those ungainly cogs the Crescent Lands

155

used. The *Gal* didn't have her name on her bow, what with literacy uncommon. She bore instead a painting, a winking blonde. Right away, though, the American saw she had no ram or ship-fighting engines.

"Your boat doesn't look like it can protect itself," he pointed out.

Gale-Baiter winced, collecting his self-control. "She is not a 'boat,' nor is she an 'it.' She's a *ship*, you see? On open sea she dances rings 'round anything not best friends with her. No southern scow can match a Mariner craft. We come alongside and board; that is the long and short of it." He took in the progress his men had made. "We will not be done by nightfall, and I won't navigate this poxed river in the dark. First light, then."

Swan billeted her troops in the dusty, deserted houses of Final Graces. For herself, she took the cobwebbed inn. Gil found her seated in a rickety chair, helmet put aside. She'd just finished writing up the day's report in her journal, and had a compact ledger open, balancing expenditures and funds of Region Blue. She looked up.

He was having a tough time getting started; she broke the silence. "This damnable war has leached away monies I needed. It was my hope to squeeze into the budget a bridge project. Trade would have doubled." She sighed. "Impossible, this year, and there will be extra hardship for that. But you didn't come to give ear to administrative woes, did you?"

He stared into heavy-lidded brown eyes. "I thought," he began, halted, then switched from what he'd wanted to say. "I thought you might not mind taking Jeb with you. You could leave him with Ferrian at Ladentree."

She closed the ledger. "I shan't be stopping there. It falls upon me to rejoin the Trustee with all speed."

"Oh." He fooled with his hat, thumbing its creases. "Will you tell me what's the matter?"

She leaned on the chair's arm. "You are being rash. Your friends may need you, in Veganá, and I mislike what is in your mien when you speak of *him*, the sorcerer. Does he look the same, do you think, when he talks of you?"

"No. I mean, he's one pretty cold fish." He lost patience. "Are you holding this against me, or what? Every Mariner alive is heading for the Isle of Keys; this whole

156

thing could be over before the Trustee and the others get the baby to her home city. Angorman and Andre don't need me, but Dunstan does. Swan, I can't depend on anyone but me. Can you tell me you wouldn't hang in for the whole distance, in my place?"

Her severity failed. "No. No, I should imagine I couldn't tell you that."

He took her hand. Rising, she pressed to him. He kissed her, taking the pins from her hair deftly, familiar with them now. She shook out the flowing blue-blackness. Her finger hooked for a moment at the chain that held the Ace of Swords to his breast. When he pulled her toward the stairs she didn't resist; events were shifting again; their respite was almost done.

They took one another hungrily. Neither had expected their exemption to last forever. They made a last denial of any truth but their own; it wasn't altogether futile.

Chapter Fifteen

Who thinks to wrest the sea from us
Or rule us with the sword?
We grappled Occhlon vessels nigh,
And gave our brief, complete reply,
"Pikes, cutlasses, and board!"
>> from "The Southwastelanders' War,"
>> a Mariner song

GIL came up the gangway just after sunrise, thankful to find the *Gal*'s deck firm under foot, forgetting she was still quayside on a quiet stretch of river.

He went to Gale-Baiter, who stood calmly by the rail. "Anything I can do?"

"Only in giving these lads room. We are overdue for rendezvous with the fleet, and shall back-and-fill down

157

this river. At least the ebb tide's with us." He sniffed the air. "It be against a head wind, though."

The American didn't know what any of that meant. He kept out of the way, along with his saddlebags and the wrapped bundle of Dirge. Crewmen were freeing berthing hawsers from their bollards, while men in a longboat readied to warp the *Long-Dock Gal* into the current. The harpooner was bawling orders aloft; Gale-Baiter's first officer had been lost in sea battle, and Wavewatcher was serving in his stead. Skewerskean seemed eveywhere, noticing each detail, his sleeves' bells sounding each movement. Gil liked the crisscross lines of laughter in the little man's face.

Swan had led her column out shortly before, one of the troopers towing Jeb Stuart's rein. They'd been near the end of any words they could say to one another.

"When I come back," he'd insisted, "I'll come through Glyffa, get Jeb, and see you in Region Blue."

"In Region Blue," she'd supported his contrivance. Then she'd taken up the mirror-bright helmet of her rank. Watching her horse being brought up, she'd added, "Once again now, you have nothing more to risk than your life."

She'd never looked back. He'd felt an awful hollowness threaten, and made himself go to the dock imitating high spirits.

The *Gal* got into the current's fairway. The longboat was brought aboard and topsails set for maneuvering. The Wheywater was green and wide here. The Mariners were calmer away from the quay. They'd be happier still on the open sea. His own discomfort, Gil thought, would grow proportionately.

Gale-Baiter didn't have many men aloft; few were needed to man the topsails.

"Note how some of them be singing whilst others are a-sulk?" the captain inquired. "After repairs were done, some of them slicked up and went to try their fortune with your Glyffan playmates. And some were kindly received, and some not. Well, this is one place where the ladies' decisions are not to be questioned; even these jolly-boys know that. I put the lucky ones up in the yards, where they are safe until the rest get over their snit."

He spoke a command that Wavewatcher relayed with a roar, "Back that mainyard! And hop to; you move like a damn bargeman!" Backing the mainyard made the *Gal* drift broadside down the current's fairway. Gradually, a bend in the river came in off the bow.

The captain had the foremast topsail backed too. Wind hit both sails' forward surfaces, and the *Gal* took a stern-board. Gil began to think they were going to back downriver.

The brig was in position to stand fairly down the Wheywater. Yards pointed into the wind that came from the sea; she floated with the current and the ebb tide, moving with beautiful economy. Ahead, the green waterway spread broader. Gil congratulated himself on bypassing the campaign for this more pleasant transportation.

Later, Death's Hold came into view around a point of land, alone on a wide gray delta to the north. Black smoke seeped from its cracked battlements and rose from its gutted spires, where the crab and the gull had dined on bloated carrion.

Gil was mesmerized by it, shivering. Death's Hold was the place he'd glimpsed in the Dreamdrowse, but this devastation hadn't been part of the vision. Gale-Baiter had assured him no Horseblooded had been found there. The American's hope, redirected to the Isle of Keys, was more the product of insistence than of faith.

One of the hands aloft exclaimed and pointed. Two smaller craft had put out from the other shore, some way ahead. One was a dory-boat, the other a longboat of eight oars. They were packed with men, the sun splashing from brandished weapons. Their course was for interception. Gil counted a dozen men and more in the longboat, plus whatever the dory held. Besides himself and Gale-Baiter, there were nine men on deck to meet them. The captain called several more down from the yards; boarding was clearly the order of business. "That lice-ridden masquerader must have kept more men hidden below decks," he rasped, "if he can afford to throw this many at us in a diversion, leaving them behind."

Wavewatcher, who'd put his harpoon away, was feeling the point of a lance with his thumb. Other Mariners collected cutlasses from the racks, took up boarding pikes or strung bows. Gil tucked Dirge behind some coils of hawser and drew the Mauser. His satisfaction in his decision to sail had evaporated. When the last few rounds were gone it would be sword's point, with him no different from anyone there. He'd have hocked his soul for a handful of bullets.

Gale-Baiter barked more orders, including one that the master's cabin shutters be secured. The fore topsail filled, and the *Gal* drew ahead, her bow swinging slowly to the fore. The two boats pulled madly, the dory falling behind the longboat. Waiting at the rail, Gil heard Skewerskean mutter something about their luck that it was only two boats. Gil didn't think their luck was running so hot. Men aloft in the yards waited anxiously for their captain's orders to fill all, but the brig hadn't cleared the river's shelves yet, and Gale-Baiter bided his time.

The longboat was preparing—clumsily, Gil thought—to come alongside. A man stood in its bow with grapnel and line. Skewerskean had taken up his re-curve bow. He drew, aimed, released. The shot was long, the arrow missing by an arm's length, but shields were raised in the longboat. The next shaft was true, but buried itself in leather plies.

The raised shields bore the flaming mandala of Yardiff Bey. The Mauser came up and blasted twice, Gil's reflex reaction to the sorcerer's blazonry, prodded, in part, by the Rage sleeping within him. The shots went wide. The Mariners were aghast, except Gale-Baiter, who'd heard a handgun at the White Tern. The American restrained himself. The shots hadn't deterred the Occhlon; perhaps Bey had prepared them for the possibility of gunfire.

Resting both elbows on the rail, Gil squeezed off the Mauser's last round. The man in the bow pitched into the water, his mail shimmering once, and was gone. Another rushed to replace him, and the grapnel whirled round and round.

Gil brought the Browning Hi-Power up carefully, resolved not to shoot unless he was certain he'd hit, and that it would make a difference. Gale-Baiter hollered, "Do for the coxswain, their steerer!" If the boat were pilotless, it might let the *Gal* slip by. Gil fired twice, too quickly. Tongues of spray leapt in the longboat's wake.

"Should've saved 'em," he rebuked himself. Holstering the Browning, he tugged Dunstan's sword free. His hand gripped, loosened, gripped tighter on it. Skimming his hat aside, he considered removing his byrnie, in case he had to swim for it. Compromising, he only loosened its lacings.

The man in the longboat threw his grapnel, missed, and began reeling in furiously, aware that the brig could soon make faster way. He waited behind a shield through the next salvo of arrows and javelins, then cast again. The grapnel missed the rails, where the Mariners might have chopped it loose, and lodged where tiller connected to rudder across the sternpost, impossible to get without someone's exposing himself to archers in the boat.

Wavewatcher saw what had happened. Gil, standing near, saw the man's big, freckled paw reach for the belt knife hanging at the middle of his back, sailor-style, where either hand might take it. Gale-Baiter stopped him, saying, "It is my place. Stand away." He took his own knife in his teeth and vaulted the rail.

Gale-Baiter let himself down quickly by the few handholds there were. Men in the longboat were hauling line rapidly, ducking under Mariner covering fire. The captain dropped the last few feet, to cling to the sternpost. The dripping line being too taut to release, he began sawing with his blade. Bowmen in the longboat hadn't shot at the Mariners on deck, having no clear targets. But now arrows began to hiss, drilling the air.

One transfixed the captain's leg to the rudder. Two more sank home, one in his thigh, one just below the scapula. Gil had one second's look at Gale-Baiter's face as the captain, pasted to the rail, realized he was dead. Falling, he tore loose the arrow holding his leg to the rudder. Rings of water sprang from his impact. The line remained. One Mariner got a leg up on the rail, meaning to retrieve his captain. Skewerskean caught his arm and flung him back. "He was dead, fool; so will we all be, if we do not stand together."

Wavewatcher was howling in anguish. He grabbed his lance again, drew and aimed. Gil saw sudden, deadly grace, synthesis of hunter, athlete and soldier. The release was one of enormous force. The lance struck through a shield, pinning the grapnel man to the boat's hull, penetrating the wood. The attackers pulled frantically, drawing themselves in under the protection of the stern while arrows rained down on them. Hidden by the stern's projection, they'd be able to climb to the deck.

Wavewatcher took up a cutlass. It was small, almost frivolous in his huge hand. "You aloft there, 'ware my commands! The rest, position yourselves about the deck."

Gil picked a spot at the portside rail and waited, one hand on a ratline, and the other still tensing, loosening on his sword. There were outcries astern, the first of the boarders. He turned, about to help, when a clambering caught his ear. He leaned over the rail slowly and nearly had his head taken off. A Southwastelander clung there, showing his teeth in a sneer. The fingers clawing the hull for purchase were blunt and visibly strong, the Occhlon nimble in his light mesh armor, his curved weapon dangling from its sword loop. Unable to reach the American from where he was, he climbed directly upward, unnerving Gil, who would never have gone against an enemy waiting with the advantages of firm footing and weapon in hand.

The boarder abruptly began to edge sideways, catching Gil by surprise, to move away from him before trying the rail. The American followed, listening to the grunted, labored breathing, unsure what he'd do when he faced the man.

The boarder sprang the last few feet, screaming Yardiff Bey's name. He had an arm and a leg over the rail when the other, galvanized by the hated name, got to him. Gil brought his heavy bastard blade around in a flat arc. The boarder could only spare one hand to raise his scimitar; the broadsword carried it backward and knocked the boarder off balance. Gil took a more resolute swing. The blade bit through the woven gorget and

162

into the neck. Dropping away, the desert man's face was awful in its disregard of his own death.

A shouted warning from Skewerskean made him spin. Another boarder, a shorter man, had dropped to the deck, ready to fight. Mariners and their foes staggered across the deck, locked in death duels. Wavewatcher had a cutlass in either hand now, the ringlets on his chest holding drops of enemy blood suspended among them.

Gil crossed swords with his new opponent, whose style relied on his edge. Yells from the Mariners told of more of the assault party making it to the deck. Seafarers raced to meet them, their bare feet slapping alarm on the planks.

Gil engaged the second man in a high line, putting down his own panic. They exchanged hair raising strokes, edges laying back and forth. The man had a long, strong arm, but his footwork was conservative. The American pressed against that possibility as blood pounded at his temples. All sounds faded but the swords' clanging and his own heartbeat. He kept control of their fencing distance, coming into range and getting out again to his own advantage. A shout penetrated his concentration; the tinkling of bells proclaimed Skewerskean in combat.

Gil's opponent was slow responding to a croise, backing up against the head ledge of a hatch, and swaying. For a moment his defense was open, though the American could not ordinarily have exploited it. But something in him drove his point in under the vulnerable throat. The boarder fell back with a flopping of limbs and that same expression of loathing. Gil paused to catch his breath, hearing Wavewatcher call, "Ho, aloft! Prepare to fill-all on my—dammit!—on my order."

The interruption had been another antagonist. The harpooner was busy both with the battle and monitoring the *Gal*'s progress downriver. With both topsails filled, the ship began to draw ahead at the wider mouth of the Wheywater. The harpooner called on the embattled men at the tiller to keep her off a little, to increase headway through the water.

There was a scraping at the ship's side. The dory had come with a second wave of attackers. Snatching up a carpenter's hatchet from a weapons rack, Gil ran farther toward the bow, to keep them from getting a line onto the *Gal.*

He was too late. Two boarders swarmed onto the deck together. With hatchet and sword he launched himself at them, swinging wildly. The world swam at him, begging combat through a red mist.

Berserkergang filled him; he coursed with a killing joy. His attack left one dead, the hatchet buried in his chest, the deck-roll playing with pooling blood. The second boarder joined Gil at the death-duel. The American felt exultation in the Rage. Dunstan's sword seemed familiar now, sending strength and cunning up his arm. Always heavy before, the weapon hefted light as a fishing rod.

Berserker blade screamed against desert scimitar. Gil's lips were drawn back, teeth locked, ears flattened to his skull in animal fury. He was hyperaware of time, distance and possibilities of slaughter. He disowned fencing to hack and hew without letup. The Occhlon was the bigger man, with a thick black mustache and angry brows. His attack was powerful and confident. But Gil, enfolded by savage depersonalization, met it, swinging Dunstan's sword with a terrible vitality.

The Southwastelander gave ground to a flurry of wild slashes, then reversed field and came on again. Both hammered with swords held two-handed, notching and blunting them. Wavewatcher's voice, bull-horning for the hoisting of jib and flying jib, trimming them by the wind, went unnoticed.

The Southwastelander's exertions left him off balance. Gil pounced on the moment's invitation, bashing the other's guard aside, thrusting with Dunstan's sword. Standing over the dying Occhlon, he knew a split second's contentment, then whirled to find more slaughter.

Battle had passed; Mariners were clearing the deck of their enemies' bodies and seeing to their wounded, but the Berserkergang didn't recognize that. Gil moved suspiciously down the deck as seafarers drew back, watching him uneasily, seeing that something wasn't right with him. Blood that had run down the fullers of his uplifted sword dribbled off his knuckles. He approached a pair of Mariners, seeing no reason why he shouldn't attack them too.

His ankles were seized from behind with a tinkling of bells, his feet yanked from under him. He sprawled flat on the deck, cracking his chin, dashing breath from his lungs. A weight like all the Dark Rampart landed on him. In a moment the Mariners had wrested his sword from him, and pinned his arms. He fought and writhed like a salmon, but this was only the second time the Rage had come to him; it couldn't yet drive him to the superhuman extremes that it had Dunstan. Eventually, the murderous fit dispersed, to be replaced, curiously, by nothing more than fatigue and calm.

"Better now?" piped Skewerskean, from where the little man held one of Gil's legs. Gil, gasping, said he was.

Wavewatcher, sitting patiently on the American's back, warned, "Whatever baresark malice you called upon, save it for the enemy. Enough is enough, agreed? Let him up, lads." Gil felt as if he'd been through a wringer.

One of the men aloft yelled, sighting a sail. The big-bellied harpooner hauled Gil to his feet effortlessly, setting him against the rail among Mariners straining for a view. The *Gal* was standing clear of the Wheywater and out to sea. Another ship had rounded the point, appearing from behind Death's Hold. A big sailing barque, she had on her foresail and mainsail the device of a golden sea horse on a red field. Spying the *Gal*, the barque had come about, wearing ship briskly. She had a brown-and-white bird painted on her bows.

Gil speculated dizzily whether he was up to an escape in one of the *Gal*'s boats, or swimming if he must. Then a triumphant cheer went up from the brig's crew. When Wavewatcher called for sail on the starboard tack, men jumped readily for the ratlines. Some broke out flags, to hoist the signal that there were wounded aboard.

More vessels were appearing from behind the stronghold. A smile had parted the harpooner's dense beard. He thumped the American on the back; Gil almost lost his hold on the rail. Wavewatcher laughed. "When you tell this tale, say you no sooner came to the sea than

165

you encountered its very overlord." He saw no understanding on the other's face. "That four-master is his
flagship; no less than our monarch, the Prince Who Sails
Forever."

Chapter Sixteen

*Many waves cannot quench love, neither can the
    floods drown it.*

> The Song of Songs,
> which is Solomon's

THERE'D been no disabling wounds among the *Gal*'s
crew, nor anyone slain except Gale-Baiter. Replacements were put aboard the brig and her own personnel,
Gil included, transferred to the four-masted barque, the
Osprey. The Prince Who Sails Forever had questions for
all of them.

Wavewatcher and Skewerskean appointed themselves
the American's unofficial custodians. They helped him
up the boarding ladder and hustled him below decks,
out of the way of busy crewmen. The forecastle was
crowded, the ship having manned for war, but the two
partners found Gil room to stow his gear and rig a hammock alongside theirs in a converted storeroom.

Osprey and her half-score escorts, smaller two- and
three-masted vessels, were working toward the Outer
Hub, scouring the coast, insuring that no enemy had
eluded them. The fleet had been late for its rendezvous
with the *Long-Dock Gal*, apparently arriving shortly
after the Hand of Salamá had fled south. The Prince
had sent a party ashore at the opposite side of the delta,
to assure that Death's Hold had been completely gutted.
The party, spying the *Gal*'s predicament as she neared
the Whcywater's mouth, had rushed to tell their Liege.

Swift ships were being sent after Yardiff Bey's even as Gil boarded *Osprey*.

Wavewatcher and Skewerskean had to make their full report to the Prince, explaining that the Lord of Sailors was eager for any news off the wind-roads.

"What are wind-roads?" Gil wanted to know.

The harpooner was shocked by his ignorance. "Why, the breezes of the air, which are thoroughfares of the oceans. In that wise, we Mariners call ourselves Children of the Wind-Roads."

"Never heard it before. How long till we get to this Isle of Keys?"

"Scuttlebutt aboard of here says this flagship will soon join the rest of the fleet at the Outer Hub. But the seas are ours once more, and many Mariners would rather put aside further enmities with landlubbers. Um, nothing personal."

"No offense."

"Most feel, though, as does the Prince, that no trace of Salamá should be tolerated, especially on the strategic Isle of Keys."

"What will the Prince do?"

"Put his recommendation before a gathering of masts, as when we voted for war after the Inner Hub was razed."

Gil made a sour face.

"Bey got what he wanted in Glyffa. Salamá is ahead of the game."

The partners frowned at one another. "The Prince will want to hear this," Wavewatcher concluded. Both got up to go. Gil stripped off his blood-spattered byrnie and reclined in his hammock.

The storeroom was dim, filled with the smell of *Osprey*'s wood and odors of a thousand cargoes and sailors, smoke of lamps, and the bite of incense. Two Mariners, off watch, were throwing dice for IOUs. They noted the stained byrnie, nodded to the American's casual greeting, and left it at that.

Osprey was making way now, her bow rising and falling on the open sea. Gil thought for awhile that he might grow seasick from the hammock's sway, but depleted by the Rage, he fell asleep instead. Skewerskean shook him awake, saying the Prince wanted to speak with him. The American rose unsteadily, having no sea legs, and followed the two through narrow passageways and ladderwells.

He emerged at last, to take his first good look around the barque. High overhead, cirrus clouds were torn and shredded by the winds, in shapes of stress and speed. Down at sea level though, there was only a light breeze to carry the sails. Low swells rolled, the color of blue ink, and *Osprey*'s bow sliced the water at a leisurely five knots.

By Crescent Lands standards, the barque was a giant, a quantum leap in marine design. She had four tall masts, rigged with what looked to Gil like ten square miles of canvas and duck. It risked vertigo for him to peer up the six courses of sail on the mainmast, to the ship's summit. The mazework of creaking rigging held the eye, bewildering it, as wheeling seabirds called out over the sheering of the barque's bow wave.

Men were scrubbing down the deck, coiling line and doing other work, but there were racks of javelins, cutlasses, pikes and shields close to hand. He made his way aft and stopped when Wavewatcher did, the harpooner calling for permission to mount the quarterdeck. An officer in trim blue silk granted it. The two partners waited behind, as Gil clambered up the ladder.

Under the curved spanker sail an awning had been set, shading cushions and a sturdy-legged table burdened with food. A man waited there, a short, erect figure with a crisp white goatee and the bluest eyes Gil had ever seen, in a crinkled brown face. He wore a uniform of white linen and held a staff almost as tall as himself, an osseous twist of narwhale horn capped with a golden sea horse. Over his heart was pinned a golden broach shaped for his ship's namesake, an osprey. The Prince Who Sails Forever.

"It is gracious of you to come," he began, "for I know you have been through much. I am Landlorn, captain of the *Osprey* and of the Mariners too, it may be admitted. Will you sit and take your ease with me?"

When Gil was seated, the Prince of the Waves continued. "Gilbert MacDonald, I believe you are named? And they call you Gil? May I? Thank you. I should be

168

much in your debt if you would relate more of the events current in this war being fought inland."

"Oh, sure, your Grace. It—"

"Ah, please! Friends call me Landlorn; will you not do me that honor?"

Gil took to the Prince from the start, to the scrupulous courtesy extended to everyone. He was sure that anyone who led the rowdy Mariners could be a hard-case boss when he had to. Soon, he was telling Landlorn his story, of the Two-Bard Commission and of Yardiff Bey, Cynosure and Blazetongue and the Occhlon, and of *Arrivals Macabre*.

In the end, the Prince said, "You shall come into your chance to see the Isle of Keys, if the Mariners second my will of it; dislodging southerners from their sea-keep is work for the Children of the Wind Roads, and therein lies tragedy, for I would rather they could stay out of it, unparticipant." His expression showed private sadness, then he roused himself. "I trust you've been made comfortable?"

"Thank you, yes. But it's all a bit strange for me; I'm a dry-land type."

Landlorn's eyebrows rose. "Oh, but I, too, am a landsman by birth."

"You? Then how'd you end up here?" Gil saw immediately that it had been a gaffe. Gil had answered the Prince's questions though, and Landlorn's etiquette compelled him to do likewise.

"I come of royalty; one of the lesser kingdoms whose name you would not know. My older brother had the throne, and there was little liking between us. He proclaimed it my duty to fetch him the bride he'd been promised by a neighboring king. I was to bring her by sea, and was obliged to swear by oaths of honor and magic that I would make no other landfall until I had brought her to him, do you see?

"Her name was Serene. On that voyage she came to mean much to me. We were attacked by corsairs and our ship burned, leaving us two adrift on a hatch cover for days. Mariners picked us up at last, a rough-handed lot not much better than pirates themselves, then."

He broke off, listening to men working to a long-haul

chantey. Skewerskean's clear voice joined in, holding to the higher notes playfully.

"We might have plead for ransoming, but I would not yield her up to my brother after all we had gone through, and Serene did not wish it either. I was sufficiently the swordsman that those nomads took me on. So you will understand, this royal scion started out lowly on the backs of the oceans. I thought the day must soon come when I should be free of my vow, and I would wait it out.

"But I had to shun the shore, so my crewmates dubbed me Landlorn. I acquired the ways of the sea, learned, mastered. I had been schooled, and so could resurrect lost lore from old books that had survived the Great Blow, and *Osprey* is one product of that. The Mariners put me at their head and I am content, though there was more to it than that. My brother is dead now, and the bonds of my vows eternal unless I become Oathbreaker and risk the magic that sealed them. But I love the oceans; much rather would I be sentenced to life at sea than the same on land exclusively. I have seen the waters in all their stations and offices; the Wind-Roads are my realm and Serene is mine, and I am fulfilled."

Landlorn was speaking absently now, staring off over the sea. Gil said a fast good-bye and rejoined the harpooner and the chanteyman at the quarterdeck ladder. He marveled at the Prince's story, wondering why it had left him with a deep, unidentified sadness.

Wavewatcher and Skewerskean gave him a hand in picking up what Mariner life was all about, and became his friends. They replaced his torn and bloodied clothes with new ones, a soft sealskin shirt and buckskin pants and jacket. The jacket had wing epaulets, sewn with metal lamellae to protect the shoulders from sword cuts.

Then the American was introduced to Mariner life. The Children of the Wind-Roads, under the care and dominion of the currents of air and ocean, were intimates with them. They had dozens of names for dawn, even more for sunset, cloud formations and portents of weather. Gil would point to swells in the morning and ask the Mariner name for them, but when he'd ask again at noon, the swells looking no different to him, the two would have a new answer. The nuances escaped him completely.

The sailors defined the subtlest variations in clouds, their height, texture, luminosity and drift. Weather predictions were extraordinarily accurate. Charts were exhaustive, and the shorelines on maps, but interiors were largely ignored; the Mariners merely called them "inlands." When Gil mentioned it, Skewerskean countered, "Does the landsman's map tell of reef, channel and shoal?"

Wavewatcher added, "And does the hawk concern himself with the rabbit's warren?"

They had their own estimations of worth. A man could be unexcelled with weapons or bare hands, but if he lost equilibrium aloft or couldn't steer by the stars, his status was lowly. Wavewatcher, who'd hunted the whale whose every part was valuable to the Mariners, was listened to with respect, but Skewerskean's chantey's made work easier, whether he sang a hand-over-hand to synchronize the tautening of the braces, or a long-haul ditty for heavier work. The little man was therefore the more welcome shipmate, with his gift for making drudgery bearable. His repertoire was staggering, though he could improvise endlessly on any subject, high or low.

"Mariners would sooner swear than discourse," he told Gil, "but they would sooner sing than swear." Tradition, law, philosophy and mythology were all bound up in memorized verses and sagas, chanteys and hymns. Restless voices poured out gratitude, humor, pride and pain.

Raised by one parent or the other, Mariner boys might spend their youngest years at sea or ashore. But early in life they began learning the lore of their peculiar tribe. When a Mariner youth took his first ship as a man, he swam to it, from shore or another ship. Naked, without one article from his former life, he made his rite of passage. His survival depended solely on his new shipmates; he might not see his loved ones for years or, in some cases, ever again. Among them he'd have to earn, beg or otherwise obtain all that he needed or wanted in life. Subsequent changes of berth would be more sedate, made as an adult. Yet, all Mariners were fond of exchanging stories about their frightening Free Plunge, as they called it, through menacing waters to an unknown world, their first ship.

Life in the closeness of *Osprey* was rigidly codified. Each person had a right to as much privacy as was feasible, under Ship's Articles. The first things the two partners taught Gil were the priorities for right-of-way on deck and in the passageways and ladderwells. As supernumerary, the American classed among the lowest groups, having to defer to officers, men on duty, and virtually anyone else with anything useful to do. The pecking order was complicated: a junior officer off watch would be expected to yield way to a crewman on duty if the weather placed certain demands on the ship. There were dozens of individual rules. Gil simply let anybody who wanted to pass him go right ahead.

Sleeping accommodations, food, free time and shares of profit were governed by strict laws of propriety. Over everything loomed the sanctity of the Ship, holy of holies. Every thought and action must be considered in the context of its effect on that common bond, shared habitat.

Osprey's crew was an elite. The barque was Landlorn's greatest accomplishment, and there was always more to learn from her. Gil lost himself in blue days and starry nights, motionless gulls shedding air from their wings, the creaking and snapping of rigging. He was making decent headway after Yardiff Bey. The Prince wanted to go against the Isle of Keys, and the Southwastelanders were being driven from the Crescent Lands. At times, he was very nearly content.

But other sails began to appear in the sea around *Osprey*, a field of sailcloth bearing for the Outer Hub, to hear the rede of war.

Chapter Seventeen

And seas, and rocks, and skies rebound,
To arms, to arms, to arms!
        Alexander Pope
        "Ode for Music on St. Cecelia's Day"

OSPREY, attended by her smaller and slower escorts, arrived at her home port on a flawless morning. The Outer Hub rested on a mountainous jut of island west of Veganá, its mammoth walls and defenses commanding the only usable anchorage there. Gil had learned that the citadels of the Mariners were called Hubs because all life and commerce of the Children of the Wind-Roads revolved around them.

Fortifications radiated from a complex perched on the slopes above the city proper. The harbor's gates were enormous, their timbers strapped and faced with iron, the blunt heads of their rivets as wide as dinner platters. They were operated by heavily geared machinery powered by teams of oxen laboring in roundhouses. There were emplacements of mangonels, ballistas, fire-casters and flame-sluices. Gil noticed most of those were pivot-mounted, and could be brought to bear on the harbor if it came to that. The walls were of immense stone blocks, and he wasn't surprised to learn that, like most of the more awesome constructions in the Crescent Lands, the Hub antedated the Great Blow.

The harbor was crammed with the gathering of masts, assembled craft of a seafaring nation, from bobbing gigs to a barque nearly the size of *Osprey*, riding stately with sails clewed up, masts dominating the maritime forest. Every ship had her emblem, a grasping kraken or sweet-faced mermaid, ram's head or diadem, pouncing black panther or four-winged gull.

Osprey anchored at the harbor's center. A longboat was put over the side for the first parties to go ashore. Wavewatcher and Skewerskean were among the first to go. The American promised to catch up later, saying Landlorn wished to see him.

The awning had been removed from the quarter-deck. The Prince of the Waves was at the rail, narwhale staff in hand, gazing distractedly at the Outer Hub. Gil pardoned himself for interrupting; the man left off his woolgathering.

"The pursuit of Yardiff Bey's ship was fruitless; my captains never caught sight of him. What thing is it, in your estimation, stolen by him from the library at Ladentree?"

"Don't I wish I knew! Important enough for him to waste an army, is all I can tell you; something he needs badly, or something he's awfully afraid of."

The Prince accepted that. "His enterprises threaten us all. Have you heard tell of our other citadel, the Inner Hub, that was destroyed? I have yet to envision what force broke her sea wall, sank her picket ships, crushed her war engines and the turrets that held them. Marry, Bey was responsible, but in what terrible fashion he accomplished it, I cannot ken. We never observed his renowned flying ship; many of our vessels mount heavy missile-throwers that he shuns." His hand swung the staff with its golden symbol. "If such destruction was loosed on the sea, the Mariners may meet it yet. I fear that."

He was interrupted. A woman had come on deck, draped with a heavy cloak against the ocean breeze. She looked younger than Landlorn, her graying hair caught back from a heart-shaped face in a long plait, fastened with pearls. On her brow was a circlet of polished coral set in platinum. Her countenance was happy but care-worn; ebullience made her appear more hardy than she was on closer inspection. Landlorn went to her, preoccupations forgotten.

She hugged him. "Well-come, husband."

"And you, wife."

Gil witnessed it with interest. So this was the woman who'd cost the Prince a lifetime exile on the sea, or rather for whom he'd chosen one. Landlorn, remembering the American was there, said, "This young ally we met up with on our voyage had a bad time of it from Southwastelanders. He is called Gil." Holding her hand up proudly, he finished, "And this is my lady wife, Serene."

Gil bowed, something he'd almost never done, even in courtly Earthfast. Serene's good-humored dignity seemed to warrant it. The Prince recalled what he'd been about to say.

"You completed part of the riddle for me, Gil. I asked myself why, if Yardiff Bey had the wherewithal to raze the Inner Hub, we saw none of it in our affrays with the Occhlon. Now I know he was engaged in his act of theft, diverted by more pressing matters."

Gil considered that. "Could be. Maybe he threw away men on the Inner Hub as he did getting to Ladentree." The thought struck sparks. "Was there a library at the Inner Hub? Archives or something?"

"Certes; our travels gather us much old doctrine, and many ancient books."

"Then it's a good bet Bey was hunting a copy of *Arrivals Macabre* there; that's why he attacked your citadel. Let's see, that would be, uh . . ." He calculated intervals, talking to himself. "It would have been just before everything blew up in his face in Earthfast. He masterminded the assault or whatever it was and netted a copy of Rydolomo's book. He brought it to Earthfast, the copy whose binder Andre deCourteney found in his sanctum. When we took the palace-fortress, Bey skipped with the pages, to Dulcet's house. When he found out he had the wrong copy, he got busy on the invasion of Veganá and Glyffa, so he could get to Ladentree. So naturally you people haven't seen any sign of the slam he used on the Inner Hub; he's been tied up with his main game, bagging *Arrivals Macabre*. But he's got it now, probably the right one this time."

Serene was watching worriedly, and Landlorn was scowling. He finished his reconstruction. "If Bey's latched onto whatever it was he wanted, we've got to get at him as soon as we can. Put if off and there might be no stopping him."

He regretted having put it all out in front of them when he saw Serene's face marred with apprehension.
175

Landlorn said, "I will be speaking to the Mariners to-night, here in the harbor. That will decide the question of the Isle of Keys."

Gil shied from asking the obvious question because Serene was present. She pursued it herself. "Will they affirm your plan?"

The Prince Who Sails Forever admitted, "It is moot. They are weary of war, and with every reason. It would be a costly battle, I trow, but if we do not go to the Isle, it will put forth its grasp to find us. Best confront it now."

His wife agreed dolorously, and Landlorn slipped an arm through hers, twirling his staff, jollying her unavailingly. Gil left them to their reunion.

Going ashore in the next boat, the salt spray putting its taste on his lips, he caught sight of Landlorn pacing the quarterdeck, Serene evidently having gone below. The last view the American had of him was the Prince's silhouette against the sky, with the wind stirring his hair, watching his people and their land, on which he had never set foot, and never would.

That evening Gil returned to the harbor, doing his best to help a half-loaded Skewerskean guide the weaving, gloriously drunken Wavewatcher. The harpooner had won a contest, hurling his throwing iron, in a whaler's tavern called the Golden Fluke, and made much of the celebration with his winnings. Gil had tagged along through the noisy, prosperously frenetic harbor town while the partners made the bars, paid off their many debts, bellowed songs, pinched cup-girls, gambled emotionally, traded lies with other Mariners and threw away an amazing amount of money. They sang him their ballads and chanteys and clamored to hear his, and taught him the hornpipe. Somewhere along the way—he couldn't remember where—he'd acquired a tambourine.

But they'd torn themselves away from it all when the hour came to hear their Prince. After boozy negotiating, a dory and boatman were hired for a scandalous sum. The two chivvied Gil aboard and loaded the cask of ale they'd brought, refreshments for the cruise. The harbor had filled and overflowed. The fleet was aglitter with lanterns and torches, spread to the sea-gates and beyond. The sky was still clear, with a slice of moon among the stars.

An immense dredging barge, lit with cressets, had been brought to the center of the harbor, where shipmasters had gathered in hundreds to sit in a profusion of costumes and attitudes, giving ear. If the popular response was too evenly divided, it would be the captains who cast ballots to choose what answer the Prince was to receive.

The boatman had to work carefully to get near the barge; the water was carpeted with craft, so that a person could have walked from side to side of the bay. As they waited, Gil told the two about Landlorn's concern over Yardiff Bey, and whatever it was that the sorcerer had done to destroy the Inner Hub.

"Verily," agreed Skewerskean, "ten thousand voices in the Outer Hub are whispering to each other about just that. One hears the words Acre-Fin."

"Well, I haven't heard. What's that?"

"Acre-Fin, every bugaboo of the oceans, the fear and dread of sailors made real, the sea's violence incarnate, its oldest denizen. New worries call up an old terror, the fish that eats whole ships and crushes islands. What the truth is, I do not claim to know, but you will hear that name tonight."

They were quiet for a time. Gil, muddled, speculated if that might be the secret of *Arrivals Macabre*. But no, the attack on the Inner Hub had happened before Bey'd won his prize at Ladentree.

Wavewatcher was humming, a fair imitation of a courting walrus. "What was that ditty you sang, Gil-O?" he rumbled. "About the watering hole on the road to the underworld that is exclusively for horse soldiers?"

Gil leaned his head back and broke into "Fiddler's Green," dolefully.

Marching past, straight through Hell, the infantry
    are seen,
Accompanied by the engineer, quartermaster and
    Marine
For none but shades of cavalry dismount at Fid-
    dler's Green . . .

He was stopped by resonant notes from a massive gong on the barge. Silence pre-empted every song, greeting, toast and argument, so the only sounds were the creak of rigging, the knock of hulls and the plaints of sea birds. Landlorn came into the circle of light; Serene was at his side. Ovation began, but he waved it aside with the narwhale staff. The Prince's face was morose in the rippling red light of the barge's cressets.

"Salutations, you Children of the Wind-Roads. I bow to you in your thousands, your ten-thousands." He lowered his head in homage. "I bear tidings no Mariner can like. Though the seas are ours again, there is unchecked danger from the land. We have ripped the Flaming Wheel down from Death's Hold, sending southern ships and sailors to the floor of the ocean, but the evil that moved them still thrives."

Murmurs blew through the crowd, fanning louder.

"I cringe to see our keels exposed to the cruel rams and rostrums of the enemy. I loathe the fire that burns our sails, and the wailing that lifts in the quarters of our slain. Our foemen are gathered, making new plans. It is my thought that we strike against them now. Thither too went Yardiff Bey, who wrought our every injury."

Gil tried to gauge the Prince's success from the faces around him. Many were dubious, drained by their battles. If they rejected Landlorn's proposal, the American would have no choice but to rejoin the Crescent Landers.

"The men of Veganá and the women of Glyffa are on the march," the Prince was saying, "and it may be that they will go beside us against the Isle, but we may not rely on it. With them or not, it falls to us to unseat Salamá from its island."

Wavewatcher and Skewerskean were on their feet now, rocking the dory, bellowing support. Others were doing the same, but many more were quiet, unconvinced. Landlorn was grim, unwilling to put war-fervor into his people.

"The Inner Hub is smoke and ruin," he reminded them. "Many of your kin and shipmates are sped. There are those who say we have taken our vengeance in full, and I would not nay-say them; what I ask is not simple

178

recompense. There must be no taint of the Masters outside their own shores."

People were vacillating. Gil was about to ask how much longer this could go on, but Wavewatcher was pointing into the sky, nearly upsetting the dory. "See! See there, in the south!"

A line of light had appeared, like a comet, brightening the night. Its brilliant head shone; its tail cut a path of splendor down through the darkness, straight at Shardishku-Salamá. Legends were preserved here, just as in the Crescent Lands. The same word being taken up at that moment before the Temple of the Bright Lady was being repeated through the Outer Hub.

"What are you guys talking about? What's the Trailingsword?"

They explained to him as the first shock subsided. It was eloquent of Landlorn's status that he had their attention again quickly.

"I cannot tell what mystical portent this is, though I hear you call it Trailingsword. Perhaps it is, proclaiming the seven times seven days left to us, or perhaps not. But it is some great sign, demanding our heed. What is your will? Do we purge the Isle of Keys?"

The Mariners split the air with their consent. Cutlasses flashed in the light of the Trailingsword as Wavewatcher, Skewerskean and the boatman chanted Landlorn's name. Joylessly content, Gil studied the Omen. With its pommel-head uppermost, it mirrored his Ace of Swords, reversed. What had Gabrielle told him months ago, that the tarot's meaning in that alignment could be tragedy?

Unimportant now. It was enough that the Children of the Wind-Roads would sail south.

Chapter Eighteen

Hope is the thing with feathers
That perches in the soul . . .
      Emily Dickinson
      "Hope is the Thing with Feathers"

FERRIAN, onetime Champion-at-arms of the Horse-blooded, Defender of Corrals, was fond of taking a scroll or book high into the uppermost parts of the library complex at Ladentree.

His wound had mended slowly, over weeks. He would never lose his limp, but he could walk, and sit a horse. The Healing Sages had advised him to stay for a time, to complete his recuperation, and he'd complied, reckoning his role against Salamá ended. The Trailing-sword had declared as much. Seeing its splendor in the sky each night, he'd been moved with a profound new mood of hope.

Now he sat cross-legged in the tower of a silent bell so large a dozen men might have sheltered beneath it. Its bronze was green, its rope decayed away long ago, for the Birds of Accord nested nearby. The place had a solemnity that appealed to Ferrian, a thoughtful freedom he held especial. At times he heard the songs of the Birds, pure trilling like no other sound in the world. There was an airy view for miles, and an intimacy with the weather he'd missed in the Chambers of Healing.

Sitting with a folio in his lap, he heard the voices of the Birds again. This time there was unfamiliar cadence to it, a disorderly intrusion of other, shriller notes. He put the folio aside carefully and rose, pulling himself up with his left hand, to spare his leg. Following the sounds, he rounded the giant bell to a far corner of the tower. He trod carefully; rotting boards made treacherous footing.

Bracing himself with his left hand and leaning out carefully, he spotted Birds fluttering at the eaves of a lesser tower, darting in at nests there. Interest became surprise; they behaved like parents bringing food to their young, but the Birds of Accord had bred no offspring since they'd been driven out of the branches of the Lifetree.

The Horseblooded cocked an ear and listened. The shriller, more disorderly notes came from beneath the eaves. He recovered the folio and hurried off to find Silverquill. The Senior Sage had been a willing tutor, anxious to hear about life on the High Ranges. It was now their habit to seek each other's company when the mood struck, a mutual privilege.

Silverquill was politely skeptical of Ferrian's claim that the Birds had hatched young. Still, the old savant dropped what he was doing—comparing several copies from original manuscripts of *Arrivals Macabre* in an effort to learn what secret Bey had been after—and went off with the brawny Horseblooded to see.

They eventually found the correct face of the right tower. The issue was partially settled before they got there; high chattering of young Birds filled the confines of the peaked roof. They edged carefully around a last beam, and saw slots of light from the eaves. Birds of Accord fed and nurtured impossibly small, vocal hatchlings.

Silverquill shook his head, dumfounded. "This is unprecedented! The Birds may breed only in the branches of the Lifetree, and it was uprooted and destroyed an age ago, when the Great Blow fell."

"Demonstrably untrue." Ferrian grinned wryly.

"Even so. But that is no explanation." They drew back, so as not to disturb that amazing scene.

Ferrian was snapping his fingers distractedly. "The Birds roosted here when their Lifetree was destroyed, and in all these years never bred. But now they have; it remains to discern why. How long is it betwixt their mating and the laying of eggs, and from that unto the hatching?"

181

"Who may say? Yet, let us venture that those are much as with other birds. What is your thought?"

"I bethink me of only one incident here in any reasonable span of time, and that is when Bey came, and we after him."

The Senior Sage stroked his trim beard. "Aye, yet what can that mean? Surely the small glamour he used on Gil MacDonald cannot be the influence that has affected the Birds. Nor can it be attributed to the Guardian, with its fiery destruction, nor to Andre deCourteney's Dismissal; they are of no nature to cause the Birds of Accord to beget."

"Perhaps the terror of the day? Many of them perished from that."

"All the less reason to think it made them bring forth young."

The Horseblooded's lips pursed. "What else then? I was wounded, and did not participate in what came after."

Silverquill studied the weathered rafters, rubbing his thumb across his Adam's apple. "The others came the next morning, the Trustee and her troops and Lord Angorman. They all met together in the rose garden and conferred. Thereafter, they parted ways."

"Hmm, that seems of no relevance either. Perhaps we are not—"

"Hold!" The savant's face lit excitedly. "There was another thing of it. All those combatants were under arms, and I bade them put those aside; Ladentree had seen enough of weapons. When Lord Angorman hesitated, the Trustee put him at ease, laying her Crook of office with Red Pilgrim, against a trellis. I remember seeing the Birds of Accord flitting round and round, alighting and hopping about, even on the Crook itself."

Ferrian's brow knit. "You are theorizing that the Trustee's staff is crafted of wood of the Lifetree? She never gave hint of that."

"True. Well, but, at least we have a glimmer of what drew the sorcerer here. The Lifetree is connected with it; armed with that fact, we may plunge into the assembled knowledge of Ladentree, and seek the rest."

The tall Horseblooded concurred eagerly. The Trailingsword had set many things in motion, he saw. "Two men are often too many to keep a secret from Salamá; more is too great a risk, for Bey may yet have ears here. This hunt across paper and parchment falls to you and me, dear mentor."

Chapter Nineteen

For all, that here on earth we dreadful hold,
Be but bugs to fearen babes withal,
Compared to the creatures in the sea's enthrall . . .
                                        Edmund Spenser
                                        Faerie Queene

COMMITTED to one more trial of war, the Mariners amazed Gil with their unanimity.

Roping needles darted unceasingly, turning out hills of extra sail. Fish and meat were salted, fruit and vegetables barreled or dried, medicines prepared and leagues of line and hawser run from the ropewalks of the Outer Hub. Shipwrights, pressed for impossible labors, delivered.

Forges clanged and glowed by day and night. From them poured new cutlasses, arrow- and spearheads, shields, grappling hooks, axes and boarding pikes, and armor and helmets hastily done up from metal lozenges on leather. Aboard the ships that mounted them, fighting engines were refurbished. The Mariners prepared their volatile fluid in giant vats for defense of the harbor. The stuff's base appeared to be naptha, but the seafarers had their own combinant secrets.

Many crafts were racheted up the ways, or hove down in bustling shipyards for swarming repair crews and caulkers. Cargo ships took Mariner treasure, to procure supplies wherever they could. More came in each day with stores for the fleet, and against blockade.

Fresh water was rationed, to build a reserve for the Hub and fill ships' casks.

Gil stayed out of people's way, impatient to leave but fascinated by life among the seafarers and the incessant buzz of their preparations. But Bey was somewhere across the water, scheming, contriving, and that seldom left the American's mind, even when he was wondering how Dunstan was or, as happened with surprising frequency, when he thought of Swan.

Even Wavewatcher and Skewerskean were busy; the Prince of the Waves filled their time with tasks, saying it was high time two such capable Mariners shouldered more responsibility.

Less than two weeks after the advent of the Trailingsword, the Children of the Wind-Roads sailed out again. It took hours just to maneuver into formation, with *Osprey* in the lead and the larger vessels around her. Tubby cargo bottoms were at the center, with lean brigs and barkentines flanking.

Gil, aboard *Osprey,* was billeted with his friends in the same little storeroom they'd used on the way out. Landlorn had yielded, for now, to the partners' pleas that they be allowed to ply their old trade as topmast hands. Serene was also in the ship's company, having absolutely refused another separation from her husband.

The fifth day out, a storm came up. In alarm, the American watched whitecaps come up and swells grow, and nausea hit him for the first time. As the ocean rose in sudden temper, ships' bows began slamming into the troughs with greater and greater force. *Osprey* and many of her sisters could have run before the wind with a good deal of sail, but it was vital that the fleet not be scattered. Landlorn ordered most canvas taken in, as the following seas exploded tons of water around the barque. The flagship did well enough, her fore topmast staysail set and the main lower topsail taken up goosewing-fashion, presenting a fan shape to the squalls, the remainder heavily lashed to prevent its chafing fully open. The Prince commanded his captains to keep careful distance but rig lanterns, and not become too dispersed. Each craft coped as her captain judged best, most of them goose-winging like *Osprey,* or rigging a three-cornered crossjack.

Gil, clinging to the lifelines, watched Landlorn clinging to a rail up on the quarterdeck, the Prince's cloak snapping around him like a whip as he surveyed his fleet. Salt spume, gust-driven, pumiced the skin like a sandblaster, numbing it in seconds. He noticed Gil, and called, "Be not so despairing. This is only a middling blow; we will ride it out."

Gil, jaws clenched on the sour taste of vomit, nodded gratefully. Landlorn, mistaking that for stoicism, smiled with approval, and motioned for the American to get himself below.

By four the next morning, when the middle watch was over, the wind had died enough for eight bells to be heard clearly. At daylight the storm was blowing itself out. The ships picked their way through sluggish seas, back to a loose formation, tallying losses.

Several vessels were no longer with them, three lost and as many more unaccounted for. Other lives had been taken by the weather as well. A great deal of sail had to be replaced, and water pumped from bilges. Masts had snapped here and there, and there was too much minor damage to calculate. That evening at sundown, Landlorn recited the brief Service for the Lost, though all hands aboard *Osprey* had survived. He told the crew—as captains throughout the fleet were doing—that their brothers were rejoined to the eternal flow of the tides, as all men would one day be. The sea, in Mariner creed, shall not yield up its dead.

Debris was cleared, and shipboard routine resumed. As were-gild for the men it had killed, the ocean granted them a fair, easy ride in the next days with a fresh, following wind. They accepted it thankfully, making the Strait of the Dancing Spar in good time.

Gil was sitting with his back against a hatch cover, enjoying the day and idly trying to calculate how much horsepower *Osprey* was cajoling from the wind, when Wavewatcher and Skewerskean went by, on their way aloft.

They stopped, and Gil asked what it was like to haul canvas ten stories up. They asked what a story was.

"Not easy to tell," Wavewatcher decided. "Why not come up and see? Sight of the Isle of Keys cannot be far off." Before Gil could say he'd give that a miss, the red-beard was calling for permission to take a new hand up the ratlines.

Landlorn came to the quarterdeck rail. "Go; encounter the sky," the Prince of the Waves told the American, curious what this fey landsman would make of the experience.

Gil put one foot on the rail, thought better of it and sat down to take off his boots. He returned to the side. It was easy enough getting around the deadeyes and lanyards, onto the ratlines. Then he looked up the shrouds, their gathering at the top only adding to the feeling of height, and had his doubts. *Osprey's* pitch and roll didn't help.

He started. The mere mechanics went okay, just demanded care that his foot was firmly on the ratline before he hoisted himself for the next step. Wind played its song in the rigging, and he found it appealing. There were spiderweb vibrations along the hard, coarse shrouds. Skewerskean raced past him, and when he chanced a look backwards, Wavewatcher grinned up at him. He steeled himself, going on.

He would have liked to look around at the play of air against sailcloth and study intricacies of the ship's rigging and running, but narrowed his concentration to ratlines and shrouds, one step at a time. He could hear the rush of foam from the keel.

When he got to the base of the tiny platform that was the main top, Skewerskean was standing on it, smirking, fists on hips. Gil knew he was supposed to do it properly, pulling himself up the futtock shrouds and angling his body out, up onto the top, but played it safe instead, snaking up through the lubber hole. He sat there, one hand white on the ratlines, the other arm around the topmast. Wavewatcher joined them, making things, in Gil's silent opinion, way too crowded.

"Well, come on," said Skewerskean.

"What 'come on'? Where?"

"Why, *aloft*. You don't think you are there yet, do you?"

"I know that, goddammit! There's a whole bunch

186

more of this flagpole I'm hanging onto, isn't there? But what makes you think I'm going up it?"

"Wanted a view, did you not?" huffed Wavewatcher. "Fie, the mess-boy climbs this high to call us down to lunch."

The idea had its appeal; if the main top was this exhilarating, what would the crosstree be like? He got, but cautiously, to his feet.

The main topmast shrouds, descending from the little topmast crosstrees, stretched almost vertically past courses of sail realized in stately arcs, were much less roomy than the first leg of the climb. Again, Skewerskean preceded him as Wavewatcher brought up the rear. Under his breath, Gil cursed the other Mariners watching from the yards, now and then calling out a jibe or encouragement.

The wind up here blew his hair around in constant fluttering. He gritted his teeth, made the dubious safety of the topmast crosstree. Wavewatcher stayed in the shrouds below, and Skewerskean hung casually to one side, a hand in the shrouds. Gil reswallowed lunch and turned his head upward. The topgallant mast waited above, shrouds bunched, ratlines far too insubstantial.

Then, for the first time, he took a good look around.

The rigging, spars and sails were a middle kingdom in themselves, with logic and beauty of their own. Below, the hull was plainly too small to need or support these regal mansions of billowing sailcloth and creaking hemp. Here, the winds themselves were divided into components, seduced to service. To the north, he could see the southernmost coast of Veganá, and to the south the hazy shoreline of the domains of Salamá.

He pulled himself to his feet, got one ratline without thinking. He never really decided to go the rest of the way up the topgallant mast; begun, the climb had its own destination. The two Mariners stayed behind, leaving him to his mood. Past memory and thought, he pursued sheer sensation.

He went painstakingly, because the ship's movements were exaggerated by the mast's height. Here, where the halyards closed in, the mast's body was slimmer. With exacting care, he pulled himself up onto the topgallant crosstree. Above him, the mast truck stood only a few feet higher, flying Landlorn's sea-horse emblem. He was level with the mainroyal yard, close to the sky as he'd ever been. Here was a terrible solitude, uninhabited but for sea birds hovering over the cryptic fluxes of the Wind-Roads.

He got his breath and pulled himself erect, adapting to the mast's sway. He burned with fierce, abstract pride in *Osprey,* then threw his head back, whooping, to a sky as much around as above him. Thronging ships of the fleet spread behind, like sheep on a meadow. He called down to his friends. They waved back, asking if he'd care to climb a little higher, and goose an angel or two.

Sounds caught his ear, coming from nowhere he could see. He heard a dry creak like a turning wheel, the crackle of flame. He craned his neck, uncertain whether or not the glare of the sun suggested a fiery mandala. Too bright; his gaze was forced down to the ocean. Before he could lift it again, something caught his attention. "What's that, another ship?"

The Mariners were instantly attentive. Following his pointing finger they saw, just at the periphery of sight, a disturbance in the sea to the far west. With no sail, no oar, and the immense displacement of water from its way, something came toward them.

Lookouts were giving the alarm. Wavewatcher turned to Skewerskean, saying, "Speedily, tell the Prince just what we see!" The little chanteyman turned, sprang lightly through the air and seized the mainroyal backstay with hands and feet, swooping to the deck in a controlled fall.

Gil began the long descent to the deck. When he dropped at last to lean on the rail, men were scurrying in all directions to bos'n's whistles piping battle stations, the timbers drumming to running feet. The entire fleet took up the stridence. A crewman, dashing by, dumped a cork life jacket into his arms. Weapons racks emptied as arms were issued out. He was gathering up his boots, life jacket under one arm, when Skewerskean found him.

"I must go back aloft," the chanteyman panted.

"What's coming off?"

"No one is sure, but it may be all our worst suspicions come real; I think it is the Acre-Fin."

"The—that thingie you were talking about? Here? Why?" Fright was an ache down his spine.

"It can mean us no good. The fleet will fight if it must, or disperse and evade. This tells us how the Inner Hub fell, but too late." He hopped to the rail. "The Prince ordered that you stand abaft by the boat station; there is little safety on the sea today." The shrouds vibrated to his climb.

Gil made his way aft as frantic seafarers dodged around him in either direction. He reached a boat station near the companionway. Swells were up, and a strong wind from the west. No move had been made to put boats over the side, but that could be done in moments. A coxswain, a man Gil knew only vaguely, was waiting by his station. To the American he said, "You are to stay here in all events, where you have been accounted, to avoid confusion."

Archers were in the rigging, and spearmen. Gil could see the catapult arm aboard *Osprey*'s sister ship, *Stormy Petrel,* being cranked down for loading. The coxswain climbed to the rail while Gil pulled his boots on and fastened his life jacket, painfully aware what an indifferent swimmer he was. The wind had lifted to a squall. Clouds raced in with the gusts, bringing light rain.

"I see a wake beyond our last ships," the coxswain said. "It sends forth a wall of water. Wait; I see it no more."

"Will it let us alone?"

A shrug. "Who may say? Yet, it—there! It broke surface, a very mountain of froth." He was yelling now, with the rising wind. "It's dived now, I think." The air flapped his shirt and tangled his rain-soaked hair.

Gil hiked himself up for a partial view. All around the fleet, fish of every kind raced blindly eastward, leaping through the spray, shivering in silver and polychrome.

Could it be another sending of Bey's? He willed himself calm; he clung to his only substance, determination to reach Yardiff Bey.

He was brought up short by recollection that Dunstan's sword and Dirge were stowed in his quarters. He

189

tugged the coxswain's trouser leg and cupped his hand to his mouth. "I'll be right back, understand?" He made his way to a ladderwell, as the Mariner called him to come back over the hundred other shouts and orders going back and forth.

Gil had to go down two decks and farther amidships. The gloom was usually alleviated by small gymbal-mounted lanterns, but these had been extinguished when battle stations had sounded. He groped along, trying doors along the port side as *Osprey* raced with the sea. Deciding he'd gone too far forward, he retraced his steps and discovered that some jerk had padlocked the room, probably one of the Mariners who shared it.

Bracing against the opposite frame, he began kicking. The two swords, one a trust and the other a clue, were too important to abandon. He stamped madly, ranting at the door.

Hinge screws gave. Two more kicks had it hanging from its hasp. He squirmed past, dug through his gear and snatched up the two wrapped swords. *Osprey* heeled, coming hard starboard; there was no time to burrow after his empty handguns. He heard the loud crack of the catapult's throwing arm on *Stormy Petrel,* stopped against its check. The shooting sent him struggling back around the door in panic, the longswords becoming lodged in the gap. He fought to extricate them, but just as they sprang free, a roar of water came to his ears.

Osprey lifted beneath his feet, listing sharply to starboard. He fell across the deck, losing the swords, to crash against the door opposite his own. It gave; he curled up automatically. In the blackness his head slammed something; lights erupted in his eyes. His right shoulder hit the bulkhead.

Osprey heaved back to port as stunning weights and stifling cloth cascaded down on him. There was a world-rattling collision, the rending of timbers. Held fast and smothered in his thrashing, he was borne down. His side throbbed in torment, his head in agony. A malign density settled over his brain. In time, he stopped resisting.

Water, cold, salt-stinging, brought him out of aimless drifting. He came to know that he'd been buried in the bos'n's-stores locker across from his quarters. He could feel spare blocks and deadeyes on him, and lengths of rope holding him, with stretches of canvas oddments over all, intertangled by the ship's gyrations. His first thought was to control his breathing, determined not to go lightheaded again from hyperventilating his scant air supply. He tried two shouts for help; when they produced no result, he stopped, saving air for other things.

Probing, he found one foot unimpeded and began worming down in that direction, bridging with his back, fending carefully with his arms. The life jacket dragged, and a length of line had caught around his thigh. It took several anxious tries and forced patience to work his knife from its sheath and sever himself loose. Inching, twisting, he got a second foot free and rested, wondering if help would show. Another shout produced none, so he presumed the Mariners were busy with other problems. At least the water that had awakened him, dripping down from the deck above, had stopped. Perhaps one of the rail-dragging swells had broken over an open hatch.

A victory; his other foot was out from under. He dug in, pulling more efficiently now, drawing with his legs, heels scraping the deck. His right hand emerged, and with it, he extracted the left, and the knife. There was more cutting, some hawser to unwrap. Then he was through.

He gulped air, sitting on a deck that was wet, but not awash. It was tilted though, as if *Osprey* were taking water in the bow and rocking in the swells. Dirge and Dunstan's sword lay near where they'd fallen. He got them and fumbled his way back as fast as he could.

But on *Osprey*'s deck there was only soaked wreckage. The Mariners had abandoned ship.

Chapter Twenty

Hie, Acre-Fin!
Foam-canyon carver!
May skewed courses spare me
thy dreaded acquaintance!
> from "The Fish that is an Island,"
> a Mariner long-haul chantey

GIL dropped both swords and stumbled to the side, where a boardingnet hung. The fleet was drawing off to the west under full sail. To the southwest, *Stormy Petrel* was nearly gone, the swells crossing her decks. *Osprey's* bow dipped too, the ocean now and again breaking over it. She rode safely enough for the moment, but must be in grievous danger for Landlorn to desert her so cavalierly. There were no boats left.

He waved to the retreating ships, impossibly far off to hail. Teetering on the rail, clinging to a shroud, he gathered all his breath and screamed to the departing Mariners anyhow.

A voice drifted up from the water, "Who calls there?" He thought it had come from astern, and swarmed up the quarterdeck ladder, its pitch steepened by *Osprey's* low-riding bow. Holding on to the spanker boom, he leaned out over the taffrail. A small boat bobbed into view, rowed by Wavewatcher, with Skewerskean in its bow.

He laughed with relief. "I thought I was alone, with one helluva wet stroll home. Come to the side; I'll climb down."

The two friends exchanged looks. "Nay, stay there," Skewerskean replied. "We will come aboard."

Puzzled, Gil returned amidships. When they'd come up the net, he resisted the impulse to babble. There was

192

something wrong beyond the immediate predicament.

"What is it?"

Skewerskean confessed, "We cannot take you after the fleet. We are not going with them."

Gil's forehead hurt. Rubbing it, he found a lump the size of a half-dollar, souvenir of his fall. He massaged it carefully, trying to comprehend what they were telling him. "Are you *both* crazy?"

Wavewatcher bridled. "Acre-Fin struck. *Osprey* and *Stormy Petrel* had to be evacuated immediately, for Acre-Fin will be back."

"Hold the phone now. Give it to me a piece at a time."

"The monster dove, astern. Lookouts in both ships thought they saw it; both helmsmen were confused. They steered closer to each other. Acre-Fin came up under *Osprey*'s port bow, lifting her into the air. She slewed down onto *Stormy Petrel*; fortunate are you not to have seen it. Men fell shrieking from the flagship's masts and decks, while the *Petrel* lacked even the time to put her boats out. Many died."

Gil looked back toward *Stormy Petrel*. Only her masts showed, and they were disappearing quickly. "What about the whatsit, Acre-Fin?"

"It took no more notice of us. It swam eastward, with all speed, for the Isle of Keys."

And Yardiff Bey, Gil said to himself. Skewerskean put in, "It will go to Him who called it up. It will come back to savage the fleet. 'Twas bad luck, that we lay in its course, or maybe the monster attacks whatsoever it encounters on the ocean. But one thing is certain, that it moved toward the Isle with purpose. We think Bey will send it back this way."

"So, let's haul ass outta here!"

The chanteyman shook his head. "The fleet must find shallow water safety if it can. The Prince will need time. So, when they abandoned ship, Wavewatcher and I caught the small boat and hid behind *Osprey*. What with all the confusion, we were overlooked, much as you were. We will delay Acre-Fin, if possible. It must be essayed; the beast will destroy the fleet, else."

Gil's jaw sagged. "I didn't see that thing, but it must be the size of goddam Pike's Peak. Catapults and archers didn't stop it, so you won't either. Now, let's cut the chatter and shove off."

"I have my whalecraft with me," Wavewatcher maintained, "and three hundred fathoms of line coiled in the tubs and poison of the Inner Islanders. I shall coat my lances and harpoon with that. With luck we can divert the monster, at the minimum. In any case, there is nothing else to do. We cannot overtake the fleet now."

The American snarled, kicking a bulwark stanchion. "That coxswain, that bastard, I told him I'd be right back."

"Many had been wounded," the harpooner reproved, "even the Prince's wife, Serene. All was chaos, and you'd been accounted present at your boat station. And the coxswain was among those lost."

Gil was rubbing the lump on his head again. His vision seemed to have blurred. "Okay, you two do what you want." *Osprey* was drifting westward, back through the Strait of the Dancing Spar. "I'm gonna throw me a raft together."

"It might be wiser to come with us," cautioned the harpooner. "If we fail to stop Acre-Fin, we may yet avoid death, but in all likelihood the beast will finish *Osprey* before doing aught else."

Skewerskean shook his friend's shoulder. "This is futile. Come, let us tack upwind, where we may yet stop Acre-Fin from reaching him."

Gil hashed that over. He wasn't about to go out in the suicide boat, but neither did he wish to die if Acre-Fin made it past the two. "Wait a second, you guys." They paused, straddling the rail. He brought Dirge to them, holding the long black blade up.

"Listen, this is Bey's. This stuff on the blade, it's all death runes, annihilation spells. Maybe it'd stop Acre-Fin."

" 'Twould fit a lance's socket," Wavewatcher allowed, reaching to take it.

"Hey, careful. Any cut it makes'll bleed until it kills you." He relinquished it.

Wavewatcher, holding the sword cautiously, eased himself over the side. "Best begin that raft, Gil-O. A sail would be wise, but take a paddle." He went down the boarding net handily.

Skewerskean gripped Gil's forearm. "Truly, if we cannot stop Acre-Fin or turn it, this will be no safe place." He followed his partner. They cast off, set their little lug sail and began tacking eastward. Skewerskean took the tiller. Wavewatcher waved.

"Hey," Gil called, "what happens when I hit the beach? Is there someplace we can hook up again?"

The harpooner smiled, teeth flashing in red tangles. "Should we fail to ride this one out, look for us beside that springlet in your song, what was its name?"

"Huh? Fiddler's Green?"

"Aye. There will we await you."

If those two don't stop that big sucker, that's just where I'm headed, too. He scanned the deck for materials. There was plenty of wood, pieces of spars and mast, rail and deck planks, and miles of rope. He thought about dragging one of the smaller hatch covers off and using it, but had misgivings about how well one would serve in rough seas.

He tried to work out a usable design. He'd never done this sort of thing before; no combination of wood and lashings struck him as stable and buoyant enough for the trip to shore. The knot on his head and the ache in his shoulder were worse. He roped two lengths of spar together and decided they weren't wide enough. Finding an axe in the ship's carpenter's locker, he chopped loose a hunk of fallen fore topmast and found it too short when he tried to fit it in.

A scrap of cloth blew along the deck, and he heard tatters of sail fluttering. A breeze had come up, from the east. The sea was roughening, *Osprey's* bow now plunging beneath the swells. He went aft, and saw that the barque had drifted farther westward. In the distance he could make out the two Mariners, who'd lowered their sail to wait. Clouds closed in, the winds heralding Acre-Fin.

He was astounded, not having thought even a monster like that could swim to the Isle of Keys and back so quickly. No wonder the two Mariners had despaired for their fleet; the ships had no chance of eluding Acre-Fin unaided.

Turbulence moved the water in the distant east. Gil knew he had no time to finish up his raft. His life jacket, he remembered too late, was back among the junk in the bos'n's-stores locker, likely under water by now.

A fish broke the water, then another. In a moment the ocean teemed with creatures fleeing the monster, some of them flopping onto the deck in rainbow spasms. When they'd passed, rain hit, pocking the swells. Shreds of canvas flapped, and the barque wallowed from crest to trough. White froth showed Acre-Fin making straight for the flagship.

He saw Skewerskean and Wavewatcher hoist their sail. The two weren't quite on Acre-Fin's course. Knifing along, wind bellying their canvas, they cut for a point of interception. The rhythm of the monster's strokes sent combers tumbling from the alpine ridge of its gleaming back. Gil could make out the tip of a gigantic dorsal fin and part of the ponderous tail, swaying through beats of incredible power. This was no mammal, but a deep-water fish. Would it stay close enough to the surface for the harpooner to strike?

The Mariners paralleled it riding just ahead to keep out of its crest, but it closed the distance quickly. The boat heeled sharply. There was a twinkle of light from whetted iron. The smooth pattern of the colossal tail fell off for an instant.

Then Acre-Fin bolted straight for *Osprey*, swimming furiously, pricked by the toggle-iron head of Wavewatcher's harpoon, burned by its poison. It bore down on the derelict like an express train. With a surge, its head broke the surface.

Gil looked on in horror. Acre-Fin's head reared. Its eyes, white-glowing circles wider than cartwheels, were without lens or pupil. Cavernous jaws gaped, and the sea broke in waves over and around spiky rows of monolithic teeth. Its underside was encrusted with barnacles and other sessile growth acquired in eons spent brooding in the sea, as if Acre-Fin itself were part fossilized. The ocean, falling back from it, nearly capsized the tiny boat pulled by the harpoon line.

Gil was up on the taffrail now, judging which way to dive. He could see water blown in banners of foam from the tips of the monster's teeth, and the spasms, deep beyond, of the twilight gullet. The wind, sucked down that abyss, made a moaning. Great lateral fins broke the surface, and it seemed they were, in truth, an acre in size.

The American decided to dive toward Veganá. But pausing for a last look, he saw the beast turn in that direction. He checked himself; Acre-Fin was coming around to see what had brought it pain. The Mariners' boat bashed along through the pinnacles of the waves behind it, the two men clinging to their mast, as line-tubs, spare whalecraft and anything else not tied down was bounced into the water.

Wavewatcher had his lance, awaiting the opportunity to use it, but the creature wouldn't give him the chance. It came about, never noticing the tiny boat, bearing eastward in search of whatever had hurt it. It returned to where it had been pricked, found nothing, and went on. The harpooner's poison would have slain anything else alive, but only burned Acre-Fin. The beast knew no enemy had come against it, and so continued the way it had come, assuming it was pursuing its assailant, unaware of the boat jouncing along behind. Gil let himself down off the rail, trembling, waiting for the next crest of water, or the next, to batter the Mariners' boat to splinters.

Acre-Fin grew smaller in the distance. For a long time it bore onward through the Strait of the Dancing Spar. The rain began to let up, the clouds to dissipate. Acre-Fin stopped, mystified that it had overhauled no antagonist. Gil tensed, knowing this was Wavewatcher's moment. It was too far away to see clearly but he thought he caught a black sparkle, as if Dirge had reflected the scant light. The ocean grew still.

There was a fountain of exploding seawater and white froth. A stupendous shape half-cleared the water, twisting monumentally, awesome in size and the proportions of its fury. It came down; waves and concussion sped from it in all directions. Then the monster thrashed in agonized circles, bent in upon its own pain. It seemed doubtful that the harpooner and the chantey-man could outlive their enemy's throes. Gil had no idea how much damage the vindictive magic in Yardiff Bey's sword would do, but sensed that the Children of the Wind-Roads would not be pursued.

The thing stirred in a final fit of torment, then cut

through the water to the east. Its stroke was uneven, conveying grave injury. He followed it until it disappeared, toward the Isle of Keys. For a time he kept surveillance, but saw no sign of the two partners, nor even a fragment of their boat. His vision had become blurry and his head ached, functions of that rap on the head below decks. Concussion was just one more worry, less immediate than his others; he dismissed it.

Leaving the rail, drained, he dragged himself amidships, where wavelets lapped at his half-finished raft. He noticed dazedly that *Osprey* had drifted nearer the shore of Veganá. Perhaps he wouldn't need the raft after all; he sat down listlessly, watching the shore with arms clamped around knees, to wait and see. The barque didn't seem to be taking on any more water. Minute after minute the current dragged her closer to the Crescent Lands.

A roaring penetrated his fog. He knew he'd heard it before. With electric fear, he recalled where. Looking up suddeny, he fell to the deck. *Cloud Ruler* was speeding toward *Osprey* on pillars of demon-fire. Insight came; Acre-Fin had in fact returned to the man who'd called it up. Yardiff Bey had seen the creature was wounded by his own sword, Dirge. He'd known who was out here on the ocean. He'd come.

Gil charged across the deck to the hatch cover. Slight hope, it was better than the unfinished raft. He heaved the edge up, got a shoulder under, and crouched beneath. *Cloud Ruler* circled in; he felt its scorching heat even at this distance, bringing steam off the water.

He lunged, biting his lip, lifting. His vision darkened with the exertion, the pounding lump on his head threatening blindness. In an effort of animal survival, he got the hatch cover up and overboard.

He was seen. The demon-ship swept through a snapping turn, the ocean boiling beneath it. Gil flung himself back, one arm to his face to ward off superheated vapor. Coughing, eyes tearing, he lurched at the opposite rail, to swim or die. Bey's craft came around, blocking that route too with fire and steam. He pushed himself away, tripping backward on the slick deck. The demon-ship hovered, unavoidable.

From a bay on its underbelly, weighted nets fell, covering *Osprey*'s small remaining deck. He clapped his hand to Dunstan's sword, but they hit first, carrying him to his knees, enmeshing him. He started sawing strands with his knife.

Vibrations traveled down the netting. Shapes rapelled quickly down landing ropes carrying swords, clubs and catch-poles. He had two strands cut when the first Southwastelander touched down on *Osprey*.

A tall, burly Occhlon, the man pounced on him. Three others hit the deck and did the same. More came after. He thrust with knife; his wrist was caught and wrenched around. There was no room to get out Dunstan's sword. Nightmare fight, its single mercy was brevity. Battered, disarmed, immobilized, he came into the dire captivity of the Hand of Shardishku-Salamá.

Chapter Twenty-one

My soul, the seas are rough, and thou a
  stranger . . .

Francis Quarles
Emblems

SAILS clewed up, the masts of the anchored fleet rested untenanted, fewer now, with *Osprey* and *Stormy Petrel* consigned to the uncaring ocean. In the distant southeast, the Isle of Keys was sunlit by a break in the clouds, as if blessed.

Landlorn had transferred his flag to *Wind Gatherer*, a three-masted square-rigger, precursor to *Osprey*. He'd already envisioned his next vessel, a lean, swift clipper, all a sailing ship should be. His drawing table was stacked with preliminary plans, where frame lines, waterlines and buttocks curved and intersected sweetly. Now they lay aside, until a time of peace.

The Prince Who Sails Forever returned his attention

to matters in question. Seated in his cabin were allies who were to help conquer the Isle of Keys. The Trustee of Glyffa and her son Andre were there, with Lord Blacktarget of Veganá and Angorman, of the Order of the Axe. Swan, the Glyffan Constable, attended too, as did Landlorn's wife Serene, who'd nearly recovered from the injury to her back taken when Acre-Fin had struck.

The tents of an armed camp covered the hills above the shore of Veganá. Hundreds of banners and war pennants had been set side by side along the beach, to let the Southwastelanders on the Isle know that the fighting wasn't done yet. Galvanized by the Trailing-sword, the allied armies had fought their way to the end of the Crescent Lands, breaking their enemies' last stand within view of the sea.

Ready to go on to the Isle, the Crescent Landers had found no boat, not even a cockle shell, along the entire shore. Landlorn's forces had been there weeks before, destroying every craft they could find to deny South-wastelanders the sea. With no way to negotiate the turbulent Strait, the allies had sat for days weighing various plans. More than half their strength was, by then, of commoners, free vassals and yeomen.

"We know Yardiff Bey is on the Isle," the Trustee was saying, gnarled fingers holding the Crook of her office. "We did not see the summoning of Acre-Fin. I sensed sorcery, but could not interfere at such a distance. The thing returned to Bey, and I could perceive only that it was wounded or dying. It no longer swims these waters, though I cannot say whether or not it survived. I doubt the sorcerer shall ever bend Acre-Fin to his will again; it will shun him, after this.

"We saw *Cloud Ruler* go forth, and later return. Would that he had tried to fly over Glyffa! How are your two crewmen, who speared the sea monster?"

Acre-Fin's throes had smashed their boat to wooden chips, leaving Wavewatcher unconscious and Skewer-skean swimming for them both. Fortunately, they'd gone unmenaced by sharks or other predators; in the proximity of Acre-Fin, no fish dared linger or hunt. The harpooner had roused at last, and together they'd managed to struggle ashore. There, they'd been met by the northerners. Landlorn had concluded that something had deterred the monster, and sent elements of his fleet for cautious inquiry. Attracted by the northerners' signal fires, they'd found Wavewatcher, Skewerskean and an army of allies.

"They are in the fo'c'sle now," the Prince answered, "as royally inebriate as when you so kindly returned them to us. I shall have to reward them, apparently; I could hardly swear a charge of disobedience against them, after all."

"And Gil MacDonald?" Andre prodded. Swan, who'd foreborn asking, waited noncommittally.

Landlorn gestured helplessly. "*Osprey* had long since sunk, of course. Skewerskean saw *Cloud Ruler* pass overhead, but whether the young man was taken or drowned, I cannot say."

"Dead is more to be expected," Angorman pronounced. "I do not deem him one to go alive into the grasp of Yardiff Bey."

"Unfortunate," Lord Blacktarget remarked perfunctorily, "but less to be concerned with than that which lies before us. How shall we whelm the Isle of Keys?"

"An arduous undertaking," the Prince admitted. "It is defended well, if not so well as our Citadel. They are stranded, and cannot withdraw. Every ship and boat was being used to sustain their war in the Crescent Lands when we caught them in open waters. Oh, no doubt some few craft escaped, but those are negligible."

Andre countered, "Time is Yardiff Bey's dearest commodity, not men. His design is twofold, to win the secret of Rydolomo's book and hinder us from following the Trailingsword to Salamá. In the first, at least, he has been successful, in part because he has been prodigal with manpower. So, I would be surprised if the desert men didn't stand and fight, ships or no. It may be that the sorcerer will do the same. His arts will be more effective there, away from the influences of the Bright Lady, and if the Five have enriched him with their favor, he will wax confident."

"Of that we shall discover," Lord Blacktarget declared loftily, hand at the hilt of Blazetongue. "We do not despair of it; the Mariners have but to take us to the Isle; we will deal with things from there."

201

No one chose to point out his arrogance, though Swan shifted in her seat. Nowadays, Blacktarget insisted that his banner go always in the van, and often took a high-handed tone with the others, even the Trustee. The Trustee permitted it, and enjoined the rest to do so. Breaking the schemes of the Five justified almost any expedient.

"But there is still the question of entrance to the harbor," the old woman reminded.

"The Mariners will accomplish that," Landlorn told her, "then bring you in, one and all. The task will be yours from there."

"And relished will it be," Swan finished softly, staring past the quarter-gallery railing at the Isle of Keys.

The Prince had a captured southern vessel brought up early the next morning. Allied soldiers were crowding aboard his other ships, many of which had been hastily converted to bear horses, and others to be packed with troops. Loading had gone on throughout the night.

The Southwastelander bottom, a big galleass with a high, creneled fighting castle in her bow and one in the poop, along with storming bridges, had been readied for Landlorn's plan. Mariners, not chained slaves, sat her rowing benches; her bow and forward tower were loaded with casks of the burning fluid the seafarers used, with more lashed near her iron beak.

The fleet formed behind the galleass and stood out into the Strait of the Dancing Spar. Closer to the Isle, the Prince ordered the casks of fluid covered with water-soaked tarps. The decks, sail and fighting tower were doused for a second time by bucket brigades of sailors.

The Isle had been filed fine by eons of the rip-currents of the Strait. Any approach except that for the sea-gates was guarded by rocks and shoals. Landlorn handed his narwhale staff to his wife and ordered all hands away, except two.

That pair was Wavewatcher and Skewerskean, who'd named, as reward for laying for Acre-Fin, accompaniment of their Prince today. When the boats were away

202

like so many water striders, he ordered, "Look sharp you two, and attend my every command."

"As we do always," intoned Skewerskean humbly.

"As you do when it bloody suits you, brazen man!" The pair exchanged wounded glances. Landlorn laughed. "Nay, take no hurt; you did serve Gale-Baiter well, and thus me. But it was ever rashly. So, enjoy this last frolic, lads; if we come through, I mean to teach you responsibility."

That put doubt in their faces. At his direction, they pulled ropes to open all mainsail clews. The broad lateen was set, stiffened in the wind. Landlorn had positioned the vessel so she'd bear in straight for the gates, before the wind. Cleaving steeplechasing swells, she held every eye in the fleet and on the sea walls.

Fire arrows and missiles lofted from the defenders even before the galleass was in range. Wavewatcher, at the tiller, surrounded by braced pavise-shields, stretched his muscles to hold course when the ship's roll or caprices of current tried to take her off it. Empty but for the casks, she moved lightly, but somewhat skittishly; it took all the harpooner's sinew to curb her in the restless waters.

Arrows began to thud into the deck at extreme distance, but the wetting kept them from spreading flame. Fireballs flung by the wall engines, unstable in flight, missed the galleass, which was still too far out for accuracy. But a huge ballista bolt drove its iron head completely through the deck, doing no other damage.

The mast and deck grew thick with a porcupine's coat of shafts; there were dozens of holes in the sail. Another fireball arced, thrown high because range was closing. Landlorn saw, and warned Wavewatcher. Setting his foot against the binnacle, the big harpooner threw his head back and bunched his muscles, dragging at the tiller. The galleass shifted for a moment, and the fireball exploded on the water in sparks and spray. The redbeard threw everything he had against the tiller, to bring the ship back on course.

The lateen mainsail took fire at last, but had been soaked well, so that the flames ate their way only slowly. On her way to her death, the galleass paid no heed to the minor hurts of stones and shafts. Gradually,

203

the distance was eaten up, as Southwastelanders readied long poles to push back the scaling ladders they still
expected to repel.

The three men crouched under showers of arrows,
javelins and toss-darts, barely able to peer around their
shields. A stone from a mangonel, bouncing from the
armored fighting castle at the bow, slammed through
the deck and hull, opening the galleass to the sea as she
came within a dozen lengths of the gates. The Occhlon,
having received no counterfire, saw now that the fighting castles and storming bridges were unmanned. Then
someone marked the casks in the bow, and a cry went
up; the southerners withheld their own fire-fluid, fearing the conflagration it would start.

The sharp iron ram bit into the timbers of the sea-
gates with hungry, resounding impact. The Prince ran
forward under a pavise-shield.

Soldiers began dropping from the wall. Many missed
the deck, sinking into the sea in their armor. Others
were stunned by their fall and didn't rise, but several
made the drop and assembled themselves. Wavewatcher
and Skewerskean took shields too, and charged after
their Liege. They engaged the southerners, sounding a
harsh chord of blades. The Prince snatched a lighted
lamp from a locker, threw aside one corner of a tarp
and dashed it against the casks. Fire caught; in moments the bow of the galleass and the sea around it
were burning. The forward castle caught quickly, becoming a roaring chimney. No more Southwastelanders
jumped from the wall.

The Mariners retreated astern, driven as much by
heat as swords. The Occhlon broke off the fight. Casks
were exploding, flinging globs of burning jelly in all directions. The water sizzled with them, and a stench of
black smoke expanded. Landlorn had arranged for the
forward tower's supports to be weakened. Now it leaned
toward the bow, spilling burning fluid, coating the
gates, creating an inferno.

Hunched behind their shields, partially screened by
drifting smoke, the three stripped off their armor. Cast-
ing aside cutlasses and shields, they dove. A dart took
the Prince as he launched himself; his clean dive became a flaccid splash. He didn't surface. The two part-

ners plunged down after him. Behind them, the sea-gates stood in a curtain of flame.

In a moment they were up again, Wavewatcher's python of an arm clamped across his Liege's chest. With Skewerskean's aid, he struggled through the churning sea, racing against spreading fire. There was no sign of the southerners who'd dropped to the galleass. The larger ships had been ordered to keep distance, but a small boat put out with shields and willing oarsmen. The wall's defenses were hidden in black clouds. Fed by the wind, held fast by her iron ram, the pyre-galleass was inextinguishable.

From *Wind Gatherer* there were cheers from men in the rigging and on deck. The boat drew alongside, and the Prince of the Waves acknowledged them weakly. Caps flew and cutlasses glittered. Men clashed weapons on shields or thumped the deck, repeating the name of the Prince Who Sails Forever.

Serene welcomed her lord back, helping staunch a wound not half so bad as she'd feared. He and the harpooner and chanteyman sat, dripping, backs against the mast, sharing a flask of rum. Serene sat by her mate, brushing away tears, the brine soaking her skirt. She mussed his hair and hugged him.

He drew her to him and planted a salty kiss. " 'Twas my last deed, I trow. Never shall I leave your side again."

The inferno blazed on, the gates' hinges weakening while the attackers bided their time. The Occhlon couldn't man their primary defenses for the heat and smoke; the galleass' forward castle had collapsed completely. With no threat of answering fire, Mariner ships moved up to lob huge stones and other projectiles.

Consumed, bombarded, the gates gave way in the end, peeling back their hinges. With a shrill hiss, still barred together, they were dragged down by the sinking galleass. The deep channel there left way for ships to advance over the sunken vessel and wreckage.

The Southwastelanders, lacking ships, had made other preparations. The first craft into the harbor was pierced by sharpened wooden piles emplaced with points beneath the surface. Landlorn called a dead halt while the stricken vessel's crew transferred to other ships. The Prince had foreseen this; scores of Mariners stripped off armor and clothing, took shipwright's saws, and slid into the water, lithe as eels. They tackled the piles, diving deep and working feverishly. A safe route was cleared, marked by inflated bladders anchored to the sunken stumps. By late morning the advance was underway again.

At the quayside it was combat on foot, with Lord Blacktarget in the van. The Crescent Landers didn't have time or room to off-load horses, and the isolated Southwastelanders had slaughtered theirs for food. The first ships at the docks were those with high, fortified decks, giving the invaders equal height with the hasty breastwork thrown up by defenders. Still, two ships were overrun and set afire, hampering the rest.

Men and women struggled and fought on the quays. The boarding pike and hooked bill, the cutlass, axe and scimitar all had their hour. Iron argument met steel rebuttal.

Swan, first among the Glyffans to land, was confronted by a willing Occhlon with a pike, its blade already showing red. He came in a low line to cut her legs away and, ideally, follow through with a stab from his weapon's steel-pointed butt. The High Constable pivoted away shield-side. She cut; the pike head came in parry with a return stroke for her exposed side. She backstepped, counter-parrying.

Instead of riposting, she slid her blade down the pikestaff and lodged it at the narrow grip and vamplate, drawing the Occhlon forward off balance. She swung the edge of her shield into his face. He fell back, but clung to his weapon. She swung and scored, shearing flesh off blue-white bone. He moaned and clasped at his wound; she dispatched him. Sisters of the Line poured past her.

Fighting spilled into side streets and alleys; neither side knew restraint. Combat went from house to house, the desert men retreated, flung back twice from new positions. The invaders kept the initiative, as cavalry began to appear from the quays.

By late afternoon, stern men and women of the Crescent Lands stalked through the smoky streets, going from clash to new clash. Where there had been no quarter asked or given, battered and demoralized Southwastelanders now began to surrender, first in small numbers when cut off, later in outnumbered companies. By sunset, the city belonged to the northerners. Only the central Keep above it remained unconquered.

Aboard *Wind Gatherer*, the Trustee turned to Landlorn. "Prince of the Waves, your share is well done. But the moment of sail and sword is past. One more enemy will be waiting, in the Keep. Time is here to test my puissance against Yardiff Bey's."

Swan was dubious. Andre challenged, "Is it wise? Here, your strength is not so absolute."

"Granted, but it should suffice. In any case, the thing must be done. He has waited; I am expected."

"Then," he let her know, "I will go at your side."

Landlorn bowed deeply. The Trustee reciprocated, and squeezed Serene's hand. Swan thought there was too much of farewell in it all. Surrounded by warriors and swordswomen, the old woman made her patient way up to the summit and its Keep. They found its portals open.

Lord Blacktarget was already there. "These doors swung wide on their own accord when you came." The Trustee, lifting her Crook, ordained that the rest must wait while she and Andre went in. Lord Blacktarget took exception.

"Madam, I will not linger behind. If Glyffans may go in, the Commander of Veganá will."

Veganáns and Glyffans muttered among themselves, eyeing one another. Blacktarget hadn't said as much, but suspected he'd be deprived of spoils and prestige.

Andre would have objected; his mother stopped him, seeing that the alliance could fall apart. "He has right, however unwise. But My Lord Blacktarget, your hardy enthusiasm for war is too fulsome for me by half. You would be well advised to be wary."

Red-faced, he blustered, "Madam, Blacktarget is well able to fend for himself."

They entered, and followed the long, unlit curve of a corridor. Behind them, the doors closed up by themselves. Then there was light from the Trustee's Crook. There was no search, no delay. At the end of the corridor, in a high, torchlit hall, Yardiff Bey waited. Andre

207

motioned for Lord Blacktarget to stay back, but the general, all in his pride, marched in, and they had no moment to prevent him.

The sorcerer stood in a limestone pulpit far above the floor, his silver occular gleaming in the crimson light. He was calm and supremely self-assured. "He is Increased," Andre discerned.

Bey chuckled quietly. "You see aright, worm. My Masters, well pleased, rewarded their servant."

The Trustee spoke. "Your mission is fulfilled? Then, why are you here? Why have you not flown back to your Necropolis in the south?"

"In due course. I knew your armies would win the Isle from those starvelings and you would deem yourself victorious and come here. Of the garrison I care not; if they cost time and sapped northern numbers they were well spent. I tarried to let you pit yourself against me."

"If your assignment is complete, yet you may have gained less than you think. The war goes against you."

The Hand of Salamá laughed, making that act ugly, his robes rippling his mirth. "Your last hope is gone. Listen: There was a final limb of the Lifetree, though its parent plant had been thrown down. Rydolomo knew whither it had been taken, and left the fact in-hidden within *Arrivals Macabre*. That could have threatened Shardishku-Salamá, but that limb's fate is known to me now; it is unmade. No other thing can interfere with the schedule of my Masters, not all the arms-bearers on earth. I have seen that gulling Trailingsword; this time it only beckons you to oblivion. There is no avail for you, you will go no farther. Not even a step."

Yardiff Bey gestured, and the floor surged up beneath them.

Chapter Twenty-two

But yet I know, where'er I go,
That there hath past away a glory from the earth.
        William Wordsworth
        Ode: Intimations of Immortality

ANDRE and the Trustee made Signs of protection against upheaval, but Lord Blacktarget had none. The general clung to the quaking floor. His two companions had attention only for the sorcerer.

The ruler of Glyffa held up her cursive-lettered Crook. An aura crackled around it, magic of the Bright Lady. Roof beams groaned, and dust sifted down. The Keep shivered to unleashed enchantment. Blasts of superheated air and icy wind chased one another through the chamber. Thunder cracked from wall to wall.

Yardiff Bey threw down the counterattack, holding his own extreme efforts in reserve, until they should exhaust themselves. Their assault was fierce, but not so much so that it penetrated his wards. The Trustee was weary, and the sorcerer's new power given by the Five would, he was positive, give him the duel.

But as the deCourteneys built their offensives, they began to reinforce each other, as with Andre and his sister. They weren't overwhelming, but the Hand of Salamá began to consider employing the wiles he'd prepared.

As mystic discharges washed around him, striving to topple him, he conceived another tactic. Resisting the deCourteneys, he took aside a little of his energies and hurled a quick spell at the vulnerable Lord Blacktarget. The general went cartwheeling, long campaigner's cloak gathering around him, constricting breath from his

209

body. Its drawstring sank into the flesh of his neck. He writhed on the stone, kicking, struggling.

Andre saw his plight. Sweat flowed from the squat wizard's face, his arts extended beyond any previous mark. Without looking, the Trustee knew what had happened. Bey's resources were in excess of what she'd expected; she was very much in need of her son's sustenance. Yet, she couldn't bring herself to make Andre let another innocent die, as she had compelled him to do a century before.

"Succor him," she encouraged, her stare never leaving the Hand of Salamá. Andre rushed to Lord Blacktarget. The general's face was darkening, eyes bulging, bloated tongue swelling in his mouth. It was as the sorcerer had intended. He'd withheld much of his prepotency; now he revealed it, lashing out at the Trustee. To Amon's gift of augmented energy, Yardiff Bey had added his own ingredient of treachery.

The old woman staggered. Flooring blocks ground together beneath her feet, and overhead a wide section of roof was flung away by backlashing of competing incantations. She mustered her fullest effort, surprising Bey; it was more than he'd estimated. Almost, it was enough. She contained his attack and launched one of her own with an explosion of blue radiance from her Crook, jolting the Hand backward with vehemence. His defense faltered. Again the Crook flared, but less brightly. Depleted, with her son's support diverted, her endurance failed. The light in the rune-written Crook flickered. Andre, toiling at Blacktarget's side, sensed it and turned to give a moment's aid to her. In that instant her will let go. She was smashed down by the spells of Yardiff Bey as by the waters of a dam that had burst.

The Crook fell from her thin hand, dimming. The sorcerer's magic flashed triumphantly. Before he could pour into her the support she'd needed, Andre had seen her life torn from her. The symbol of her Trusteeship lay dark now. At the same time, the cord tightened around Blacktarget's neck, killing him.

From Andre's throat came a wail. From depths of instinct, he invoked a wizardry that crashed black fury at Bey's defenses. The sorcerer's most trusted protections were in jeopardy; his antagonist's attack, more vicious than Yardiff Bey had thought him capable of making, was barely turned. The Hand of Salamá had to shore up his endangered wards.

Andre, in his wrath, called down his curse in a voice of such volume that cracks shot along the stone walls. His enmity beamed at the Hand, who was pounded backward a second time, bewildered at this new ferocity.

Andre raised up his left fist, and blue lightning spat and snapped. He cried a spell of destruction so terrible that the roof beams began to split and pull themselves down. Bey parried desperately, bracing them back by his arts. Andre lifted his right fist up, howled again, and blue magic of the deCourteneys shone from it like a beacon. The stone floor fissured open with a rumble, belching deep-earth fumes, tossing Yardiff Bey to his knees. For the first time, the sorcerer thought of opening the ocular, but wasn't sure that even that extremity would help.

The limestone pulpit tottered. Andre summoned up blue, plasmic hatred in a last dreadful bolt. It was insignificant if the Keep were broken in pieces and swallowed up, or the Isle itself consumed by the ocean. In primal malice, he cared only that Yardiff Bey die.

An arcane aura swirled around him. He gathered it in, hands outstretched. The sorcerer saw with amazement that all his newfound energies were no match, in this moment, for deCourteney's stark emotion. But he had a last, hidden recourse, short of the ocular. Reaching behind him, he drew up the captive who'd lain, dazed and motionless, out of sight at the rear of the pulpit. Andre's hands swept around in unison, funneling their forces.

Gil MacDonald felt himself hauled up, sick and weak, from half-dreams of storm and lightning. He remembered little since the Southwastelanders had taken him, beaten, into captivity, to be held in occult sedation. Now Yardiff Bey's unnaturally strong hands used him as shield.

Andre spied Gil at the last instant, as his bolt went out, too late. He blurted a Dismissal on the heels of his own spell, but was only partially effective. The American's body arched backward in spasms, wreathed in vines of azure light, as Bey snatched his hands back. The wizard broke off his attack. Gil went stiff, eyes rolled up into his head, tongue bulging in his gullet. No pain had ever been as bad as the one in his chest. Awareness slid away.

Andre, appalled, stood motionless, hands slumped to his sides, mouth agape. Bey had the American's body up again, in front of him, backing away. At the rear of the pulpit, he escaped into pitch darkness, taking his hostage.

The ground shuddered beneath the rent floor. Roof beams groaned, splitting, raining slivers of wood. Andre shook himself from his disorientation and saw he couldn't repair them. He'd done things in his transport of fury that he'd never match or undo in any sane moment. He bent, took up his mother and her Crook in one arm and Lord Blacktarget over his shoulder, and lumbered, ungainly, for the entrance.

Outside, in gathering night, Swan and Angorman were preparing to enter. They'd held back, hearing the conflict, knowing there was little they could do, but their anxiety had gone past their control. Just in that moment, Andre came.

Seeing the Trustee in death, the High Constable lost all color. Men of Veganá clustered to their slain Commander.

The Keep's roof collapsed, and the stronghold fell in on itself, into the earth-cleft. Clouds of dust and subterranean gas rose, and the Isle trembled under their feet. The shocks sent other portions of the fortifications into rubble, with creneled turrets and ramparts following the donjon into the earth. Waves in the harbor tossed the anchored Mariner fleet around like toys.

From the ruin a silvery shape lifted on streamers of demon-fire. *Cloud Ruler* swung southward; the sorcerer only wanted the Isle of Keys behind him. There would be ample time to deal with deCourteney; next time, the wizard would have no tidal wave of emotion upon which to draw.

At the lip of the crater where the Keep had vanished, Andre bent over his mother. Swan ordered her Sisters of the Line to build a pyre, thinking of her brother Jade's words. "The last of the Old have passed away,"

212

she whispered. Men of Veganá began mourning dirges for Lord Blacktarget.

Andre shut out his grief and called Swan and the other captains. He issued directives for disposition of captives and departure. The subordinates looked at one another uncertainly. Some bridled at orders from an outlander.

But the wizard's mien was locked, with unspeakable anger riding his brow; no one would risk defying him. Angorman proclaimed, "The rein has passed to your grip."

Swan went to do as he'd said. The men of Veganá, seeing it, did the same. "Tell the Prince of the Waves to make him ready," Andre said, "and begin reloading our picked forces at once."

"The winds give that no favor," Angorman cautioned.

"There will be wind to overfill all sails, I vow." Andre took up the Crook of the Trustee, and removed the arming girdle and scabbarded Blazetongue from Lord Blacktarget's body, slinging it over his shoulder. He looked south, where Yardiff Bey had gone. The Trailingsword hung in the sky there; he shook his fist toward the Necropolis, and it left a blue glow in its wake.

"We come! If that Lifetree is destroyed, and you are invulnerable, I care not. Salamá, we come."

Two days after the invasion, one of the Isle's taprooms had been revivified. The place had been called the Dogfish; its shrewd young proprietress had buried barrels and cases of her best under a false floor in the celleret when the Occhlon had come, months earlier. She'd dug them up and reincarnated her establishment, naming it the Broken Yoke. She'd scarcely unlocked her door when two Mariners crowded in, and began depleting her modest stock.

" 'Tis the source of no small bitterness," Wavewatcher complained a little later, "this reaping unkindness where the harvest ought to have been gladsome thanks." He was squiggling doodles on the tabletop with moisture from their tankard rings.

"If our intermittent shortcoming has been disregard

213

of orders," Skewerskean added, "why, 'twas done holding the Mariners' best interests uppermost. Most times."

Foxglove, the proprietress, she of the tumbling sable locks and swaying hips, was bringing their next round. "Wherefore are these complaints? Is it so perishing unpleasant to be put in authority over your own ship?"

The harpooner growled, "Life becomes charts, schedules, manifests—"

"He feels worse about it," Skewerskean confided to her, "because he was named captain."

"Pay calls, customs men, pilot's fees—" the redbeard droned.

"And I am first officer, purser and supercargo."

"—ship's log, inventories, credentials—"

"We can embark on compensatory business ventures only, or the Prince promises to make us grease-boys in the sculleries."

"*And,*" finished Wavewatcher, pointing to the ceiling, "just try getting a goddam shipwright to pick up a mallet without letting him hold the mortgage on your oysters!" He plucked up another drink.

"Oh, la!" Foxglove commiserated, "the weight of the world, hmm?"

"We always saw that it threatened," Skewerskean admitted, counting out her exorbitant price, "and avoided it also. But the Prince had replacements to appoint, and we are both qualified." The chanteyman held her hand now, playing his fingers over her wrist. She gave a preliminary tug, not completely unhappy with that intersport. "Telling no to a Prince is one of those matters better left unassayed."

The door's opening, admitting another customer, interrupted the game as Foxglove whirled her hand free. Wavewatcher, scrutinizing the man framed in the light, let out a snort. "There; all courses cross in time, just as is said by the old grand-daddies. You are a long haul from your Earthfast, old son, and farther yet from the High Ranges."

Ferrian took a chair with them, the toll of diligent riding apparent on him. "Your memory is spry. I congratulate you on the news I had at the docks, that you two have arisen in this world. I was seeking a ship and, hearing your names, thought it could be no others but you."

"Pray waste not those well-wishes," Foxglove advised from behind the bar. "Success depresses them."

The Horseblooded told them, "I arrived at the coast this morning, and ferried over on one of these supply ships that are ending the starvation here. I am informed I am too late to speak to Andre deCourteney."

"As all will attest," replied Skewerskean. "The wizard enlisted our Prince's further aid, half by plea and half by statement inflexible. They sailed for the South-wastelands, and all those allies and mounts with 'em, in great haste and with precious little ullage. The Trustee was slain in combat with Yardiff Bey, as was Lord Blacktarget, but the Crook and that especial sword Blazetongue go on with Andre deCourteney."

Ferrian was nodding. "I had the tale from a Glyffan woman, and heard this news of Gil MacDonald as well. I thought the balance of these hodge-podge soldiers would go along soon, but there are some to garrison the Isle, and others to be set back on the Crescent Lands."

"Aye. That wizard did insist, all speed and mobility was his preoccupation. Hence, most foot soldiers stayed here."

"Where will the fleet make landfall?"

The chanteyman was playing with his tankard. "Not near here. Observers report amassed southerners, frustrated with their lack of passage ships. The Prince and deCourteney, avoiding them, were making southeast. The wizard called up the very air, filling all sailcloth. Common thought has him landing farther east, where he can drive toward Shardishku-Salamá with less resistance."

"And the Crescent Landers put themselves under him?"

"Well, the Sisters of the Line are under their commander, that Swan, and the Veganáns have some interim general, but they did indeed obey the wizard. All of them were angry for the deaths of the two great leaders, and time and again Blacktarget and the Trustee publicized that the Trailingsword must be heeded. And so, too, thinks the Prince Who Sails Forever. Off they all sailed."

215

Ferrian leaned forward. "Everyone, is that so? Angorman too? Well, my hearty sea-rovers, it falls to me to catch up to that fleet as soon as ever I may. Is it enough to hear that many lives ride with it?"

Their faces perked up. Until this moment life had been a dreary sentence of sober industry. For the Horse-blooded's words there was the enthusiasm reserved for stays of execution.

"We can accept only offers of business," Skewerskean reminded his friend and captain, "on the Prince's order."

The tall Rider frowned, left hand burrowing in his pouch. He came up with a pair of copper bits, all the money he had left from what Silverquill had managed to find for him. He laid the little pellets on the table, where they clicked together, a preposterous sum with which to purchase passage.

"They'll do," Wavewatcher announced, and scooped them up. Foxglove shook her head unbelievingly.

"But can you overhaul them in the fleet?"

"Horseman, meseems 'tis fundamental; breezes that drive them eastward must pass us. Or if not, we may still make our attempt."

Skewerskean warned, "The Prince will see us hung." But he threw back his drink, rising to go.

Over his shoulder, Wavewatcher called to Ferrian, "Meet us on the quay in the half-hour, and all will be ready." To the chanteyman, he philosophized, "Remuneration is remuneration; nobody ever said anything about *profit,* witling."

Ferrian watched them go, then chortled down into his drink with the humor of long sleeplessness. He caught Foxglove staring at him quizzically, and raised the toast to her. "Here's to as perceptive a pair of businessmen as this old world ever saw, and to good ends for two-penny rovers."

PART IV

❦

Proprieties of the Apocalypse

Chapter Twenty-three

And when fate summons, monarchs must obey
> John Dryden
> *MacFlecknoe*

THERE was no elation to be had from this rallying of blazonries, clan totems and banners of war at Seaguard. Coramonde, generations' labor of the *Ku-Mor-Mai*, was coming undone in rebellion and civil strife.

Springbuck had been working toward a time when, his realm secure, he could gather a host here and sail for Shardishku-Salamá. But he hadn't envisioned it this way, a desperate rush to gather what troops he could and confront the Masters while it still was possible. He'd left trusted Honuin Granite Oath in command, yet even Earthfast was no longer secure.

Springbuck's decision to cast all his strength southward, and not stand fast in a wasted effort to subdue Coramonde, had come hard. His every instinct had told him to hold on, as his ancestors had done, to grip the suzerainty with the martial fist. But, from what he knew of Bey and of Salamá, Coramonde couldn't be saved if the Five worked uninterrupted.

"Can I expect further loyal contingents?" he asked his Warlord.

Hightower sighed, raising frosty-white eyebrows. "Communication has fallen apart. Some have sent you knights and scutage and men at arms, and posted the call along to those they trust. The strike force that was Bonesteel's own before his death stayed true, made a forced march here, flying the crimson tiger and your own stag's head.

"We may expect no more from Honuin Granite Oath either, than that he hold Earthfast and some of the suzerainty. So, we have a quiltwork. There are archers from Rugor, Clansmen from Teebra, four of the war-drays of Matloo dispatched by loyalist septs, and your personal guardsmen who number less than two companies. Oh, and members of the Constabulary of the Way continue to drift in. There is also Balagon and his One Hundred, the Brotherhood of the Bright Lady, along with a good part of the Order of the Axe. Strange, to see them more in comradeship now than enmity. But those are all you have, and a goodly part of Coramonde in chaos."

"As it would be," informed Gabrielle deCourteney, "whether you stay or go. Salamá has many intrigues incubating in Coramonde, and cares not which ones hatch, so long as there is discord and confusion." Her wide mouth smiled, dimpling, sardonic. "Put aside any idea that you two could have held on here, my desperadoes; that is what the Five would most have liked to see."

Springbuck's chin was against his chest. "But our roster here is short. Militarily speaking, this is farce."

"Practically speaking, it is inescapable," she parried. "You not only lack the means to shore up your throne. You lack the *time*."

He resettled himself in his plush chair, considering that. The three were met in the palace of the King of Seaguard, who'd kept fealty to the *Ku-Mor-Mai*. Though the drapes were fastened against night airs, the conferees could hear the gulls mourning over Bold-haven Bay. "The Mariners are waging war on the sea, and winning against the Southwastelanders. The King of Seaguard would give the ships needed."

"Few as we are, we have small hope to conquer the Southwastelands," Hightower reminded him, "much less lay siege to the Masters."

Gabrielle, exasperated, tapped her toe. They knew it was a danger signal, and listened. "You do not understand yet, nor does Springbuck; your goal is to penetrate *through* to the Necropolis, and *not* in order to mount some crude siege.

"I told you of the séance with Gil MacDonald, when I gave him the Ace of Swords. Since that night I've had my busy ear to the half-world and the tidings its creatures carry. I have read auguries and scrutinized the stars, deciphered the fall of the knucklebones, and taken the meanings of entrails." Where she was usually light-spirited, even in the gravest matters, she was somber. "This upheavel is conceived to fend us off from the Five and their pursuits; it is the sort of thing about which Andre warned. The Masters think you two can launch no offensive, all in your disarray. Before we can act, they are confident, their real labors will bear fruit."

Springbuck played with the basket hilt of his sabre, Bar. No more ceremonial trappings for him; he'd chosen to wear his old attire of an Alebowrenian bravo on his excursion to Seaguard. He'd undoubtedly have more use for vambraces and war mask than brocade and silk.

"What would be their crop?" he wondered.

"Ultimate spellbinding. It could wipe away the world."

"Can it be stopped?"

"Everything can be stopped, even time itself, *Ku-Mor-Mai*. But this endeavor cannot be foiled from here. Shardishku-Salamá is like some smelting furnace of magic; it cannot be extinguished by half-measures, or from afar. We may go to it and do what arms and enchantments can, but from Coramonde we can achieve nothing."

Springbuck clicked his tongue and tapped Bar's pommel. "Then you prevail, Gabrielle. I'd hoped to avoid this war for a time."

Hightower was on his feet. "As easy to reject the flood or deny the avalanche. Spare us your regrets; you know little enough of what awaits you."

His tone dropped. "We may yet see a time of cataclysm like no other. Drums tell the world to march. Cast out your wise men, *Ku-Mor-Mai*! Drive them from you and listen to the epistles of your flesh; the gales of war speak *your* name tonight! Take the rede your hackles send you; study the writ of your bowels. There's where verity resides now."

"My Lord Hightower." The sorceress stopped him. "Cast no more shadows. Salamá has thrown quite enough of those."

He subsided, going to monotone. "Preparation may prove futile, and forethought will be no protection; I did

220

but warn him." To Springbuck he added, "There will only be the guidance that lives in the marrow."

The younger man rose. "If that's the shape of things, we'll do as best we may, to stop this thing unknown by thaumaturgy or hand-strokes. But first we must look upon it."

She whirled on him, enraged. "Unknown to you!" In a temper she was capable of anything, and a Protector-Suzerain was no safer than any other man. Springbuck held himself carefully.

"We have had our glimpse at it, your Warlord and I," she continued, her hand to the old man's cheek. Hightower's chain-mailed arm encircled her. Springbuck left, closing the door behind.

His name was called. Captain Brodur caught up, breathing hard, his bared sword in his hand. It was he who'd brought the first warning of revolt, because his home fief had been first to be lost. Brodur, visiting his family, had risen from bed to enter the fray in breeches and shirt, without bothering to take up armor or arming girdle. He and his family had been driven out though, their land taken. Brodur had made the painful recognition of his duty and carried the news. He was carefree no more; men called him "Brodur-Scabbardless" for, having begun with a bared blade, he'd vowed not to cover it until his family had their lands returned.

Now he gasped his message to come and see what Omen had appeared. They found a hallway window. Moonlight and starlight over Boldhaven Bay was outdone by a new illumination. Seeing the Sign hanging in the southern sky, Springbuck shouted for Hightower and Gabrielle. They came running, the Warlord with his two-handed blade half drawn.

Gabrielle confirmed that it was the Trailingsword. "My brother and the rest discharged their commission. Now you have a higher edict, Springbuck; the men left to you will go with you southward. Reacher will have seen it in Freegate, as will any who hate the Masters. Whether those will be enough or not, we shall learn, in seven times seven days."

Springbuck drew Brodur-Scabbardless aside.

"Call together all leaders of the diverse elements.

221

Have the King of Seaguard invited. You may pass my word: Soon many swords, like yours, shall leave behind them the estate of the scabbard."

Every scrap of their patience, stamina and imagination was subject to test, those next three days.

"Your Grace, the septs of Matloo refuse to embark without their war-drays. I ask you, where have we room for those oversized wagons and horses?"

"Hmm. Fill each dray with cargo, captain; they are capacious enough. Pack more in around them once they're secure. Thus, we sacrifice little space. We may need those fearsome wagons. The horses will fit somewhere aboard the vessels designated for mounts. Some men of Matloo may accompany them."

"My Lord Hightower, the *Ku-Mor-Mai* directed me to you on a subject. A special tax is levied on profits of those buying goods from the departing Lords and soldiers. Where can be the justice in this? I am an honest man, seeking to aid our great cause, and take due earnings from that. The Protector-Suzerain would lack funds, had not we merchants opened our coffers, converting goods and deeds of land to hard specie."

Hightower's reply blew the userer's hair back. "Slight good will your monies do you, coin-caresser, if we fail! When before this have you bought bullocks so cheaply? When has land been rented or sold to you outright at such low sums? Bah! Better men than you are sailing in one more day while you, squealing piglet, are best gone from my sight, else I hang you by the heel at the ramparts."

"The problem is as follows, *Ku-Mor-Mai*," said Brodur-Scabbardless. "The men of Teebra object that the volunteers from the Fens of Hinn are allowed to fly their flag. They say rebellious Hinn is rightfully theirs, and this should not be permitted."

"The men of Hinn promised they would be first to the gates of Salamá if they could fly their standard. Besides, the Grand Council of Teebra had grown hardhearted to them, for in their shared religion, Hinn is more orthodox, making Teebra uneasy. See what you can do to soothe the Teebrans, but do not let them forget their fealty to me."

The captain made a note. Looking him over, Springbuck asked, "What device is that you bear upon your shoulder?"

It was a stylized emblem, a longsword picked out in white, beaming hilt uppermost, on a field of stars. "Everyone seems to wear the Trailingsword now." He made to go.

"Just a moment, Captain; there is one matter the more. Lord Hightower will command the expedition under my lead, but will also general our regular legions. He needs a good man over all his cavalry elements. He selected you."

Brodur was evasive. "Lord, I have never even commanded a squadron, let alone regiments!"

"You avoided it. It was permitted until now, but that is no longer tenable. Oh, I know you would rather keep peace of mind, but you'll learn to live without it, as I have. Surely after the war you can go your own way once more."

Brodur, ruffled, denied that. "There will be no peace, once my fine aptitudes are disclosed." The *Ku-Mor-Mai* barked with laughter, but wondered how the captain would react when he was in charge.

"Lord Hightower, many men take exception to these new rules. Being told to boil drinking water, and how and where a man may take his relievements, and the things they must do with their rubbish, and how they must bathe with soaps the apothecaries concocted, those lay much against their pride."

"You are a brave and able man, Lord Bantam. I remember your volunteering to stay behind and command my family's garrison against siege during the retreat to Freegate last summer. But what happened? Half the men who remained with you took ill. The Hightower and its defenders would have fallen if Yardiff Bey's general had had more time to spend on you. Attend me; these rules, as strange to me as to you, were given to Springbuck by the outlanders Van Duyn and Gil Mac-Donald. We will be careful about our drinking water and our—our sanitation, as they put it, and no man will stop short of our goal for sickness if I can help it. If you must, tell them it has arcane meaning. Or again, provoke their honor; this is part of their service.

"And pass along my warrant that these rules are holy doctrine hereafter. The man who ignores them and his superior will both hear from me in strongest terms, clear? My gratitude, Lord Bantam."

Men grew sick, stomachs emptied their contents into the sea, and the leeward side of any troop vessel was a noxious, crowded place to be.

The sailors of Seaguard's flotilla were hugely entertained by so many landlubbers coming to grips with the sea at once. There would have been fights, Springbuck was sure, except that few of his soldiers wanted to do anything but lie or sit in their misery. On advice from older officers, he ordered that everyone was to stay topside whenever weather permitted during the day. Lingering below invited disease and apathy, and dampened morale worse than salt spray ever would.

Hightower and Gabrielle spoke to him with more ease now that their renascent love was open fact, but usually preferred one another's company to the *Ku-Mor-Mai*'s. Springbuck either talked to Brodur or the officers of his flagship, a ponderous fighting-carrack, or stood on the aft fighting castle.

Though Brodur-Scabbardless had ample opportunity to gamble, he had little time, worrying about his new command and fretting about their horses' well-being. A part of his outgoing spirit returned, but he still carried a bared blade.

Nearly two weeks out, they sighted the Inner Hub. They asked one another what could possibly have made those immense breaches in the sea wall, and torn the harbor gates away so completely as to leave no trace of them. This was the older, the first of the Mariners' citadels, and had boasted walls of marble and of beryl, gardens, halls and libraries and temples. Now there was smeared ruin. Mast trucks poked blackened pennants out of the surface of the harbor, grave markers. Ash and wreckage drifted restlessly on the water. Springbuck could only hope that, as Gabrielle had predicted, the Mariner vengeance would occupy the attention of whatever Southwastelander ships plied the sea.

He was on the rear tower of the carrack, named *Oakengrip*. Hightower and the sorceress were on the forward castle, she sheltered under the long, warm sweep of his cloak. A gulf of loneliness yawned, even as a cold, analytical side of Springbuck came forth, telling him it would strengthen the expedition's resolve to see this devastation and think what it meant in terms of home.

Pulling his own cloak tighter, he paced to the other side of the deck and peered forward, toward the southern horizon. Unsteady in the unfamiliar rhythm of the sea, he'd been on deck most of the day, letting men know he shared "the ship, the weather, the situation altogether," as the Mariner rhyme had it.

The next day the sea became rough again, sporting whitecaps, and all landsmen who'd missed the agony of seasickness the first time coped with it now. Those who'd already dealt with it refamiliarized themselves. No ships were lost, and only a handful of careless men. The *Ku-Mor-Mai*, was thankful he'd gotten off so easily. A day came, just short of three weeks after the Trailingsword's appearance, when land hove into view.

Chapter Twenty-four

The virtue of adversity is fortitude.

Francis Bacon
"On Adversity"

IT was a peninsula of struggling, sunburned orchards and crops. Springbuck's poor vision gave him only the vague details of modest white huts fronting a bleached, broad beach. Fishing nets had been draped to dry, and long canoes were pulled above the tide's mark. The flotilla was on full alert; there was little information about this side of the Central Sea. The strand was unnervingly quiet, with no sign that their arrival had been noted. Unwelcomed, unopposed, they were used to no third alternative.

Hightower ascended the aft castle. "Someone must go ashore, and there is not much time for it." The *Ku-Mor-Mai* agreed; an alarm might already have gone out. The Warlord finished, "It is my intention to do so."

"I'm sorry, my Lord, but you are too valuable to risk at preliminary scout. Send someone whom you trust."

Brodur, a pace behind the old man, offered himself at once. Hightower insisted, "I will take any others you choose, Lord, but mean to go myself. It will fall to me to give the command to disembark. I must see what is there for myself first."

The younger man couldn't dispute that. He conceded the point, and Hightower was soon in a longboat with Brodur and a dozen other volunteers. Springbuck followed them through a spying tube, squinting elaborately to make the scene come clear, but after they'd secured their boat and gone past the first line of houses, he lost them.

A half-hour passed. Springbuck ordered more boats readied, selecting a larger party to come ashore with him. Just then the longboat put out again from the beach, and in its wake came the canoes. Men of Coramonde loosened swords and tested bowstrings, but heard no war cries and saw no weapons or armor flashing.

Hightower's boat pulled alongside the flagship, but the others stood back. Their occupants had been warned that Coramonde, come to wage war, would be quick to misconstrue an act as provocation.

The people were small, brown-skinned folk whose boats were painted in bright colors and fanciful designs. Most wore a sort of short kirtle; many had flowers woven in their hair, and there was a good deal of simple jewelry, childlike works of coral or shells. The *Ku-Mor-mai* noticed, at this close range, that many were scarred, missing a limb, maimed, bereft of an eye or ear, or otherwise afflicted. Still, they sang a happy-tempoed tune of greeting, for all the fact that their faces were sad and wary.

The soldiers and sailors didn't know what to think of these little people, but called to them good-naturedly.

Hightower and Brodur brought a representative to the Protector-Suzerain, a slender brown man older than most of his people, wearing a dignified chiton. He was in awe of *Oakengrip*. "O *Ku-Mor-Mai*," Hightower boomed formally, "I present Kalakeet, who is Speaker of these people, which call themselves the Yalloroon."

The Speaker smiled, but clearly had misgivings. Springbuck was to learn these people had good reason to fear strangers. Kalakeet told him, "The great Lord Hightower has said thou art called Protector-Suzerain, and we beg thee to take us under the soldierly wing of Coramonde."

Springbuck was stuck for reply. Could he, in fact, be a Protector? "Why do you ask it of me?"

The Speaker's face lost composure, as if a hope faded. "We are tormented by an enemy, as beasts of the pasture or cooped fowl. In our whole history we have been unable to throw off the collar of Shardishku-Salamá, and we had thought, when the Trailingsword lit our sky night after night . . ."

Thinking what it must have meant to have the Masters blight their lives for generations, Springbuck's impulse was to tell Kalakeet's people deliverance had arrived. But he had no wish to lie, and he spoke the only thing a *Ku-Mor-Mai* could dare to, the truth.

"There is no wing mighty enough to preserve you in surety against Salamá, but if you will it, you have found determined allies."

Those listening thought it a good response, except Hightower, who clenched the hilt of his greatsword. Kalakeet seemed as if he were awakening from a dream. "I should have foreseen this; no plight like ours is thrown down in a day. My people saw this arrival with too much optimism, I should say, without meaning to offend." He squared his thin shoulders. "There are many items we can tell one another; wilt thou come ashore?"

"Thank you, yes." He took a map from an aide. "First, we would like to know precisely where we are. Can you tell us?"

They'd been blown east of their destination. That event was benificent, in that the Yalloroon were hospitable. While Kalakeet was apprising Springbuck's navigators and pilots of inaccuracies in maps and charts, the *Ku-Mor-Mai* took his Warlord aside. Hightower confirmed that the city was empty of armed men. Springbuck gave the order that unloading begin at once.

Arrangements were formulated for some vessels to beach and others to unload by boat. Warships dropped back to form a defensive cordon. Blocks creaked and tackle groaned as supplies and equipment piled up on the beach. Those craft transporting horses took high priority; armored fighting men were the backbone of warfare.

The town had no walls or defensive works at all; those had been banned by the Southwastelanders. Springbuck ordered three ships to disgorge their full cargoes of infantry, an augmented brigade of hard-bitten pikemen from the late Bonsteel's legions. The *Ku-Mor-Mai* would feel better when he had a ring of them around the city of the Yalloroon. Sharp-eyed archers of Rugor positioned themselves and their mantlets, hammering in their stakes, for supporting fire.

Leaving the rest of the operation to subordinates, Springbuck repaired to Kalakeet's austere little home. Gabrielle came along, and Balagon, Divine Vicar of the Brotherhood of the Bright Lady, Angorman's rival. But Hightower said he had off-loading to supervise.

When they'd gone, the Warlord turned and stalked away, his visage fierce. He'd heard the story of the Yalloroon's suffering; it had lifted him to a pinnacle of rage. He nearly trampled Bodur, who jumped from his way. Hightower scarcely registered it. "Brodur-Scabbardless, commandeer me the first twoscore horses off the ships. Then handpick thirty-eight more men, best of our very best. We are going riding."

Springbuck and Gabrielle made themselves as comfortable as possible in Kalakeet's dirt-floored common room, along with Balagon. The *Ku-Mor-Mai* had not had much chance to acquaint himself with the ageing warrior-priest. The Divine Vicar was a figure out of fables, leader of the renowned One Hundred. Well along in years, like Angorman, he was a canny and vigorous man. His sparse white hairs were gathered by a simple leather circlet, and he wore black ringmail under his white vestments. On his right forefinger was the heavy seal ring of his station, and at his hip hung his famous two-handed blade, *Ke-Wa-Coe* which, in the Old-Tongue, means Consecrated of the Goddess.

It was strange for the son of Surehand to be in Gabrielle's company again without Hightower. She, on the other hand, gave no indication that she felt the same.

The food the little Speaker put out for them was pitiful, crusts and oddments of meat scraps, and runtish vegetables along with some puny fish. Kalakeet apologized, explaining Salamá didn't leave much. Springbuck expressed surprise that the Yalloroon didn't live under closer control.

"At times we do, in closest arrest, and at other times not, according to the whim of the Five. Yet, there are worse things than short rations, or going homeless, or coming to steely harm, *Ku-Mor-Mai*."

Gabrielle asked what he meant. Kalakeet elaborated. The Yalloroon had lived under Shardishku-Salamá for an uncertain time, since they were forbidden records. Once, they'd lived peacefully at the ocean's shore. Thus, they'd been unable to resist armed conquerors, adherents of the Masters who'd ground them down with painstaking intimidation, torture and execution. The Yalloroon had fought back once, disastrously. None who'd taken up arms were punished, but every other man, woman and child was, and many of them were killed. Some rebels committed suicide out of remorse and others simply became despondent; no uprisings occurred again. Several groups set out to escape, by land and sea, but all were brought back, saying they'd found no place not controlled by Salamá.

The Yalloroon became playthings in a game of transcendent cruelty. They suffered ever-new terrors, humiliation and pain, being tested, they concluded, in some cold experiment to learn how to separate people from pride, from hope, from any other quality that might inhibit total submission.

They'd considered racial suicide. But one woman had stood up at one of their meetings, saying, "There is only one reason they could wish to erase us so utterly. They know we are better than they."

The weaker and less angry knew they couldn't bear

229

it. Many took their own lives or each other's by agreement. Those who were angriest, though, vowed to keep the things Salamá wished to destroy. So, while the Masters could quite easily have them killed, or broken with physical torture, or compelled by direct duress, separating the Yalloroon from their self-worth had met insurmountable resistance.

Springbuck was amazed. In some way, Shardishku-Salamá itself had lost face, its clinical subjects refusing to behave as they ought. The Yalloroon had been unshakable in their belief that they were being tormented simply because they were better. From it had flowed the strength to resist. Erring, the Five had converted these unimposing people into a human alloy capable of being shattered, but never bent, the diametric opposite of the intended result.

"But then," interrupted Balagon, "as far as you know, we could be of Salamá, and all this, even the Trailingsword, a ruse."

"As happened generations ago," responded Kalakeet. "An army came, and declared us liberated. There were celebrations and thanksgivings. After a week, they revealed the terrible truth, a sudden and subtle blow that started a more severe round of atrocities."

"You have little reason to believe us then," Springbuck observed, "but you are no longer alone."

"And whether that is true or false, *Ku-Mor-Mai*, we welcome thee. If it is betrayal, that is thy crime, not ours." He said it in an old, formidable dignity. The *Ku-Mor-Mai* bowed homage to that.

"When deeds are tallied," he answered, "none will match those of the Yalloroon."

Balagon voiced agreement. Splendid Gabrielle took Kalakeet's hand and inclined her head over it.

Springbuck began asking questions about the area. He answered Kalakeet's questions about Coramonde, but told nothing of his actual plan; information could be extracted from the bravest man. A cartographer arrived with revised maps for the Speaker's review, and the Protector-Suzerain ordered the expedition's healers to move among the Yalloroon and be of whatever service they could. Night and the Trailingsword came on, and Kalakeet lit hoarded stubs of candle.

The door banged open. Hightower filled the frame, reeking of the fight, with new damage to his armor, eyes smouldering. The first engagement with the Southwaste-landers on their own soil had already been fought.

He sat, to tell them about it. Hearing Kalakeet's story, he'd become infuriated. Seeking release, he'd reconnoitered the countryside with Brodur and select men at his back. They'd encountered three times their own number in enemy cavalry, stumbling into them by chance in a winding pass. The Southwastelanders had been astounded but Hightower, with no more hesitation than it made to drop his lance level, had gone in among them, irresistible. His men, with scant choice, had borne in after. The southerners, less heavily armored and without room to maneuver, had stood their ground.

The Warlord had driven completely through their ranks. Springbuck could picture that; he'd seen the old giant in combat, where getting in his way was tantamount to suicide. Gabrielle's face wore a pride the *Ku-Mor-Mai* couldn't begrudge.

Hightower and his men had cut the Southwastelanders to pieces, and sent them reeling back down the pass, shivering in fright of these terrible new foemen, found where there ought only to have been helpless Yalloroon. The men of Coramonde had ridden back to the city singing, with a foeman's head on every lancetip.

Springbuck set his hand to the Warlord's hilt, pulled the greatsword from its sheath. It was streaked with the dark blood of enemies, red coming to brown in the candlelight.

"Lord Hightower has delivered the first statement of our long communiqué of war."

The Speaker reached out timidly. The very ends of his fingers reached the cold blade, rested there for a second. He drew them back as if burned, awed at the brown stains on them. Then he buried his head in his hands, weeping.

Wrestling within the son of Surehand were loathing of the squander of war, against satisfaction in the delivery of the Yalloroon.

Chapter Twenty-five

Who asks whether the enemy were defeated by strategy or valor?

Virgil

THE Lord of the Just and Sudden Reach gauged the dust of enemy horsemen. One of the riders of his advance party, doing the same, estimated, "They will be here in perhaps forty minutes, Majesty."

Reacher shook his head. Those were swift desert chargers, bearing lightly armored Southwastelanders. They would arrive at the little way station here, where the men of Freegate had stopped, sooner than that. He looker to the courier who'd just come up from the main body of his army.

"How far back are my sister and the array?"

The man answered unwillingly, knowing it was bad news. "No less than an hour and another half, my Lord. They are harried by unarmored bowmen on fleet steeds who, firing at them, outrace pursuit. The Horseblooded might have chased and caught them, but the Snow Leopardess would not allow her force to go asunder. She will come as quickly as she can. It might mean delay, your Grace, or it might mean a fight."

"It is Katya," Reacher replied. "It will be a fight." But she was handling things entirely correctly. It wouldn't do to let the Horseblooded become separated from the slower-moving mailed warriors of Freegate, risking piecemeal combat in unfamiliar country. She couldn't know this way station was here, deserted by its few sentinels, commanding high ground that would be defaulted to the thousand or so Southwastelanders coming at full speed.

Reacher had come ahead with two hundred men to

scout the terrain in depth, only to find Southwastelanders within minutes of this strong position on its high ground, approaching from the opposite direction. He studied the hill, its grass burned brown by the overbearing sun. To the west, enormous broken teeth of stone formed a jagged hedge, sloping away toward the uneven, ravined land that led to the Central Sea. The position was secure enough there. The way station and its outbuildings were close by the side of the Southern Tangent, at the crest of the rise; from there the hill fell away to the east. It descended into gullies, draws and washes etched from the earth. That it wasn't more heavily fortified was due to the fact that it fronted league after league of barren, uninhabited land to the north, guarding the farthest parts of Salamá's domain. South of here, the Southern Tangent was said to stop, vanishing beneath a region of desert.

The way station was indefensible by two hundred men against a thousand or more, but that same thousand might hold it against many times their number. The Lord of the Just and Sudden Reach dismissed the idea of trying a useless holding action. That only left it to come back with his whole army and dig the desert men out, using precious time and costing a toll of men.

"We leave now," he told the soldiers who waited tensely. They relaxed a bit, hearing it. "Have all buildings been searched?" he added.

"It is being done, my Lord," said the captain in charge of scouts. "There are some outbuildings left; it is nigh accomplished."

"Where is the Lord Van Duyn?" The American had been eager for a look at the Southwastelands, asking to come in the advance party as a favor Reacher could hardly deny.

"He is gone up onto the roof of the way station," one said, "to see the lay of the land."

Edward Van Duyn eased the hauburgeon that always seemed to drag at his shoulders, rubbed dust from his gold-rimmed glasses and rechecked his estimate of the enemy's rate of travel. The prevailing wind blew down the slope, out of the highlands behind him, toward the

233

plains. Distances were difficult to judge with the brazen sun directly overhead.

Van Duyn might easily have remained back in Freegate, or returned there when Reacher had made his decision under the Trailingsword to go south. In the capital, he would have had the contiguity device close to hand, ready for escape from this Reality if the Masters should prevail. But Katya was accompanying her brother, not to be kept from his side in time of danger even by her feelings for the American. Threatened by prolonged separation from her, Van Duyn found himself unwilling to accept it.

There was another reason for his going, less subject to analysis. He'd found himself recalling Coramonde's Highlands Province and how, at the end of a day's toil at the model farm or surveying for the new dam, he and the Snow Leopardess and many others would gather in the community bath and sauna they'd built. There they'd baked out the chill, laughing, joking, buffing themselves lobster-red in the heat. They'd spun a hundred plans and dreams, more than their tomorrows might bring, but no less worth conceiving.

He'd had something then, challenges and ideas, accomplishments and hopes. He'd been accorded the friendship of the Highlanders, seldom given to outsiders, a thing of bedrock palpability, irrevocable. He'd thought of that often since the Province had been swallowed up by the polar magic of the Druids. To be sure, there were incalculable other Realities to which he could withdraw by Contiguity; he was frank enough with himself to own up that, in doing so, he'd sever a part of himself. In this line of thought, he'd been drawn more and more into the effort to cast down the influence of the Masters.

Reacher was suddenly standing beside him, having come up without the slightest sound. Van Duyn stifled his surprise. The King never meant discourtesy; it was just that, peerless hunter and tracker, he went with an unlabored, unthinking stealth. Standing just over five feet, lean and broad-shouldered, Reacher, it was said, could cross a field without disturbing any blade of grass. His wild, simple upbringing left him uneasy in the company of most people. His preference for passing among them inconspicuously had given him a rumored talent for invisibility.

Besides that there was, Van Duyn suspected, the matter of the King's reflexes. The American had never been able to measure Reacher's response time, but it was vanishing small. What attitudes and outlooks would he have developed, moving through a world of comparative sluggards with something like instantaneity? Anyway, nothing to make him outgoing.

"How soon?" asked the King forthrightly.

"I should say less than half an hour. They can catch us on open ground if we withdraw, can they not?"

"Unimportant; they will not pursue. They will occupy this ground." He tugged at his high, ring-mail collar. Reacher disliked panoply, being used to the brief hunting gear of the Howlebeau who'd raised him, and whose foster brothers were the huge wolves of the steppes. The King had often run with the packs, a member among them. For that he was sometimes called "Wolf-Brother."

After the conference at Earthfast, Reacher had led his armies far down the Southern Tangent, to the edge of Freegate's boundaries. The Horseblooded had come, keeping their compacts with the men of the Free City and the strong bonds their hetmen had with the King. Southwastelanders had been raiding and sacking far into Freegate's territory, and retribution had been overdue.

The King's scouts had ferreted out the southerners' advance base, hidden in the heart of the wastes. Reacher had made a long march and taken the place by surprise. On the same night, the Trailingsword had burned in the sky for the first time.

The Masters were using a young and warlike race, the Occhlon. Though prisoners had been reticent to the point of fanaticism, it had become clear that the Five weren't simply fostering border troubles. This was some major effort, wherein they were fielding every man-at-arms they had. Andre deCourteney's warnings in Earthfast stayed prominent in the King's mind.

Though communication with Coramonde had been lost, Reacher had heeded military imperatives, decrees of legend, and his own wilderness instincts, letting the

235

Omen lead him toward Salamá. The Freegaters and Wild Riders had sent the desert men flying, unable to match the northerners' numbers. This way station marked the end of lands to which neither side had any claim, and the beginning of the Southwastelands.

"If they reoccupy this place they'll hold us back, won't they?" Van Duyn more stated than asked.

"For a time. We here are too few to repel them." He pulled the mailed coif up over his blond hair. Van Duyn picked up his Garand and they went back down the cylindrical stairway.

Departure was interrupted. From the last building to be searched, two warriors emerged with a struggling man braced between them. The captive, sobbing and pleading, was thrust on his knees before the King.

"This one was bound, gagged and hung by his sash," explained the captain, his longsword drawn. "There was a pair of laden donkeys also, which he says to be his." The captive waited like a mouse among snakes.

Reacher examined the Southwastelander curiously. The man was no soldier, and hardly a spy. He was dressed in overused robes, his conical hat battered and dusty, his beard matted and dirty. Around his neck hung a medallion stamped of brass.

"What else is there?"

"In the stable, my Lord? Nothing more." The captain's gaze went south, where the enemy's dust was nearer.

Reacher pointed to the medallion. "What emblem is that?"

The southerner's eyes slid away. "Only my employer's."

"A minor official's medal, Lord," supplied the captain, who knew something of Southwastelanders. "This man would be an area newsgiver, and collector of tribute."

"And what news did you give the sentinels here?" Van Duyn asked. The King was pleased his question had been anticipated. The prisoner hesitated.

The captain's edge flicked up under the newsgiver's chin. The prisoner squeaked and gabbled, "That all is well, and our armies in firm control of the wastelands. Th-that victory is assured."

Van Duyn grinned. "Only, as you passed that encouraging dispatch, we were seen riding down; made you a liar, didn't we? So the angry sentinels left you for us, apropos of your falsehood?"

The collector-newsgiver admitted it. The American chortled. "You poor sucker. Your employers never told you what happens to propagandists when reality catches up, did they?"

"I did believe it to be the truth, I swear upon my father's eyes! Why else would I have stopped up here before turning south? Eee, spare me my life, I beg; I can make good recompense."

"What payment is that?" pounced the captain.

"Do you but bring my donkeys, and I will show." When the animals were fetched, he unpacked a long, thin sack. He opened one end, and spilled out a thin stream of red powder.

"Earnai," the captain said, "Dreamdrowse." He rattled the newsgiver by gathered lapels. "Why did the sentinels not take it?"

"Have mercy! Am I a madman, to risk my life by telling those provincial scum I was transporting the product of a season? And later, before I could buy back my freedom, I was gagged unspeaking."

Reacher turned to go. The discovery had no tactical significance. Maybe, he thought, the Southwastelanders would find it and make themselves stuporous, but he doubted that. The collector-newsgiver, released, slumped in astonishment. They had no time to go slowly, with a prisoner, and it wasn't the King's way to slay offhandedly.

But Van Duyn was stirring the red powder with his boot. He called the Wolf-Brother back. "We could put this to work, you know." Getting no response, he continued, "This is the form they call 'mahónn', am I correct?"

"It looks to be," the captain agreed. "It is from the Old Tongue, meaning 'rescue.' "

"Very concentrated," Van Duyn went on, "quite flammable. Suppose we burned it upwind, when the Southwastelanders came?"

They all struggled to absorb the idea, except the King. Arms folded across his chest, he strolled over to look down the slope to the south. "Would they not avoid it?"

The American frowned. "Very well then, scatter it among the grass and fire it. Or better yet, egg them into charging upslope, and fire the mahónn as they pass through it."

The captain spoke up, "If it does no more than afford us time it will be much, my Lord King."

Reacher turned back to them. "We have only some minutes," he warned; "therefore, let us do this thing with all speed."

Prepared in the form of mahónn, the Dreamdrowse wasn't effective until burned. Still, Van Duyn and the others tore strips of cloth and masked themselves against the dust they would raise sowing their bizarre seed. It was stored in long, thin tubes of canvas. Holding one end of a sack, they slit a corner at the opposite end and cantered along, shaking Earnai in among the tufts of grass, losing little to the wind. There were a dozen sacks in all, the area's entire refined product of "rescue" for this growing season. The captive couldn't bear to watch; he sat rocking and wailing with the hem of his robe to his eyes. At the bottom of the slope, sheltered by rocks, Reacher and fifty men waited to bait the trap.

Van Duyn finished, gave the command and sped back up the hill. The American and Reacher's captain crouched and marked time.

They'd barely made it. The Southwastelanders' formation, less disciplined than was the northern habit, appeared. It had extended itself in the course of a hard ride; Reacher had counted on that. He slammed down his visor, dropped his lance and charged, leading the way, but left it to his men to take up the war cry. The Wolf-Brother and his little wedge of armored men hewed into the southerners' left flank, throwing dozens of them down with their first strikes. Then they fell in among the surprised desert men with swords, maces and cavalry picks. There was the wild, random exchange of blows. From the crest of the hill Van Duyn watched sunlight flicker on metal and heard the screams of the wounded and dying. The Freegaters had gotten to close quarters before the Occhlon could use their mancuverability, and Reacher's strongly armored men prevailed.

But more Southwastelanders came up quickly behind the first. The King gave his trumpeter a yell. Retreat blew, and Reacher raced from the fray, his standard-bearer and trumpeter close after. They swept up the hill, their horses still fresh. Only a handful of desert men gave immediate chase; few really knew what had happened.

When they topped the hill, the men of Freegate turned and gave battle again. The captain spurred up in support, with the other northerners. While a milling skirmish broke out beside the way station, the rest of the Occhlon regrouped at the foot of the hill, and followed. Van Duyn noticed the southern banner for the first time, a black scorpion on a crimson field, the device carried by Ibn-al-Yed, the sorcerer who'd died during the battle of the Hightower.

Reacher slid from his saddle and took the bow and fire-arrows that had been readied. He took his first arrow, with its collar of oil-soaked straw tied by wetted gut, and lit it from a fire-pot. He nocked, drew until the nock lay under his right eye, sighted and released in smooth series. There were three more arrows prepared, burning. Before the first had landed, he'd fired them all. Downslope, they thudded in among the clumps of sun-browned grass, scattering embers.

Smoke appeared, the wind nurturing it, as Reacher completed his pattern with three more shafts. The Southwastelanders, pouring up the slope, ignored the burning grass as being too low and dispersed to stop them.

Van Duyn unslung his Garand, holding it at high port, watching the charging cavalry worriedly. The King held up his hand though, to keep him from shooting. "That might deter their charge," he said. "Few enough more will make it through."

Prevailing winds rushed the fires down toward the enemy. The smoke took a reddish tinge as the Dream-drowse was consumed. First wisps of it blew into the body of the Occhlon. Van Duyn prayed the breeze wouldn't shift.

The charge wavered; some desert men actually drew rein. Then insanity broke out in what had been a deter-

239

mined, competent attack. Horses threw their riders; men fell or jumped from the saddle, colliding with one another. They ran screaming from imaginary terrors or sat weeping. They cringed from each other or lunged together with murder in mind, or sprawled out in a drugged stupor, depending on their turn of mind, tolerance, and exposure to the mahónn. Some in the rear weren't affected and, divining that the smoke was more than it appeared, retreated. But the major part of the force was engulfed.

Van Duyn stayed to one side, as defenders on the hilltop finished off those Southwastelanders who'd made it to the top. He watched men below stagger through the smoke in tears, nausea, hallucinations and hysteria. Those who were able to lurched off the field to escape southward.

After several minutes, the smoke below began to thin as the fire burned itself out. The victors gathered. "That was no clean triumph," the captain alleged, "but smacked more of conjuror's tricks."

"You have the high ground," Van Duyn grated, "and your casualties are small. The enemy's in route, and has lost heavily."

Reacher, watching stricken Southwastelanders crawl from the field or huddle down close to the ground, said nothing.

The last prisoners had been herded together when Katya arrived, the main body of Freegate coming in ranks behind her. With her was great Kisst-Haa and several of his kin, the reptile-men. Bringing up the rear were the laughing, unregimented Horseblooded, singing and cavorting among themselves. Spying Reacher, they forged ahead, calling, "Wolf-Brother, we are here!" They had given him that sobriquet, as they'd named his sister *Sleethaná*, the Snow Leopardess.

Now she vaulted from the saddle and caught Van Duyn and her brother up in a boisterous double hug. "I did worry," she admitted, "but mounted archers were hitting us side and side, and outran even our fleet Horseblooded there, where southerners alone know the twisty canyons. I perforce set them a little trap. Staring hard, you may see the carrion birds from here. How went matters by you?"

"Well enough," Reacher allowed. He held up a captured standard, the black scorpion on crimson field.

She puzzled aloud, "Why is this emblem still flown?"

The Wolf-Brother didn't know, but was concerned as
much as she. But he remembered to say, "Congratulate
Edward; his inspiration gave us the day." She bussed
Van Duyn soundly; he hung an arm around her and
returned it enthusiastically. She was first to stop for
breath.

When she got around to checking the lay of the land
to the south, she was delighted. "There is no fortress or
impediment as far as the eye can see; only open plains.
With Horseblooded outriders and heavy Freegate
knights, we will make good way."

Reacher was still distracted. With Van Duyn's arm
around her waist, the Snow Leopardess took her brother's hand. "Leave off; a day's work is done."

The King went with them then, letting the defeated
banner fall. But the black scorpion had awakened a disquiet he couldn't set aside.

Chapter Twenty-six

*In desperate matters the boldest counsels are the
    safest.*

                                                    Livy
                                                    Histories

SPRINGBUCK and Hightower sweated, coaxed, ranted
and had the army off-loaded within a day and a half.
Shifts of men trudged burdens through breaking surf.
Flailing, blindfolded horses were set down by winch,
knee deep in the waves.

Among those was Fireheel, Springbuck's favorite.
The long-legged gray, ill-humored from shipboard confinement, went high-stepping, eager for a hard ride.

Hightower sent out deep patrols while craftsmen assembled carts, water barrels and other equipment from parts they'd brought. In the meantime, men worked staleness and stiffness out of themselves.

In planning the route, Springbuck made himself think more as burglar than invader; contact was to be avoided, and standup combat eschewed, unless there were some clear advantage to it.

Early on the second morning after their landing, horns sounded and drums beat. Tents were struck, columns formed, and for the first time the *Ku-Mor-Mai* saw his entire corps drawn up. They were formidable in their thousands, but hardly a match for the hordes rumored to be in the Southwastelands.

Except for the war-drays, water wagons and baggage wains, the column would be entirely made up of horsemen, including infantrymen who'd dismount to fight afoot if needed.

Springbuck left the unmounted portion of his infantry as security for the city, hoping to keep an escape path open.

Most of the men had removed part of their armor or cut up light blankets to supplement the protection of their tabbards. Springbuck accepted Kalakeet's offer of a light robe makeshift-tailored for him. To the spare Alebowrenian outfit, he'd added a hauberk of light rings suitable for the warmer climate. Though it was early morning, the sun was hot, a demonstration of what was to come.

He met Hightower and Gabrielle, who waited at the head of the formation. The sorceress wore a white burnoose, untroubled by the heat as she sat her sidesaddled mare. At her cantle hung her brother Andre's sword, holding within its pommel the gemstone Calundronius. Nearby stood Balagon, who'd mustered the One Hundred of his Brotherhood. Springbuck called Brodur, and they trotted in hasty review.

The Legions were ready with the preparation of a lifetime's professional soldiering. Rank on rank of light and medium cavalry, mounted pikemen and bowmen and panoplied knights, they were used to biding their time against the order to march. Behind them, Alebowrenian bravoes joked and boasted, decked out in their finery, calling greetings to the *Ku-Mor-Mai*. Next, archers of Rugor tested their bowstrings and squinted at the morning light.

The men of Teebra, hardy mountaineers, had raised their animal totems, and worn their war bonnets of eagle feathers. Over their hauberks they'd donned their necklaces, strung claws and fangs of beasts of prey.

At the rear, the war-drays of Matloo were drawn up. They were sturdy wooden wagons, faced and strapped with iron. Their bodies were halved, articulated, to make them more maneuverable. Their wheels, fitted with spikes, slashing rims and hub-blades, could do terrible damage. Each was pulled by eight giant armored war-horses bred for the job. The driver held his handfuls of reins in a turret at the wagon's prow, and his riders could either close their side plates for protection or open them for the use of spears, bows and the overlong swords they used. At the fore, astride the lead horse, sat the Lead-Line Rider, practicing the most perilous, prestigious calling there was for a man of Matloo. Without him to control and direct the team, the driver's guidance might be inadequate. In rigorously puritanical Matloo, no one was more esteemed than the champions who rose to that rank.

The men of Matloo were set to depart, all Lead-Line Riders in their high-cantled saddles, but around them a dozen of the Yalloroon had gathered. Springbuck and Brodur stopped. Drakemirth, the grim old step-chieftain who led the contingent, was at words with Kalakeet the Speaker. Drakemirth was almost the size of Hightower, his slate-gray hair and beard plaited and clamped in dozens of small braids. He stood with mail-gloved fists on hips, listening to pleas that he let some of the Yalloroon go with him in the drays. Noticing the *Ku-Mor-Mai,* he said, "Your Grace, here is a decision for you."

Springbuck got down. The little Yalloroon repeated the request. "Kalakeet," the son of Surehand said, "I promise your people will go with the ships if trouble comes. What would it profit for you to come with us into the heart of Salamá?"

Kalakeet was unswerving. "Protector-Suzerain, we do

not ask all to go; only a few. Who has endured more at the hands of the Five than the Yalloroon? Who has a better right to send witnesses, to bring back the tale of this faring? Any of us would risk it, but we know only a few may go. Is that so much to petition?"

Springbuck found himself conceding that it wasn't. "What think you, Drakemirth?"

"We can tuck along such small passengers as these," he granted. "We have four drays, room enough for two of them in each. Speaker, mind you, do as you are instructed and be no distraction to us, should battle come."

Kalakeet bowed low, but the Speaker's voice held an amused note. "Exalted Drakemirth, calm in the midst of peril is our single aptitude."

They went with all the speed they could maintain, raising choking dust in the heat of the wastelands, discovering the special rigors of travel there. Scouts came across what seemed to be a well-traveled route. It was decided that the army would trace it to its source, paralleling it but keeping well off it. It was Springbuck's order that they cold-camp each night.

On the third evening, the value of that was proved. They'd stopped early, on the edge of a long plateau, to keep the advantage of high ground. Toward dusk a long file of men and animals wound its way up from the south. It settled down for the night, not three miles from them. Hightower pointed out that the northerners had a clear advantage of numbers, saying they should take this camp for the information they could gain.

Springbuck let another factor decide him, that there were many strings of spare horses among that column, while his own forces lacked a single remount. The men of Coramonde quietly resaddled in the gloaming. When night had come on, they made their careful way down, and formed up on the plain. The wagons and war-drays were left behind for consideration of noise. Advancing at a walk, the army came stealthily to within a quarter-mile of the camp.

For the first time, the battle flourish of the *Ku-Mor-Mai* sounded south of the Central Sea. Heavy lances were clenched. Men whooped forward at the gallop.

There were a few guards in wicker armor wound in leather, carrying light target-shields and slim, straight-bladed swords. Most had the simple sense to dive for cover. The ground shook from iron hooves drumming in the darkness.

The attackers hadn't hit a military unit, but rather a supply caravan headed northwest. Only a handful of its escorting soldiers ever got to their saddles. Women who'd been cooking dinner or kneading camel dung into rings for fuel, and men who'd been tending this or that chore, screamed and flattened to the ground. Giant northern chargers soared out of the darkness, hurtling campfires. Pack animals brayed in fear, fighting their tethers, their harness bells ringing. Any man who raised a sword was struck down. Captives, most of them caravaners and their families, were rounded up and guarded. The freight was unremarkable, provisions and livestock bound for an army in the field.

The desert men's gabbled responses were barely coherent, the only clear fact being that they'd traveled for many days now.

In the largest of the tents, Springbuck assembled all the documents and maps he could find. He'd learned from Gil MacDonald what a treasure house of military information captured papers could be. He called in Kalakeet, who'd stayed back with the war-drays and whose knowledge of the area, vague as it was, was superior to his own. As the *Ku-Mor-Mai* and the Speaker bent over the papers, Gabrielle came in, cooling herself with a silken fan.

As best Springbuck could make out, there lay between the northerners and their way south a mountain range some dozens of leagues long, the Demon's Breastwork, one of Salamá's great natural defenses, a palisade of jagged, impassable cliffs. To the west, it descended into a low-lying, searing desert called Amon's Cauldron. Much farther to the southeast, the Demon's Breastwork ended, but that circuit was a well-traveled convoy route, much patrolled, on which the northerners would run a high risk of battle. The caravan had departed a major fortress somewhere south of the Breastwork, its destination the northwestern tip of the Masters' domain.

"You have been south of the Central Sea before," Springbuck said to the sorceress. "Have you any comment?"

"I came by a far different path," she replied cryptically, "and went by it too. Yet, that is the terrain as I heard it."

Springbuck was holding a document that, composed of paragraphs and lists and bordered with official seals, had the look of an orders letter. Neither he nor Gabrielle could read its southern characters, and Kalakeet's people had been forbidden literacy, but at Springbuck's urging, Gabrielle labored over the date of signature, set down in the eccentric lunar reckoning of the Southwastelands. It was four days previous.

The *Ku-Mor-Mai* ruminated, "There is some discrepancy. The orders would have come at this fortress we hear mentioned, not somewhere en route. Yet, how could a shuffling caravan skirt this Demon's Breastwork in so brief a time?"

"There was once a passage through these mountains," Gabrielle recalled, "or so the story runs in my family. But that was said to have been destroyed, to further isolate Shardishku-Salamá. Not destroyed, perhaps, but only hidden? And now, when it is so vital to speed supplies up to their army in the Crescent Lands, in use once more?"

"A question for the caravan leader," said the *Ku-Mor-Mai*.

Hightower brought the man, whose teeth chattered as he refused to give any information, his terror of the Masters outweighing any threat the northerners could bring against him. Gabrielle moved the *Ku-Mor-Mai* and the Warlord apart with her soft white hands, slipped an arm through the astonished captive's, and walked him out of the tent.

They watched her draw him aside a short way, fanning herself and speaking in words too soft to hear. He listened, then shook his head no, violently. She spoke again, leaning close, holding a palm up. The blue glow of deCourteney magic came up off it, illuminating both their faces. She let it fade, and bespoke him again. This time, he seemed to yield. Leading the sweating, trembling caravaner back as if he were her swain, she smiled. "This one has seen the blue light of reason. There is indeed a way through the Breastwork. Salamá

246

is using it more and more to hurry troops and materiel to its campagin."

The caravaners had been taken through a tunnel under the Demon's Breastwork. What had been a passageway ages ago was now known as the Gauntlet of Ibn-al-Yed, because Yardiff Bey's mask-slave had converted it into a death trap. The travelers had been blindfolded and taken through the Gauntlet by two guides, each of whom knew only half the way. Guidance must be heeded exactly; the passageway was filled with lethal pitfalls, snares and other deadly tricks. Each guide had gone blindfolded in that part of the tunnel that wasn't his to know. Once the caravan was through, the guides had gone back the way they'd come, to the fortress called Condor's Roost, beyond the mountains.

Hightower maintained, "Going straightway under those cliffs saved them a week and more. Can we not do the same, guides or no?"

Gabrielle, unperspiring, fanned herself slowly. "The traps were engineered by Ibn-al-Yed. What that son of the Scorpion has worked, I can unwork."

"Failure would earn us graves under the mountains," reminded the Warlord.

"Time's unsparing," Springbuck argued. "The days of the Trailingsword are half spent. A shortcut is worth any dare."

The *Ku-Mor-Mai* never ceased to marvel at how problems could come up, and amaze him, in retrospect, because he hadn't foreseen them.

His most immediate difficulty was keeping his prisoners alive. His soldiers had met the Yalloroon and heard their sad story. Now, they wanted nothing more than to rip into some Southwastelanders in retribution; some even cried "Havoc!" in defiance of Springbuck's command. It took shouted explanations, and more than one man stretched out by the flat of Hightower's sword, to quell the uproar. To forestall mass murder, Springbuck disarmed and released all the desert men except the caravan leader, appropriating their horses, but leaving them their dromedaries and camels. That word of his landing would go abroad mattered little; before southern troops could come down on his track, he intended

247

to be beyond pursuit, closing up this Gauntlet behind him.

They were up at first light. Rows of horsemen moved through the dawn, honed lanceheads playing reflective games with the intense southern sunlight. Bits jingled and snorting horses registered impatience with tosses of their heads and quick digs of their flashing hooves. The men of Matloo, under Drakemirth, had spent part of the night fitting their dray-wheels with extenders, broadening them, to make travel over the sandy stretches easier.

The Yalloroon had used all their available silks to make coverings for their deliverers' armor and sweating horses. Springbuck wondered how taxing the climate would be under combat. Worse than Coramonde in its hottest months, he knew. His best scouts, prowler-cavalrymen, led the army through winding ravines. The way was worn with the use it had seen since the war's outset; the prowlers would have found it even without the southerner to show them. Faster than a caravan, they arrived by late afternoon.

The army came to what seemed a cul-de-sac, but its end, hidden to the side, was the mouth of Ibn-al-Yed's Gauntlet. Gabrielle made them all draw back and went alone into the darkness. The *Ku-Mor-Mai* and his Warlord both had reasons for objections, but suppressed them.

An hour passed, while the sun sank lower and occasional bursts of the sorceress's magic lit the end of the ravine. One by one she felt out the snares and traps, extending her perception and control over them. She systematically took over the Gauntlet, bringing all its perils under her own command, holding them in abeyance wth spells and words of Enforcement.

Afterward, she walked back to them, the strain bracketing her eyes. "The way is safe, and I will hold it so. Yet, do not linger; Ibn-al-Yed's devices are many." Hightower gave orders; torches and lamps were kindled, and Gabrielle's horse brought. The Warlord lifted her up, his big hands encircling her waist.

Springbuck detailed Balagon and his One Hundred to insure that no one stopped or faltered. Brodur-Scabbardless was given charge over the rearguard. Total silence, except for relaying instructions, was the inflexible rule. With Springbuck on one side and Hightower on the other, the sorceress entered the Gauntlet.

The passageway was cool and dank after the desert, but filled with a sickening stench. They'd expected to see bats or crawling things, but no living creature would dwell in the Gauntlet. Hoofbeats echoed hollowly on rock, and red torchlight wavered across it. "I like not this burrow," whispered Hightower against his own orders.

The way wound on, partly through natural chambers in the mountain, but more often tunneled. Horses snorted and were nervous, hating it here. The Gauntlet seemed to go on endlessly. But at last, a breath of air reached them, wriggling the torch flames. Gabrielle, reining in, halted them. "This is more than midway," she declared. "I will stay here and put forth my influence in both directions. Make all haste."

Hightower took the van. Springbuck, loathing it, knew he must stay in the Gauntlet until all his troops were through. The ranks moved on, horses sometimes tossing their heads and fighting the bit. Men's eyes, in the shadows of their helmets, darted constantly. The son of Surehand peered continuously for Brodur, but knew the rearguard would be a long time coming. In the damp coolness, he sweated worse than he had on the desert. The mass of the mountains hovered over him.

The clans of Teebra clopped past. He was distracting himself by trying to recall where they were in the order of march when Gabrielle screamed. Her cry, as if she'd been injured or more, bounced back and forth in the passageway. Frightened horses fought their riders, and men yelled in alarm. Springbuck roared for silence. The sorceress swayed, a hand to her forehead, then slumped sideways. The *Ku-Mor-Mai* caught her, hearing the rock around him grinding against itself.

In a moment she came to, her breathing unsteady. Her hand gripped weakly at him. "Springbuck, some calamity is come. There was a great disturbance in the magic of the deCourteneys, and now an abyss. I fear my mother is slain!"

Springbuck ignored everything but immediate danger. He shook her. "Can you maintain the Gauntlet?"

"I—I think it so. But there is . . ." Her voice trailed away; he felt convulsions threaten her. He commanded the march to continue, full speed. His every nerve shrieked; his entire army was in danger of being cut in two, or entombed. Gabrielle reasserted herself to gasp, "My energies are failing, they flow away. Andre! Andre throws the whole of our magic at some enemy, more than he has ever used before. I can barely withhold any."

Springbuck's flesh crawled as he heard the ponderous shifting of stone. There was a crash, splintering wood, the death cries of men and horses. Fireheel half-reared under him, the whites of the stallion's eyes showing.

The *Ku-Mor-Mai* called for all to be silent, hold ranks, but the terrors of cave-in were there. Men and their mounts bolted forward while Gabrielle's face showed the contortions of effort, holding back the mantraps. Springbuck pulled her back out of the way, sheltering her and her horse with himself and Fireheel. He swept out Bar; it caught the light of passing torches and even in stampede, men were wise enough to give it wide berth.

The sorceress' features were crosshatched with pain. "Can you hold, Gabrielle? *Can you hold?*"

Her lower lip was bleeding, where she'd bitten it in the throes of her struggle. She nodded weakly. "For the moment." He took hold of the hilt of her brother's sword, hanging from her saddle, where Calundronius was kept, thinking the gemstone might help. "No!" She batted at his hand feebly. "It would only dissipate all magic in here, mine included."

One man blundered into him, and Springbuck seized him and held Bar at his belly, demanding to know what had happened.

"I had been near a wain bearing barrels of water, but when I looked, it was there no longer; the stone had dropped away beneath it, and it had fallen into the breach. We never heard it hit, nor could we see any bottom to the gulf. The gap was from wall to wall, too long for any horse to hurdle."

Springbuck, numb, let him go; the rest had escaped already. Gabrielle's face, usually pale, was bloodless now, her hair clinging in damp scarlet ringlets to her sweating cheeks and brow. Her eyes were screwed shut in effort, lip again clenched in her teeth.

He started back, to see if there was some way to bridge the pitfall. Fireheel was unruly, unwilling. Gabrielle's eyes snapped open. "Springbuck, no! There is no way back."

He stopped. Hightower appeared, torch held aloft. Seeing the sorceress, he called her name. Her gaze went to him; the Gauntlet's hidden machinery could be heard.

Fireheel reacted. The gray's gathered muscles uncoiled; tons of stone crashed down where he'd been. Gabrielle, attuned to Ibn-al-Yed's ancient devices, flung her hand out, crying "Hold!"

He reined in brutally, and Fireheel's hooves struck sparks from the tunnel floor, skidding to a halt. A long metal shaft shot from a concealed hole, its point digging deep into the rock wall opposite. It just missed him, blocking his way. He backed the horse, to see how he might get around or over it, and a second shaft sprang from the floor, burying its head in the ceiling. Now two poles, perpendicular, stood in his way.

Thinking he detected a pattern, he started to back again, afraid the next spike would spit him where he sat. Gabrielle wailed his name again. "Come forward, forward!" Breath failed her. He rushed up to the crossed shafts and two more, obliques, intersected where he'd have been without her warning.

Hightower rode up, greatsword in hand. It shone wetly in the dimness; he'd thought there was betrayal, and killed the luckless caravan leader. Putting all his weight behind it, he sheared one pole in half, the pieces falling away. Springbuck took his best swing with Bar, the sword called Never Blunted. He cleaved the second shaft. Behind him, the sides of the tunnel collapsed. Debris and fragments ricocheted.

Gabrielle exerted her will over the Gauntlet again; most of the powers of the deCourteneys had been exhausted in the last few minutes as, hundreds of miles away on the Isle of Keys, Andre launched a near-successful assault on the Hand of Salamá. Unknowingly, he had wrought disaster upon the army of Coramonde as well.

"I hold the Gauntlet," she panted, "but it cannot be

for long. Too many triggers have been sprung, trip wires broken, counterweights activated. The ultimate deadfall, the mountain itself, will crash down when I let go."

"Release your hold on those behind us as we go," Springbuck said, "and thus, conserve yourself." Those who'd been caught on the other side of the first pitfall, if they'd been able to do so, must have gotten clear by now; she'd held out long enough for that. He sheathed Bar with a clash and leaned low to take up a dropped torch.

He and the Warlord slipped their shields onto their arms. Again, they took places at her sides.

They galloped off, taking with them their circle of light and the tattoo of hooves. As they went, Gabrielle loosened her hold on the traps they'd passed. Steel darts whizzed in clouds, ceilings and walls collapsed, floors dropped away, smoking acid showered down, and boiled into the pitfalls. Deadly fumes curled up, too late, in their wake, and impaling-stakes sprung. Burning fluid lapped across the rock floors, and poisoned arrows whistled. Ten thousand murders were aborted.

The three burst from the southern mouth of the Gauntlet. The Trailingsword hung brighter, nearer in the night. Gabrielle, at the end of her enormous strength, lolled and swayed. Lynchpins, keystones, counterweights and latches, freed from her will, brought down their last trap. The mountain collapsed with a rumble. Men and horses lost balance as the earth shook. Dust, gas smoke belched from the tunnel's mouth.

Springbuck, face blackened, dismounted to stare back at it. "Is the area secure?" he asked an officer offhandedly.

"Yes, *Ku-Mor-Mai*. We found no sentinels." Indicating the Gauntlet, he explained. "They thought they needed none."

"My Lord Hightower, what do you think they'll do there, on the other side?"

The Warlord, looking up from tending Gabrielle, tugged his beard and thought. "There is old Drakemirth back there, and Balagon, and not least of all is Brodur-Scabbardless. They will take the long way, or perhaps even essay the shorter way through Amon's Cauldron,

252

but they will come, doubt it not. With them will come the far greater measure of our manpower."

"How fares Gabrielle?"

"She is spent, yet she will recover."

Springbuck stared at the Trailingsword, blurry to him. "Then, our route-sign beckons."

A wide, mountain-flanked valley guarded the way south. Flat and scorched a lifeless yellow, it reminded the crouching *Ku-Mor-Mai* of nothing so much as a brass skillet. At its far end, just short of the pass that gave access toward Salamá, stood the fortress at which the caravan had gathered, among its rearing ochre escarps, salients and battlements, Condor's Roost.

All told, Springbuck had less than two thousand souls in his separated element. Only five water wagons had come through the Gauntlet, and almost none of his lighter cavalry; he'd brought his heaviest chivalry through first, to resist any attack that might have sought to throw him back. There were none of the regular infantry he brought along on horseback, no pikemen, and too few archers. Still, it had seemed likely the collapse of the Gauntlet would draw investigation, and so he'd moved away from it. His scouts had left subtle signs for their counterparts with the rest of the army.

Some fortune had offset the tragedy of the Gauntlet. A strong simoon had come up to swirl sand and dust, obscuring the telltale cloud the army raised. It had made riding hard, driving grit into mail-links, eyes, ears and clothes, but Springbuck had greeted it with grudging pleasure.

Gabrielle lay on a litter in one of the few baggage wagons they had. She'd regained her senses, but was exhausted by the siphoning of her energies. She'd also entered a depression brought on by her mother's death, of which she refused to speak. Andre's singular demand on the deCourteneys' mystic bond had lapsed, and the sorceress was slowly recuperating. The simoon had died down a few hours before, and now, at late sunset, the air was eerily calm.

Condor's Roost was an impressive feat of construction in inhospitable wastes. The late caravaner had said it possessed capacious cisterns, fed by both springlets in the mountains around it and the infrequent rainfall. Springbuck, beginning to appreciate how pivotal water was in the Southwastelands, considered the need of water the major reason to begin against the fortress now, rather than waiting. His scouts had found no other source of it, and men and horses were using what they had at an alarming rate. Too, there was the deadline proclaimed by the Trailingsword.

But as intimidating as Condor's Roost was, it didn't quite span the pass from side to side. The land to Springbuck's left was fissured, textured from quirks of upheaval, defying fortification.

"An assault on those walls will cost us dearly," predicted Hightower, himself a master of entrenchments. "We cannot mount the frontal assault that will carry that pile by storm at the outset."

"Our scouts report no other way south," Springbuck replied.

The Warlord's brows knit. "And what will transpire, should the defenders duck out their back door and bring aid?"

"Disaster, maybe. It cannot be permitted."

"More lightly described than delivered, *Ku-Mor-Mai*."

Springbuck squinted, eyesight badly hampered by the distance, at those crevasses to the left.

"Bring me a man with the eagle's gaze. There may be a way."

A sharp-eyed archer from Rugor confirmed what Springbuck had thought. Those wrinkles in the earth's mantle might hold a way past, if men went carefully and on foot. They could take the pass behind the fortress. Holding it would be another question entirely.

"It would be a desperate position to man," Hightower said doubtfully, then shrugged off misgivings. "It can be accomplished though, I trow. Hah! Whosoever holds there will have a siege of his own to fight."

"I concede that, my Lord, but I think some resupply could be done by traversing the back hills and ridge lines. What other way is there?"

The Warlord's iron gloves slammed knuckle to knuckle in a decisive clang. "There is none," he said.

Chapter Twenty-seven

Let the gods avenge themselves.
                                    Roman legal maxim

THERE was the subdued rattle of manacles. Four field marshals of the Southwastelanders were ushered into the tent of their captor, the King of Freegate, Lord of the Just and Sudden Reach.

They were attired more as kings than conquered. Their armor, covered with the skins of the huge snakes and lizards of the deserts, shined with gems and gilt-work. They were Occhlon, a cruel race fit to prosecute the wars of Shardishku-Salamá, and they waited with elaborate indifference. After the victory of the Dream-drowse, Reacher had taken their force unprepared.

There was disdain in the captives' manner for this rabble of mongrels who'd dared enter these sacrosanct lands. The Occhlon had ridden out against invaders, thousands of spears catching the sun, scorpion banners in rippling life. There had been a collision in arms lasting a day and part of the next before going the way of the invaders.

The field marshals studied their enemies covertly. None of them knew just which was this monarch of Freegate. No single figure had been identified as commander. Alert, impatient in the brittle way of jungle beasts, they anticipated humiliation. Subordinate officers and aides were coming and going, and men of the Horseblooded, those amazing riders.

There'd been a shock of recognition between Occhlon and Horseblooded. Born to the saddle, the two races had fought encounters of incredible savagery, with feats of horsemanship and daring approaching insanity.

Senior among the Occhlon prisoners was a burly general named Aranan. He quickly sorted out the functionaries and lower echelons, and scrutinized the remainder. He thought he knew who his opposite number must be, that tall one, whose thick mustachios spread across his face like wings. The northerner took reports and gave terse orders, his forehead furrowing often in thought.

Besides those who might be this Lord of the Just and Sudden Reach and his subalterns, there was a strangely matched trio speaking softly together to one side. One was a sour-faced man, skinny, and not looking the part of a warrior. Moreover, he had an odd metal framework hung from his ears, which held circles of glass before his eyes. Doubtless a warlock.

The second was plainly a savage of some type, wearing only a cincture and gloves, a heavy cestus on his left hand and a gauntlet with long, curving claws on his right. The third was more noteworthy, a woman decked out in armor, with knives strapped to her hips and a sword slung at her back. Her blond hair, bleached nearly white by the desert sun, fell to her waist. A woman, thought Aranan, allowed to go about as if she were a man? Really, the perversions of these outlanders! He hid his shame and fury, that a lowly female should witness the disgrace of an Occhlon general.

In anger, he squared off before the tall warrior he assumed to be King. From habit, Aranan set his left hand on his empty scabbard. "We stand as your prisoners today, my Lord of the Just and Sudden Reach, but you would do well to remember balances; there is symmetry to war, as to the Wheel of Fate."

The man of Freegate looked him over carefully. "What would that mean, pray?"

"That your grasp has overextended itself, and will be lopped off in due course. You have come too far."

"So? Never would we have raised the banner of war to you, but that you did so to us."

The Southwastelander's face reddened under sunbrowned skin. "My sword would answer you, were we on the field. We are Occhlon, a warrior race, premier in duty to our Masters!"

"Among others, you mean?" the outlander asked with honest interest.

"Lions among warriors!" the desert man barked.

256

"There are the Baidii, but they are ancient, decadent and unworthy. And there are the Odezat, who fight more for pay than pride, but before all others there are the Occhlon."

"Your race lives for war, then?"

Aranan's chest puffed with pride. "Inspired to arms, we rose as the new champions of Salamá."

The mustache moved, a smile showing beneath it. "The field is ours today."

"Your reversal is forthcoming."

The northerner caught his lip between thumb and forefinger. "Our full strengths are yet to be matched."

Aranan spat on the carpet. "Strengths? Match yours against mine then, dung-eater!" He held his right hand out, daring the Freegater to try wrists. The northerner looked the hand over speculatively, but restrained himself.

Another came forward, the savage whom Aranan had noticed. He watched the Southwastelander for a moment, then threw his left hand up and took the challenge. His fingers, in their cestus, interlaced with Aranan's. "If you would try your might and main with the King of Freegate, your wish is now come as fact."

The Occhlon's eyebrows shot up. "You?"

Reacher saw no need to repeat it. Hands bore down and wrists flexed. There was a slight quivering as they stepped up their efforts. The southerner was shocked at the absolute resistance he met. Aranan, ever a winner at the wrist-duel, huffed and strove, but never gained a hairsbreadth.

Reacher exerted himself. A sudden yielding, and their hands flip-flopped. It was the field marshal's hand bent up and under, and he who cried in pain. Reacher let go and turned from him at once. Guards moved to take the prisoners away, but the general resisted, addressing Reacher's back.

"Go into Mother Desert then," he invited, "go find your end. We are many, and we are ready. And forget it not, that you are rousing older, more terrible wrath. Do you think we fly the banner of Ibn-al-Yed idly, or that all his magic died with him? Mother Desert, and the Five who rule her, have many, many secrets to bring out in their good time. The Scorpion Flag is not thrown down so rudely."

Reacher, back still turned, gestured. The guards hustled the prisoner away. The officer who'd refused Aranan's challenge said, "Will there be aught else, sire?" The King shook his head. They bowed, though he didn't face them.

His second-in-command, Katya, came to him. "Surely you pay that blusterer no mind?" she pressed. "We have broken them; they have no men left in this land to send at us."

"Which, I believe, is what your brother's fretting about," interjected Van Duyn. "The Masters have sent the majority of their manpower elsewhere, it seems, and you've dealt with what was left. Still, I'd say it's obvious that they're determined to buy time. Now, with no mundane resources left, to what will they resort, d'you suppose? Reacher's wondering what else they might have in, um, reserve, just as I am."

The King confirmed it. The Snow Leopardess shook her head, white-gold shimmering. "Borrow no trouble, brother." She took her casque up. "I will make the rounds."

Van Duyn said he'd come, and she accepted cheerily. She wanted to hear more of the tales he'd been telling her from medieval Japanese history. She thought highly of that culture.

When they'd left, Reacher went to the flaps of his tent. The sun was setting on the Southwastelands. He wished he were back with his lupine foster brothers, running the High Ranges. What, indeed, would the Five send against him, now that their armed resistance had been thrown back?

The King, stretching his fingers in their cestus and clawed glove, was plagued by that.

Making his uneventful circuit of the camp, the guard swayed now and then in the saddle. Protracted battle had sapped the strength of every man in the army of Freegate, and the Horseblooded as well.

His mount stopped, sniffing the slow breeze. He could see nothing there, but became more alert. It might be some jackal or other scavenger from the battlefield below, but again it might be an enemy. He clucked and advanced beyond the torchlight ring to investigate.

His death, punctuated by his screams, roused that end of the camp. Two more guards came, shields up, lances ready, to see what had happened to their comrade. From the darkness came a rasping, like the uneven release of some immense, ratcheted wheel. Red points of light gleamed. One sentinel veered toward those, lance-head going before.

His weapon was seized and snapped like a splinter, he and his horse flung aside with absolute force. The second rider bore in on the intruder's side, though he couldn't make out clearly what it was. His lancehead was stopped as if he'd ridden into a boulder, lifting him from his saddle; his horse foundered for a moment, was grasped and raised in the air. There was a sound like rusty, grinding metal, and the animal's sides and neck were crushed.

Horns blew, raising the alarm. Relief sentries grabbed torches and rode out behind their watch commanders. In Van Duyn's tent, the Snow Leopardess and the American awoke. They slipped on clothes, took up weapons, and threw back the door-hangings. From there, they gaped out at the cause of the furor.

Some Power had dispatched a servant against the invading army, an old and dreaded guardian of Mother Desert. While men rode in circles around it, waving firebrands and yelling half in provocation, half in terror, the enormous scorpion moved with purpose toward the slope leading to the King's pavilion. This servant of Salamá had been set to slay the King of Freegate, removing the motivating force of the invasion. Katya saw that the thing didn't swerve from its course when archers swooped in to loose their shafts at close range, nor did it stop to rend the fallen with its chelicerae and feed on soft tissues and juices. Its pharynx pumped, anticipating food, and its mouth frothed, but there was only one man in the camp who would sate its hunger.

Arrows bounced off it; spears did no better, and sword cuts rebounded unnoticed. Strident raspings of its pedipalps against its walking legs announced its anger, but it wouldn't be turned aside. A horseman came too close; the monster picked up his vibrations through its pectines, pivoted with amazing agility and trapped him in its claw, snipping him neatly in two. His companions fell back in horror. The scorpion dropped the pieces and scuttled on quickly.

"He's seen it," the Snow Leopardess said. At the summit of the hill, Reacher had appeared, staring down tight-faced at the monster. Katya wasn't so contemplative; she took the first horse she came to, sword in hand. Van Duyn, looking around, could find no other mount. Shouldering the Garand, he went off after her at a trot.

The camp was fully aroused, and more coherent defense took shape. A line of pikemen grounded their weapons' butts and formed their hedge. The emissary of the Masters crunched in among them like a machine though, and the polearms were turned aside or snapped off by its thick chitin. Several of the heavily armored horsemen had been stung, and now the envenomed tail darted in among the infantrymen, everywhere at once, passing through their mail. Soldiers heaved in convulsions, their autonomic systems paralyzed. The blue of cyanosis was in some faces already, from the massive doses of poison meted out. Death was nearly immediate.

Kisst-Haa and another reptile-man lumbered up to block its way, their armored tails thrashing. Kisst-Haa's first blow missed; the scorpion's movements were too quick. It struck him down with a claw, and he lay still. The sting curled in, quick as thought, transfixing the other reptile-man, piercing the scales of his breast. He went down, filled with poison; the monster clambered on over his body.

Off to one side a ballista cracked, one of the many captured war machines. Its long shaft went true, but rattled off the thick plates covering the creature.

Katya broke through the lines of demoralized soldiers. She galloped behind the thing, knowing its pedipalpi and stinging tail could only strike to the front. She cut at the busy tail as hard as she could, but only notched her sword. The scorpion whirled in an instant, catching her horse's leg. She jumped free, but the animal died with a pitiful whinny. The thing started for Reacher's pavilion. The King waited, analyzing its attack.

Van Duyn came up with his M-1, to bar the way. The Garand belted against his shoulder over and over, empty shell casings flying from its breach. He used a whole clip, but the scorpion was unscathed. Its tiny median eyes and the smaller clusters on its side margins might be vulnerable, but they were impossible to hit at this range in torchlight. The monster swarmed past the helpless American.

Alone now in his pavilion, Reacher collected a pair of javelins and a long firebrand, and loped toward the captured siege machines. He knew scorpions usually lie in wait and seize their prey rather than give chase, and had incorporated that in his plan. Moments later the monster plowed into the deserted pavilion like a reaping machine, flailing and snapping with its pedipalpi, shredding thick fabric, crushing tentpoles. Finding its prey gone, it reversed field and backed out of the ruin, its pectines listening, making its rasp of agitation.

The monster had detected Reacher now, charging off on his trail. The King had gotten to the ballista, now left unmanned, its crew gone to join their captain. Dropping his javelines and propping his torch in the sand, he began spinning the winch to prime the colossal bow-engine, his back and arms bunching with effort. Hand over hand he turned the wheel that drew the great nock back.

He heard rasping and left the machine as the scorpion flailed out of the night at him. Reacher grabbed the torch and a javelin and dashed out onto open sand, moving over it lightly, his stride resilient. The creature came after, wallowing a little in the looser sand, away from the summit of the camp. The King raced in a wide arc, drawing it along. When he had a fair lead on it, he dug his heels in to stop in a spray of granules, and grounded the torch.

He poised, took a few running steps and cast hard at his pursuer, then sped away again. The weapon clattered at the thick carapace, glancing near the tiny median eyes. The scorpion stopped, rasped in furious challenge, then hurried after. But Reacher had dashed ahead, circled and come back to the half-cocked ballista. He jumped to the winch, taking the wheel through full turns at a time.

Other warriors caught up now, but he waved them back; no weapon they carried could serve his purpose. The clash of chitinous armor came from the night. The King found the last prop he needed, a thick-beamed brace, like a sawhorse of logs, part of a disassembled trebuchet. He jerked it cleanly, to carry it at chest height, walking step by slow step to set it in front of the ballista.

As the scorpion came into the light again, on his fleet trail Reacher snatched the remaining javelin and another torch. The scorpion sidled around to block him, anticipating his moves now. He broke to the right, releasing the other javelin, pivoting off his follow-through. The barbed head struck in among the foaming pharynx, making a wound this time. The grating of the monster's wrath drowned out all other sounds, as it ripped out the javelin.

It tried to close on him, but its claws clacked shut on empty air; Reacher had circled off to the right. They began a hair-raising dance, the King trying to stay away from his foe by staying close in behind it, the scorpion whirling madly to catch him. Van Duyn and Katya arrived, but couldn't intervene or shoot in the darkness and constant, unpredictable motion.

Reacher leapt, backpedaled and changed field. Spinning on its pairs of walking legs, the creature came near but never quite caught the monarch of Freegate. Bit by bit he teased and baited the monster to the position in which he wanted it.

He skipped to the right, ducked under the claw that swung at him, and threw the torch into the chattering pharynx. The scorpion hissed, but he disappeared just before the sting smashed into the sand where he'd stood. Reacher whacked the sickle tail with his cestus and, spinning on his heel, dashed away.

The scorpion scuttled after, driven mad by the taunting. Reacher sprinted toward the ballista, arms and legs pumping, head rising and falling in steady rhythm. Behind him came the pounding of the beast's walking legs, the creak of unlimbering claws eager for his flesh.

Just before he got to the ballista, he took to the air like a hart, and used the brace as a springboard. The scorpion, an instant behind him, scrambled up with its pincers spread. The King perched on the ballista's long muzzle for a single glance back; the monster was hauling itself up hastily, all in its rage, sure it had him. Its walking legs clicked on the brace, its pincers clamped on the ballista's huge wooden stave, tilting its snout down.

Reacher gathered himself and dove flawlessly over the rear end of the siege engine, catching the halyard as he passed, tugging it free. The titan's-bow released.

The shaft, longer and heavier than a knight's lance, tipped with steel, sprang point-blank into the scorpion's underplate, where its carapace was joined. The monster's breath whistled; its limbs thrashed, and it toppled, to writhe on its back in the sand. Sluggish juices ran from it. It struggled to right itself, the primitive nervous system surrendering to spasms. Soon, all its movements were random, erratic. Gradually, they became feeble. The King edged closer; Van Duyn and the Snow Leopardess joined him, along with revived Kisst-Haa. The side-margin eyes seemed to pick the little monarch out, burning with impotent hatred.

The tumult had been heard in the prisoners' tent but, shackled to their tentpole, surrounded by glittering spears, they were ignorant of what it meant. Aranan thought he knew though; in a way, he felt sorry for the King and his men, that they must go down to a Summoning, and not the proper force of arms.

The curtain was tossed back. The King of Freegate strode into the room. He had Aranan unchained, then hauled him to his feet. Reacher turned and went back out; a foot taller than the King, a hundred pounds heavier, the general was tugged along helplessly, like some gangling adolescent.

Reacher dragged him down the slope and flung him headlong to the ground before the quivering body of the scorpion. Its legs and terrible claws waved aimlessly, all but still. The long ballista iron rose from its carapace like a bare flagpole. The general tried to form words, but no sounds came.

The King went down on one knee beside him, taking the edge of his breastplate and yanking him close. As ever, the words came softly.

"There is your emblem itself cast down." Aranan mouthed like a fish. Reacher shoved him, and he fell back in the sand under the stars and the Trailingsword. "Tell me now," Reacher invited, "how your Mother Desert will deal with me."

Aranan, in a fit of childish pique, burst out, "Hold this deed in your heart; you will have no other like it. Brave acts of arms will avail nothing if you are ill-starred enough to win through to—" He caught himself.

"Go on with it," the King provoked him, "finish your threat."

Aranan yielded to the baiting. "March south then, you overweaning savage. Shardishku-Salamá has that protection through which no mortal may win, the Host of the Grave."

Reacher, his emotions veiled again, left the man there. He went to stand among the wreckage of his pavilion, head bent in thought. The phrase took up residence in his apprehensions: *the Host of the Grave.*

Chapter Twenty-eight

All in a hot and copper sky,
The bloody sun, at noon . . .
　　　　　Samuel Taylor Coleridge
　　　　　The Rime of the Ancient Mariner

THERE'D been no patrols from the southerners. They must fear little, Springbuck thought, here at the inner door to their heartlands. The *Ku-Mor-Mai* had thought to lead the flanking party himself, but Hightower had gruffly pre-empted him.

Ironically, the added light of the Trailingsword became a complication. Hightower decided to minimize the danger of discovery by keeping to the shadows along the base of the crags forming the valley. He'd

264

gone among the thousands, picking whom he wanted, five hundred men with infantry experience.

Armor had been lamp-blackened, boots muffled, and metal sollerets and all needless trappings abandoned. Scabbards were wrapped with dark cloth to prevent sound. Each man had a light pack of provisions, climbing rope and water skin. Most bore lances to serve as pikes, but some had bows and quivers.

They set out under a new moon, bent to inspect the ground over which they must find their way, each within arm's reach of the man in front of him. At the fissures, they would rope themselves together. The gradual coiling of their march went slowly. Springbuck, seeing how difficult it was, hoped they'd have time to reach their goal and dig in before daylight. Scouts had already been sent to find another way, however precarious, to the end of the valley. The chaotic peaks and falls of the region made it dangerous, even for practiced mountaineers.

Two hours passed, during which Springbuck constantly revised his estimate of the positions and speed of his flankers. He went back to his concealed camp twice, to inquire after Gabrielle's condition. She'd left the trance or coma into which she'd fallen and entered natural sleep.

Came the glowing of fire, with distant shouting. The fortress' gates were thrown open. A patrol exited, passing burning cressets in the bailey. The *Ku-Mor-Mai* waited for their traveling lanterns to send back just one fatal reflection from his Warlord's contingent. But the patrol passed down the valley, fifty strong, without incident. With it came strings of spare horses, replacements.

An officer voiced Springbuck's own thoughts, "Lord, if they go that way they will certainly come upon their ruined Gauntlet."

"Aye, but it isn't to be helped. They aren't many, and there are none in this territory to whom they can take the tale. But we must beware that they don't come down on us by raid or sally."

He wished he could send some men after that patrol; he badly needed horses, and the intelligent, courageous war mounts of the southern breeds would have outvalued mere gold and gems. However, he needed every

265

man, and held them at their places. Tired as they all were, they got little sleep. The first remote hint of dawn lifted their spirits somewhat.

The air brought a resounding crack of boulders shifting, the tremor and scrape of a rockslide. Springbuck knew Hightower and his men, heaving and levering with lances, had managed to block the pass at least partially. Men in the ramparts could be heard faintly, calling to find out what had happened.

The northerners were all ahorse, meals gulped and prayers recited, by the time day was bright enough to be of any use. They cantered out to wind their way down onto the flatlands below, blowing trumpets and unfurling banners. The tip of the sun watched the scene in minor arc. They drew up and gusted their challenge. At first the enemy commander thought them mad, but knowing something had happened in the pass at his back, he reserved judgment. He sent a mounted party out the south gate, to look into the disturbance he'd heard last night, and kept the rest of his men ready, some at the ramparts and others assembled on horseback in the bailey.

Springbuck came forward after a time. His trumpeter blew defiance, and a herald showed the snarling tiger banner of Coramonde, crimson on black.

"What alien blazonry is that you do display?" the commander shouted.

"Coramonde," Springbuck supplied.

"You are a long way south, stranger; a foolish trip, only to die."

"There is scant office for words here, southern man. We mean to pass through this place."

"Do you? Demand our swords from us then, and you shall have them, but not hilts first!"

"As you wish. We are at your disposal; prove your words on us." He threw an offhanded salute, but the commander ignored it. The *Ku-Mor-Mai* thought that the enemy, if he were wise, would wait and see how the situation in the pass looked before committing himself. Springbuck pictured it as he went back to his men. A scouting party going up the pass would meet the jumble of boulders, still-shifting gravel and blowing dust from fallen, powdered rock. They'd be permitted to come close before men of Coramonde struck in ambush from high ground. Arrows, boulders and other debris would be as deadly, thrown from the heights, as the guns of Van Duyn and Gil MacDonald. It would be a mauled reconnaissance detail that returned to the Condor's Roost.

Passing time, the *Ku-Mor-Mai* had his men withdraw to the opposite end of the field and dismount to rest horses. The sun climbed and grew warmer. Many men broke out the light silken awnings given them by the Yalloroon, to spare themselves the heat. Seeing the distance an enemy must sally to reach them, Springbuck made no objection.

It was late forenoon when the distant sound of drums and cymbals came. The men in the fortress knew they were under siege. Awnings were snatched down with wispy haste from the lances supporting them. The orderly confusion of preparation was carried out in seconds. Springbuck led his men out again, shifting his grip on his lance, settling and resetting his shield on his arm. His supple mail had become uncomfortably warm.

The sunlight had become acute, wincing-bright. As always, the *Ku-Mor-Mai* had sharp-eyed aides nearby to inform him of anything his own poor vision might miss. The castle's drawbridge dropped. Southwastelanders came out with a whooping and howling, whirling scimitars and longswords over their heads in gleaming circles, their lances carrying many battle streamers. These, prisoners had told Springbuck, were Baidii, men of a race that, unlike the Occhlon, had lived in this region throughout history, longtime retainers of Shardish-ku-Salamá. They were fewer than a thousand, so Springbuck gave the order that one-third of the elements left to him stay back in reserve.

The Baidii came in thick groups, not the precise alignments of Coramonde. Their panoply featured flaring ridges and much scalloping; their headdress-helmets were upholstered with silk and linen and leather, to shed heat. The northerners found intervals and spacings and continued a slow advance; the *Ku-Mor-Mai* wished to conserve his horses.

When he saw the gap was small enough, he gave the word and touched spurs to Fireheel. The gray shot forward as the battle flourish blared. Visors clanged down, lance points aligned with the foe, and rowels went into flanks. In each man's mind the wide valley became an arena, his own corridor of it filled with a thousand perils and possibilities. Fallow yellow earth was gouged by flashing hooves as horses, scenting combat, lengthened stride.

Springbuck felt the eroding confidence he always knew before mass combat. His imagination was too vivid not to toss up scenes of his death.

The two groups crashed together. The weightier men of Coramonde bore through lighter-armored Baidii. Lances hunted for direct routes past shields; many found them. The uproar came, compounded of neighs and screams, jockeying hooves and striking steel.

Men kept to their standards as best they could, the Coramondians with more discipline than the Southwastelanders. They went together over and over, zealots of war. Springbuck's spear turned from an hourglass-shaped shield, the Baidii's own lance sliding from his. They came around and went at each other a second time.

The southerner, perhaps thinking the *Ku-Mor-Mai* lacked skill or heart, swung his lance in the long, side-sweeping stroke that could only be used safely on an inferior opponent. Springbuck knew what it meant about the man's estimate of him. He grasped his spear with conviction, tightening at the last moment, and struck just when he should, clamping knees to Fireheel and keeping his seat in drill-field style. His foe's longer, side-on stroke hadn't reached him yet.

The son of Surehand slipped his point past the hourglass shield. The lance struck through the man's pauldron and drove him back off his horse, Fireheel's speed and power delivered along its shaft. The weapon, fixed in the Baidii's chest, was torn from Springbuck's grip.

He looked around; the fight was about even. The Baidii, more lightly armed, were born to the saddle, masters with lances. But now the moment of the lance was over, most spears being broken or left in an enemy's body. Men of the north worked with heavier broadswords, picks, maces and axes. They could take

268

and deal greater punishment, and that decided the melee.

Springbuck, with Bar drawn, kept close by his standard, trying to watch what was happening. The sabre was busy, as Springbuck made the acquaintance of the southern scimitar. He dealt a thrust, standing in his stirrups as Fireheel battered, teeth bared, against a southern charger. He never heard the braying of the ram's horn that called the Baidii to break off battle.

They withdrew in good order, too fast for the jeering men of Coramonde to catch. The enemy commander had seen all he wished. Now he'd consider his next move, letting Mother Desert do his work in the meantime.

Coramonde carried its dead and wounded from the field. The clash hadn't lasted ten minutes. Springbuck had the southern dead dropped at the far end of the valley, just out of bowshot of Condor's Roost. The few Baidii wounded who hadn't managed to withdraw with their fellows asked, and were given, the grace-stroke, knowing they were of no further use to Salamá.

The full weight of the sun's glare came down. The northerners spread awnings again and found or made what shade they could for their horses. Waterskins were passed. The *Ku-Mor-Mai* was forced to order that men conserve water, for their own and their mounts' sakes both. There was no fuel for fires, but they were content to dine on cold food and talk of victory.

The sun soon had them loosing their armor. Springbuck allowed it, but forbade any man to remove his panoply. He himself stayed fully ready, though he wanted nothing more than to lie in the shade with a little something to drink. Instead, he squatted with his buttocks on a rock and a scrap of silk draped over his head, plumed war mask on the ground at his feet. It would take more men to settle a true siege. If Brodur and the rest were long delayed, this effort might end in disaster. He rose presently, and went among the injured.

Late that afternoon three scouts came back. They'd found what they thought to be a roundabout way to the pass where Hightower held, but it could only be negotiated by descending a cliff face and climbing another. Springbuck took aside a dozen men of Teebra, who

269

were at home hunting and fighting on rocky crags. He ordered them to contact the Warlord, whatever it took to do so. Other scouts reported no water sources or alternate routes past Condor's Roost.

Night came on, and the Trailingsword. Springbuck shivered in the darkness, still surprised at how cold these sun-broiled lands could become, calculating the time it would take the rest of his corps to arrive. Seven days, with luck? More like ten, or even fourteen, if they met intense resistance. He commanded that all water be put under a senior captain, whom he designated Water Officer, and rationed out each day to the leaders of the various elements under him.

Wind rustled sand against his heels. Now he perceived that other enemy, ally to the Southwastelanders. How many men, he asked himself, had Mother Desert vanquished before she'd come to grips with him?

Springbuck's vision wouldn't keep focus. It hadn't come to his attention before, because rising waves of heat played with every image meeting the eye in the inferno that was midafternoon. As always, the sky was burned a cloudless blue.

It was the eighth day following the battle before Condor's Roost. Rations of water were down to sips per day. Men stinted their energy, not moving much. They ate lightly; dry, parched throats made it difficult and left even greater thirst in the wake of food. Everywhere, horses stood with drooping heads under awnings the men had been forced to erect to keep the sun from them. Unused to the desert's oppression, some of the chargers had already died. The animals, too, were on drastically short water allotments. The last of the oats and feed had been eaten days ago. Now horses dined on what their masters could spare.

The desert furnace sucked strength from the *Ku-Mor-Mai* as he sat. His lips, like everyone's, were swollen, cracked and peeling. His tongue moved viscously in his mouth; talking was an increasing effort.

Gabrielle was in the improvised tent he'd had fashioned for her. She'd regained much of her strength, but her arcane energies were gathering to her more slowly.

270

He'd asked if she could help their situation, but after an evening of effort, she'd confessed that she could avail little. Condor's Roost had been imbued with its own wards and defenses against occult assault. She would be able to penetrate them, given time, but not soon enough to be of use. Her one attempt had endangered her with total collapse.

In another day or so, Springbuck knew, there'd be no option but to try frontal attack, unless it was to try to get through the pass at night, past now-vigilant Baidii. He'd sent a second group of mountaineers, two days before, to ask his Warlord if they oughtn't withdraw completely or link up, but had received no reply. He had to presume the message had never arrived. It mattered little now; they'd never make it back through the desert without water. Their only chance of getting some lay in making it through the pass or, if they could get into it, in Condor's Roost. For the latter, he'd lost most of his hope.

He damned the delay in his reinforcements, more by rote than in passion. Vultures rested in the heights, waiting for the carrion due them from their Mother Desert. Several men had tried to catch one, to drink its blood, but the birds were wary, and the *Ku-Mor-Mai* had ordered it ceased, to preserve energy. That had been yesterday; now he didn't have to command anyone to keep still. His men were surviving on their last reserves. Before evening, he must make some decision.

His bolder subordinates counseled storming. But there were no rams, no towers or ladders or catapults, few archers, a total absence of cover and little stamina. Still, that was rapidly becoming the only option.

He heard cymbals and shook his head, thinking his hearing had been affected. They came again on heat-distorted air, with the paying out of heavy chain. He dragged the silk from his head and got unsteadily to his feet, shaking men around him and pulling them to theirs.

The gates of Condor's Roost were opening, its drawbridge lowering across the dry, stake-defended moat. Springbuck went to Fireheel, whose head was lowered in unaccustomed indifference. The big gray

271

barely responded as his master climbed clumsily into the saddle. But then Fireheel snorted, and livened somewhat.

Men were scrambling ahorse now, awkward with haste and depletion. They fell in, not the same iron warriors who'd ridden so fervidly against the Baidii that first day. Mother Desert had daunted them.

Gabrielle stepped from her tent. Seeing Springbuck, she half-raised her hand, as if she would have waved, then let it fall. He'd had a horse prepared and left for her, with some water and a few provisions. It made him less despondent, thinking she, at least, might leave the valley alive. With the camp so crowded and privacy so scant, he'd avoided her. Now he wished, too late, that they'd spoken.

There were more Baidii today, he saw, supposing the garrison was out to end the siege at one blow. Perhaps Hightower still had the southern route sealed; Springbuck no longer cared, hoping the old man would find some way to get south with what was left of his unit.

The Southwastelanders formed ranks more carefully this time, archers at the rear. Springbuck had his men drawn up, but knew they could never charge. The horses' endurance was gone; they could only save what moment's vigor might be left, and deal with the Baidii at close quarters.

The *Ku-Mor-Mai* wondered if the rest of his army, if it still existed, would be stopped, to end the expedition against Salamá entirely. He was bitter; Salamá had done well against him, while he'd barely gotten to strike.

The Baidii advanced, undulating eerily in the heat waves. Men of Coramonde readied themselves, but didn't move. Springbuck took one last look around, execrating Mother Desert. His shield dragged at his arm; chain mail weighted him. Men around him hoisted their swords and bucklers; there weren't many lances left among them.

The Baidii hit like a flash flood into a hapless orchard. For dozens of the Coramondian chargers it was the last exertion. Unable to cope with heat and dehydration, their hearts failed and they fell even as they tried to answer the bit one last time.

The surge of battle sparked hidden remains of Springbuck's endurance. He met his foe with a good, accurate strike. The man's falling weight dragged the lance from his hand, and he yanked out Bar. He was glad the enemy hadn't stood back for an archer's duel; the Southwastelanders wanted to repay their injuries sword to sword, a transaction Springbuck welcomed.

They filled the plain, losing formation, gathering to this or that banner to go against some other. The Baidii were darker and leaner than the Occhlon, burned by centuries in the oven of the desert. They were ready to retest themselves against the invaders. Men of Coramonde responded with cold fatalism, taking whatever strokes or wounds they must, patiently waiting out their chance to lash out again. The Baidii, out to prove they could stand their ground against the northerners, found that in truth they couldn't. Their pride and confidence in Mother Desert had brought them to grips with tenacious, dogged enemies. Springbuck and his men, accepting that they were to die, were borne up by that terrible emancipation.

Fighting was ferocious and all-encompassing. The Baidii, in their vanity, ignored the drums that ordered them back. If they hadn't, archers could have sent showers of steel-headed death at the northerners. But arrogance won; the Southwastelanders elected to stay and test their mettle.

Springbuck's arm began to ache, something that hadn't happened to him since he'd been in training as a boy. More and more northern horses were dropping from exhaustion. Everywhere, men of Coramonde began to show signs of final fatigue, but struck in heavy, killing blows that clove light desert armor and dark southern skin. Blood from both sides covered the thirsty sand and splashed on horses' fetlocks.

At last Springbuck drew back, telling his standard-bearer to follow. He meant to withdraw what men he had left, and form a last line. A cry went up from the enemy, to see the remaining banners carried back, clustered in desperation. There were no more than eight hundred northerners against half again that many Southwastelanders. Springbuck had no brave words, and couldn't have shaped them through his swollen throat if he had.

The sun seemed to be burning its way through the back of his war mask. With it came eerie calm. The son of Surehand thought a lobster might feel so, in the pot where it meets its boiling end. The Baidii came on again, though their officers forbade them halfheartedly. The Southwastelanders were ordinarily well disciplined, but now they were at retribution, not war.

Men of Coramonde, stirrup and stirrup, withdrew step by slow step, backing their horses. They surrendered one hundred yards over the next quarter-hour, the hardest fighting Springbuck had ever seen. Suddenly patience and common sense ended. Death was the only coin in which he cared to traffic.

His standard-bearer was resisting the mandates of wounds that must, the *Ku-Mor-Mai* knew, claim him. Springbuck snatched his crimson tiger banner, throwing aside his crumpled shield to take it up. Fireheel, feeling his rider's moribund mood, pushed forward. The *Ku-Mor-Mai* voiced a challenge through his tortured throat and went among the Baidii, with the sword called Never Blunted hewing his way.

Behind him were men of Teebra. In the custom of their tribes, they threw down their own shields, drew out the heavy short swords that hung at their sides, and accompanied their Protector-Suzerain with bright blades in either hand. In a moment the entire remaining force had cast itself after him.

Springbuck slashed and drove, dully curious. From which quarter would the final enemy come? Then he felt a certain change in the tenor of the engagement. Dismayed cries spread through the southern ranks from the rear.

Up from behind them came a frost-haired giant on a coal-black desert charger, and the men who'd stood at the pass with him, weapons rising and falling with fresh enthusiasm.

The Baidii, outraged at what they took for some warped deception, turned to fight on this second front. The *Ku-Mor-Mai* collected the men left to him and held his ground. Many Baidii ran. They couldn't imagine what kind of maniacs would fight until they were nearly obliterated, for a military deceit. They didn't know Springbuck and his men were as surprised as they.

In time the onslaught stopped, Hightower faced Springbuck as yellow dust settled, and the younger man slowly considered the fact that he was still alive.

Springbuck pushed himself from the saddle and half-dismounted, half-fell. Sitting there, he wrenched his war mask off with a sigh and threw it from him. Many others did the same, blinking as if awakening from sleep.

Hightower unhorsed. He offered the Protector-Suzcrain a scrap of dampened cloth and Springbuck drew it across his tortured lips, squeezing excess water into his mouth greedily. Only then did the Warlord offer him a short drink from a small skin at his belt. There were other waterskins; Springbuck's troops thronged to be next to drink.

"How?" was all Springbuck had the strength to wheeze.

"Not easily," conceded Hightower. "Come to your feet and walk a bit. 'Tis improper for a leader to sit about when his men have not been seen to."

"It isn't for this one," Springbuck husked, in his abused gullet. Still, he let the white-maned hero pull him to his feet.

The story came in starts and stops as Hightower gave orders for them all to withdraw to Condor's Roost. He and his few hundred had taken it. He sent a detail to fetch the wounded and bring Gabrielle.

From his position, the Warlord had looked down at preparations for the sally out of the fortress. As Hightower had known he must, the opposing commander had stripped his command to put together the force he needed. The Warlord had, in preceding days, readied scaling ladders for this time. That confused Springbuck, who'd seen no trees worth the name.

"Well, I know something of war," Hightower admitted, "and old ideas sometimes serve." Using long, stout lances, he and his men had bound up serviceable ladders with climbing ropes and strips of leather cut from empty drinking skins and their own gear. Springbuck later saw one, with cleverly leather-hinged tripods for legs.

"But still, those walls are so high," he said.

"Aye, high and hazardous. But I evened that considerable with another rockslide; it took us days to prepare that. We had long lines on the ladders to steady 'em, but two toppled anyway and I lost men. The walls cost us too; these Baidii are men for a fight, regular razors when they are aroused. Someone was drumming for the men out there on the field to retreat, but they thought it had to do with the fight in front of them, so they kept at it from pride. We took the horses we needed, and here we are. Are you fit to ride now, my Lord?"

They all rode or limped or carried one another to the fortress. Motionless bodies on the ramparts and in the bailey attested to the heat of the struggle to take Condor's Roost.

The *Ku-Mor-Mai* stayed awake long enough to command that the injured be tended, the dead buried, scouts sent out, guards posted, horses cared for and all the other things that would have been done anyway. There were drinking spigots and troughs, and men crowded by these and waded into them, too weak to rejoice, dousing themselves and gulping reverently. Hightower posted some of his own troops to make sure no one made himself sick.

Springbuck trudged off, leaving Hightower in charge. He found at last the quarters of the enemy commander, who'd died resisting the Warlord's sally, and bolted himself into it. It was set off a cool courtyard, shaded and quiet. Water trickled from a fountain into a cool, green basin. He plunged his head in, and his crackled skin ached wonderfully. He drank slowly, then filled a goblet from it. Torpidly, he stripped mail and gambeson, boots, vambraces and sword from his body. Cool air began to lift the reek from his naked skin.

He lay down on a couch, unclothed to the fragrant breeze that came through the fretwork. With a last sublime sip from the goblet, he fell asleep.

The lock-bolt slid back softly on its carrier, obeying a disembodied will. The door opened silently on oiled hinges. He flinched awake, sweat covering him, alarm on his face.

Gabrielle stood there, looking down. She regarded

the bruises, cuts and lacerations, his sunburned face and raw, split lips. She studied his eyes in their hollow settings. She drew the sash from her waist and opened the burnoose, shedding her clothes like white plumage.

He hid his questions from himself and took the moment as it occurred, fearing that if he spoke it would elude him like an evaporating vision.

She joined him on the couch, for a passage at love that proved their flesh had forgotten nothing. She drew away as much of his pain, healed as much of his suffering as lay within her province to do.

In time she told him, "I came south with him long ago, Springbuck, when Hightower was all in his prime, and together we strove. From the best motives he presumed to overstep the things the Bright Lady had said we might accomplish. For that he was made blind. Hightower remembers what he and I had between us then as love, and who am I, who owe him so much, to deny it? Yet loyalty and indebtedness are not love; and I understood that when the traps almost took you from me in the Gauntlet."

Afterward he slept. She rose, took the billowing robes and left him, closing the door softly after her. Condor's Roost was aswarm. She found Hightower where he was in conference with subordinates. He saw what had happened from her expression; she discerned no disapproval in his. She stood near him, taking his hand, her head on his arm. They communed unspoken grief.

Chapter Twenty-nine

Hark! from the tombs a doleful sound

Isaac Watts
Hymns II

EXCEPT for those duties considered indispensable by Hightower, the army rested and tended its wounds for two days. They slept, bathed, ate and slaked their thirsts with as much water as they wanted.

Condor's Roost kept a bulging pantry against time of war. They dined on unfamiliar southern dishes; jellied meats, shrimp in sweet syrup, spits of highly garnished goat and dog, and honeyed parrot. Debris was cleared away from the pass to open the way south. There was sufficient manpower to rotate crews frequently, so no man had to work more than an hour or two each day.

The fortress' forges came to life, as northern smiths began reshoeing those horses needing it. Gear was being repaired, food and water supplies readied. Springbuck threw himself into preparations, determined to keep the appointment of the Trailingsword. There were now two weeks left in its seven times seven days.

On the third day following the end of the siege, he was called to the ramparts. Hightower was there, shading his eyes against noon's punishments; he showed the *Ku-Mor-Mai* where, at the end of the valley, a column of fours had come riding. An alarm was made. This could as easily be bad news as good.

When the newcomers were halfway down the valley and the fortress' walls were crowded with its former besiegers, sharp-eyed watchers began to call the blazonry that was arriving, the snarling tiger's mask. But there were many others, more soldiers than there'd been in the sundered element. Springbuck directed that the gates be kept closed and the drawbridge up until they had proof that this was no ruse.

Another device could be seen, a green unicorn. Gabrielle strove to see who was under that flag. The end of the column appeared, the four war-drays of Matloo, and Springbuck's misgivings began to subside. Another emblem was visible, a raised fist holding a length of broken chain, showing Freegate was there.

On the open ground outside Condor's Roost, there were unexpected reunions. Brodur was there right enough; Hightower thumped him on the back like a proud father, for having brought his men through. With the Scabbardless was a haunted Andre deCourteney bearing Blazetongue on his hip, and Reacher, King of Freegate with his sister Katya and Edward Van Duyn and allies in thousands. But it was clear that they'd been through bitter battles.

Andre saw that Gabrielle already knew the very worst tidings he had for her.

The arrivals' formation dissolved rather than being dismissed. They pitched camp in the valley, with the men of Coramonde giving what help and hospitality there was. The newcomers had fought all three of the races who served as military arm to Salamá. Now they rode with Odezat war banners for saddle blankets, and jeweled Baidii daggers or Occhlon scimitars hung from their cantle guards. There were profusions of bright silks covering such armor as they chose to wear. Still, it was clear enough that this was an army in retreat.

After the disaster of Ibn-al-Yed's Gauntlet, Brodur had decided, in concert with Drakemirth and Balagon, to skirt the Demon's Breastwork at its southwest end. He'd sent word of what had happened back to the city of the Yalloroon, then begun a forced march.

But not all bad luck had come to light by that time. There'd been survivors, apparently, of Hightower's very first skirmish, and they'd managed to escape to the west. Occhlon and Baidii, massed all through that region to repel the landings they'd expected after losing the Isle of Keys, had made an instant move to throw Coramonde back into the ocean. The ships from Seaguard had stood out to sea, safe for the moment, with the remaining troops and the Yalloroon aboard, and

Brodur's messengers also. There'd been no time to get word back to the Scabbardless.

The following day, the Mariner fleet had come on the scene, propelled by winds called up by Andre deCourteney. When matters were sorted out, Andre had decided to go on, making his landing nearer the end of the Demon's Breastwork, where he could rendezvous with Brodur. The vessels from Coramonde were to stay on station off the city of the Yalloroon, in case any part of their army attempted to withdraw in that direction.

But Occhlon trackers had evidently picked up Brodur's trail, though he was unaware of them, and the bulk of the southerners had gone after him. The Scabbardless was moving as quickly as he could, not knowing how well or ill the *Ku-Mor-Mai* had fared beyond the Gauntlet. As he'd neared the end of the Breastwork, his scouts had begun to pick up signs of a Southwastelander ambush. The trap had been directed the other way; Brodur had nearly blundered into it from behind.

Reacher's army was coming down from the northeast. The southerners were laying the sort of trap they preferred, built around the water holes and oasis at the end of the Breastwork; strategic ground was of less importance to them than control of water. Reacher, in search of both a way south and water for his army, had been led by the terrain straight into the ambush; even his Horseblooded outriders had failed to discover it. But Brodur had struck from the enemy's rear, dislodging the Odezat, Salamá's mercenary divisions, from their positions. The engagement had lasted a day and most of the night, ending in the annihilation of the Odezat and the linking of the two northern armies.

With that Andre deCourteney had arrived, looking for one ally only to find two. He'd given his news to them, and scouts had confirmed that the major part of Salamá's army was coming on from the west, with the four or five men for each Crescent Lander.

With the Horseblooded, Glyffan lancers and other light cavalry buying time and hampering the enemy advance, the allied armies had dashed south, determined to keep the schedule of the Trailingsword, though it had meant letting themselves be bottled up, away from the sea. By the time they'd gotten to Condor's Roost, their pursuers had been no more than a day behind them; it had cost many lives to win even that little lead.

As they tallied it all up, assembled in the fortress' officers' mess, the various leaders who didn't know one another came to do so. There were stories ancillary to it, told in brevity, but one that was recounted in full was the fall of the Trustee of Glyffa, illustrating Bey's increased prepotency and the Masters' feelings of invulnerability. Gabrielle had already cried all her tears; she listened to it now, unflinching.

When Andre had done he turned to Swan. The High Constable still wore her white-winged, mirror-bright bascinet, and the blue cape of her office, but her armor had seen so much use and damage that she'd appropriated an Occhlon general's, a fine suit cut from the scaly skin of a giant wastelands serpent, all sinuous browns and blacks and grays. She rose now, with the Crook of office the Trustee had carried since the old woman's adepthood, covered with sigils and scrollwork of Power. Swan bowed, and put it into shocked Gabrielle's hands, saying, "Now the daughter takes up what the mother has bequeathed. Glyffa attends your words, oh Trustee."

Gabrielle took it, and it was as if her mother were near. Much of her grief fell away; the Crook felt familiar in her white hands. She looked to Swan, whom she'd never met, but whose name had reached her in her mother's communications. "I will need all support, to employ this well."

Swan clasped her hands behind her back, as was her habit, thinking of all that was left to accomplish both in Glyffa and the Southwastelands. "Your legacy will be human weal, and fulfillment." A tear caught in the long lashes; she repeated the pronouncement, "And your name will live forever."

Gabrielle made no remark, but was willing to wager Swan could play a demanding game of chess; the Trustee had chosen her lieutenant with typical perception. Even Katya, who'd had her frictions with the sorceress, beamed cordial approval.

Springbuck thought one of the more notable events of the gathering went unnoticed; Balagon and Angorman sat side by side, and if they weren't overly

281

friendly, at least they had put their animosities to rest. On the weary, perilous ride south, their two sects of warrior-priests had, of necessity, come to the mutual peace of allies. A reconciliation of the two leaders seemed only logical; the two accepted it in the Bright Lady's name.

All courses were locked in now. The *Ku-Mor-Mai* said, "Gathered, we may, at the minimum, have the satisfaction of confronting the Five. But it will only be if we go with greatest haste."

Andre replied, "Speak with more hope. The Trailingsword conjoined us in this certain time, under precise circumstances, by the Bright Lady's ordination. Salamá has much to fear from us, even without the Lifetree. As for their armies, the Occhlon and the others are kept together by fear of the Masters; if we can diffuse the power of the Five, Southwastelander alliances may well unravel."

Andre tried to feel as hopeful as he sounded. Reacher had mentioned that phrase the Occhlon general had let slip, the Host of the Grave, but no one recognized it. Hightower thought it might be another name for the huge armed array now following them south, but Andre privately doubted that.

Van Duyn was considering the news of Gil MacDonald. Somehow that made the scholar feel tired; he'd very much have liked to be back in the Highlands Province, building a life.

They moved through the pass that evening, after stripping Condor's Roost of whatever provisions, water, weapons, horses and fodder and feed they could use. Crews worked through the night, reblocking the pass with every rock they could pry loose. Word came down to discard all excess burdens; Mother Desert had taught them her lessons. The first Southwastelander scouts were seen coming into the far end of the valley by the last men to come down off the heights.

In the area they entered there was more greenery, and more water. They cantered along past fields and irrigation ditches, meeting no resistance, but abundant eye-popping. Many workers ran for their lives, but most stared in undisguised astonishment. Defended by

Mother Desert, they'd never seen an invading army before, only their own men riding out to serve Salamá.

The army went quickly, no longer troubled by the hardships of the wastelands. Springbuck kept outriders, mostly prowler-cavalry and Horseblooded, far in advance and wide on either flank, and maintained a well-manned rearguard. They kept strong security when they bivouacked, but no attacks came. The country had been drained of virtually every man able to bear arms. Now it was the very old and very young men, along with the women, who kept life going in the Southwastelands.

Gabrielle seemed a different woman now. She rode with the Sisters of the Line around her, the Crook of office in hand, conscious of the weight of responsibility that had fallen to her. She kept intimate company with no one now, not the *Ku-Mor-Mai* or his Warlord either. And when she spoke of Salamá, there was a light in the sorceress' eye that belonged in a hawk's.

Swan kept close, to advise or assist her. The Constable's horse, cleaned and curried now, was recognizable as Gil MacDonald's chestnut, Jeb Stuart. Springbuck, who'd heard something of her involvement with his friend, made it a point not to bring the American's name up, unsure if she thought of him as dead or alive.

They came to the end of the thriving farmlands in a week, having passed through the eastern corner of them, and entered an untilled, arid stretch, unpopulated and frequented only by the occasional vulture or jackal. Springbuck became nervous, and stepped up his patrol activity.

But when they'd been in the badlands for four days, disheartening word came from the rearguard. Southwastelanders had pursued them down through the fertile regions, closing much of the lead the northerners had gotten at Condor's Roost. The desert hordes were less than a day behind, outnumbering them badly. Springbuck's allies were split into two schools of thought. One espoused by the Snow Leopardess, urged that a portion of the Crescent Landers stop and hold back the southerners while the remainder went on to Salamá. The other faction, led by the deCourteneys, said every man and woman might be needed in the Necropolis; splitting up their force would invite ruin. The *Ku-Mor-Mai* held this the wiser course, to push on and strike with full strength at the Five. Reacher concurred, and Hightower and Swan. Katya accepted it, though she'd meant to command the delaying action herself.

They picked up their pace, hoping the enormous corps behind them would be slower. Rearguard scouts reported that the gap was closing, though; the Southwastelanders had stripped themselves of all their slower elements. Within another day their vast dust cloud was visible.

At the end of the arid stretches, the northerners came to a plain that extended as far as they could see, like the bottom of a dry, dead sea carpeted with gray ash, hot and still. Banners hung limply, and the moisture on their skin and in their mouths was cooked away as soon as it formed. Looking up to estimate the time, Springbuck saw the sun was gone. The sky was light, but as monochrome as a bowl of lead.

Gabrielle said, "We are come to the precincts of Shardishku-Salamá." Andre's hand felt of the scabbard of Blazetongue.

The northerners rode out onto the plain, but as soon as the last of them had come, they all heard a sustained skeletal rattling, as if uncounted bones were clacking together. Not even the deCourteneys could guess what it meant. The Crescent Landers went on, but they'd passed beyond day and night. Here, it never became dark, although no special spot of light in the gray canopy indicated the sun.

In their wake, many hours later, came the hordes of the Southwastelands. The desert men drew up before the desolate plain, spent from their chase. They looked among themselves, arrogant Occhlon, aristocratic Baidii and wily Odezat, having followed as far as they dared. This place was under the direct scrutiny of the Masters, prohibited to all. The rulers of the Necropolis would exact punishment now, and doubtless show displeasure to their lapsed guardsmen, the Southwastelanders, as well. It would take much penance and sacrifice to appease them.

The desert men reined around and went back the way they'd come. There was nothing else to do; in their minds, the intruders were already dead. No one could survive or escape from the lifeless plain where lay Salamá. The southerners passed back up into the arid regions at a lesser pace, sparing their beloved horses, but anxious to be gone. When they'd left, and their dust had settled, a single man led his weary mount out of concealment. He'd come south behind them, unable to pass them and their patrols to join the northerners.

He climbed tiredly into the saddle, his horse bravely summoning what reserves she had. Ferrian, once Champion-at-arms over the High Ranges, patted her dirt-encrusted neck. He'd had to steal her, last of the many horses he'd ridden since he'd come, late, to the Southwastelands. She'd carried him courageously, but he wasn't sure she had the stamina to overtake the other Crescent Landers. He had long since stopped regretting that Wavewatcher and Skewerskean hadn't overtaken the Mariner fleet before its troops had disembarked. He couldn't think of setbacks now, though; the final remnant of the Lifetree had gone in beneath the umbra of Shardishku-Salamá.

In the rose garden of the Library at Ladentree, Silverquill looked up. His mouth fell open. The Birds of Accord gathered in a great flock, circling the Library.

As he watched, they turned south, called by their ties with the Lifetree. The Sage shaded his eyes, watching the Birds vanish to mere specks, and whispered the most earnest prayers he knew.

The plain was dead, antiseptically so, without so much as an insect to be seen. The northerners came to feel they'd left the world of the living altogether. With no way to take bearings, Springbuck was given directions by the deCourteneys, who appeared to sense where they were going. He lost count of the rests the army had taken, and had no way to measure progress accurately. Water supplies dwindled steadily, and everyone began to show signs of exhaustion except Reacher, Gabrielle and Andre.

A crunch under his hoof made Fireheel flinch. The *Ku-Mor-Mai* flicked at the ash with the tip of his sword. A length of brittle bone, a human femur, was there, broken by the gray's step. Springbuck stared at it for a moment, then stirred up the soot around it. The rest of the skeleton, unguessably old, lay among scraps of harness and bits of metal trapping. Hightower had come up and his horse, too, snapped bones beneath its tread.

They'd wandered into the last resting place of a slaughtered army. Probing the soot with lances and swords, they exposed rotted shields and corroded armor. One skull was still circled by a gleaming fillet, holding a big black pearl to its white brow.

No one was inclined to scavenge. Springbuck got them moving again; for more than a mile they wended their way among remains, hearing the fragile cracking of an army they took to be a kind of predecessor. Once beyond the relics, the *Ku-Mor-Mai* took his followers a long way beyond the bonefields before he let them stop again.

Andre was first to notice it, an indistinct irregularity on the horizon. As time went on, it became a serration-line of silhouettes, eerie designs difficult to discern. The still air made distances deceptive, and their approach toward that outline seemed to take days.

Then they had their first sight of Shardishku-Salamá, the city taking on definition of a perplexing, somehow distorted sort. Some of the structures there were lit with wavering flame.

A dark line had appeared, extending across their route, between them and the city. Some began to say it was a treeline, end of the desolation. Springbuck couldn't make it out, but Hightower could, saying he thought it no treeline. In time, they realized it was another army, nearly spanning the horizon, coming closer.

They gaped in disbelief at the sea of foemen. Numbly, they groped for shields and donned armor once more.

A half-mile separated them when the opposing force halted. They flew no banners, and there was no sound of horns or challenges. Springbuck could see little, except that his force was outnumbered overwhelmingly. He called for Hightower and a standard-bearer, and rode up. Reacher fell in beside him, and the *Ku-Mor-Mai* was glad for his company. He felt a chill despite the hot, stagnant air.

No parleying group came from the other side, so Springbuck rode on. He heard a sharp inhalation from the herald, and his own caught in his windpipe. His nerves, trapped between the primal need to run and a firm decision to go on, threatened to fail him. Drawn up before him in their terrible ranks were those who could only be the Host of the Grave.

They stretched away to either side, as far as he could see, eyes glowing in black sockets. They waited in perfect silence with nothing to say, nothing to fear, desire or question. Severed forever from happiness or grief or thought, they waited, ideal household troops of Shardishku-Salamá, like so many statues of slate.

Springbuck summoned up saliva, licked his lips. "Do you contest our passage?"

One figure broke formation and advanced. He was wearing panoply that had once been rich and burnished, beautiful to see. Now it was green, crumbling with age. He sat a cadaver-horse, whose eyes were lit like its rider's. A reek of charnel decay wafted from them both.

Springbuck's skin crawled as if it were too tight on his bones. Fireheel snorted and dug at the sooty ground. The corpse was implacable and unhurried. Springbuck's horror fought hard to take control of him. The face he saw was rotting, areas of bleached skull showing through. The voice, when it came, was toneless, a whispering rattle from a throat-box long unused.

It said, "Where your horses' hooves stand, that is as far as you ever go toward Shardishku-Salamá."

With defiance he didn't feel, the *Ku-Mor-Mai* answered, "That has been said before. We have come for our just returns."

The whisper-rattle came so mutedly that they had to bend forward to hear. "We tend the affairs of the ages here. Die."

There was the metallic complaint of its sword, grating out of its sheath.

"Back to ranks!" shouted the *Ku-Mor-Mai*. All four of them yanked their reins, and rushed madly back in a shower of soot. Hysteria went at their backs. What good would lancers, swordsmen, war-drays and warrior-sisters do, when their opponents were already slain? Springbuck cast one look backward, and shrank from what he saw. The corpse-army was coming on, not slowly and not quickly, but irresistibly.

When Springbuck and the others reached their own lines, their enemies had covered half the distance in pursuit. The *Ku-Mor-Mai* snapped orders to arrange his formation. He'd thought for a moment of withdrawing, but to what avail? The dead would never tire or pause; they'd simply roll across the plain until they eventually engulfed their exhausted enemies.

He explained quickly what they faced. "Gabrielle, can you do anything?"

She balanced the Crook in her hand and traded glances with Andre. "I do not know," she confessed, "how can one affect shadows and carrion-meat?"

Springbuck racked his brain for a way to stave off that attack or escape it. Then, on his own, Fireheel caracoled, and again, turning and rearing at the onrushing Host, whistling his fierce invitation. He didn't care who was coming; the gray only wanted the chance to fight.

Springbuck whipped Bar, the Obstructor, from its scabbard; the sword left a white swath of light in the gray air. Hightower bellowed invective of his own, sweeping free his two-handed greatsword. Red Pilgrim came up, and Blazetongue and the myriad weapons of the Crescent Lands. Some found comfort in a gesture, crouching behind lances or dropping visors. Others just eyed the Host, seeing that the die was cast, and accepted it in their hearts.

The Host of the Grave made little sound, riding as if from nightmare. The living dreaded their touch more than the bite of their swords, but spurred their horses on.

That singular onset began, men and women in death-lock combat with corpses. Beyond the desolation, in timeless Shardishku-Salamá, the Five, assured and imperturbable, awaited the battle's inevitable outcome.

PART V

❧

Symmetries of
the Firmament

Chapter Thirty

Pale Anguish keeps the heavy gate
And the Warder is Despair
                    Oscar Wilde
                    "The Ballad of Reading Gaol"

GIL MacDonald passed some intangible landmark that told him he was leaving behind something too sinister to be called unconsciousness. He felt excruciating pain in his eyes.

He tried to move, but couldn't, and so tried some more. In the end he did, but his fumbling hands were slapped away brutally. The pain returned. He tugged, tossing his head, fighting blindly. There were immovably strong hands clamping his head steady, thumbs pressing in at his eyeballs. He thrashed, moaned, and the hands retreated at last. Much of the pain remained. He rubbed his tortured eyes, and finally blinked them open.

Light blinded him. Peering through the narrowest slits he could manage, he saw a room in darkness, but he lay in a cone of light. Beneath him, he felt rough stone. He heard a raspy voice he didn't like at all. "You see, my Lord? Enough pressure on the eyes would awaken a man even from the Dreamdrowse."

A second voice spoke. "Adequate, Flaycraft." The tone was placid, fear-provoking, as the cold malice of a snake. Shapes wobbled into definition. The first person Gil saw was the closest. He shook his head, disbelieving. This one was of the tribe of man, maybe, but a simian extreme. Squat, with long, shaggy brown hair that was almost a pelt, he slouched, bandy-legged. He was heavy with muscle, beady-eyed beneath ridges of thick bone. His fingers were long, hirsute and black-nailed. From him came the odors of instinct, of life at animal level. It came as no surprise than he was un-clothed.

Gil tracked his gaze to the other, making himself confront him. Yardiff Bey was calm, secure in his own environment. The cold ocular shone in the dark room; Bey's face held an icy pleasure.

Gil's stomach contorted in fear, and his bowels threatened rebellion. He doubled over for a moment, but the spasm passed. He couldn't imagine how long he'd been out. He sat up and swung his legs around. He was sitting on a stone slab that managed to combine the clinical with the sacrificial. His head spun, and he could see nothing outside the cone of light.

Yardiff Bey watched the play of the outlander's thoughts, each predicted, in sequence. The last of them, renewed fear, pleased the sorcerer. The creature, whom Gil took to be Flaycraft, was toying with something on his chest, a necklace. Gil saw it was the Ace of Swords, on its chain. Flaycraft grinned, displaying long yellow canines.

Gil lurched, grabbing for his tarot. "Okay, ape-guts; give it here." Weak, he lost balance. Flaycraft, shorter than the American but broader, eluded him easily and kicked him as he went down. He curled up and groaned. The beast-man seized him by his hair, yanked him to his feet, flung him back on the slab. Gil filed the information that Flaycraft was one strong animal.

"So, that is your tarot now?" Bey asked. "The Ace of Swords? Reversed, I should think."

Gil rubbed his aching head. "Where's Dunstan?" he managed.

"Near." Something like a smile crossed Bey's face. At his side hung Dirge, recovered, apparently, from the wounded Acre-Fin. Those events all came back in a jumble.

The sorcerer purred. "You do Dunstan and yourself ill service by being difficult. The regimen here is strict-est compliance; punishment is Flaycraft's trade. You erred in going against me and the convections of destiny. Your friend's well-being as much as your own rests in your submission."

The dark-robed Hand of Shardishku-Salamá glided

away, silent and stately as a manta-ray in deep water. Gil wanted to answer, but was preoccupied with the twin assertions that his friend was alive and that he, Gil, must behave. It begged the question, why was he still alive? The sorcerer would only tolerate him for some well-defined purpose, and was obviously using the Horseblooded for leverage. *Goddam Bey, always knows just which button to push!*

Flaycraft watched him now, a cat with a new mouse. *Got a crazy one here,* Gil reminded himself. The beast-man caught his arm in an excruciating grip, shaking him like a doll. "Disobey once, I entreat you. Then, I can school you in lessons of torment. Already, I have taught your friend Dunstan!"

He let go. Gil's arm throbbed from that one brief squeeze. Flaycraft went off behind his patron. Gil wobbled after them a few steps, stopping at the edge of light. He saw Bey framed in orange radiance at the end of a passageway. Flaycraft went to stand by his side. Yardiff Bey waved a hand, and the passageway walls rumbled inward. In seconds, the corridor had contracted shut with a vibration that traveled through the floor.

Gil took a few steps, groping at the blank wall. All he could feel was solid rock, nicked and chipped by ancient tooling. He blinked up owlishly at the light, but it was far overhead; he couldn't make out just what it was or how it worked.

Then he realized he wasn't alone. In the silence left by the closure of the passageway, he heard breathing. He edged back to the slab. His pulse pounded behind his ears and beat at his temples.

"There isn't cause for alarm, Gil MacDonald. This is a sad thing, seeing you here."

Gil strained to see. The voice had been quiet, familiar. "Dunstan? Hey, Dunstan?"

"Yes, I, my friend." Gil stumbled into the dark again, tracing the words. "Just ahead of you. Pause a moment, sit, accustom your eyes to the dark."

Gil felt his way to the wall. A low shelf, like a bench cut from stone, ran along it. He sat. Gradually, he made out his friend's outline. Dunstan was seated with his back to the wall, vague in the dim wash of the beam focused on the slab. Finding Dunstan lifted some of his anguish and fright, but robbed him of words. He blurted, "Oh man, man, I'm sorry. I was going to spring you, but I screwed it up good."

He couldn't see the Horseblooded's wan smile, but heard it in his tone. "Berating yourself is unfair. Few men ever came alive to Shardishku-Salamá; none ever imposed his will here."

"Salamá? This is it? Lay it out for me a bit at a time, okay?"

"You broach two long and separate stories."

"Oh. Look, let's go back into the light, huh? I'm not much for the dark, personally." He labored to his feet, but Dunstan stayed seated. "What's wrong?"

The other was long in answering. "I have been confined here far longer than you, Gil. Bey proved his genius, restraining and punishing me with a single spell."

Gil groped for him. "What are you, tied or something? Maybe I can—" He snatched his hands away. *"Oh, sweet Jesus Christ!"* He'd felt down the Horseblooded's arms for shackles or bonds, but where the wrists should have been, he'd felt only columns of stone. He touched again, gingerly. "Dunstan, your arms; what's wrong with your—"

"Not arms alone. It's as I said. Yardiff Bey fettered me by his arts, as only he would think to do."

It was true. The flesh of Dunstan's arms gave way to cold stone, and his legs were the same. The sorcerer had joined him to the perpetual custody of naked rock. Gil backed away and sat, head hung in defeat. "How long have you been like this?"

"I do not know, and do not wish to. My foremost aspiration has been to forget time. I think I was close to success, but perhaps I was only on the rim of madness. I am in no pain, and hunger and thirst do not come to me, nor any agony of the body. But the unknown progress of time, that was a terrible affliction."

Gil began to tremble. "Does that mean I'm gonna be . . . will he do that to me?" He was ashamed, but it was his overriding thought and stark terror.

"I think not. You were awakened for a different purpose than torment."

Awakened? The last thing he recalled, and that none

293

too clearly, Bey had plucked him up. He'd thought he'd recognized an astounded Andre deCourteney. Then something had hit him like megavoltage.

"Dunstan, I've been down for the long count, haven't I?"

"Yes. You were brought to Salamá unliving, I understand. I only heard a little besides what passed between Bey and Flaycraft. A mystic bolt and a Dismissal struck you concurrently, and balanced one another."

"I died?"

"No, you are no ghost. Magics in contention will eliminate first those elements common to both. When those forces are canceled, the remaining energies compete. But in your case, both the bolt and the Dismissal were Andre's, and held all forces in common. Thus, all energies, all influences, were neutralized. All activity stopped; you were neither dead nor alive, until Yardiff Bey quickened your life once again. There is one who wishes to speak with you, you see."

"With me? Who?"

"His name is Evergray. He is a Lord of Shardishku-Salamá; not one of the Masters, but high in authority."

"And he's why Bey brought me around? But what's it for?"

Dunstan sighed, resting his head on the stone behind him. "After Yardiff Bey captured me, he fled to Death's Hold in *Cloud Ruler*. It was the only place that would receive him; a few of his adherents still lurked there in hiding."

"Yeah, Gabrielle and I thought you were there. She did this thing, this séance-like."

"I was interrogated by Flaycraft. Under his hand, I told whatever little I could. I was put to great pain, and lost all bearings. I gather that Bey regained his Masters' favor, and I was moved here, to Salamá, but for long and long I thought myself still to be in Death's Hold."

"What about this Evergray?"

"I was placed here by Yardiff Bey, but one day Evergray came, having heard about me from Flaycraft, who is his servant. Prisoners, outsiders of any kind, are almost unknown in Salamá. He wished to question me about the world. Until then I had sat in the dark, for there was no light until Evergray came. I used to sit and sing, sing every saga and ditty and ballad I knew, just to fill the blankness."

"And Evergray?" Gil encouraged gently.

"Yes. He wanted to know what my songs were, at first. He treated my every word like a report from an undiscovered continent. On one visit he mentioned that there was another outsider here, enemy of Yardiff Bey, in a mystic coma. He asked me if I knew the man, but when he described you, I said I thought not. When last I saw you, Gil, there was no burn-mark on your cheek, nor any scar cut in your brow."

"Got 'em in Earthfast the night we raided."

"Ah. I was in the Berserkergang then, and took no notice. Strange to say, the Rage has never come upon me again since that night. There were many moments when I might have welcomed it."

"It isn't in you anymore, Dunstan. It passed to me."

The Horseblooded was silent for a few moments. "Now I must make apologies to you."

"Not your fault. It saved my life once, I think. Anyway, it doesn't matter here. But why'd they stick me in with you, if Bey was keeping you shut away in the dark?"

"Because Evergray wanted it, perhaps. Or it may be that the Masters are eavesdropping on us. I don't know, but your company is welcome, even though I'm sorry to see you here."

Gil rubbed his hands together, feeling them wet and slippery. "That passageway's buttoned up tight, huh?"

"I have never been able to inspect it, but I presume so, yes."

The American found he felt constricted. "I was never locked up before, y'know? I mean, I've been confined to barracks and like that, but nobody ever shut me in before. Hard to take."

He felt stupid, complaining to a man who'd once had the freedom of the High Ranges and then been fastened to the rock in unending night. Dunstan asked, "How fared my kinsman Ferrian?"

"They couldn't save his arm of course, but they pulled him through. He came south with me and Andre deCourteney and some others. We had to leave him with the Sages of Ladentree, but he didn't seem too put out about it."

Dunstan chuckled, a strange sound. "He always loved chinwagging, and old stories. Odd, in a Champion-at-arms, to be so—"

He stopped, interrupted by vibrations in the walls and floor. A vertical crack of orange light materialized where the passageway had been. Gil scrambled to his feet and stumbled toward it, planning to take whomever it was from behind when they entered. But he was stiff and sore. Before he could do it, Flaycraft sprang into the chamber. The torturer moved nimbly, but without grace. He had a long wooden club, studded with spikes, in one hairy fist. He saw Gil, and gave a moist, grunting laugh.

"Yes, try it! Try often; bare your teeth, little mutt!" He waved the club over his head, making the air whistle. The American, still weak, knew Flaycraft would maim or kill him, given the chance.

Another figure came up behind, filling the passageway, blocking most of the light from it. Flaycraft's club lashed out again, and Gil jerked backward. "Little mutts do not stand," the torturer snarled, "when Lord Evergray enters a room."

Gil leaned back against the slab, goggling at Evergray, scion of Shardishku-Salamá.

Chapter Thirty-one

When half-gods go,
The gods arrive.

> Ralph Waldo Emerson
> "Give All to Love"

HE—if Evergray was in fact a man—was tall, close to seven feet. He wore loose robes that broke different colors from their highlights, and a complicated metal headgear, half crown, half helmet, with loops, spires and projections; it seemed just a bit loose.

His face was long and inexpressive, a smooth face without wrinkles or creases, a mannequin's face. Eeriest of all were the eyes, red-pupiled, with whites showing all around them, as if their owner were in a constant state of fascination.

The American muttered, "What have we got here?" Flaycraft made an irrigated guttural sound, starting forward with club raised. Gil backed away hastily.

Evergray waved the beast-man aside. "Stay your hand, good Flaycraft." His voice resonated in the room, immediate to the ear, but without the bass pitch Gil would have expected from a giant. When he moved to inspect the American more closely, Gil decided to stand and see what was going to happen.

Flaycraft snarled. "He should be on his ugly face before you, great Evergray."

The giant stopped a few feet from Gil, examining him. "Of what value is his obeisance to me, faithful one?" The torturer shot Gil a look of sizzling hatred. Evergray went on. "Is it true, what has been said? Are you, in fact, from a place outside this line of Reality?"

Gil hedged. Information looked like his only commodity of life right now, and he wanted the best rate of exchange he could wangle. "Why should I tell you?"

"Flaycraft can make you tell. He would enjoy it; he detests you."

"Then yeah, I come from another Cosmos."

"But you have free will?"

"Uh, I guess so. Why, don't you?"

Flaycraft yelped, "You are here to answer, not ask!" He charged forward and rammed the tip of the club into Gil's belly, too fast and strong to avoid. The American folded and groveled on his knees, distantly registering Dunstan's words.

"Matchless Evergray," the Horseblooded said, "please understand: He is a stranger, unfamiliar with proper decorum. I shall explain, and he will mend his ways."

Evergray wasn't paying attention, though. His face was half turned, as if he were listening to something from the passageway. The others heard nothing. "The Masters summon me," the giant said. "This discussion will wait." He exited.

Flaycraft, who'd been hoping for the command to continue his work, relaxed now. Panting, Gil sat back on his heels, holding his stomach. He gasped, "This isn't . . . over yet, ass-face . . . You and me are . . . gonna go round and round, one day."

Flaycraft chortled, and followed his Lord. The passageway thundered shut. Gil grabbed a corner of the stone slab and hauled himself up. He staggered back to Dunstan. "Thanks for talking up. Flaycraft was about to put a monumental hurting on me."

"He enjoys pain, and hates you."

"What for?"

"He knows you are Yardiff Bey's enemy, and he is Bey's servant as well as Evergray's personal attendant. And he is jealous, I think. He resents the Scion's interest in you."

"Well, they're welcome to each other, for all I care."

"Are you feeling better?"

"A bit. I picked up assorted dents and dings, getting here." He fingered the swollen injury on his head, from his fall aboard *Osprey*. "Listen, what's that nut talking about, this 'free will' stuff?"

Dunstan explained. Evergray had held long, questioning conversations with him about the nature of choice, and volition, and whether men truly possessed them. He was obsessed with the topic. The Horse-blooded told Gil, "For him, all things center upon Evergray; he has been taught to think that way. Notwithstanding, he has also been taught it is the nature of Reality to limit free will. Our fates are all determined for us, or so the Masters hold it. Evergray has begun to doubt that, though, and wants to know if free will exists. When he heard that you come from outside this Cosmos entirely, he pressured Yardiff Bey to awaken you."

"That doesn't sound like Bey. He might want to keep me around for a hostage, but he'd leave me on ice."

"But he is Evergray's father; you are now in Yardiff Bey's mansion."

"Evergray is Bey's third child? The one in the prophesy?"

"So it is said. Evergray will talk about himself endlessly if he is inclined. He is not a true offspring, in the sense of being born of the body. He seems to be a construct of sorts, brought into existence by Bey's magic, animated by the Five."

"A construct? Like a machine?"

"More the product of occult skills and alchemy, as is a golem. I am Horseblooded, Gil; I can't explain, for I don't ken it myself. But Evergray is alive by Yardiff Bey's skills, and looks upon him much in the way of a child toward a father. His thoughts do not operate as ours do, and I find it hard to comprehend him."

"He wants my advice, sounds like. How do we use that to get out of here?"

"I am at a loss as to that. My plight is less easily remedied than is yours."

"A lot of people will be gunning for the Masters soon; when I was with the Mariners this Omen appeared, what they called the Trailingsword."

"The Trailingsword? Peculiar tidings indeed."

"When he nailed me, Bey said the Trailingsword doesn't matter. The last piece of the Lifetree was destroyed; nothing can stop the Masters."

"Only a renewal of the Lifetree can end Salamá's influence, I understand, but the Five can still be foiled or frustrated."

"Lifetree, Great Blow, Trailingsword—what have they got to do with Evergray?"

"Of that I am as ignorant as you. Centuries ago the Lifetree bloomed very close to this spot, fed by the one arcane spring whose waters will sustain it. Rooted in the earth, reaching to the sky, it kept the world in harmony. There were celebrated wizards and warriors here in those days, the Unity.

"But some hungered for overlordship. Amon sought them out. They worked treason by night, uprooting the Lifetree and destroying it, striking down the most powerful members of the Unity. Then they began the incantation that would liberate the hordes of the Infernal Plane, the Great Blow. An antithetical spell was shaping in what is now Coramonde. The Bright Lady set the Trailingsword over the place where her supporters gathered. Whoever opposed the new Masters gathered there to defend, while her adherents worked their counterspell. In seven times seven days, the final contest of magic came to pass. The Great Blow was stopped, but the world was upset and tottered, and changed."

"And Bey's afraid a branch of the Lifetree survived. Or was. It would have stopped the Masters for good?"

"And stripped away every strength they have acquired over the centuries."

"You said the Trailingsword appeared, uh, forty-nine days before the last bout. I must have seen it weeks before I was bagged. I'd give my right arm to know how much time went by while I was out."

"In any case, the Trailingsword promises momentous events."

"The problem's how to use that on Evergray." The passageway ground open again. This time, Gil stayed put. Flaycraft waddled in, club in one hand and a bucket in the other. He laid the bucket on the stone slab and brandished the club at Gil. "Exalted Evergray will question you later. Therefore, hold yourself ready." He turned to go.

"Hey, Flaycraft," Gil called. The torturer paused. "Was your mother really raped by a fur carpet?"

The beast-man growled and raised the club. He saw

the American brace himself, and laughed. "You will be most, most unhappy when mighty Evergray has no further questions for you!" He backed into the passageway. Seconds later, it closed.

In the bucket, Gil found a bottle of water and a bowl of cold, gooey stuff like gruel. The purpose of the bucket, in a featureless stone room, was evident. He offered some of the food to Dunstan, but the Horse-blooded shook his head. "I've no need of it."

"You're not missing anything. I've squooshed tastier goop out of bugs." He forced himself to eat a little, and drank greedily. "What do you suppose Evergray's doing?"

"From time to time he is summoned by the Masters of Shardishku-Salamá."

Again Yardiff Bey stood in the ring of light. But where he'd been the Accused months before, he was once more the Hand of Shardishku-Salamá. With him stood Evergray. The Masters' incorporeal voice came once again, speaking to the giant.

"Scion of Salamá, are you prepared to begin your Assumption?"

Evergray's head remained erect, light splashing from the horns and projections of the crown-helmet. The Masters pursued their point. "Why do you not respond? The subject here is a majestic legacy."

"Why was I interrupted?" the giant burst out. "I had questions yet to ask the mortal."

The collective voice of the Five betrayed cold irritation. "Mortals will wait, but the affairs of the ages will not. Soon, now, you must be filled like a water vessel with Our great power, to wield it over the earth at Our command."

"But that moment is not yet come, when you Five will Ascend to the godhead."

"Neither is it far off. Transference of our energies will be done by portions, for to do it all at the once would overtax even you. The first portion will be done now. Go to the chapel that is appointed for you and await it."

Evergray didn't budge. "Tarry not," the Masters told him. "Submit to Our will, as you were created to do."

301

The giant stared into the blackness with wide, red-pupiled eyes.

At last he said, "The Masters' wish has always been law in Salamá." He left the ring of light. Bey waited patiently, head thrown back in thought, the ocular gleaming. When he was sure his progeny had gone, he spoke.

"Have no misgivings. All is well with Your great plan."

"Our Scion becomes truculent. It must not come to disobedience."

"And shan't; I have arranged against that. The mortal will be the key. Through MacDonald I will insure Evergray's hatred of free-will creatures. The Scion will yield himself up to your designs."

"We tolerate no miss-moves. We will be endowing Evergray with great forces for safekeeping, forces of which we must divest ourselves in the final moments of our Ascension."

Bey nodded impatiently. And when They had Ascended to godhead, Evergray must accede to them. "It will be so. The Lifetree is perished," he reminded them, "and there is no counterforce."

"There is no counterforce. The alien will behave as you plan?"

"He may do any of several things, but all are foreseen, and serve my purpose. I perceive that the Rage has passed from the Horseblooded into this one, and that makes him altogether more suitable. Far better Evergray believes he has chosen to obey, rather than risk injuring him with Compulsions."

"He must bend to Our will, and turn others to his. Your part in this will not be forgotten."

Bey bowed deeply. "As you new gods shall serve Amon and his infernal deity, so Yardiff Bey will serve you, and so shall Evergray rule the Crescent and Southwastelands by your command." He bowed again, ecstatic, on the brink of every ambition.

Gil spent an unknown period waiting for Evergray to show up. He ate, slept, had marathon talks with Dunstan, and began the cycle again. His sleep time changed, in circadian adjustment, into naps, and the tension of imprisonment penetrated his dreams. His vitality came back and he began to exercise, though he felt guilty that Dunstan couldn't.

Flaycraft, when he came, told them nothing. Gil baited him, but stopped short of provoking a fight. Reacher could have taken the beast-man apart; Hightower would certainly have broken him over one knee; but Gil was nowhere near their class, and had been drained by the things he'd undergone. The torturer would bear his canines and make ominous threats, then leave a new bucket, taking the old one away. Afterward, Gil would find his hair on end, his hands shaking.

Finally, the Scion of Salamá appeared. The passageway rumbled open and, backlighted by the orange radiance, Evergray beckoned to Gil from beyond it. The American came haltingly, not quite believing he was permitted a small taste of freedom. He had a moment's indecision about leaving Dunstan alone, but figured he'd have to play Evergray along.

Outisde, Gil blinked in the light of a corridor as wide as a city boulevard. The cell-side of it was solid rock; the other wall was opaque glass or crystal, lit from the exterior by a molten orange luminance, rearing up hundreds of feet.

The passageway shut, and Gil could see no opening where it had been. But indicating its position was a glowing rune, suspended in air by the stone wall of the corridor.

"We will speak elsewhere," Evergray said. "The confines of your chamber are not pleasing to me."

"Dunstan and me don't think much of it either."

The giant had already started off. "We will not discuss that; it has no importance to me." He was more imposing now, with a more distant air. His red pupils had shrunk to mere pinheads, and he radiated strength. The crown-helmet was steadier on his head.

They passed through a series of galleries filled with curious and odd objects the American couldn't identify, some like abstract sculptures, others like small icons that stood in niches in the walls or on stands. Perspective and the sizes and shapes of the objects and the rooms had been tampered with, distorted.

They came onto a broad terrace, looking out over

Shardishku-Salamá. It was built of towers and monoliths, pylons, obelisks, bizarre palaces and structures inexplicable. One was a building constructed in the image of a spread-winged bird of metal, its feet planted among the other structures, its mouth opened to show a forked tongue. Next to that, a tower rose, fashioned from what looked like colossal bones. The building beside that had hundreds of minarets, showing different colored lights in each. Beyond was a titanic globe of basaltic rock, iron, ivory, gold, jade, and chalcedony; from its top a crown of flame roared into the air, the orange fire that had lit Bey's glass-walled corridor. On the wall of another, Gil saw a heroic bas-relief, hundreds of yards on a side. In it, figures swarmed and soared around a tree that grasped and clutched at them like a malign octopus. The figures were striking at it with thunderbolts, tearing at its roots, fighting bravely. This was the Masters' depiction of their treason to the Lifetree.

Bey's mansion itself was a single block of stone, a gigantic cube set down in the middle of the city. Farther along the vast balcony, *Cloud Ruler* sat, its fires cooled. "Where is everybody?" Dunstan had told him the few citizens of Salamá hadn't many mortal servants, or much use for them, according to Evergray. But Gil hadn't expected the place to look so empty.

Evergray pointed to the flaming globe. "There, in their Fane, the Masters called me, and I must go again soon. Yet I have more questions about free will."

Gil said he'd try to answer. Evergray sat on a wide bench of flint, chiseled to his proportions. "What has your free will done for you? Has it answered enigmas, ennobled you, extended your spirit or increased your powers?"

"I . . . it doesn't work that way. It's only doing what you want. It's only about being able to pick."

"One does anything at all, on impulse?"

Gil held up his hands helplessly. "In theory, I guess. Evergray, I can't see what it is you're leading to. Are you telling me you never made up your own mind about *anything?*"

"Only in the smallest sense of choice among preselected alternatives. Never in the greater sense of invoking change of my own."

"But you want to?"

"I am unsure. It is a capacity I have, but will not be permitted, when the Masters rule. Yet it is a part of me, of my greatness, I think. I have the ability; it seems undesirable for any aspect of me to go unused. My every facet is the function of perfection; why, then, must part of me be suppressed or ignored? It is inappropriate."

"How'll you lose it?" Gil was amazed; this wasn't ego Evergray was displaying, it was psychosis.

"The Masters will accomplish their spell soon, and their powers will be remanded to me. Then, untainted by earthly ties, or energies of earthly origins, they will rise and fill themselves with the might of the Cosmos. They will reshape the face of the Crescent Lands and the Southwastelands, and rule their new domain. Over them will be Amon, who will control all planes, serving his Infernal Deity, our ultimate Lord. And I will control all mundane things in the name of the Five."

Gil was dumfounded, and his thoughts became dense, trying to cope with what Evergray had said. The red haze he'd known came down over his vision. In the storm of his emotion, the Berserkergang began to take hold.

Evergray noticed. "Ah, is this some seizure of the free will? But no, I see: It is simple, unmonitored Rage. Uninteresting." He waved a hand; the Rage was snuffed out like a candle.

The American stood, gaping as if he'd gotten a bucket of ice water in the face. He rocked back on his heels.

Evergray made no summons, but Flaycraft had come up to them. "Take him back to his chamber," the giant said, "for I must go to receive more of the legacy of the Masters." Flaycraft stepped toward Gil, who brought his hands up.

"Evergray, at least take Bey's spell off Dunstan, won't you? He's been helpful to you."

The giant sounded angry for the first time. "Submit! Offer no resistance to my faithful friend." The torturer gave the Scion a look somewhere between gratitude and adoration. "He is my cherished, steadfast Flaycraft," the giant went on, more calmly. "I will speak to you again when I have more questions. The Horseblooded is of no importance to me."

As Flaycraft herded Gil away with glee, Evergray stood and gazed at the Fane of the Masters, fingering the crown-helmet on his head.

Chapter Thirty-two

I have seen them gentle, tame and meek,
That now are wild, and do not remember
That some time they put themselves in danger
To take bread at my hand.

Sir Thomas Wyatt
"They Flee from Me"

GIL related everything in detail, partly to tell Dunstan what their situation was, and partly to consider it more closely himself.

"This tells us more of Evergray," Dunstan admitted, "yet, of what use is it?"

"I'm not sure; what do we know? First, the Masters are aiming for divinity, or something like it. Second, to do it, they have to 'Ascend,' whatever that means. They have to get rid of any taint of their own humanity. So third, they're going to put all their earthly power in Evergray and make him their stooge, ruling by their instructions." He stopped, considering. "But why allow Evergray free will?"

Dunstan leaned his head back against the stone. "He is to exert control, is he not? Then, a certain capacity for will is implicit. How can an unquestioning machine dominate, as Evergray is to do?"

"You got it; a zombie's no good to them, and the Masters can't rule directly because it would taint them again. That's probably why Bey, and not the Masters themselves, brought Evergray to life; their power and Evergray's will be separate. It will make it easier to keep him in line."

The Horseblooded nodded. "It was clever of them to have Evergray created, rather than entrusting Yardiff Bey with their power."

"Hell yeah. He's too liable to figure out a way to buck them. So, fourth, Evergray's been kept in Salamá, almost incommunicado. Wait a minute; is Flaycraft a free-will type?"

"He is indentured to Yardiff Bey by his soul."

"I see. Well, Evergray's got this oh-wonderful-me attitude, and he's getting muley. The Masters must be nervous; without him they're stuck, Lifetree or no Lifetree. But once they put on their new godhood they'll be in absolute command. And maybe that's why they really want him to have free will. Without it, they haven't got a slave, just a dummy. And the Masters need their slaves, or how could they be Masters?"

"Quite reasonable."

"Our wild card is Evergray. He's already gotten some of their force; he's got this aura, like electricity." He saw Dunstan didn't know the word. "He almost looks— No, no, he *is*; Dunstan, he's *bigger!* When he came here that first time after I woke up, that crown thing he wears almost brushed the passageway ceiling. But this time, when he called me out from the corridor, he was hunkering down to look in. And the crown itself is tighter now. He's grown!"

"Swollen with his legacy, you mean?"

"Oh, and get this: He stopped the Berserkergang."

"Impossible. It may be shortened, but not Dismissed. The Rage isn't possession, but rather a venomous side of the individual taking over. It is a susceptibility, not an affliction."

"Tell that to Evergray. He flipped his hand at me and stopped the fit dead."

"That is prepotency indeed, which even the deCourteneys couldn't match. His prepotency comes upon him now."

"Yeah, he's changing fast. We may not have much time."

"It is my fear, my friend, that we have none at all."

Gil made a thorough inspection of their cell, but found no opening or seam to it, even where he knew the passageway must be. The walls offered no hand- or footholds, so he never got to climb high enough to see just what kind of arrangement the cone of light was. He presumed there was ventilation of some kind, but that it, too, was out of reach.

Monotony set in. Now Gil began stalking around and around their chamber, working arms and legs, doing sets of exercises from sheer frustration. Then the two would re-dissect what they knew of their situation. After a time the American would eat, nap, and begin again.

"In taking our pleas to Evergray," the Horseblooded pointed out, "you will encounter one obstacle over and over: Yardiff Bey."

"That's it. Bey's smarter than I am, smoother than I'll ever be. For everything I say he'll have twenty counterattacks and rebuttals."

"Unless," the Wild Rider proposed, "you make no declarations."

"Huh? Oh, you mean just use questions, right? I dunno though; I'm no shrink."

"There exists no alternative."

"Just one, and that's jumping Flaycraft when he comes in. If you get his attention for a second, maybe I could put him away. I don't think he'll be looking for it."

"His sort always expects violence. And he is more dangerous than you think. More; even though our words have been soft, they may yet have been overheard."

"But it's the only other way out."

Dunstan didn't reply. Gil knew he was thinking about the utter solitude he'd have to endure again. "Dunstan, we've got to go with what we've got. When that passageway opens again and Evergray comes through, call out to him. Make a racket."

The Horseblooded sounded despondent for the first time. "Very well. But sit and rest; it may be some time."

Gil sat near the spot where the passageway would open. He felt alert and strong again. He'd only planned to relax, too keyed up to rest, but somewhere along the line he fell asleep.

Dunstan's warning snapped him awake. "Gil, beware." The passageway opened again. Gil waited to one side, balanced, hands and feet ready. Evergray's voice echoed loudly from the corridor. Gil went warily.

This time there was no doubt that the Scion of Salamá was metamorphosing into his new form. He was two feet taller than he'd originally been, and his eyes were blazing crosscurrents of red and white. He was surrounded by a crackling aurora, and the crown-helmet was very nearly a perfect fit.

"I have come into much of my legacy," he told the American. "Soon I will receive that last and greatest measure. But I wish to hear you respond to my questions." They went again to the balcony to look at the Fane of the Masters. Evergray wanted to watch it as he awaited the command to join the Five for the final time.

"Mortal, what have you to tell me about the free will? Yardiff Bey has said your claim to it is false, and you, too, are moved helplessly by events. But I think you have free will. Is there any value to it that you can mention?"

"One or two; it's a mixed blessing. But think for a minute. Is there any other facet of yourself they want you to abandon?"

"None. My strength and intellect, my imagination and perceptions are to remain my own."

"D'you think your free will could be some kind of fault then?"

The response was angry. "I am without flaw."

Gil pretended elaborately that the next thought was impromptu. "Evergray, could the Five be jealous of you?"

The Scion's fist hit the balcony's rail, making it quake. "This thought may be so! I feel I have their enmity, and harbor that same suspicion."

"They've never dared to let you decide anything for yourself?"

"No. Always, the will of the Masters has been set down."

"But what could they gain, barring you from using free will?"

"Mortal, they would keep me from being all that I might."

"But they're already making you their prime servant. Do you deserve to be more?"

"Yes, and yes again! I am worthy to be their equal!" The enormous hands were clamped on the rail now, and hatred was in the radiant eyes.

"Well, then," Gil suggested softly, "why don't you exercise free will?"

Evergray calmed a bit. "I am unsure. The Five have always worked for my well-being. Defying them, I risk disaster."

You understand better than you think, Gil observed, but said, "Is there any other way to use free will?"

"None. When they have Ascended to the godhead, the Five will control my every act, forever."

"How much time is left?"

"It is already begun. Do you not hear the festive music? Soon I go to the Masters."

Low and far away, it could barely be heard, an eerie, dissonant music that rose and fell unpredictably, celebrating the Ascension. "Evergray, couldn't you perform one act of free will? You'll never have another chance, will you?"

"No, but it is too late. External assault has failed, and the Masters' plan proceeds."

"What assault? Where?"

The giant pointed. For the first time, the American noticed shadowy mass movements on the desolate plain. "There, beyond the Necropolis, an army of mortals is come. Soon now, they will be trampled under by the Host of the Grave, which is our guard."

This is it, Gil thought. He asked, "Evergray, couldn't you just walk out? Take charge of that army, make your own destiny?"

"I am Scion of Salamá. At least the Five will permit me to rule. What would those creatures out there offer?"

Gil plunged ahead with a lie. "Loyalty, worship, acclaim. You're perfection itself; we need a leader like you, Evergray, to guide us and rule us all."

"I find that difficult to accept, sensible though it is. Your kind is intractable, impossible to deal with."

"Ask Dunstan! Go on, ask him."

"I cannot leave. The Five will summon me at any time."

"Then let me bring him to you, and he'll tell you the same thing I just did."

The giant inspected the American for a moment, eyes flashing, aura pulsing. Then he raised one big hand. "It is done. Go, fetch the Horseblooded here. Haste; the music rises, and the final moment draws nigh."

Gil dashed away, through turns and angles of the deserted galleries of Bey's palace, apocalypse at his heels. He came to the last chamber before the corridor. It was a wide, vaulted room with levels of balconies stretching away above, its walls lined with figurines and icons.

In the center of the room, blocking his way at the worst possible moment, was Flaycraft, toying with the Ace of Swords that hung around his neck. A hate-mask grin split his face. There'd be, Gil saw, no reasoning with him.

"Well, little mutt, will you run away from me now? Go! Your last run is started!"

There was no way around, no time to appeal to Evergray. Gil pushed down astringent fear and stepped out into the room. "C'mon; there's no wall between us."

Yardiff Bey's servant launched himself across the room with a howl. Gil braced to meet him. Ducking grasping paws, he bobbed up behind the torturer and landed a chop to his ear. Flaycraft roared, whirling.

Gil stayed just within jabbing distance, tagging two shots to the other's face. Flaycraft stopped short, more in surprise than pain. The American bore in, knees bent low, delivering the bottom of his elbow in an upward blow under the edge of the beast-man's sternum, his forearm and fist coming up like a goose neck. He followed with the heel of his hand to his opponent's chin, reversed directions and spun-kicked Flaycraft's stomach going away, a perfect little demonstration in hand-to-hand.

But Flaycraft didn't go down. He wasn't even hurt much. He came after Gil, ripping at his shirt. The American abruptly saw what he'd gotten himself into. He pivoted back around and launched a side-kick to the torturer's groin. The flat-footed authority of the kick stopped Flaycraft.

Gil back-fisted his knuckles into the beast-man's face, and chopped at his throat. Flaycraft screamed, shook his head angrily and locked his hands around his foe's throat, bearing him backward, knocking over a pedestal, sending a figurine bouncing. His brute strength was amazing; the hirsute body hid the power of an animal, or a madman. Feeling that, Gil panicked. He locked his hands and struck at the other's wrists. Two swings did no good, and his wind was shut off. Long black thumbnails had broken the skin at his throat. He was only conscious because the blood flow to his brain hadn't been pinched off by the clumsy choke.

He thought the blurring of his vision was unconsciousness coming on. Then he knew it was the first wave of the Berserkergang.

He brought one foot up and set it at the juncture of Flaycraft's hip and thigh, swinging his other leg through the torturer's. Rolling backward, holding handfuls of brown chest hair, he flipped the beast-man over his head. The deadly grip peeled itself off, backward. He was free, gasping, holding clots of long hairs. Flaycraft slammed down, but bounced up again, very much the angry primate. Gil struggled to rise.

Flaycraft tackled him, bearing him down. Sounds of their struggle drifted up among the darkened balconies. They sprawled, and the beast-man's grip swelled at the American's throat again. Gil tried to sit up, heels scrabbling for purchase, but Flaycraft rammed him down. In moments, blackness would close in for good. Gil slapped out his hands to break his fall; his right hit something hard, and fumbled to grip. Small and heavy, it filled his palm, the figurine that had fallen. He swung it blindly. It connected with Flaycraft's head, and the choke weakened for an instant. He swung again, and again. The hold faltered, fell away. Gil surged up, free.

Flaycraft held his head as blood welled from his scalp, matting his thick hair. Panting, Gil threw the figurine as hard as he could. It ricocheted from the torturer's shoulder. Flaycraft wiped blood from his eyes and a growl started low in his chest. Gil backed away, hyperventilating both from the Rage and to recover from the choking. He wouldn't have left the fight now if he could.

Flaycraft charged again. Gil backpedaled, working hand combinations dredged up by the Berserkergang, chopping and snap-punching, evading clinches. He tried for the nose and piggish eyes, but heavy ridges of bone protected them. The torturer's scalp wound, looking worse than it was, had covered his face and shoulder with blood and marked the tarot at his breast. Gil kept chipping away, using elbows and knees when he could, ducking and sidestepping. His nerves jumped and hummed with hatred. He was unaware of how much his expression resembled his enemy's.

He blocked reaching hands with a wide, rotary motion and threw a snap-punch to the high ribs, index knuckle cocked forward. He had enough room to slam an elbow in after it.

Pain ignited Flaycraft. He threw himself on Gil, unstoppable, yellow canines snapping close to the jugular. Gil caught the chest hair again, holding him away, trying for a hip throw. They were too intertangled. Gil changed grips to the shaggy ears, to hold Flaycraft's head steady. Then he crashed the top of his own skull into the snarling face. He felt bone give, and was himself staggered.

Flaycraft reeled back, his broken muzzle reddened, his wide, flat nose shattered. Gil blinked, seeing stars, and retreated to bring his back up against a wall.

He understood the match dimly. Flaycraft wasn't, and never had been, a standup fighter. His trade was abusing prisoners already bound and subdued. He was unaccustomed to open combat; but the beast-man was willing, and horribly strong and determined.

The moment's intellectualization was swallowed up again in the Rage. Flaycraft teetered, wiping blood from his bone-visored face, left eye swelling closed. He growled through torn lips. "You have a bite, little mutt," he slurred, "but now it is time to leash you again."

Gil heaved his shoulders, standing free of the wall. He topped Flaycraft by a head, but sensed, even in seizure, that the other would tear him apart if the match

313

went on much longer. He brought his hands up again, but his vision wavered.

The beast-man rushed him, arms spread. Gil faked left awkwardly, ducked right and put everything he had into a stiff-fingered left to the other's midsection. He chopped with the right, but it might as well have been a pat on the head. Flaycraft, arms wide, caught him in a bear hug that ended breath and threatened to splinter his ribs.

Gil dug thumbs under the lower corners of the torturer's ears, behind his jaw, but Flaycraft persevered. The American swung cupped hands in to pop them into the beast-man's ears in detonations that must have burst his eardrums. He only tightened his hold. Gil was starved for air.

Gil's nose was bleeding, as were his many lacerations from Flaycraft's nails. His eyes had focused down to a narrow circle surrounded by darkness; his head wobbled aimlessly. But the Rage bore him up with ferocity. He pushed his thumbs into the inner corners of the torturer's eyes.

The beast-man tried to avoid it, burrowing his bloodied head into Gil's chest, trying to sink his fangs in. The American forced his thumbs past the muscular opposition of lids, into the vulnerability behind them. Flaycraft screamed in pain. Gil ripped his thumbs away, tearing before them all that was in their way.

The torturer released him, stumbling away, hands clapped over both eyes. Gil fell to the floor and breathed in huge gulps, desperate for a few critical seconds' consciousness. Flaycraft groped back toward him with no other thought but to kill his enemy.

He tripped over Gil's legs and they both rolled on the carpet, one trying to keep distance, the other to close. Gil scrambled free. Flaycraft jumped to his feet. Blinded, deafened, he waited for smell or some vibration to tell him where his antagonist was. His face was unrecognizable; blood flowed from his ears, and his eyes were sockets of ruin.

Gil now believed the torturer could go on indefinitely, but the Berserkergang whispered that death would end it. The American spotted the figurine's fallen pedestal, a double spiral of metal rod with small circular base and platform, and went for it. Flaycraft sensed that somehow, charging with a roar. The beast-man took him from behind as he stooped for the weapon. Fingers locked on Gil's throat again. With no more than four or five seconds left, Gil swung the pedestal wildly over his head, unable to aim. There was blunt, violent collision of bone and metal. The grip weakened. He fumbled clear, swung again, and grazed his enemy.

Flaycraft shook his head angrily, dazed. Gil's world was blacking out; the Rage couldn't keep him going much longer. He brought the pedestal over his head in an arc of calculated hate. Even the beast-man couldn't take the blow without damage. He fell, the side of his skull opened, blue-white bone dashed in. The carpeting was sodden with his blood.

Gil, too, had fallen to his knees with the force of the swing. The torturer swayed before him, gurgling and growling, ruminating somewhere in the depths of his fury. He extended a cautious hand sightlessly feeling feebly, still seeking the grip that would let him kill.

Gil shifted his hold on the pedestal and swung again. It was his last effort; he never felt it end. He only saw the hated darkness rise.

Lying headlong, he held his aching throat where blood ran from nail wounds. Near him lay Flaycraft, sprawled dead. Between them was the pedestal, bent in the middle from the last blow, its base stained with blood. Some of Flaycraft's brown hairs still clung to it.

He toiled to his feet in the weakness that followed the Berserkergang. Something caught his eye, the Ace of Swords covered with Flaycraft's gore. He leaned over unsteadily, took it and put it on with bloodied hands, hiding the tarot under his shirt. He passed down the long gallery slowly, breathing deeply.

But at its end he realized that, in taking the Ace, he'd left proof positive that he'd killed Flaycraft. If Evergray noticed it on him, the Scion of Salamá would be suspicious, even if he didn't know what had happened to his servant. With a sudden thought to hide the body, he returned to the other end of the gallery.

One look around there convinced him it was futile. There was blood everywhere and no immediate place of concealment, even if he could move the torturer's bulky corpse. His breathing had begun to even out; now he heard the celebratory music of the Masters, louder than before, as if its crescendo were near. He lifted the beast-man's head and tossed the Ace of Swords beneath it.

"You wanted it, Flaycraft. Now you've got it." Listing dizzily, he went to free his friend.

* * *

Chapter Thirty-three

All theory is against free will; all experience for it.
                                        Samuel Johnson

GIL went along the rock face of the corridor until he came to the rune hanging in the air. Nothing more was necessary. The passageway dilated by Evergray's previous command. At the far end, a figure was outlined against the cone of light.

"Dunstan, c'mon; you're sprung."

The Horseblooded shielded his eyes from the orange light. He leaned weakly on the edge of the passageway. The gaunt face, like a sad clown's, achieved joy and sorrow at once. "The words you needed must have come to you."

"I made a few points, but he's not convinced. Wants to talk to you."

Dunstan stood upright, gazing at his hands. "I heard a voice call my name, and I was whole once again. Do you suppose I was never truly part of the stone? Perhaps Bey only made me see and feel what he wished. Mayhap I was imprisoned by what I believed, and could have walked free at any time."

Gil had been working with his tongue at a tooth that had been loosened in the fight. He spat it to the floor with a gobbet of blood and saliva. "What's it matter? You're free now."

That fact penetrated at last. "I am free!" He threw back his head, crowing his triumph. He leapt into the corridor and began a jig, hopping, stamping his feet. The music of the Masters swelled, but he used it for his fling, locking elbows with the protesting American, swinging him do-si-do. And what matter if the tune was played in demon's tri-tones? He laughed and sang, clicking his heels in the air, his long horsetail of hair flying; Gil's objections went unheard.

Then he saw the red stains on Gil's hands and clothes, and how he had his arm clamped to his side, feeling as if some of his ribs were cracked. Dunstan stopped. "What's happened? What have they done to you?"

"That's what I'm trying to tell you! Evergray sent me to get you, but Flaycraft tried to stop me. It was him or us, so it was him."

Dunstan's face was bleak again. "Almost, I could hate you for that. Simple death was ten thousand times easier than he deserved; it was damnable largesse."

"Give it over; the clock's running out. Evergray's got to go back to the Masters for his last session any time now."

"Come, lean on my arm."

"I'm okay. I'll fill you in as we go."

But when they re-entered the gallery, Evergray was standing beside the torturer's body, with Yardiff Bey nearby. In the Scion's hand was a greatsword nearly his own height.

And that's the end of it, thought Gil. Evergray no longer showed a smooth, emotionless face; now it was taut with righteous anger. He saw the two.

"Mad creatures, this was my friend," he boomed, his voice hurting their ears. "He was my teacher, my companion, my guardian, my servant. What have you done?"

Gil didn't evade. "Only what he would've done to me, *tried* to do to me."

"Of course you did, MacDonald." Yardiff Bey transferred his calm stare from the mortals to his progeny. "I knew it as soon as I happened upon the corpse. It is in his free-will nature to slay and maim, and bring suffering without thought or pause." Gil glowered, knowing his

317

appearance must suggest the red-handed butcher Bey was making him out to be. "How many lives have you taken, MacDonald? You murdered in those first seconds that you were in Coramonde. You have been murdering ever since."

"Shut up, Bey! What about *you*? For God's sake, what about your killings, centuries of them?" He floundered, unsure that it was any defense at all.

The sorcerer's tone stayed calm as a tranquil river. "I? When have you seen me kill?" He knew the American had been too dazed at the Isle of Keys to note the death of the Trustee.

Gil couldn't find a retort. For all the deaths with which Bey was connected, Gil could cite no time when he'd seen the Hand commit murder personally. As he'd told Dunstan, Bey was smarter, smoother. The sorcerer spoke to his creation again.

"Understand, child of my arts; free-will beings are treacherous and ungrateful. I knew that when I besought you to arm yourself. It will be no loss when the memory of free will is wiped away forever before the glorious New Order. There is death in everything they touch, just as there is ruin implicit in that tarot MacDonald wears."

Gil broke in. "Spare the tears, Bey. How many people died to suit your plans? Quit splitting hairs; you're just as guilty as—"

Insight came to him. "Oh, *right!* You're not here by accident, and neither was Flaycraft. You bastard! You set me up again, didn't you?" It was clear now, Yardiff Bey had used Gil one last time, to dissuade Evergray from his stubbornness about free will. The sorcerer had arranged the fight.

"Evergray, don't you see what's going on? You, me, Dunstan, Flaycraft; Bey's played us all off against each other. If Flaycraft killed me, fine and dandy; I'd have looked erratic and everything I'd said goes out the window. And when I won, it was all the same: You still end up hating mortals and going along with the Masters. It's fail-safe."

"He is mad," Bey intoned placidly, "and the mad will claim anything."

Gil snarled furiously. In the back of his mind, something had been yammering for attention. Then he had it.

"Bey, what did you just say, something about the tarot I wear? Flaycraft took that from me. Why did you think I was wearing it again, *unless you saw me take it off him?*"

He grabbed the ragged front of his shirt and tore down the rotting sealskin. Flaycraft's toothmarks were all he exposed. Bey was nonplussed. "He arranged it all. He must have watched from somewhere up there in the dark, one of those balconies. Evergray, he witnessed the fight. Yes, I took the Ace, and he saw it and left to get you. But he wasn't there when I came back and left it here."

The sorcerer had composed himself. "It was only misstatement. No minor confusion of mine can palliate what you have done—"

He was drowned out by the American, screaming to Evergray: "Roll Flaycraft over!"

The giant brushed the squat body over with one hand. The Ace of Swords lay in a red puddle. Yardiff Bey's disclaimers stopped. Evergray clenched his fist, shrieking into the air. The other three clapped hands to their ears, their hearing jeopardized. He pointed a long finger at the sorcerer.

"My one companion, my only friend. His life mattered not at all to you. Now hear my troth: Your plan will never come to pass!" His head snapped around, listening to his Masters. At the top of his lungs he bellowed, "Never!"

He pointed at Gil and Dunstan. "These death-lusting mortals are unfit to shape their lives. In like wise, the Masters are worthy of no godhead." A circle of radiant, crackling energy sprang up around the horns and projections of his crown-helmet. "There is only one entity with the power and sanity to bring order to the world, and he is Evergray. *I* am the synthesis of Might and Right. Both sides will be abased to me. To me!"

He faced Yardiff Bey. "Stand aside. The armies of the north are engaging the Host of the Grave, but I shall take them under my command. The Spell of Spells will be stopped, and all will yield to me."

The sorcerer stood to stop him, half-drawing Dirge. "What my magic has made, my magic can unmake." Evergray raised his own weapon. Bey hesitated, seeing it. The Scion snatched Dirge from the sorcerer's grasp, handing it aside carelessly. Gil took the deathblade with all caution. Bey's fingers flew to the ocular he wore where his left eye had been.

Evergray set his feet firmly, his aura crackling brighter. "Use that last desperate resort, father, but be warned; if you do, your life lies upon it."

Knowing Evergray was filled with the energies of the Five, Bey let his hand fall from the ocular. His shoulders drooped. Gil stooped and snatched up the Ace, shoving it into his waistband. It had brought him a convoluted turn of luck; he was unwilling to abandon it. Then he stood, Dirge in hand, to face Yardiff Bey.

But a tempest came up in the sorcerer's mansion, the Masters' efforts to stop their Scion's defection. They'd put too much of their power into him though, and he defied them. Wind and lightning broke around him, but didn't touch him. The fury of it drove Gil, along with Dunstan, into the shelter of Evergray's magic. When the American looked again, the sorcerer was gone.

"Come!" Evergray commanded over his shoulder. The two fell in close behind, having to trot to keep up with the aroused giant while the wrath of the Five crashed around them.

Evergray led them out onto the balcony, to *Cloud Ruler*. No guards appeared to interfere; if the Masters couldn't halt Evergray, no show of arms would. He spoke a syllable, and the flying craft's hatch rolled open. They boarded.

Inside, Gil and Dunstan gazed around at the rich appointments of the command chamber. The giant seated himself before an enormous lens, straddling the command chair which was too small for him. He put his sword aside, set hands on knees, and went into deep concentration, breaking the vessel free of Yardiff Bey's control. *Cloud Ruler* shuddered, belched flame and lifted off slowly.

The demon-ship rocked turbulently for a moment, then steadied again. Evergray laughed. "He tried to liberate the fire-elemental entrapped in *Cloud Ruler*'s bowels, but I contained it again instantly, by my arts. I am mightier than the Hand of Salamá!"

Gil peeked around Evergray at the lens. Salamá shrank in its convex fish-eye. The American could see dark masses moving on the desolate plain. Off in the distance was the hill where the Lifetree had bloomed.

One lone figure came out to stare up from the balcony. From this height, Bey looked insignificant, almost pitiable. After all the centuries, Yardiff Bey had made his greatest error. Eager to summon Evergray and accuse Gil, he'd left the gallery too soon.

The only time you've ever been careless, Bey, and now it's all coming unglued. The American found he couldn't savor the irony. The tiny figure was barely visible.

Don't go away; we'll be back.

Chapter Thirty-four

The glories of our blood and state
Are shadows, not substantial things
                              James Shirley
                              "Death the Leveller"

ON the desolate plain, swords rushed in ritualistic curves, approaches and interplays of war. With no effort to defend themselves, the Dead attacked relentlessly.

Springbuck's first match was definitive. The dead soldier came at him, eyes glowing, skin decayed, armor corroded. It swung a notched sword; the *Ku-Mor-Mai* blocked with his shield and responded with Bar. In a moment, they were trading strokes. The corpse-warrior wasn't particularly strong, nor certainly a clever swordsman, but its offense was ceaseless.

Springbuck and his opponent wheeled around each

other, angry Fireheel setting his shoulder against the spectral mount's. The *Ku-Mor-Mai* saw the Dead would be as avid to fight, unwearied, an hour or a day or a year from now as at this second. His army could match any mortal opponents, but how long could they stand against these insatiable foemen?

He caught the sword on his shield and got a blow in. Bar dug deep, severing an arm. The specter dropped its shield and plucked a rusty mace from its saddlebow, coming on again. Springbuck intercepted the mace, the blow numbing his shield arm, and buried his blade deep in the corpse's side. The dead man twitched with the impact, but lifted its mace again.

The *Ku-Mor-Mai* tugged wildly to free Bar. The mace fell with unflagging resolve. Springbuck was able to hold up his battered shield long enough to ward it off. The Obstructor came loose; he cut again. This time the hand that held the mace dropped, parted from its arm. The corpse fought on, grinning, ghastly, clubbing with the stumps of its arms. Springbuck caught its rotting harness and pulled it from its saddle. It crashed to the ground and began to flail its way to its feet. The son of Surehand leaned low and struck off its head with one slash. The head rolled in the gray soot, but the body continued to struggle, losing balance and falling, never stopping.

Springbuck backed Fireheel out of the way, to see what was happening. Up and down the front, it was the same; the Dead couldn't be stopped short of dismemberment. The northerners were cutting their horses or their legs from under the enemy, or literally disarming them. Sometimes it worked, and sometimes not.

Springbuck saw Angorman not far away, leading the Order. Red Pilgrim whirled and cut around him, felling the Dead with its steel mandates. By Angorman's side, Balagon swung *Ke-Wa-Coe,* the broadsword he'd consecrated to the Bright Lady. The Order and the Brotherhood, select champions of the Crescent Lands, hacked and hewed. In their section of the battle, the Dead made slow headway.

Rank after rank waited to fill gaps in the line of the Dead. They would triumph by attrition; the northerners were far too few to carve them all. Springbuck could

322

order a withdrawal, but to where? The Host of the Grave would run the living to the earth.

Engaged along a wide front, the Crescent Landers met enemy after enemy. The war-drays of Matloo careened through the fight, hub-blades threshing through the Host. Heavily plated Lead-Line Riders guided the armored teams on; the crews licked out with their long, two-handed swords. The Dead fell in rows. The Yalloroon crouched inside the wagons, their terror outweighed by their awe of the outlanders for daring challenge Salamá to come out and fight.

The other northerners were falling back as they battled; they couldn't stand their ground with severed arms clawing at their horse's shanks. Springbuck was thankful his army was mounted; infantry would have been engulfed. The living sustained losses; the Dead fought and silently fell only to be replaced by other uncaring, animate corpses.

A wide breakthrough occurred, the Crescent Landers' line pierced by a wedge of the Dead. Brodur-Scabbardless saw it and, cursing the luck that had given him the responsibility of command, brought up all his reserves, three squadrons of heavy cavalry. With those thousand ironclads at his back, he cast himself into the gap. The Host rose to meet them, and the Scabbardless was swallowed up in the melee. The breach closed for the time being, and more reinforcements were hurried there, but only a part of the reserves could fight free again, and Brodur had fallen.

Reacher's flank, at the extreme right, was falling back in good order. His mainstay, Kisst-Haa and the several reptile-men, plied their colossal blades and flayed with their flanged, armored tails. Their foemen were stamped flat by broad, scaled feet, halved or cut off at the knees by broadswords, plucked up and torn by mighty claw-hands, or smashed by caudal armor. Even the Dead were no match for them, yet Kisst-Haa and his kinsmen must tire in time, and couldn't hold the entire flank themselves.

Even wildhearted Katya saw this was no time for charge and sally; she fell back with Van Duyn and her brother. When the Horseblooded had seen that their wailing arrows were of no avail, they'd swept out keen scimitars.

Reacher, the only man afoot, leaping and dodging in the midst of it, slashed with his clawed glove and struck with his cestus, hurling corpse-soldiers aside. Seeing how hard it would be for his men to resist the Host, he tried to be everywhere at once, helping as many of them as he could. It was a mistake; no one man could do it, not even the Wolf-Brother. He found himself encircled, standing atop a writhing pile of cadaver parts, lashing out to every side. The mound grew as he fought, but more and more of the Dead turned toward him.

Katya saw, and rode in to bring her brother out. But a sword took her horse in the side, and she went down. Kisst-Haa, who'd been following her with one eye, made a steam whistle of alarm. One of the Dead loomed over the Snow Leopardess, an ages-old axe raised.

The reptile-man bent, picked up the spiked-ball head of a broken mace, reared back and threw it with all his muscle. It passed completely through the dead man, hurling the body back ten feet. Van Duyn appeared, to raise his shield over her and help her up. Reacher leapt down to them, and Kisst-Haa and his kin moved in, greatswords thrashing. The Snow Leopardess recovered her weapon, and the group withdrew in hedgehog fashion, defending at all points.

Springbuck, trying futilely to keep his line dressed in withdrawal, saw Andre and Gabrielle in among the Glyffans. He left his place, and Hightower held the gap with enormous sweeps of his blade, swinging a morning star with his left hand.

"There is no hope but you," Springbuck told the enchanters. "Our lines will dissolve soon. We've no reserve, nor any place to take a stand." He noticed that Andre wore his own sword again, brought south by Gabrielle. He was holding Blazetongue in his hand. "Andre, your sword has Calundronius in it. Would the gemstone work?"

The wizard shook his head. "It might clear some small space against the Dead, but not defeat them in numbers."

"Then, what of Blazetongue?"

The wizard was surprised. "What of it? It has done its last office, calling up the Trailingsword. We lack the means to summon its lesser fire."

"Is there nothing you can evoke from it?"

Those words brought back the Trustee's. Andre turned excitedly to Gabrielle. "Our mother said she thought Blazetongue might have a last service left in it, to render up when it is unmade."

She considered that. "But can we accomplish it?"

"Its magic is akin to ours. And surely here, directly beneath the Trailingsword's marker, we have a propitious place, even though that Omen isn't in view."

"Try, try!" pleaded Springbuck, seeing that he must return to his place. Andre hefted Blazetongue; Gabrielle lifted the Crook, which glowed with the blue magic of the deCourteneys. Brother and sister went forward, holding their talismans high. Swan and the Sisters of the Line came to guard their Trustee.

Hightower opened a way for them. The Dead, pouring in, were stopped at once by the brilliance of the Crook. They persisted though, falling in piles before Gabrielle deCourteney. She had a hard time urging her frightened horse forward, so Springbuck rode in to take its bridle, leading it on. Andre was at his sister's other side.

When he'd gotten to the center of the melee, Andre dropped from his saddle, Blazetongue in hand. Taking the greatsword by its thick quillions, he stabbed it deep into the sooty ground. Gabrielle had dismounted too, in a ring of swordswomen. She struck the weapon's hilt with the Crook, and blue sparks shot out; struck it a second time, and beams of light shone from it, making the Dead shield themselves. She struck Blazetongue with the Crook a third time; the sword turned to blue incandescence, not burning, but discharging all the energy bound up in it. Flames spread outward, consuming their way through the Host of the Grave, driving them back from the living, guided by the deCourteneys.

The balefire spread left and right, racing along the battle line. Any of the Dead whom it touched became momentary torches, dropping into piles of ash. Men held their cloaks or shields to fend off the heat, but the fire didn't seek them out. A barrier of blue burning

325

sprang up from the dust. The bulk of the Host of the Grave was held back by it, unable to get at their antagonists. But there were still many of the Dead on the other side, the Crescent Landers'. Springbuck demanded, "Will it hold, this wall of magic?"

"While there is anything left of Blazetongue," Gabrielle assessed, "but then it will end."

Unearthly combat continued, the living taking the offensive mode. Those of the Host left on the northerners' side of the flames were now outnumbered. The living rode them down with charges and a rising and falling of arms. Many of the Dead had been consumed by Blazetongue's released energies, but many more waited beyond a curtain of flame that now burned lower. Springbuck, gazing out at them, saw their hungry, glowing eyes, like a night of stars. They were biding their time until they could take up where they'd left off.

A shout came from Hightower, "See!" They searched, and saw it riding high up, a silvery shape on red pillars of demon-flame. Springbuck thought of Bey, watching and gloating aboard *Cloud Ruler*, and channeled his resentment into his right arm.

But the flying vessel swooped lower, and lower yet. It banked and came back, its fire splashing off the ground. Ship of the holocaust, it trailed its red blast through the Host of the Grave. It withered the Dead like insects in a bonfire.

Cloud Ruler cut a path of annihilation from one flank of the Dead to the other, leaving behind it the stench of cremation. The Dead wavered. *Cloud Ruler* came around for another devastating pass, and a third. The northerners hewed down the Host remaining on their side of the conflagration like so many executioners. The demon-ship swung back and forth, carpeting the ground with the seared Dead. Springbuck couldn't speculate how that vessel might be coming to his support, nor could Andre, nor Gabrielle. At the moment, that was unimportant.

Evergray brought the sky ship around for another run. Gil and Dunstan had lost count of the passes he'd made through the Host of the Grave. There were a few stragglers escaping *Cloud Ruler*'s purging fire. Except for those few, though, the ancient sentinels of the Five had been incinerated. *Cloud Ruler* circled for a landing.

Below, the last of the curtain of flame was dying. Where Blazetongue had been planted, there was only a hole, the ground around it a glassy fusion. The Crook of the Trustee was quiescent. Breathing was a trial; fumes were the residue of the Host of the Grave, a thick, smoky reek that permeated hair and clothing and choked the lungs. When they disembarked, Gil and Dunstan coughed, rubbing their eyes and staring at the charred field. Evergray stood, fists on hips, satisfied with what he'd done.

"In this moment, the Masters must feel their weird upon them," he declared loftily.

Springbuck arrived with the deCourteneys, Hightower and the others from Coramonde, Glyffa and Veganá. The *Ku-Mor-Mai* dismounted and rushed to the American and the Horseblooded, pounding their backs, gripping hands and shouting amazed greetings. Gil was careful with Dirge, unsure if its spells were still active. Questions and explanations were lost in the confusion, but the deCourteneys became concerned, seeing Evergray, who was smiling, his aura flickering.

Swan arrived, and Angorman. She saw Gil and called out his name; even in the tumult he heard it. She came down off Jeb Stuart, removing the bascinet, its white wings and mirror brightness smudged now. Her snakeskin armor showed signs of the battle, and he was still marked with Flaycraft's blood. Neither of them knew what to say.

"You found your friend," she ventured at last. "Did you slay your enemy, then?"

"No." He looked to Dunstan, who was joyous as his nature ever let him be, talking to Springbuck. "But I guess it's all right. You?"

"The Trustee fell in conflict, and Gabrielle has taken her place. Yes, I have survived; more than many were allowed to do." He brushed her hair back at the side, where the birthmark ran. She flashed her smile and took his hand.

Evergray broke off his gloating, interrupting reunions. "Who reigns here?" The words hung, imperious, in the smoky quiet. All looked at last to Springbuck.

"I am Springbuck of Coramonde, *Ku-Mor-Mai*. There are only free equals, met here. Yet I have led as much as any."

"That being the case, you may marshal all the free-will forces for me. But all other decrees will be mine."

Gil saw the anger that drew all around. "Hold it, Evergray. They want what you do, to stop the Masters; you just can't take over like this though. Outside Salamá they do things differently. We're all—"

"Silence!" The giant's face shone in fury, eyes blazing. "No free-will creature may defy me. I am Evergray of Shardishku-Salamá. I will stop the grand design of the Five, and impose my will on them, as they would have done to me. My authority transcends all others." He shook his enormous broadsword at the city. "Be ready, then, to perish!"

"And your word outweighs all others?" Angorman spoke up, leaning on Red Pilgrim. "And the gods?"

Evergray's burning gaze went to him. "You mortals never saw how the gods' destinies hinge upon your own. When I have thrown down the Masters, I will topple the shrines of the gods, and none will survive!"

Angorman brought his greataxe up in a flash. "For the Bright Lady!" He rushed the giant.

Evergray brought his weapon around, stopping the legendary axe with a blade-to-blade intrusion. Sparks shot from the meeting. Before anyone could act, Evergray drove his point through the Saint-Commander. Angorman sank with a shedding of blood. Gil, horrified, called the old man's name. The warrior-priest's eyes fluttered shut.

Hightower attacked, his sword uplifted, but Evergray parried and, as they went *corps-à-corps*, dealt a blow with his free hand that flattened the Warlord. Swan was calling for archers.

There was an explosion of arcane blue, as Gabrielle's Crook spoke. Evergray shrugged it off, and sent a counterspell at her. The Crook strobed harsh colors.

Gil saw that Evergray could never endure or even understand the mortals he'd decided to rule. And it was Gil MacDonald who'd brought him here. The American brought Dirge up before he himself became a target, and sank the deathblade deep into the giant's side.

Evergray threw his head back and screamed in agony. Dirge hummed angrily; black smoke roiled from the wound. The giant spun, yanking the hilt from the outlander's grasp, and slapped him to the earth like a rag doll.

"You," the Scion accused, unbelieving, "whom I freed!" He was swaying, leached by Dirge's malevolent enchantments. He pulled at the sword clumsily, but it resisted him. At last he yanked it loose, fighting for balance, knowing what terrible wound he'd taken.

"MacDonald, did you mean my death from the first? Ah, you have gulled me. Die with me, then!"

Hightower, back on his feet, leapt to interpose himself. But Evergray, even wounded, was too strong and fast. Bey's sword struck through the old Warlord's guard and his armored body, driving him down to the dust atop the stunned Gil. Dirge slid on, out the back of Hightower's mail, into the American's side, irresistible invasion of steel through complacent flesh.

The Warlord groaned and writhed; Gil felt as if he'd been butt-stroked in the ribs. There was a rushing sensation to it, noise and feeling both, air leaving his punctured left lung.

Evergray drew Dirge out brutally, eliciting another cry from Hightower, to strike again. Now Gabrielle blocked his way, and she struck Dirge with her mother's white wooden Crook. There was a bright splash of magic, staggering Evergray, who dropped his weapon and closed his huge hands on the Crook. Archers held fire, and even Andre couldn't interfere where the Trustee's Crook was concerned. Strands of mystic brilliance played up and down the rod of office, flickering over them both, as she diverted the giant's energies, drawing them to her through the staff. His aura grew dimmer, while hers increased.

Andre, Dunstan and Springbuck eased Hightower off Gil. The wizard and the *Ku-Mor-Mai* looked to the Warlord while Swan and Dunstan bent over Gil, all of them wary of the duel erupting nearby. When they saw the damage Dirge had done Gil, the Horsebloodcd's sad clown face seemed about to come apart from grief; Swan made a low sound of woe, suppressed far back in her throat. The American got himself up on one elbow, keeping his good lung, his right, uppermost to help breathing. His wound sucked and bubbled with his respiration. He clapped a hand to it, sobbing in pain, eyes bulging. With a flood of horror he realized that the weapon Evergray had used on him was the dread blade Gil himself had carried south.

Evergray harbored more power than even Gabrielle could absorb. She released her Crook, sinking to the ground, but the giant stumbled back and forth, unable to let loose of the staff. He couldn't stop the outrushing of his own vitality. Brighter and brighter he flared, like a nova. Then the light went out.

He fell, blackened, the crown-helmet tumbling from his head, no longer fitting him; he'd shrunken with the loss of his power. The Crook of the Trustee was now a row of cinders.

Gil lay near, fighting shrilly for air. Evergray focused on him stuporously. "I truly had no allies, had I? Nor kin, nor friend, nor any who wished to be."

The crosscurrent radiance in his eyes died. Gil, also under Dirge's sentence, hung his head down in defeat.

Chapter Thirty-five

For better than never is late . . .
                    Chaucer
                    "The Canon's Yeoman's Tale"

THERE was an explosion on the plain; *Cloud Ruler* disappeared in a red fireball. Yardiff Bey had removed his spells from the elemental within it; now that Evergray's no longer held it, it burst free. Hovering for a moment, a searing, raging globe, it took its bearings while those below crouched from its heat, then blazed into the sky, away from its long imprisonment.

From above, from all around, a choir of frustration

and venom filled the air. The Masters lamented for themselves, and the Spell ruined by Evergray's death. Their hatred rolled across the plain, trembling the tatters of cloth that clung to the fallen.

Gabrielle sprawled in the dust by Hightower's side. The old man couldn't staunch the blood that flowed from him, though his clamped hands shook with the effort. She tried her enchantments, though she knew nothing would reverse Dirge's malice.

Van Duyn arrived, with Reacher and Katya. With them came some of the Yalloroon, staring wide-eyed at the aftermath of battle. Two of the little people had died, along with the crew of the war-dray in which they'd ridden, when their vehicle was overturned and overrun by the Dead.

Swan knelt by Gil's side as he tried to hold his breath and re-expand his lung by pressure, hand covering his wound. But the function of Dirge's magic made it impossible to seal the injury. He gave up and looked at the High Constable.

"You were right in Final Graces," he labored, breath short. "About risk."

Springbuck appeared over Swan's shoulder. His eyes flicked to the wound, then met his friend's candidly, holding no hope. Gil tried to smile, but failed. "I know. I should have listened to you. Forget it. Bey's still back there in the city."

Andre had left Hightower, for whom the wizard could do nothing. Now he led Balagon away from where the warrior-priest had closed Angorman's eyes forever. The Divine Vicar had taken up Red Pilgrim; Andre took it from him gently, handing it away to Van Duyn, who stood nearest him. Hearing Gil, Andre nodded. "That is no less than true. There is still Bey. Gabrielle?"

She still held Hightower's hand, but said, "The Masters await. There is yet time to act."

"Are you not spent?" Springbuck asked anxiously.

"Not so," she replied. "I took in a measure of the force escaping Evergray. The rest is fled at random. The Five's resources are diminished, but they will draw more to them, or be given of Amon's. We have only this moment."

Hightower sighed weakly and squeezed her hand in approval.

Their losses had been heavy. Because some must care for the injured and because the number of horses was reduced, Springbuck had fewer than seven thousand functioning mounted troops. He began rapid orders for assembly. Then he halted as an emaciated mare bore toward him through the drifting smoke and stench. She came to a stumbling stop and her rider dropped to his feet.

"Ferrian!" Dunstan flew at him. "Kinsman!" They gripped forearms.

"We are peculiarly met," observed Ferrian, eyes sweeping the scene.

Many Wild Riders came to their former Champion, saluting, pressing his hand in theirs, but he broke away, and came to Springbuck. When he'd heard what had happened, Ferrian motioned to Gil and Hightower. "Though Angorman and many others on the field are beyond help, these two here are not, for in Ladentree I learned many things. Yonder, east of Salamá some small way, is the hill where the Lifetree blossomed. Down within it lie those particular waters which fed the Tree, and would remedy Dirge's magic."

Andre was unconvinced. "Those are for the Lifetree. I doubt any other influence could summon them forth."

"Carnage wrought by ordinary steel cannot be undone," Ferrian answered, "but these of an eldritch nature, these might be. It would be ill of us not to try."

Gil knew a flash of hope so poignant it stripped him of his stolid resignation, slim as the chance was, and Swan's face came alive.

Springbuck knew he must be the one to say it. "The Masters will not defer that long, Ferrian. An hour's delay will be the death of us all." That same hour would kill Gil and Hightower. He searched Gabrielle's face for vindication, desperate that she understand two lives were balanced here against many, as well as the fate of the Crescent Lands.

Ferrian shook his head. "The gods have us on schedules all their own. But there is a third choice, *Ku-Mor-Mai*. Let those who must press on to Salamá, and let but a few of us detour, bearing these two comrades to the hill."

Dunstan seconded it, saying he would go. Springbuck's expression showed how welcome that proposal was. "Well thought on. But how to transport?"

The latecomer pointed to where the overturned wardray of Matloo had been righted. Its tongue-hitch had been twisted and broken, but the team had been recovered, and hasty repairs made by septmen. "There is the method."

Springbuck ordered the dray brought over. Gabrielle took Swan aside. Low, she commanded, "High Constable, go with them. I hold little more confidence in this than Andre, but it must be tried." Swan didn't conceal her eagerness to obey.

As the dray was brought up, Ferrian turned to Van Duyn. "You are Gil's only countryman. Will you not come too?" The older man hesitated, then murmured that, of course, he assuredly would.

Katya took his arm. "We both will go. And Reacher too, will you not, brother?" The King affirmed it, staring strangely at his old friend Ferrian, his wilderness sense telling him there was more here than was being said.

Springbuck asked if they would need a driver from the men of Matloo, or an escort. "No," Ferrian answered, "for all danger here will be directed at the deCourteneys. The last contest will be of magic, and in Salamá; thus we should go unmolested." Ferrian thought for a moment. "Still, my kinsman Dunstan is unarmed. If Andre will not need his sword, perhaps he would lend it to a weaponless man?" He fixed the wizard with a strange look.

Obeying a sense of inspired impulse, Andre unhooked the scabbard from his belt and gave his sword to the surprised Dunstan, commenting, "I wish no one to be . . . unprotected."

The dray was beautifully made, meticulously planed with its joined timbers reinforced with armor plate, braced and strapped with metal. It was articulated, flexible in its center, to lend maneuverability. Its port-plates were raised, from combat against the Dead, and there

333

were red stains on its polished wooden deck and bulk-heads, drying to brown.

For this ride, the northerners agreed, they needed no Lead-Line Rider. Being lifted aboard, even by so many careful hands, made Gil wince in pain. Van Duyn knew that wound was killing his countryman quickly, filling the pleural space with blood and pressure that had probably started a mediastinal shift, pushing toward the uninjured side, straining the heart and placing even greater demands on the overworked right lung. Gil hadn't gone into shock yet, but that might happen any second, and against the magic of Dirge, no conventional technique of aspiration or drainage could avail.

Hightower was even worse. The steady loss of blood had covered his midsection, and coated his mailed legs. Gabrielle helped strap him in on one of the benches that ran the length of the dray, while Gil was eased down on the other. She kissed the Warlord, patted the American's shoulder, then walked stiff-spined to her horse.

"To Salamá," she said.

Katya and Reacher rode up, leading Van Duyn's steed. Ferrian took Red Pilgrim from Van Duyn and handed it aside to Dunstan, who crouched in the dray. Swan had mounted Jeb Stuart.

Springbuck groped for words. "Grace of the Lady upon you," he finally bade them.

Ferrian answered, "I bid you good fortune, son of Surehand. Here under the shadow of the Five, where every word and deed is heard and seen by them, I say it. May the deCourteneys carry the day." He climbed into the dray as Dunstan stood to the vehicle's armored prow and gathered handfuls of reins.

The men of Coramonde were drawn up in their squadrons, interspersed with the other war-drays of Mat-loo. Behind them were women of Glyffa and men of Veganá, units of Freegate and gathered clans of the Horseblooded. Springbuck joined the deCourteneys at the head of them all.

Gabrielle needed no divination to read his mind. "Would your presence not mean much to MacDonald?" she inquired. "And to Hightower?"

"The armies must be led," he evaded.

"We deCourteneys have a smattering of talent for

that, as has been seen. But you can do little in Salamá save sit and wait. Go with your friend."

Andre spared him further agonizing by shouting the order to ride, slapping Fireheel's croup. The big gray sprang aside as the ranks moved by. Joining the others at the dray, Springbuck found that a weight had left him. Dunstan clucked, flicked the reins, and started off eastward as the rest fell in behind and beside.

The northern armies rode through the obsidian arch, a quarter-mile span, that was the entrance to Shardishku-Salamá. Andre had a small contingent fall out here, to guard and keep watch on the plain.

Then they continued, clattering up boulevards hundreds of yards wide, past the vacant palaces and deserted towers of the city. They met no opposition; the Masters, guarded by the Host of the Grave, had never thought they would need any defense but their own powers. Now, after the huge drain caused by the death of Evergray, the Five were conserving those. They might have made feints, or even tangible attacks, but that would have cost critical amounts of energy, and the outcome would have been in doubt. In their own arena, in their own time, the Five would confront Andre and Gabrielle, whom they held to be the only serious threat.

The armies flowed between the soaring structures of the city. In silence, they viewed the stupendous bas-relief depicting the destruction of the Lifetree. Most of the residents had fled and others had expired when the Masters, pressed by demands on the strength left to them, withheld it from their subjects.

The Crescent Landers drew up before the Fane, its vast curve sweeping out above them. Its doors had seemed small, in proportion, from the far end of the boulevard. Now they stretched upward, higher than a donjon, of cold dark metal that gleamed like onyx. Here the deCourteneys left the massed warriors, telling them to stay back from the magic that dwelled within. They were well and quickly heeded.

Leaving their horses, the two spread their arms before the doors. They sensed the might of the doors, the Masters' first test.

"Masters of Salamá," Gabrielle challenged, "we are

335

for earnest combat. For preliminaries, we care no more than this!" With that, she spat on the doors. Where it landed, blue essence of her magic sizzled and popped, spreading to the hairline crack between the two portals, racing up and down. The doors quaked, caught in the conflict of wills between the deCourteneys and the Five. Thick hinges rang like tuning forks. In that first contest, the Masters found that the new Trustee was indeed worthy of her office. The Five didn't exert every effort, but let the deCourteneys put theirs forth. The doors burst open, swung wide.

Andre and Gabrielle walked together into lightlessness. When they were within, the cyclopean portals swung shut. No one outside tried to stop that, nor could they have done so.

Though Dunstan kept the ride as smooth as he could, the passengers were still swayed and jounced. Gil was feeling cold, his respiration shallow and fast, his chest screaming for air. Hightower seemed to have lost consciousness. There was a yelp from Ferrian who, for some reason, stared back across a flat landscape at Salamá rather than ahead.

"The glows of thaumaturgy are there," the Horseblooded shouted. Dunstan hauled on the reins. Ferrian, with a hair-raising Horseblooded whoop, dropped through the rear hatch while the dray was still rolling. He pointed back toward the Necropolis, calling jeers to the Five.

The others looked. Ripples of enchantment and antispells disrupted one another, sending multicolored distortions through the skies over Salamá. Springbuck and the others turned worriedly to Ferrian, and Dunstan clapped a hand to his shoulder.

"Kinsman, have your senses fled?"

The other Rider shook his head, the long tail of his hair flying. "Oh cousin, no. I held back a secret from you all, for the Masters hear every word and see every deed here, in their inner domain. But their battle with the siblings deCourteney is in full career. I will explain all, as I dared not do before."

They heard him out in assorted states of skepticism or befuddlement, even Gil, who watched through the

336

rear hatch. "When I was recuperant at Ladentree, I saw a strange thing. The Birds of Accord had brought forth hatchlings, yes, a thing they can do only under influence of the Lifetree. I bespoke Silverquill, the Senior Sage, and he remembered the Birds had lit on the Crook of the Trustee. We reasoned the rod of her office was wood of the Lifetree itself."

"The Crook was consumed," Katya pointed out, "stopping Evergray." Springbuck closed his eyes in sorrow, seeing salvation appear and disappear in moments.

"But hold," Swan objected, "the Trustee had been many times in Ladentree. Why did the birds not respond before?"

"The same occurred to us, and so that scholarly process of elimination came into play. We started with a different, theoretical answer, and proved it by diligent research through the library, piecing together Rydolomo's secret in reverse, as it were, and had a bit of information even Bey lacked. At the Lady's instigation, a limb of the Lifetree, cut to Her likeness, went northward as figurehead to the bow of a ship. Do you understand?"

Gil blinked. *Shaped like the Bright Lady?* "Angorman's axe," he blurted. It lay where Ferrian had put it, under Hightower's bench.

"No other. The helve comes of a fragment of that figurehead. Wildmen burned the rest but did not know, and hence Bey never learned, that one vestige survived." Ferrian drew the greataxe out of the dray, its haft looking like ordinary ashwood.

"The Lifetree," he declared, "come south by dint of the Trailingsword, when the Masters think it safely consumed." He pointed eastward. "And under that hill are those healing waters it will call forth, and in which it will thrive. We must take it there, sink it into the ground. If our star fails us not, it will flourish again."

Hightower, clinging to life by insistence alone, produced from somewhere in his ruined depths a spasm of a laugh. "Now must yon webmakers of Salamá be a-spin! Duped, like any bumpkin, by the Lady!"

"I should have brought more troops," Springbuck muttered.

"Untrue," Ferrian corrected. "The Masters can only

337

stop us by their arts, if at all. Thus, I took this." He handed the axe to Springbuck and showed Andre deCourteney's sword from its scabbard at Dunstan's side. Unscrewing the pommel, he pulled out the mystic gemstone Calundronius. He held it up, chatoyant on its chain. "This will negate all spells, but can protect only a few. So, I contrived a purpose to keep our number small. Our only word now is haste, our one purpose to see the Lifetree replanted. Not all our lives nor any other price matters against that."

"We should tell the Trustee," Swan suggested.

"No time," Gil coughed, head spinning. "It's just us. Springbuck?"

"Precisely. If no one objects, I will go in the fore with the stone, and let the rest range round the dray."

As Ferrian relinquished Calundronius, Katya asked, "What if the Five muster some pursuit? Were it not sound policy for one or two to stay back, to repel that? Edward and I are well suited." Van Duyn cleared his throat, resettled the M-1, and agreed.

"And," added Ferrian, "the team will need a Lead-Line Rider now, a job for a Horseblooded."

Ferrian drew himself up onto the wagon's tongue. Nimble as a tightrope walker, he made his way along, flipping shut each horse's blinders. Used to that, the huge animals waited, knowing they'd be expected to do their hardest work now. Ferrian mounted the special saddle on the left-side leader's back. In the Lead-Line Rider's perilous station, he whistled sharply.

Swan had stopped long enough to lean in and brush Gil's lips with hers. Hightower exerted himself to say "That's it! No one will take this life from us now, laddie!" But his own face twisted in pain.

Springbuck, settling Calundronius around his neck, wondered if the deCourteneys could engage the Five for the needed time. If not, what hue and cry might the Masters set on the northerners' heels?

Chapter Thirty-six

*The desire of rising hath swallowed up his fear
    of a fall.*

Thomas Adams
Diseases of the Soul

AT the center of the Fane, supporting the stupendous
bowl of its roof, was a titanic column of granite, dozens
of paces in diameter. A small ring of light showed, far
up the looming pillar, a spread-eagle figure, hung upside down by the ire of the Five.

Yardiff Bey, shorn of the accumulated powers of
centuries, had been set there to wait. When the moment's emergency had been dealt with, the Master
would exact a slow, precision-pain revenge.

But that must be postponed; the armies of the Crescent Lands were already within the gates of the city.
And if the might of the Masters was decreased, if the
day had already seen reversals undreamt of, still the
brooding Five, defended by their spells and their Fane,
had few misgivings. Here, of all places, the Five
couldn't lose.

Yardiff Bey, bones vibrating, sinews close to snapping, stifled his pleas. Almost, the subsequent punishments of the Masters would be anticlimax; they'd done
the worst when they'd stripped him of every favor and
cast him aside like used goods, discarded by the Lords
of Salamá.

The Masters readied themselves, in that cold unanimity Bey had always idolized. Their common will began
to coalesce; and weakened as their prepotence was, it
still awed the sorcerer. But in the midst of that amazing
marshaling there came a sound that even Yardiff Bey
had never heard.

The Masters, in one voice, wailed dismay. A single image slipped through their guards and Bey caught what the Five had sensed on the plain outside their city, a sky filled with singing, soaring Birds of Accord.

There were multifold things in the gathered minds of the Five then: confusion, panic, anger. And there was a hatred of the sorcerer, for this, too, was a failing of his; he'd assured them that the last of the Lifetree was burned. The Birds, drawn by instincts of their own, proved the Lifetree was coming again to its accustomed waters.

The Lords of Salamá grasped it no sooner than their apt Hand. Bey achieved a strangled laugh. "Masters of Shardishku-Salamá," he shouted, "how will you crush the deCourteneys if the Lifetree takes root, and sends all your powers back to thin air? Which of you is willing to go prevent that, leaving the spell-forged safety of this Fane, and your mutual protection? And who will stay, with strength diminished, and face the wizard and the Trustee? Decide! The Crescent Lands are at your doors!"

It was true. The Five had acted in concert throughout the ages, and dared not separate now, with their powers so reduced. And now the deCourteneys spread their arms before the doors of the Fane. Yardiff Bey had seen the only solution even before his Masters.

He was freed from his bondage, eased down lightly to stand in the ring of light at the foot of the granite column. On him the Five must fasten all their hopes. "Go forth, with the forces with which we shall arm you," they instructed, "and be foremost in our goodwill once more."

Chafing his arms and legs after their stresses, he sneered. "There is a higher price on your Hand. Make me one among you; promise a station coequal with your own, then I will do as you desire. Oath-take that now. Refuse and you perish, nor cares Yardiff Bey."

They howled their wrath, but their terror was greater. The Five made hurried, irrevocable vows, concretized by their own infernal sources. Satisfied, he agreed. All the energy of magic, all the power of will that the Five could bring themselves to surrender, flooded into him, expanding his strength beyond anything he'd felt before.

He'd been processing this information about the Birds. The last known wood of the Lifetree had gone north, and only recently it must have come through Ladentree. Bey's agile mind leapt that gap in a flight of speculation. "Where is the axe called Red Pilgrim?" he asked them.

The Five stretched out their perceptions, ascertaining it, and told him; in the dray, bearing hard for the mound of the Lifetree. Even then he found a moment to admire the subtlety of it all.

So much attention had been diverted to Bey that the deCourteneys had triumphed in the issue of the doors. When the tall, wide doors of the Fane closed after them, the siblings refused to permit the darkness to continue. The insistent blackness fell back before their blue glow. Wrapped in azure light, they made their way to the heart of their enemies' stronghold.

As they rounded the huge column Bey, guided by the Masters, slipped around the other way, undetectable in the overwhelming presence of the Five. He knew that the Masters must prevail, so long as the Lifetree was eliminated. Until the deCourteneys were fully engaged, he would wait in the shadows. He must not become embroiled in this battle.

Gabrielle's voice broke the ponderous silence. "Why do you Five love the night so well? We do not fear to behold you." She broadcast the light of her enchantments. The Masters bore down hard; their art kept hers from illuminating the farthest limits of the temple, where they waited. But their bloated outlines could be seen, moving clumsily. No longer human, distorted by their own deeds and traffickings, and made horrible to see, they hid from view.

"Nor do we hesitate to name you!" she proclaimed. Andre added his imperative to hers; the walls of the Fane trembled. "First, Skaranx, whose high charge and honor was to guard the Lifetree, and who chose instead to destroy it."

To one side, a long, serpentine shape writhed, hearing its name and crime.

"Temopon, seer for the Unity, who vowed sound counsel but rendered lies. So did your will become Amon's." Next to Skaranx, the barely seen form of

Temopon stirred uncomfortably, like a slug near a flame.

"Vorwoda, who was her husband's buttress and confidante. Poisoning his mind, you made him ripe for tragedy, earning demon's gifts." The reigning beauty of the world in ages past, Vorwoda gave a scream from the shadows, thrashing grotesque, insectile limbs in her mossy bed.

"Kaytaynor, the Supreme Lord's most valued friend, who slew him from envy and lust for Vorwoda. Your love is long since turned to abhorrence. Did you think to steal what you did not merit?" Kaytaynor, his swollen body twisted and bent, tried to reject what he heard, radiating his resentment.

"Lastly, Dorodeen. And where are there words to denounce you? Not brave enough or wise enough for the loftiest seat in the Unity, yet clever enough to breed treason, and so bring it down. Worst of all are you, for you loved the Unity, but cast it low because you could not rule it." Dorodeen, the Flawed Hero, who had ended an entire civilization to salve his own inquietude, moved not at all. He repressed the only thing he feared, his memories, and waited, impassive as a crag of ice.

The Masters were assailed by a second excruciating, lucid understanding of what they'd become. Then they hid from it, and struck at the deCourteneys with all their weight of evil.

But their strength was less than it had been. Andre and Gabrielle pooled their powers, and withstood it. Furnace heat and arctic cold skirmished, and the Fane rumbled. But the interlopers deflected every onslaught with anti-spells of their own. Then deCourteney magic erupted. Riding the crest of their emotions, the two counterattacked.

The energies warred, unseen by the eye but palpable enough to set Gabrielle's fiery hair floating, riding their currents.

This was Bey's moment. He extended his arms, while militant winds cracked his black robes around him. First, he'd need a means of travel. With puissance he'd never known before, he ripped aside the curtains of the half-world, and summoned it to him. In an instant his desire was filled, rearing above him, taking the shape of

342

a horse of smoke, of night-black substances of dread borrowed from dreams. It was even taller at the shoulder than a dray horse of Matloo, its breath hot and sulfurous. Its eyes beamed yellow malevolence, and its restless hooves of polished jet left the rock beneath them glowing from their touch. The nightmare horse shrilled, then bowed knee to Yardiff Bey. He scrambled up to its back, sinking his fingers into the coarse tangles of its long mane.

He swept out across the Fane. The Masters redoubled their assault on the deCourteneys, so that the sorcerer would go unhindered. Outside, the northerners ran for safety as the mountainous doors crashed open. Bey blurred past with such speed it seemed a black wind had blown by. The soldiers heard his demoniac laugh echoing back along the boulevard.

The detonations of the doors, slamming open, rolled across the Fane in a shock wave. Gabrielle spun, thinking it an attack from the rear. Sensing that, the Five spent a major effort. But the offensive burst like a comber off Andre's stubborn wards; he'd let his concentration fail once, on the Isle of Keys, and had vowed it would never happen again. Alone, he held, sweat streaming down his face, nails digging into his palms until blood seeped. He was driven backward bodily, pressed to his limits.

All that was in the moment Gabrielle turned. Now she was back, supporting Andre with her arm, shaping a shield against which the Five could do nothing. She dispatched enchantments that rocked the foundations of the Fane, far down in the roots of the earth, and lit the entire room. Shrinking from the light of her sorcery, the Masters sped their total fury at her.

Gabrielle deCourteney, reaching her zenith, bolstered by emotions not unlike the Berserkergang, converted the Fane of the Masters into a crucible of magic.

Chapter Thirty-seven

*Yet is every man his greatest enemy and, as it were,
his own executioner.*

Sir Thomas Browne
Religio Medici

YARDIFF Bey bore down on the arch of Salamá's entrance. One of the men on watch just found time to leap
aside; the other, frozen in his tracks by surprise, was
trampled under the hooves of the hellhorse, his flesh
crumbled and scorched by its passing.

Yardiff Bey drew to a halt out on the plain. He
turned his heightened, one-eyed gaze to the east, seeing
farther and better than mortal sight. He descried the
war-dray far off, throwing out a plume of dust. Its way
led through low, gutted hills from which much stone
had been quarried and cut for use in Salamá. Beyond
those rose the bare little mount upon which the Lifetree
could thrive.

He sensed an emanation he'd come across before;
Calundronius, accursed gemstone of the deCourteneys,
was there. No simple spell would stop his prey. And
even with his infernal steed, Bey could not overhaul
them in time; they'd gained a commanding lead. It
would require extraordinary measures to halt them, or
at least impede them until he could catch up.

He ordered his thoughts, sorting out the things he
must invoke, flows he must tap, oaths to bind and vows
to make. He used a forbidden tongue, his aristocratic
hands darting through the passes of his Shaping. The
hellhorse, scenting sorcery, reared high, beams of amber
light arrowing from its eyes. Ears flattening to its skull,
it screamed its excitement; not an equine sound, but
rather the cry of a giant feline.

344

Van Duyn and Katya, having dropped far behind the main party as rearguard, heard that sound. They turned, and saw a horse and rider, tiny in the distance, coming at uncanny speed. They brought their horses around, the American unslinging the M-1, to do whatever they must to buy time for those riding with the Lifetree.

The main party thundered down into the lowest part of the valley, their horses lathered with sweat, flinging up the earth in clots. They passed striated cliffs and deserted stoneyards, catching sight of low-lying excavations where ground water had formed pools. That an open body of water could exist here proved their destination was close.

Springbuck's heart was alive with hope; all victory seemed possible. Then Fireheel slowed, his senses sharper than his rider's, testing the breeze, ears pricked forward, moving with quick, high steps, head swiveling. Springbuck scanned for danger, taking Calundronius from his chest and holding it by its chain. He saw nothing approaching from any direction, and the sky was vacant.

The brown earth jumped, like a horse's shoulder-twitch; Yardiff Bey's sorcery was taking hold, Shaping this most inert and difficult of the elements to his purpose. Rising in a mound, as if a baker kneaded dough, it folded and refolded, swelling. Here, where the earth had already been opened and raided, Yardiff Bey had found pliant material, receptive to his arts.

The earth-elemental found its feet like a drunkard, the problems of balance and motion altogether alien to it. It came from quiescent soil, used only to movements dictated by simple gravity and the patient adjustments of the substrata. It was twice as tall as the tallest of the humans, crudely wrought. Headless, it worked its arms and legs slowly, with a rain of dust and gravel, chance minerals and bits of rock.

To the right of the road was the valley's side, and to the left, a jumble of stone blocks in the abandoned yards, leaving no room to go around. The eight bulky dray horses reared and neighed, kicking, threatening to break their cracking swingletrees. Gil and Hightower could do nothing but endure the rocking and jolting grimly.

Dunstan had himself braced in the curve of the driver's waist-bar, fighting the reins. Fireheel had shied away from the apparition, but now Springbuck forced the gray close, holding Calundronius out. The thing sensed the gemstone and its power. It stomped clumsily, gathered more earth to it and flung it at the *Ku-Mor-Mai*. Sand, dirt and shale hit Springbuck like a wall. The stallion and his rider were blasted backward, falling; Fireheel whinnied in fright, and Calundronius was torn from the Protector-Suzerain's fingers. Swan lofted a javelin that drove deep into the creature's side, then began to slough out again without effect, telling her no mortal weapon would avail.

Dunstan and Ferrian were working together to back the neighing, bucking team. Reacher rode up to seize the right lead horse's bridle.

Sorcery drew the elemental to the axe, guiding it in its only purpose, to stop the Lifetree. It lifted a boulder, hurled it at the dray. Its aim was off; docile earth, it was unused to something as bizarre as trajectory. The boulder missed the team, but smashed into the dray, snapping a wheel rim, crunching its spokes.

The elemental went to the wagon and, without sign of effort, it began to topple the vehicle over on its side. Dunstan clung to his place at the prow a moment, then the reins were dragged from his hands and the weakened hitch broke. The eight horses milled and reared. Ferrian, arms and legs gyrating, was tossed headlong. Reacher managed to break his fall by leaning far out of his saddle, but the King's own horse, flinching in fright, robbed him of balance. Both went down. The team broke and ran blindly, and with them went Reacher's horse. The King scrambled madly to pull Ferrian and himself from beneath the great hooves, but his leg was struck, and Reacher's left leg hung useless, crushed and numb.

Inside the dray, men tumbled as wall changed place with ceiling and floor. Gil managed to catch himself by a handhold ring, igniting white agony in his side. Red Pilgrim lay nearby, having narrowly missed his head.

Hightower's restraints came loose, and he met the wood with a thud.

The earth-being began to pry at the dray bed, not understanding what it was, but only that the object it sought was within. Clumsily conceived arms hunted the chassis for purchase, to sounds of sliding soil and gravel. Its weight tilted the war-dray still more. Those inside struggled to the rear hatch, but its lock was jammed, and the prow had been crumpled in. There was a roof hatch but it, too, resisted them.

Swan was out of her saddle, helping dazed Springbuck dig himself out of the soil that half-covered him, hoping to find Calundronius, as the Shaping commenced tearing at the bed of the overturned dray. Tugging the limp *Ku-Mor-Mai* free, she found his fingers empty and condemned the luck; Calundronius was the one thing that would help now. She began scooping dirt furiously, looking for the negator.

Planks were torn away from the dray bed. The elemental began working its crude hands in for a new grip. Gil was helpless to aid Dunstan, who was throwing himself against the rear hatch.

There was a creaking from the roof. Inch by inch, the hatch there bent open, as the monster gradually pulled the floor away. The roof hatch parted further, and Gil saw the King of Freegate, Lord of the Just and Sudden Reach. His right foot was planted against the roof, back bowed in exertion. Now he threw his head back, face bracketed with strain. He'd peeled one corner back, and now the latch gave. The hatch popped open.

Reacher, asprawl, thrust his hands in, took Gil's shoulders and yanked. The American was pulled to momentary safety with a shriek of pain. Dunstan came behind, dragging the bulk of Hightower in short, desperate tugs. Then Reacher seized the Warlord, hauling him out in one motion. The Warlord's blood ran copiously from his mouth.

Half the dray's bed came loose in the elemental's hand. Dunstan, grabbing up Red Pilgrim, was last to tumble through the broken hatch. The Shaping broke off its efforts on the dray, pushing it aside, rolling the wagon over onto its roof. Reacher, with one leg numb, had to move quickly to keep Gil and Hightower from being trapped beneath.

Holding the greataxe, Dunstan ran for the nearest horse, Jeb Stuart. The elemental followed close after, and the horse shied and bolted from it. With nowhere else to hide, Dunstan made a frantic dash for the mazework of quarries and stoneyards. The monster pursued.

Swan left Springbuck to dig for the negator. She plunged into the stoneyards to help Dunstan, pausing only to pick up a flake of rock with which to blaze her route through the jumble.

Reacher had already recognized that he couldn't follow; he hopped and hobbled back to Ferrian. The Horse-blooded sat holding a gash in his temple that had come close to his eye. The King began to tear his old companion's vest into shreds for bandage. Gil lay back, wearily cursing the luck that had stopped them so near their objective.

The stoneyards were filled with unused pieces, from monolithic cubes the size of a house to keystones no bigger than a scent box. Lying where they'd been left, they formed a labyrinth terrain of roofless corridors and cul-de-sacs. Dunstan, weaving among them, Red Pilgrim clutched close to him, tried to quiet his own breathing, listening for sounds of the thing following him. He chose his path by guesswork, hoping he was moving the right way. The melancholy Horseblooded hoped the plan he'd conceived in transit, as it were, would work.

He heard the calls of Swan, but withheld any answer, unsure if the creature could hear. Then Dunstan heard scraping, tons of stone being moved by illimitable strength. The elemental was close, guided by the decrees of Yardiff Bey that had targeted it on the Lifetree.

He finally found what he'd sought, an excavation filled with murky ground water, surrounded by high blocks. Dunstan cudgeled his brain, twisting his sad face in thought. Which would be the best place to wait, one that would give his pursuer no long corridor of approach? He plotted the grating, grinding noise of dislodged stone, and positioned himself.

Swan's voice, nearby, made him look up. She'd ascended a series of blocks to stand high above the rest of

the maze, and seen his plan. "That way," she called
through cupped hands, then pointed. "It comes, no more
than thirty paces!" She turned, jumped, vanished from
sight. He stepped to a better location. There he waited,
sweat beading his long features and staining his shirt, as
the thing heaved stone tonnage aside to get at him.

Dunstan's gaunt face worked urgently. He'd come
with the vague idea of luring the monster into the water,
but if he waited on the brink, might it not catch him
first? He was of the High Ranges, and could barely
swim, but if he dove into the water now, could the thing
not kill him and bury the axe with stones flung from the
land? He berated himself; hadn't that lifetime-night of
captivity in Salamá even taught him to *think*?

The block fronting him began to move, even as he
heard Swan's halloo. He hazarded a quick look over his
shoulder and saw her there on the far side of the pool, a
dozen paces from him, watching him expectantly. Her
look brought home to him the fact that he was not in
the Rage, that he'd thought and acted, under great pressure, and not yielded up control of himself. He was
again Dunstan, and nevermore Berserker.

Then his mind became cool, his course of action
clear, his arms steady and strong. He fired the terse order to Swan, "Stand ready, Red Pilgrim flies!"

As the last block was moved away and the earth-
elemental lurched toward him, he took a two-handed
grip at the end of the greataxe helve. He waited until
the creature was nearly on him, a precise calculation.
Then he heaved the weapon up, over his head, as high
and as far as he could, and immediately threw himself
between the elemental's feet, curled in a tight ball.

The creature's limited senses remained with Red Pilgrim, as the axe spun and glittered through the air over
the pool. The thing moved after its prize, prodded by
dim-witted singleness of purpose. It plunged off the lip
of the excavation, into the water. The axe descended,
clanging to the stone near Swan.

The water heaved and surged with earth and stone
swirling through it as two antithetical elements met.
Waves and foam pounded, a miniature hurricane in
narrow confines. Dunstan got to his feet, brushing dirt

from himself. The waves stilled, and the pool's surface became as smooth as it had been before.

Yardiff Bey, a wraith of murderous intent, flew at Van Duyn and Katya; his horse's hoofbeats left a trail of glowing prints in its wake.

The American had dismounted, to snuggle the butt of the Garand firmly at his shoulder. The hellhorse grew larger in his sight picture, cannonading the ground. The sorcerer was crouched behind the beast's neck, clinging like a thistle in the whiplash banners of its mane. "You must wait until he is nigh, Edward," the Snow Leopardess advised, "or he may distort what you see."

He fixed his cheek to the rifle stock, steadied his sight blade. He fired carefully, as he did all things, leaning into the recoil. The first shot was high. The second kicked up dirt, an overcompensation, but the third hit. Bey's eldritch mount gave its feline cry as it lost vaporous, foul-smelling blood from a wound in its left gaskin. Katya, seeing Bey could hide behind his steed's neck, told Van Duyn to hold fire; her reckless courage had hold of her again.

Rowling her horse, she went at the Hand of Salamá, shield up, ironbound lance pointing the way. But Bey's mount was demoniac in its speed and strength, and feared nothing. It swerved away from her lance like spindrift, its snapping, sulfur-smelling fangs barely missing her arm. Its enormous weight slammed her horse's side, knocking the Snow Leopardess and her charger through the air, discards of battle.

The rifle came up again; Van Duyn fired with metronomic punctuality, one round per second. One whistled through the beast's forelock, but others struck deep in its neck and chest. Though Bey was protected from the gunfire, Van Duyn stood his ground resolutely. It almost cost him his life; he just did manage to dive aside. The hellhorse swept by, its wounds fuming and sizzling.

As dust settled around him, Van Duyn climbed shakily to his feet. Katya was already picking herself up, throwing off her fall. "I am unscathed," the Princess assured him, peering eastward after the vanished sorcerer, "but the day seems mapped for disaster."

Springbuck, finding Calundronius, had raced for the stoneyards to rescue Dunstan and Swan, only to meet them as the two emerged. The *Ku-Mor-Mai* sighed his relief, shaking the lean Horseblooded by both shoulders.

The others were at the rear of the ruined dray. The King pointed toward Salamá; Springbuck couldn't quite see, but the others described for him the horseman coming with supernatural speed.

"That'll be Yardiff Bey," grated Gil, certain. He was glassy-eyed, his skin blue with shortage of oxygen. Hightower was propped against the wagon, eyelids closed, yet they fluttered open at the name.

The Warlord spoke to the heart of matters in a quavering voice. "Time is short, and I see but one horse." Fireheel stood waiting, the only one not driven or frightened away. "*Ku-Mor-Mai,* finish this ride."

There was no counterargument. Springbuck took Red Pilgrim from Swan. "Fireheel is brawny," he declared, gathering the gray's reins, "and can bear one more beside."

"Then, let it be Gil MacDonald," the old man bade, words coming in a gargle of blood. "I am late in years, and have my death-wound."

They hoisted Gil into the gray's saddle and used the baldric of Ferrian's scimitar to hold him to the high cantle, seeing he was half-fainting. Springbuck rode behind, carrying the axe and steadying his friend. Swan removed her gleaming, white-winged bascinet and wrapped its chin strap through Gil's belt. "If you can fill this with the waters of the Tree and bear it back, Hightower's life may still be saved. I will try to find a horse, and follow, if I can."

Springbuck nodded, but doubted she had the time. He spoke to Fireheel gently, asking one last effort. The stallion complied. And so the two, the ruler of a mighty suzerainty and the displaced alien, became, of all the thousands who'd answered the Trailingsword, the ones to cover the final stretch.

The other four turned to await the sorcerer. Dunstan was still armed with Andre's sword, and Swan had drawn hers, taking up Springbuck's fallen shield. Ferrian brandished his flashing scimitar, and Reacher leaned against the dray, balancing on one foot, holding Swan's javelin.

A fey calm settled over them. Soon, the salvoes of the hellhorse's hoofbeats could be heard.

Fireheel churned to the summit of the steep, grassy slope. Springbuck, who'd barely been able to hold Gil in the saddle, slid off, unfastened the baldric, and eased his friend down. The American couldn't stand, couldn't breathe or speak. He lay on the ground, clawing at his throat, as the pressure in his chest choked life out of him. Springbuck, beyond knowledge and beyond prayer, took Red Pilgrim in a woodchopper's grip, and with a broad stance, raised the axe.

When he sighted the four waiting for him in the road, the sorcerer recognized that his options were exhausted. The hellhorse was beginning to falter, and there was no time for spell-casting. He must unleash that weapon he wore where his left eye had been.

He'd lost the eye, long ago, in mortal combat beneath the earth. He'd wrenched from its socket the single Orb of his monstrous opponent, and made it his own in replacement. Now he leaned to one side of his mount's neck and flipped open the ocular.

The Orb seemed to turn the whole world a harsh, unendurable white, abolishing all color. There were only outlines to be seen in its brilliance. The pain Bey felt, liberating those energies, threatened to rob him of consciousness. Dust swirled up, and the air was superheated. The four mortals fell away, covering themselves, seared and blistered.

But the Hand had already elevated his awful gaze up the mound. There, its venomous light caught Springbuck full in the back as he raised the greataxe. Calundronius didn't protect him; the Orb was no enchantment, but a living property, like dragonfire. The *Ku-Mor-Mai* pitched forward, but brought the axe through its arc. The crescent bit dug deep into the earth. From that crease water gushed, to fountain and flow.

Bey had already clicked the ocular shut, clinging to his horse's mane; the Orb was fueled by its user's life, and a moment's exposure had nearly cost the sorcerer his. He barreled past the dray and his downed opponents like Death, the Hunter. Near the top of the hill though, his steed came to the end of its unnatural endurance. As it sank to its knees with a resentful sibilance like a snake's, he slipped clear and continued afoot.

At the summit he discovered Springbuck stretched out full length on the ground. Not far from him, Gil MacDonald's body lay face down in the runoff from the hill's mystic waters. But that runoff was becoming less and less; between the two forms, the Lifetree stood.

Angorman's axe haft had awakened from the sleep of centuries and put forth roots, growing with preternatural speed, as if years were passing like minutes. Even now, it was less a helve than a sapling, knurled with the promise of limbs.

Yardiff Bey smiled; he was in time. The Tree was still young and vulnerable to his powers. His hands danced skillfully, calling sorcery to him, but without effect. Then it came to him that Springbuck still wore Calundronius. He started for the *Ku-Mor-Mai*, meaning to hurl the gemstone off the hill, but stopped dead. There was a gurgle, a watery snort, movement, a gust of exhalation.

Gil MacDonald rolled out of the runoff, shaking water from his eyes, spitting, coughing. He'd been healed, not drowned, by those rarest of waters.

The last thing he remembered was an unbearable light that had downed Springbuck; the first thing he saw was Yardiff Bey. He bounced to his feet, forgetting he'd been as good as dead, but recalling he was unarmed. Bey's hand went to his ocular. He would risk its use one more time; Lifetree and enemy would both fall.

Gil concluded that the ocular was connected with whatever ray had struck the *Ku-Mor-Mai*; but too much distance separated him from the sorcerer.

"The episode ends well," allowed the servant of Salamá, finding the catch of his ocular.

A white puff of feathers struck his cheek. He recoiled instinctively. Another streaked past, as several more hovered before his face. Suddenly, the air was alive with piping, swarming Birds of Accord, like a snowstorm of wings and song. Bey swatted them away, wildly angry, and made to unlatch his ocular.

Gil MacDonald was no longer there.

The Hand of Salamá spun, searching in the blinding, deafening blizzard as Birds blundered into him. Gil hit him blindside, taking advantage of the unseeing ocular. They grappled on the ground, the American's punches and chops hardly hurting the sorcerer. Bey's strength was immense; he struck away a groping attempt for a choke-hold on his throat, but Gil got his wrists, holding his enemy from behind in a leg-lock, moved not by Rage, but rather by outrage.

Still, this was Yardiff Bey. Irresistibly, his hands came to the ocular. It would serve him one more time, and win him all his desires.

Something pressed hard at Gil's side as he wrestled; Swan's helmet. He released his hold, and Bey's hand flew to the ocular. Gil tore the helmet loose, grasping it by its white wings and, as the Orb shone forth, jammed the glittering bascinet down backward over the sorcerer's head, holding it fast.

The Hand of Salamá arched backward, squealing in horror. Smoke, glaring white light and the crackle of mystic fire escaped around the helmet's edges. Gil clung, literally, for his life. Then he had to yank his hands away, as the bascinet became too hot to touch.

It lasted only seconds. Bey slumped, paroxysms ended. The Orb, unpowered, went out. Gil worked up the meager energy to shove himself free.

As he did, a gale sprang up on the hillside. A chorus of gloating, gibbering voices came on it, invisible, circling the hill. Then there was a new voice, surrounded by ranting and wailing in the manner of the damned. Gil recognized it: Yardiff Bey's. Sobbing, pleading to no effect, the sorcerer's soul was borne away to pay unholy debts.

Then calm returned, and the Birds of Accord resumed their waiting.

Chapter Thirty-eight

I cannot rest from travel; I will drink
Life to the lees.

Alfred, Lord Tennyson
Ulysses

IN the Fane of the Masters were whines of utter despair. The Lifetree had taken root, exerting its equilibrium.

The influences of the Five pulsed erratically against blue deCourteney enchantments. Andre spread his arms wide with a gusty laugh; Gabrielle's luminance was renewed. They'd been beleaguered, but now the attacks were dissipated like so much mist.

Gabrielle's green eyes narrowed. Arrogant Masters who'd been within an instant of godhood were naked to her. The sorceress' unquenchable will, supported by her brother's arts, dragged her enemies from their places. Their dreams of deity were broken, leaving only their obscene shapes. Skaranx, faithless watchman; Temopon, deceitful advisor; Vorwoda, hateful lover; Kaytaynor, friend-slayer; and Dorodeen, flawed hero; they came in a semicircle around the deCourteneys as failed, petty spirits.

One by one, Gabrielle called their names. They came to touch their heads to the floor at her feet, monstrous shapes bending to an unforeseen task.

No words passed, but the same sharp aspect was in both the deCourteneys' miens. Gabrielle raised both hands high, a very empress of magic. A final radiance broke from the two. The central column vibrated, a webwork of cracks appearing all along its granite height. The deCourteneys turned to leave their enemies. The

Masters made a tentative move to follow. She whirled back; they were cowed by her glance alone.

The stone pillar was wrapped in a sleeve of blue glory, held together only by Gabrielle's imperatives. Brother and sister came to the doors, which Andre opened with a motion of his head and a word of Compulsion. Men fell back, averting their eyes from the unbearable light. Framed in it, Gabrielle made a last Dismissal. The central column came apart in a shower of stone and dust. The roof cracked, enormous chunks of it breaking loose. The immeasurable weight of the Fane collapsed.

In that penultimate moment, the Five shook loose from the ages of their plotting, resigning themselves to death with a perverse curiosity, as their Fane crashed down upon them.

Returning down the road from Salamá, Andre and Gabrielle and the army came to the broken dray. There, Ferrian and Reacher kept watch over the body of Hightower.

. Gabrielle went to him slowly, stooping to kiss the Warlord's leathery brow. "He was at peace, at the end," Ferrian told her gently.

Her eyes were brimming. "It was granted us both to know why we failed against Salamá so long ago. Seeing the Lady's whole plan was a measure of compensation."

Healers were seeing to Ferrian's temple and Reacher's leg, applying demulcents to the burns they'd gotten when the Orb had opened against them. They had no news yet of what had happened on the hill, so wizard and sorceress hurried on, as Van Duyn, Katya, Dunstan and Swan already had.

Riding up, they saw a blackened area in the grass, not knowing it was the spot where Bey's hellhorse had fallen and evaporated as its unnatural life was consumed.

At the top of the hill, the rest had gathered by the Lifetree. The Tree towered over them, already crowded with caroling Birds of Accord. The timeless artificial twilight of Salamá was dispersing, and honest night breaking through.

Swan, Van Duyn and the Snow Leopardess stood

over them as Gil and Dunstan knelt by Springbuck's unmoving body. Andre grieved anew, thinking this last death might be more than his sister could bear. Then the *Ku-Mor-Mai* groaned, drawing up one knee. Gabrielle ran to him, as Gil recounted the events of the chase. Sisters of the Line crowded around their High Constable, pressing ministrations on her, and on the others' wounds as well.

Of Bey's body there was little remaining except dark powder; its spirit had preserved it all these centuries.

"The water stopped running before I could get to it," Gil told Andre sadly, "and now the Tree's taking it all; no more runoff."

" 'Twould do Hightower no good," the wizard admitted. "He died even before you came to the mound." He gazed to one side, and saw the double-bitted axehead, its collar snapped open by the insistent growth of the Lifetree.

"What about the Masters?" Gil wanted to know. Gabrielle pointed back toward the city. Shardishku-Salamá was consuming itself in fires leaping upward toward the sky.

"I've got to see," he announced. Jeb Stuart's hurts, and Fireheel's, were being attended by knowledgeable cavalrymen. Gil was about to borrow a horse when Springbuck, struggling to his feet, called for two.

"Where is the injury so grievous it will keep us two from seeing this sight?" he demanded. No one contradicted him, or pressed to be taken along.

By the time they'd gotten to the city, the fires were burned out. There were only minor drifts of smoke; of the Necropolis there was nothing. The sky was nearly dark now, but the light of dawn was coming up in the east.

"So fast," Gil murmured, "how could it have gone up so fast? Even the stone is gone."

Springbuck shrugged. "The Masters endured long after they should have died, and so did their magic, and the things it built. All this destruction, held in abeyance, was accomplished in quickened time."

Gil dismounted. "Coming?" Springbuck followed suit slowly, babying burns, aches and wounds.

They passed where the gateway arch had been, and stopped at the spot where the Fane had dominated Shardishku-Salamá. The place was flat, with no block, no timber, not so much as a potsherd to show a city had stood there. It was now a table of scorched earth. The American felt his side, where the wound had disappeared; something told him Dirge, too, had ceased to exist. Springbuck looked straight up, but there was no sign of the Trailingsword. He was unsurprised. Gil took the Ace of Swords and let it fall to the cauterized earth.

They made the long hike to their horses, mounted, rode away and never glanced back. Pale dawn had begun.

The armies had encamped around the base of the hill. Warriors of both sexes had begun ascending the hill, to bear witness of the Lifetree.

The deCourteneys and the others came down. Andre, guessing Gil's thought, indicated the Tree and said, "By evening it will achieve full growth. It's uppermost branches will be in the clouds, its roots deep in the earth."

Springbuck was speaking to Ferrian. "Friend Rider, your timing is harrowing-fine."

The Horseblooded grinned, adjusting the bandages on his head. "Victory is its own excuse, as we say on the High Ranges. I came to the Isle of Keys just after the Mariner fleet set out. Andre, you rule the winds all too well!" He struck his thigh with his left hand. "For fact, I did, in haste, neglect to say something to Gil." He looked to the American. "The ship I took was under two who said they knew you, said you needn't seek for them yet at, um, 'Fiddler's Green,' but might find them at the Golden Fluke."

Gil laughed, then noticed Swan watching him. He sobered. "How would you like to see the *Outer Hub*?"

Her face was fond, but unhappy. "Region Blue has been without a High Constable long enough," she declined. Catching Gabrielle's eye, she added, "And Glyffa, far too long without a Trustee."

The sorceress returned the appraisal. "Region Blue will have a new High Constable, in sooth." Swan was startled; Gabrielle finished, "I cannot squander my best administrator on one area." She saw Gil's frown, and laughed. "No hangdog faces! You may visit, but there is the Reconciliation to consider." To Springbuck she moved her glance, pretending still she spoke to the American. "We have much to do, you see, though there will be leisure too."

The *Ku-Mor-Mai* held her eyes. "One mustn't neglect affairs of state."

Reacher surprised them all, saying, "I, for one, do not answer that plea of politics."

Katya puzzled, "What now, brother?"

"You are clever, sister, and willful. And as formidable as you have to be." He eased his injured leg. "Therefore, you have a season in which to do as you like, be it going with Edward again or returning with me to Freegate. But when that is done and this leg is sound, I would like you to take the throne, if you will. I am for the High Ranges."

Van Duyn made a sour face. "The whole Crescent Lands are upside down; don't plan a vacation yet." He took the Snow Leopardess' hand.

"But much of our plight came of Salamá," Andre reminded, "and will lack a driving force now, though there remains the demon Amon."

"And the Southwastelanders?" Springbuck prodded.

"Their center is failed. They are a factional people; our strong armies, going north without doing harm, might go unmolested."

Gil seated himself on a rock, where Swan had set herself with a waterskin. He took a pull on it, the brackish water tasting sweet to him.

"There is work for you too, brother," Gabrielle was telling Andre, "in Veganá. They need all help rebuilding there. What better place to go awhile, until the Reconciliation, when Glyffa's call is upon you once more?"

"I'd hoped for Andre's assistance myself," Springbuck interjected. "There are the Druids." The wizard looked torn.

Van Duyn sat down next to Gil. The younger man passed him the waterskin. "What are you going to do, Ed?"

"Finish what I started in the Highlands Province; I hate to quit anything like that. But there's this business of Katya taking the throne. If you want to go home, you'll probably have to come looking for me in Free-gate."

Swan stared at Gil as Van Duyn wandered off. Her face was soft and warm. To one side, Springbuck was gesticulating with Gabrielle, Andre and Katya, saying, "We are the most coherent force in the Crescent Lands. Disorders, rebellion, lawlessness there may be, but these we can overcome. In time, we might forge another Unity. What worthier labor is there?"

Swan asked Gil, "You have a plan too, Seeker?"

He rubbed the dark powderburn tattoo on his stubbled cheek. "Yeah; I'm gonna grow a beard." She didn't even smile. "All right, no, I have none, Swan." He hung his head for a moment, then looked up. "But we have a long ride back, to talk about it."

She flashed her grin. "A sensible beginning."

Down where the war-drays of Matloo were laagered, the Yalloroon had gathered, joining hands, to dance and sing in jubilation. They'd seen Salamá burn, and were free. Gil was watching them when Springbuck came over. The *Ku-Mor-Mai*, too, inquired, "What will you do now?"

He shrugged. He hadn't forgotten that the Berserker-gang hadn't come to him when he'd fought Bey. Had the Lifetree's waters healed that too, the arsenal of the Rage?

Andre deCourteney had run down to take part in the Yalloroon's dance, dragging with him Gabrielle, who protested only halfheartedly. The little Yalloroon giggled at them with delight; the wizard played the buffon, flapping his arms, twirling on his toes. The sorceress curtseyed, and moved light-footedly.

Ferrian joined their circle, moving slowly with a modest skip, and Dunstan, who was roaring his amusement. Gil glanced to where the Lifetree climbed, almost visibly, in the sun. He stood, took Swan's hand, led the High Constable to her feet. "I'm going dancing. You?"

About the Author

BRIAN DALEY was born in rural New Jersey in 1947. After an Army hitch and a stint of odd-jobbing and bumming, he enrolled in college and began writing while working on his B.A.

The Starfollowers of Coramonde is the author's second novel. He has no permanent address as yet.

You'll find all that is possible and more...in the fantasy of Evangeline Walton and Katherine Kurtz.

Available at your bookstore or use this coupon.

The Books of the Welsh Mabinogion

Adventure stories from old Welsh mythology dramatically retold by master storyteller, Evangeline Walton. "These books are not only the best fantasies of the 20th century, but also great works of fiction."

—THE SATURDAY REVIEW

_____ PRINCE OF ANNWN	27737	1.75
_____ THE CHILDREN OF LLYR	27738	1.95
_____ THE SONG OF RHIANNON	27801	1.95
_____ THE ISLAND OF THE MIGHTY	27967	1.95

The Deryni Chronicle

Sweeping tales of romance and sorcery in a quasi-mortal race whose extra human powers at once bless and threaten mankind. "It is clear that Katherine Kurtz is a great new talent in the field of fantasy. The books have the promise of Tolkien . . ."

—BESTSELLERS

_____ DERYNI RISING	27599	1.95
_____ DERYNI CHECKMATE	27102	1.95
_____ HIGH DERYNI	27113	1.95
_____ CAMBER OF CULDI	27597	1.95

BB Ballantine Mail Sales
P.O. Box 100
Westminster, MD 21157

Please send me the books I have checked above. I am enclosing $_____ (please add 75¢ to cover postage and handling). Send check or money order—no cash or C.O.D.'s please.

Name_____

Address_____

City_____ State_____ Zip_____

Please allow 4 weeks for delivery.

L-47